CW00498741

CROSSING THE WHITEWASH

CROSSING THE WHITEWASH

NICK RIPPINGTON

Cabrilon Books

Copyright © 2015 Nick Rippington

The moral right of the author has been asserted.

All rights reserved.

No part of this publication may be reproduced, stored in a retrieval system, or transmitted, in any form or by any means, without the prior permission in writing of the publisher, nor be otherwise circulated in any form of binding or cover other than that in which it is published and without a similar condition including this condition being imposed on the subsequent purchaser.

Published by Cabrilon Books

ISBN 978-1-5143-6217-4

Typesetting services by BOOKOW.COM

For my mum for giving me my love of books
My dad for backing me in everything I do
Jean, for all her help and support
My wife Liz for putting up with my rants
My daughters Jemma and Olivia, for being them

Acknowledgments

Thanks to everyone along the way who has helped me turn this from a series of incoherent thoughts into a body of work, but specifically my editors Phil Davies and Liz Rippington for taking the trouble to read, advise and sort out my grammar mistakes; authors Richard Blandford, Kerry Wilkinson, Jill Marsh, Chris Brown and Ian Sutherland for their shrewd observations and steering me on the right track; Jane (J-D) Dixon for her wonderful cover design and willingness to make numerous changes on demand from me, and finally Steve Passiouras at Bookow, the fount of all formatting knowledge (or should that be font)...

PROLOGUE

THE rat sniffed the air as the kid watched, spellbound.

He'd never seen one running free before.

Some of them could grow as big as cats, he'd been told.

Not this one. This one was so malnourished you could see its ribs. Hungry as it was, though, it wouldn't go near the decomposing organic lump that lay in that corner of the room.

"You think they're gonna rape you?"

The cellmate's words broke the spell. "You've been reading too many stories, kid. They ain't gonna rape you, they're gonna fucking kill you... That's what you should be worried about."

If the younger man was concerned, no flicker of emotion crossed his baby face. He kept his eyes fixed straight ahead, doing a quick inventory of the fat fuck opposite him. The bloke was 18-stone of pure human junk, ugly tattoos plastering the top half of a flabby, uncovered torso. Some sort of snake wrapped itself around his throat, slithered over the jaw and entered his mouth while two mythical dragon-like creatures fought for supremacy across man boobs and an over-nurtured belly. The names Shaun and Wendy could just about be picked out amid the chaotic artwork. Children, or victims?

The snake moved as the older man expelled a burst of staccato laughter. It stopped abruptly, as if the power had been cut to his brain. He stared off into the distance, the only sound that of long, diseased fingernails scratching at the scabs that ran the length of his arm.

The kid checked on the rat. In the tales he had been told they were always black, always big and always dirty. Rats were to be feared. They would eat anything.

A-ny-thing.

Which was why this one was such a disappointment. It wasn't black for a start but covered in sporadic tufts of grey hair. It certainly wasn't big and it wasn't helping itself bulk up by turning down the meal on offer. If it had a family, it was letting them down, too. Dirty? It was about the cleanest thing in the cell. Sniffing the air again it wrinkled its nose and aborted its mission, scurrying out of sight.

Watching the rat reawakened his own sense of smell. He almost gagged. The foul stench reminded him of chicken bones left too long in a dustbin, mixed together with substantial quantities of body odour and raw sewage. He resisted the temptation to squeeze his nostrils shut with his fingers, though, believing it to be a sign of weakness.

"They're offering a good package," said the fat fuck, faulty circuits reconnecting. It was as if he was describing a new private health scheme rather than an invitation to kill a man. Grimy fingers made a pointless attempt to groom a shoulder-length tangle of greying hair. "They're insisting on a proper job. Maximum violence. The client wants someone to 'rip your head off and piss in the bastard hole'," he made quote marks in the air to frame the vivid description. "They might rape you after that, but I doubt you'll feel a thing."

Though the words were delivered with the expert timing of a stand-up comedian the kid doubted his fellow prisoner had a funny bone in his entire body. He wanted a reaction, but since his arrest the kid had learned to keep his emotions in check. A whole cabal of 'interested parties' had been wheeled in to assess him and he had stared blankly at them through eyes of cobalt blue crystal – a human mirror revealing nothing. As a result, evaluation reports put before the judge were useless. With nothing to go on she applied the going rate for crimes of this nature – 12 years. The crown dropped the murder charge to spare the taxpayer the cost of an appeal.

Manslaughter? Murder? Same difference, really.

The kid stretched his wiry frame in the grey jumpsuit which hung off him like an older brother's hand-me-down. The wonky wooden chair screeched as he transferred his weight and patted away a yawn. "You heard about this in the exercise yard?" he asked in a cockney accent as thick as London smog. "Could someone be blowing up your backside and telling you a hurricane's on its way?"

"It's for real," said the big man. "Someone's offering a lifetime's worth of Product. Weed, brown, chemicals; people use whatever it takes to make the time go faster in here, you know? Of course you do. That's your line of business, right?" The kid didn't bite. "Anyway, whoever wants you in the ground put feelers out. It got the yard all excited. The psychos talk about nothing else. They've been counting the days. You clocked the reception committee? All the fresh meat gets some kind of welcome. When you spend day after day staring at the same bastard walls, it's nice to see something new. We could have sold tickets for you, though. You're box office."

Again the laugh, a throaty chuckle as if half the larynx had been stripped away over a lifetime of inhaling noxious chemicals. It grated with the kid but he needed to maintain the dialogue. Things were starting to make sense.

He had entered the main wing earlier to a mind-fucking din, the kind of white noise he imagined they piped into a terrorist's cell day after day in order to extract a confession. The chink-chink-chink of sharp objects scraping across metal bars, banging and stamping, taunts and abuse, gangster rap lyrics without the tenderness. He chose to keep his gaze on the yellow-white walls in front, knowing that if he raised his eyes to the landings above it would make matters worse.

As he made slow progress through the wing he began to filter out different sounds: wolf whistles, cries of "Hello Sweetie" and "All right Precious", 'mwaah, mwaah' kisses, insane whooping. The one shout that settled in his head and stayed there, toying with his imagination, delivered in a baritone growl: "Hope you remembered the lube, sweet cheeks!"

Reaching his cell he was greeted by this fully signed-up member of the dregs of society, perched on the bottom bunk rearranging his pubic lice with nicotine-stained sausage fingers. Withdrawing them slowly from his trousers he proffered a handshake it would have been rude not to accept.

"What the fuck did you do anyway?" The cell mate was asking now. "They claim you brained a granddad with his walking stick, killed him outright. That's considered poor form – even by people in here who've done despicable things. The psychos will believe they're doing a public service, offing you."

"It ain't true."

"What ain't true?"

"It wasn't a pensioner. It didn't happen like that."

"You don't have to convince me... I salute you, kid. I'm a big fan of euthanasia..."

You're coming close to getting some, thought the kid. "I told you it ain't true," he said, knuckles forming into fists.

"Whatever you say. Still, I'll give you credit. It's rare someone's reputation gets here so much earlier than they do. Respect."

He held out the knuckle of his right hand, which was inked with "Hait". Jeez, thought the kid, if you're going to get your skanky girlfriend to do your tattoos on the cheap, at least make sure she isn't illiterate. He left it hanging there, unfamiliar with the American gesture of fist bumping.

The hand was withdrawn. "Suit yourself."

The younger man couldn't care less about hurting the slob's feelings, but needed allies. "Sorry," he said. "That was rude. I'm just fucking knackered, ain't slept for weeks."

"That won't change in this shithole," said the cellmate, waving his hand around like a guide at an historic museum. "This is Wano mate. Worst prison in Britain. People shout out in the night. The victims. They're being bullied, beaten up, ass-fucked. It's too overcrowded man and the lunatics really have taken over the asylum. Sleep with one eye open."

No proper sleep, then, for another eight years, best case scenario. Fuck. "So when I doze off you slit my throat?"

"You don't doze off," said the big man, unblinking. Then he leaned across and slapped the kid on the knee, laughing again until the cough took over and his face turned crimson. The kid waited for the attack to subside. "Ah fuck, sorry, I'm playing with ya," said the cellmate, removing a cigarette paper from his pocket and pulling strands of tobacco from a pouch on the bunk. "Shit, I guess you don't know who I am."

Don't tell me, thought the kid. Yorkshire Ripper? Ronnie Kray? Rose West after the op? He was tired of playing games.

"I'm a mate of your old man's. A business associate. We done some projects together in the past. When I heard you were on your way I thought I'd best keep an eye on you... even bribed the guards with a bit of weed to get you put in with me."

"Why should I believe you?" asked the kid, pointing at the older man's track marks. "You've got a habit."

"Hey, do it your way if it makes life easier for you. Your old man, or old dear for that matter, would vouch for me. When you speak to 'em say you've bunked up with Cozza. Anyway, why would I upset your little gang. They've got a bit of a reputation. I don't want a bunch of eager little twats chasing me around in me old age." He sniggered but stopped abruptly as he felt another coughing fit coming on. "Look, tell you what I'll do." Cough. "I'll see if I can find out more." Cough. "Ask some subtle questions. Deal?"

"Sure. Deal. Thanks... Cozza."

"No problem." He hauled himself up and headed for the door. "Get yourself settled. Unpack your stuff. Sauna's down there, first on the right, next to the Jacuzzi." He did have a sense of humour, then.

The kid was pretty sure he already knew who had put up the reward. He had fought a long-standing drugs war with one particular crew keen to encroach on the pill-popping East London estate where he conducted his business. It was tactically astute for them to strike now, with him behind bars and his firm in flux. Alone now, he took a closer look at his cell. It was top-of-the-range decrepit; the furniture wooden and distressed, the walls plastered with dark poetry and will-sapping graffiti. "Leave hope at the door," one prophet had scrawled in something red. There was a tiny window which, when opened a few inches, struck up against metal bars, obscuring the view of the solid brick wall behind. To his right a separate cubicle housed a seat-less toilet, but any suggestion of privacy had been removed with the door. A dusty portable TV with a cracked screen nestled in the corner by the rotten food, wires exposed and connected to a mobile phone he assumed belonged to Cozza. Tugging the sheet in place on the top bunk, only now did he notice the stains on the mattress which hinted at stories no civilised person would want to hear. It certainly would be a miracle if he could overcome his sleep problems in these surroundings.

As he started to rise, stretching his back, he caught sight of his reflection in the bed frame. He had convinced himself he'd dealt well with the trial and remand; that he was hard, seasoned and prepared for what was to follow. Hollow cheekbones framing eyes sunk into shadow told a different story.

Suddenly, there was a shift in atmosphere – shouting then a pounding of feet. He caught a glimpse of something reflected in the metal bedframe that wasn't supposed to be there, span around and lifted his arm just in time. A jolt like an electric charge passed through the wrist and warm liquid spread up his sleeve. The sensation wasn't unlike peeing yourself as a kid, and he felt strangely embarrassed even though he knew it wasn't urine. It was blood... a fuck of a lot of blood.

He ducked as the attacker came in swinging again, the weapon slicing the air above him. He thought he'd escaped unscathed until the elbow followed through and cracked against his forehead, blurring his vision and jarring like a bitch. His assailant felt the impact, too, cursing loudly. "Fuck!" Time froze before the noise poured in like water from a jet washer, playground chants of "Kill the fucker" and "Fuck him up" flooding the cell. Hazy figures squeezed into the doorway, preventing a quick getaway.

His brain made calculations in fractions of a second, factoring in the audience, the surroundings, the assailant. Huge. Shaved head. Mixed-race. Biceps developed over long hours lifting weights. Ideal for tests of strength, not speed. Unsuited to brawls in confined spaces.

The kid's arm throbbed – boom, boom, boom – like something was trying to burst out. He reminded himself he'd had worse. Moving quickly, he caught his opponent off balance. "Oof!" The muscle man expelled air and energy as the head rammed into his gut. Following up quickly the kid grabbed a steroid-enhanced arm and sank teeth deep into the flesh above the wrist, shaking his head like an animal tearing at a tough cut of meat. A high-pitched sound, part-scream, part-moan, pierced the air, followed by the clink of the weapon dropping to the floor.

Fuelled by adrenaline, the kid threaded the meaty, bloody limb through the bed frame before sending his head crashing forward again. It collided with something soft, which buckled and cracked under the force. Still moving, he sank teeth into a tough piece of gristle, twisting and turning, ripping it off and spitting it to the floor, the taste of blood familiar to his pallet.

"Snuh, shuh, fuggin cun, you bit off my fuggin ear," said his shocked victim through a broken nose.

"Pardon!" shouted the kid, having fun. He rendered the other arm useless, grabbing fingers and bending them back on themselves until the crack echoed like a gunshot, quietening the audience for a second. His opponent incapacitated, the kid reached down and retrieved the weapon – a home-made shiv constructed from razor blade and plastic toothbrush moulded together with the flame from a cigarette lighter.

Rising to his toes, he barely noticed his own pain. He felt invigorated, light-headed, triumphant. He loved the blood-pumping, all-consuming rush of the fight and struggled to remember the last one he'd enjoyed this much. Then he chuckled. Idiot. It was the one that had put him in here in the first place. The smile slowly crossed his face, but slipped away before reaching his eyes.

"Look, shnuh. I'll help you, shnuh. Be yo' bodyguard, shnuh," the beaten thug pleaded, blood in his sinuses making breathing and talking difficult.

"Yeah," said the kid. "God help me If I need you as my bodyguard you useless piece of scum. You ain't a hard man. You're small fry... and my old man says when you got a fish danglin', you don't let 'em off the hook."

Behind him there was a scuffle as the screws arrived fashionably late, the fight over. In the background an alarm bell rang incessantly, warning him he didn't have much time. Moving the weapon's sharp edge to within a centimetre of the lifer's right eye he spat out his demand: "You want this back, nigger?"

In response his victim blinked wildly, realisation spreading across his face. "Why don't you take it then..?"

The kid plunged the blade home.

AFTER the noise died down, a familiar shape re-entered the cell. The rat wondered where the caged animals had gone, particularly when there was food to be had. Scampering forward, it sank its teeth into the discarded piece of meat.

A bit tough, but better.

Fresher.

Its family could eat tonight.

Part I

1996-2006

ONE

GARY MARSHALL would always remember the first time he met his stalker.

Some recalled exactly what they were doing when those planes crashed into the twin towers or Princess Diana died, but world events mean little to 13-year-old boys. Being threatened with a blade for the first time by someone who wished to relieve you of one of your prized possessions, however, is bound to have a lasting effect.

A happy lad, Gary had set about his day-to-day chores that morning in a brighter mood than usual. His joy seemed to be shared by the entire country, too, an outpouring of national pride which he had rarely encountered in his young life. What's more it was centred around his home, London, and even the tower blocks on the estate where he lived seemed cheerful, their grim exteriors transformed by flags bearing the Cross of St George hanging proudly from windows and red, white and blue bunting trailing across balconies.

He had finished his round later than usual, unable to resist taking a peak at the back pages of those papers he was supposed to be delivering. They told of how England's new footballing SAS strike force, Shearer and Sheringham, had dismantled the hotly-tipped Dutch 4-1 in Euro 96. Grumpy old Ron, who ran the newsagents, didn't even complain about his tardiness. Instead he chose to delay his departure even further by discussing the game. "Those strikers are something else, ain't they?" he said.

"I like Gazza," Gary confided. "He's my favourite."

"Aye, he's a bit of a show-off, though. Can't be trusted. What about that booze business before the tournament started, eh? You mark my words, he's a wrong 'un. Still, I can understand why he'd be your favourite. That's what your mates call you, ain't it? Gazza? Your old man is always telling me you're destined for great things."

"Yeah, well..." Gary blushed. His dad boasted about his football abilities to the point of embarrassment. To be fair, he'd done well for the local Under-14 side as a midfield playmaker, playing in a role not dissimilar to Gazza. That was where the similarities ended. While the footballer was broad shouldered and rumoured to be partial to the odd Mars bar Gary was tall for his age, gangly and lithe. He was also a natural blond as opposed to Gazza, who had dyed his hair. Some kids teased Gary, calling him a "ginga". His mum assured him otherwise, compromising with "strawberry blond".

"You're a good lad, Gary," said old Ron in a rare moment of tenderness, rubbing his head, "now be off with you or your mum with have my guts for garters." Gary laughed, having no idea what garters were.

When school was over his mind turned to going for a kickabout at the local rec. He was bound to find some of his mates taking advantage of the warm afternoon sunshine, but first he had to return home to get changed and dump his bike.

The estate he lived on was known as the Boxers, the flats having been erected sometime in the 1950s, but given a token makeover 30 years later by some council clever clogs who chose 'inspirational fighters synonymous with the East End' as a theme. Standing next to the brick monstrosity of Minter Towers, a block named after the former world middleweight champ Alan Minter who staged many of his early fights at the York Hall in Bethnal Green, were identical buildings clad in various shades of insipid pastel known as Walker, Cooper and Stracey. The buildings certainly resembled fighters, but rather than in their prime, these were shabby and punch-drunk, with graffiti like badly-drawn tattoos decorating their exteriors. A big black mark like a bruise crept up one beige wall of Minter, the result of an abandoned car being set on fire.

"So what have we here, man?" A boy stepped into his path just as he was about to push his way in through the entrance to the lifts. He looked about a year older than Gary, was brown skinned and wore an American basketball vest to emphasise developing biceps. Four of his mates emerged from the shadows.

"I live here," said Gary. "My flat's in this building. Excuse me." He tried to edge past, but the boy mirrored his movements like a bulky centre-half barring the route to goal. Gary felt uneasy. He'd heard his mum telling a neighbour that people had been accosted on the estate, mugged and relieved of their valuables and cash. "Look, my mum will be out searching for me if I'm not home soon." The excuse sounded weak even to his young ears.

"My mum will be worried," mimicked one of the other boys in a whiny voice, his pals laughing.

"You'd better hand over them wheels then, pal, if you don't want her coming down here to pick up da pieces," said the leader.

Gary inched backwards, the youths following him. He knew he was in trouble but was determined not to give the bike up. It was a racer with gears and his dad had saved up a long time to get it for him, making the purchase from a mate at Walthamstow market. He thought about riding away but couldn't summon up the guts. His stomach rolled, fear gripping him like that first time he'd been invited to jump in at the deep end during swimming lessons. When the sun glinted off something in the gang leader's hand he thought he might pee himself. It was a knife, and he was holding it sideways in the way movie gangsters held their guns.

"Bike, bredren, or I'll stick you." There were uneasy chuckles from his mates.

"Oi!"

Gary physically jumped at the sound. It came from his right and he took his eye off the gang leader for a split second to register the scruffy looking kid in a tracksuit two sizes too big for him standing on a raised area of tarmac a short distance away. Great, he thought. Is he involved, too? That might explain a few things.

The kid's name was Arnold. He went to Gary's school and lived in one of the houses just down the road from the Boxers. His dad had money, by all accounts, but people said he had obtained it illegally. The father wasn't a nice person, anyway, according to the rumour machine. He had a violent reputation and Gary had witnessed this first hand when he had seen the bloke chase his dad across the estate, waving a training shoe above his head and calling Stan Marshall a "f'ing cheating cunt!". Not that this was an unusual state of affairs where Gary's dad was concerned. Thugs regularly turned up at the door to 'have a word', only for his mother to send them on a wild goose chase. His mum said people were jealous of their dad's ability to bring home good money at a time when others were struggling to make ends meet. Gary was happy to accept the explanation, the alternative being that his dad was a rip-off merchant who conned his customers.

It wasn't just the boy's thug dad that made Gary uneasy. Arnold seemed to have taken more than a passing interest in him person- ally. When Gary played football he often caught glimpses of the kid standing among the sparse audience on the sidelines, and he also felt him watching from afar in the school playground. Just like a stalker.

Perhaps the boy was lonely, but if that was the case why didn't he summon up the courage to say hello? To be truthful, Gary wasn't sure how he would feel about that. It was a bit off-putting that Arnold always had that heavy-set, squat dog at his side. It was with him now, straining at a metal chain being utilised as a lead. Had Arnold been after his bike all the time? Had he been "casing the joint" as they said in films?

"Who's dis mug?" The leader's question surprised Gary. It meant that he and Arnold weren't connected.

"Dunno Naj," a couple of his minions replied.

"Looks like someone who has a liking for hospital food, yeah?" He slapped the hand of his nearest compatriot then looked Gary in the eye. "You stay here, bike boy, Ain't finished with you."

The entourage parted and Naj hobbled, gangster fashion, towards the new arrival, knife tucked against his leg. "Why don't you an' your little doggie mind your own bidness?" he shouted. Rather than running off, though, Arnold Dolan maintained eye contact with the gang leader and started speaking to him quietly. The other boys were distracted, trying to follow the conversation, and Gary realised this was his chance. Cycling away now would be the sensible thing to do, but he didn't want to be branded a coward at school.

He held his ground as the boy Naj suddenly lunged at Arnold, who lurched backwards then tugged at the chain. "Millwall," he shouted and the dog sprang forward, snarling and rearing up on its hind legs, spittle spouting from between sharp teeth. Bundling the gang leader onto his back its mouth closed around the youth's leg and he screamed, flapping his arms wildly as he tried to manoeuvre into a position where he could use the knife. Advancing, Arnold dragged the dog aside then swung the chain fiercely down on the gang leader's knife hand. With an exclamation of pain he dropped the weapon and lifted his hands to cover his face.

The metal links rained down again and again, the other gang members not so sure of their ground now, hesitating in no man's land as the snarling dog turned to face them. No longer frozen by fear, Gary realised he had to help his surprise ally. He leapt on his bike and rode in the direction of the fight, swinging his school bag like an Olympic hammer thrower. He caught one of the lagging gang members on the side of the head with it and the boy fell to the floor. Two of the others turned too late, Gary administering a well-placed kick to the stomach of the first one, then punching the other in the ear. That was enough to send the fourth gang member legging it for the car park exit. Momentum slowing, Gary skidded to a halt next to Arnold, who showed no sign of tiring as he brought the chain crashing down again and again.

Blood scarred the tarmac and the boy's face had been disarranged in such a way that he might have been peering at a distorted reflection in a fairground hall of mirrors. One eye was fully shut, caked in blood where the metal links had cut through the eyebrow. "Mate... Mate, you'll bloody kill him!" said Gary, tentatively putting his hand on Arnold's shoulder.

Arnold turned wild eyed to look at Gary and for a moment he thought he might be next in line for a beating. Then the other boy seemed to realise who Gary was, smiled and dropped the chain to his side. "Shouldn't go out armed then, should he?" said Arnold. "My dad says you must show 'maximum force' retaliation, so they know you're serious. What did you think he was gonna do with that blade, clean your fingernails?" The boy called Arnold smiled as he watched the raggle-taggle army head for the car park exit as the dog turned manic circles, barking at them, drool lubricating its muzzle. Lifting their leader by his jacket lapels he spat in his face. "Listen here, and listen good," he said. "This is our turf – it don't belong to you mugs. You've just made the mistake of tangling with the Boxer Boys. If we see you around here again it won't end so well for you. Tell your mates they don't come back here unless they have a death wish. Understand?" The boy nodded, his expression vacant, his bloody mouth hanging open. "Fuck off with you then!" Arnold flung him in the direction of his mates. Then, putting his fingers to his lips, he whistled loudly and the dog trotted up to be treated with a rub behind the ear. "Good boy, Stevo, good boy!" He turned to Gary. "You OK, champ?"

"Yeah, um, thanks. Thanks a lot. You call your dog Stevo?"

"I know… funny ain't it? Named him after the Irish super-middleweight boxer Steve Collins. He's a real warrior. I met him once, honest. He lives down Southend. You're Gary, ain't ya? I seen you about. Everyone talks about you. Bit of a footballer, ain't ya? You seem all right. Come down Upton Park some time, with me and me brothers, it'll be good. Oh, I'm Arnie." The words came scattergun, as if he had locked them away for weeks and only now had the chance to release them.

"People call me Gazza," said Gary.

"Like the footballer?"

Gary nodded. "You're West Ham, too? I thought I heard you shout Millwall."

As he said the word, Stevo growled.

"Well trained that dog," said Arnie. "That's his attack word, just in case I get in trouble with them south London bastards. Took a bit of training to get him to react to it, but it works a treat."

Gary looked at the dog uneasily. Its tongue was lolling out to the side and its eyes were bright and sparkling. He could hardly believe it was the same animal that had attacked the knife-wielding thug with such ferocity. "Don't you fear he might, um, turn on someone, though? Attack a mate or..."

"Oh, don't worry," said Arnie, patting the dog and ordering it to sit. It obeyed immediately. "He's a right softie. Wasn't always the case, mind. I rescued him from these blokes over the rec, Russians or something. They were training him to be one of them fighting dogs, hanging him from a tree branch by his teeth. It's meant to toughen the jaws up, y'know? When he fell they laid into him real bad, with sticks an' all. Bastards! Couldn't let that carry on, could I?"

"What did you do?"

"I followed them to this yard, right, where they had him chained up. I broke in and stole him. He was a bit fierce at first, did this to me." He showed Gary a four-inch scar on his wrist. "Bled like a bugger but I won him over with treats and stuff. Now he's mine. Loyal as fuck. Them blokes did come sniffing around to get him back, but dad caught them snooping and he and some mates taught them a proper lesson. He don't like foreigners anyway, me dad, so he was happy to do it. They ain't been back since." He paused, looking lovingly at the dog. "Glad I got him, Stevo. He'll do anything to protect me and if he knows you're a mate he'll do the same for you ... God knows I need him. It's getting a bit lairy round here. There are plenty more douches where they came from." He indicated in the direction of the car park entrance, the gang long disappeared. "Me and you should stick together."

Arnie's eyes were attracted by something on the floor which glinted in the sunlight. He bent down to pick it up. It was a knife with a six-inch blade. "Looks like that loser left something behind," he said, slashing the air with the weapon. "Think it's about time I started carrying a nice, sharp knife. Stevo's great, but he ain't gonna stop a bit of cold steel."

He shoved the blade into his coat pocket and peered off into the distance for a second, seeming to lose his thread. Then the life returned to his eyes. "What about it, anyway? The Boxer Boys. Sounds good don't it? Came to me all of a sudden. That's who we are, ain't it? Boxer Boys. Hey, nice bike. Give us a backy would ya? I'll be late for me tea. Stevo can run alongside."

TWO

ARNIE unhooked the chain and Stevo ran off into the house, almost bundling over an attractive blonde woman in black and white checked mini skirt and fishnet tights, the crows feet around her hazel eyes betraying her age. "Oh Arnold!" she exclaimed. "Did you have to do that, love? His muddy paw prints will be everywhere and I've had the cleaner in today... hey, what's happened to you?" She inspected his blood-encrusted knuckles.

"Somalis I think they was," he replied. "Tried taking Gary's bike so I sorted them." He moved aside and ushered his new friend into the house. "He gave us a lift home so I invited him in for a drink and some grub. Hey, Gar, this is me mum," he stood aside and the woman looked him up and down.

"I know Gary," she said. "I've seen him around, anyways. You live over on the estate don't you love? Your dad works down the market, runs the stall with the cheap trainers. Got some nice bargains."

"Mum should know," butted in Arnie. "Always down there, she is. No wonder. When you have to kit out five kids it must cost a bomb." He laughed. "Spent so much on that fuckin' stall Dad banned you from going there, didn't he?"

"Hey, don't swear in front of your guest," his mum said, looking embarrassed. "He's kidding, Gary love."

"Very pleased to meet you Mrs Dolan," said Gary, adopting his polite voice, the one he reserved for other children's parents. "I expect you know mum too. Sheila Marshall? She works part-time down the bakery."

The woman gave the question a moment's thought. "Nah, can't say I do, love. Sorry. Anyway, let's get you boys your drinks. I imagine all that 'activity' has made you thirsty."

She went to a large fridge/freezer unit in the corner and pulled open the door, retrieving two cans of pop from inside. Gary looked around. Everything was shining chrome. He made a mental comparison with the small DIY kitchen back at his flat. His dad had spent months knocking it together from a flat pack picked up on the cheap, only for it to fall into instant disrepair. Surfaces were already scarred and drawers poorly fitted. You had to open them carefully if you didn't want one of them dropping on your foot, a real hazard for someone with plans to become a professional footballer.

By contrast, the kitchen in the Dolan household must have set them back a fortune. It shocked him simply because if you looked at the normal, semi-detached house from the outside it was just like all the others in the street.

"Come and see me room," said Arnie, grabbing the drinks. He led the way through the dining room to the hall passageway. As they headed for the stairs a young girl in school uniform with bunches in her jet-black hair approached in the opposite direction. "Get a move on Anj!" said Arnie.

"Get lost!" she said equally playfully, thumping him on the arm as she jumped off from three steps up. He grimaced and feigned injury, then twisted and tugged her hair as she started to walk away. "Oww! I'll tell Mum," she protested, promptly shutting up when she noticed her brother had a companion. Shooting Gary a coy look, she bit her lip.

"This is Gazza, sis, me new mate," said Arnie. "Gonna see a lot of him about. We're forming a gang." She tutted, declared: "Boys are stupid" then moved on down the corridor, taking a doorway on the right which Gary guessed led to the lounge. She was carrying a book and he could just about read the title: The Hobbit. It was one of his favourites, a primary school teacher having read it to his class a few years back. He thought about talking to her about it, but sensed Arnie's impatience.

"She's all right, my sis," he said, charging up the stairs. "I get on better with her than the other idiots. God, if anyone touched her..." He shook himself out of his daydream. "Come on, I've got Resident Evil upstairs. It's the biz. You ever played it?" Gary shook his head. He only had a cheap computer console and a handful of games. It wasn't really his thing. Still, Arnie seemed enthusiastic and he decided to go with the flow. When they reached the top of the stairs they faced a door guarded by a "Keep Out!" sign.

"Lot of good that does in a house like this!" Arnie said, pushing through. Gary was greeted with wall-to-wall posters of boxers and dogs in equal measure. Pride of place belonged to a full-length pho- tograph of the heavyweight champion Mike Tyson, who had beaten the great British hope Frank Bruno for the second time earlier that year. Steve Collins, Chris Eubank, Nigel Benn and Michael Watson also shared space on the wall, next to a collection of dogs in a variety of sizes, shapes and colours. Pressed up against the side wall was a bunk bed.

"It's all right, I guess," Arnie said, looking around as if seeing the room for the first time. "I share with me younger brother Bruce but it ain't so bad. He has to let me do what I want or he gets one of these." He held up a fist and threw a punch at an imaginary rival. "It could be worse, I could have to share with one of the older ones: Chuck or Sly."

Gareth's mouth fell open in surprise. "Your names: They're a bit ... unusual."

"Ha. I know, I know. We're named after film actors. Dad's a big action movie fan and mum went along with it. Even when Anj came they named her Anjelica after Anjelica Houston, the actress."

"So, let's get this right," said Gary. "You're Arnie after Schwarzen- neger, obviously. Bruce is... Willis?" Arnie nodded and filled in the blanks.

"Sly was named after Sylvester Stallone and Chuck, well, that's Chuck Norris... not that I know much about him. One of me Dad's favourites though. Hey, you into boxing?"

Gary nodded, not wishing to offend. He could take it or leave it. It couldn't compare with football and he found it a bit brutal but he didn't want to upset his new friend. "Hang on!" Arnie reached under the bed and pulled out a pair of boxing gloves. He threw them at Gary then pointed. In the corner of the room, Gary noticed the punchbag for the first time. "I'll get changed. Put them on, and I'll give you some tips on how to punch properly, do the maximum damage," he said. As Arnie lifted up his shirt Gary was shocked to see large areas of the boy's torso were covered with bruises of different shades and colours.

"It's all right," said Arnie, registering his unease. "I'm just toughening myself up, like me dad told me to. He says you never know when someone's gonna come at ya... just like today. These immigrants want to take over our country. Dad says we gotta keep them in their place, all them foreigners. They come here, take our jobs or sponge off the state. We got to send home the blacks and Pakis – keep Britain Great." He prodded a faded mark that covered his ribs. "These don't hurt, not really. They make me more determined to defend myself, get as good as I can be. Know what I mean?"

Gary nodded, though he didn't have any concept of the problems Arnie talked about. His own father had loads of mates at the market who had originally come from different countries. Despite their skin colour and chosen religions they got on brilliantly, went to each other's family events like weddings and birthdays, and as far as he knew none of them had taken anyone else's job. Anyway, wasn't Arnie's dad a career criminal? It was unlikely he had a proper job to lose. His new friend's statement seemed at odds, too, with the fact he had surrounded himself with posters of boxers who were, in the main, black.

It wasn't just the racist remarks that made Gary uneasy. The bruises didn't help and he wondered how Arnie had come by them. "Where is he now... your dad?" Gary asked, looking around nervously.

"Oh, don't worry, he ain't like Kato!" said Arnie, laughing at his own private joke. When he realised Gary didn't understand what he was talking about he explained. "You never seen them Pink Panther movies?" he asked. "Dad's favourites: he's got them all on VHS. They're wicked! Kato's this Japanese bloke, right, and Inspector Clouseau, the French detective, employs him as his self-defence instructor. He has orders to attack at any time he thinks the Inspector is off guard. He jumps out of wardrobes or springs from under the bed when the Inspector's with a woman... it's proper funny. No, our old man is away for a bit. 'On holiday at Her Majesty's Pleasure', me mum says." Arnie laughed.

"Eh?"

"No, you numpty! Ha ha," said Arnie. "I don't mean the Queen's paying for him to go on his holidays or anything. It just means he's in prison. They stitched him up for some armed robbery shit. It's the risk you take, he says. The job pays well and we ain't done bad for ourselves seeing this area is a shithole. I'm 13 now, though, and the longest he's been out of nick since I was born was two years. That was up until the Old Bill turned up to cart him off again a couple of weeks ago."

"Don't you miss him? If it was my dad I don't know what I'd do."

"Yeah well, I guess your dad and my dad are different people... damn is that the time?" said Arnie, looking at the clock. "You said you'd have to be back by six or your mum would be worried. Put those gloves on and let's have a sparring session. No point wasting time."

Gary did as he was told, but he couldn't help thinking his friend had deliberately changed the subject.

THE TWO BOYS became inseparable over the next three years, striking up a special bond others tried to break at their peril. The Boxer Boys became a real thing. Pete Vickers, a long-time schoolmate of Arnie's, was an early recruit, along with a boy called John Fallon, who picked up the nickname Fancy Man for his penchant for 60s-style clothes inspired by the mod generation. Of course, then there were Arnie's older brothers Chuck and Sly, who always seemed to be around when there was trouble.

The gang went to football matches together, stood side-by-side at parties and discos, and sneaked into the local public house for underage drinking and pool. They were getting their teenage kicks and life was good.

THREE

"NUTTERS!" Pete Vickers forced his way between them.

"You wanna play, Pete?" said Arnie, headbutting the peacemaker.
Vickers shrieked and fell backwards, landing on an old sofa.

"Serves him right for interfering, eh?" Arnie threw his arm around
Gary's neck and laughed. "Now, where were we?"

Gary pulled away. "I'm bored now, Doles," he said. "Give it a rest,
I've got a headache."

"Tssh, lightweight!" Arnie was smiling, though. "Reminds me of
that time in my room, remember? You had the boxing gloves and I
invited you to take a swing. Belted me right in me bruised ribs, for
fuck sake, so I gave you a Glasgow kiss. You crashed into the bunks
and the fuckers collapsed. I was laughing so much I didn't see you
get up. Butted me back, you did, and Stevo didn't like it. Next thing
I know I'm having to pull him off ya."

He took his arm from around Gary's neck and scanned the surroundings. It was Thursday night at the community centre, a gathering the adult do-gooders had the cheek to call youth club. In one
corner a couple of local kids were whacking coloured balls across a
carpet of ripped baize, while from the other side of the room came
the click-clack of table tennis balls being hit across a net. With little
else on offer, the two friends had been making their own amusement
in the form of a headbutting contest.

"Hey, I can't see him. Where is the little git?"

"Bruce? Think he went out front," Fancy Man said, turning up to
find out why Vickers had cried out like a girl. He was dressed in his

trademark parka coat, drainpipe jeans and brown, tasselled loafers. He'd got all the mod gear from a catalogue that Arnie's eldest brother Chuck had on subscription. It made him stand out from the crowd, the other Boxer Boys happy to wear an assortment of sweatshirts, polo shirts, jeans and leather jackets. "Last time I saw your little'un he was with that spotty goofball, whatsisname? Tigger, that's it."

"Oh, that ain't good," said Arnie. "That little oik's a sly bastard. Mum'll kill me if I lose her little baby. Let's have a shufti, see what we can see." He led the way to the front door, Gary, Fancy Man and Vickers following.

"Go outside boys and you can't come back in, those are the rules," said the balding man at the small table by the doorway, a metal money box open in front of him.

"Sod you and your rules, Gramps," said Arnie, flashing him two fingers. "This club's shite anyway."

"So don't come back again then, you little ruffian... matter-of-fact, you're barred."

While the old man's attention was diverted, Gary pocketed a handful of coins. "Hey!" The club helper suddenly realised what was going on. Before he could apprehend the thief, though, Gary's mates shielded him and hustled out through the open door.

"Rebate!" shouted Gary and they all laughed.

Vickers bashed Gary on the arm. "What you go and do that for?" he asked. "You'll get us all in trouble."

"Sorry," said Gary unconvincingly. "It was just there, winking at me."

"Share the wealth, I fancy some smokes." Arnie materialised, holding his hand out.

"Get your own," said Gary.

"Aww, don't be like that."

"You know what I think about smoking, Arnie. Makes you unfit."

"Oh, listen to 'im," said Arnie, "old Gazza." He dug his elbow into Vickers' ribs, triggering a coughing fit. "Oops! Sorry Vickers, you old woman. Maybe no ciggies for you then. Why should the rest of us miss out, though, just cos our Gaz fancies himself a sportsman. Bet some of them footie players smoke, anyway. That Gascoigne, for starters." He tapped the side of his head. "Idea," he said. "How about cigars? They ain't dangerous if you don't inhale. What d'ya reckon?" He glared at Gary so keenly that he relented.

"If you must, go on then."

"Come on, it'll be a buzz." Arnie had won the argument but wanted to ram home his point. "That Malcolm Allison. He's a football coach, right, but he smokes them, don't he? And that other fella, Big Ron. They wouldn't do it if it was dangerous, now would they?"

Gary had lost the will to argue. When Arnie was in this sort of mood you couldn't win.

"What are those little buggers doing?" said Fancy Man, pointing along the street. A group of youngsters had formed some sort of huddle. Arnie's young brother was among them.

"Dunno," he said, "Let's find out." He held his finger to his lips and began tip-toeing along the fence at the side of the pavement. The others followed his lead. When they got to within 30 yards of the group he shouted: "Now!" and broke into a sprint. Leaping among the younger boys, he saw most of them had their hands out offering Tigger money. Fancy Man locked the centre of attention in a bear hug, pinning his arms to his sides.

"What the holy fuck's going on here, Bruce?" asked Arnie of his younger brother.

"Uh, nothing, bro," replied Bruce timidly.

"Nothing. Yeah, right." He moved across and punched Tigger in the gut. "Our Bruce don't seem to be talking to me, so you'd better help me out." The boy with the lank hair and spots doubled over, gasping for breath. Arnie grabbed his hands and forced open his fingers, the boy letting out a squeal as a cracking sound splintered the night air. "What's this?" Arnie asked. The others gathered around to look. Tigger had some small transparent packages in his hand, containing a white powder.

"I asked you a question," he said, lifting Tigger by the hair so their eyes were at the same level.

"It's coke, Doles," volunteered Vickers. "Cocaine. Makes you feel special, they say. Want a try?"

"Don't need no drugs to tell me I'm special," said Arnie, keeping his eyes on his prisoner. "You selling this fucked up shit to my little brother, Tigger, you scum?"

"Uh, no, fuck mate, no. Aargh! Think you broke me fuckin' fingers. Ow! Look, your brother just volunteered, that's all. He's helping me and I'm paying him."

"Oh, so you're turning him into a drug pusher, are ya?" said Arnie, wrinkling his mouth in a sneer. "What's the going rate for that then?" He shoved his hand into the back of the boy's trousers and pulled out a wad of paper. Behind him, Fancy Man whistled. Gary estimated there was at least £200 in scrunched up banknotes in his friend's hand. "Well, well, well," Arnie said, stripping away a couple of twenties and handing them to Bruce. "Here's your wages you little fucker. Now sod off home and be grateful I don't tell Mum."

Bruce headed in the direction of the house.

"Come on, Doles, let's get those cigars you were so keen on," said Gary, fearing what his friend might do. "We don't want anything to do with this."

For a second Arnie didn't respond. Then Gary noticed a familiar look as his friend's eyes glazed over. "You run along now and I'll catch you up in a minute," said Arnie. "Me and Tiggs just need a quiet word."

FOUR

GARY HANDED the coats to his sister. "Glad you could make it!" he said to Anjie. "And, um..."

"This is my best mate Janie," explained Anjelica Dolan, indicating the broad-shouldered girl in the flowery print blouse. His eyes were unavoidably attracted to her cleavage. It was more pronounced than most girls her age. The blouse was teasingly low cut and she had complimented it by a tight black mini-skirt which showed off a shapely pair of legs. Anjie wore a more modest ensemble of black trouser suit with a white blouse, a few buttons open but little on show to attract the leers of the young bucks in attendance.

"This, Janie, is Gazza," said Anjie. "Our Arnie thinks the sun shines out of his arse, so he can't be that bad!"

They all laughed.

"Drinks?" offered Gary.

"You do know we're only 14?" said Anjie, biting her finger coyly and reminding him of the first time they met.

"Of course, we've got soft drinks, though. I didn't mean..."

"It's a joke!" she interrupted, slapping her hand against his chest. "You boys, so gullible. I think that's why I like you Gazza, you'd believe anything I say. We'd love a glass of wine each, or even a vodka and coke if you got any."

"I'll see what's in the kitchen," he said.

"Oh, and Gazza..."

"Yeah?"

"Don't forget that birthday kiss."

Even in the dim light the girls could see Gary Marshall's face turn a darker shade of pink. They giggled as they watched him wander off.

"You fancy him, don't you?" asked Janie.

"He's all right. Fancy him's a bit strong. We're friends really. It wouldn't work anyway, with him being me brother's best mate. Arnie wouldn't approve, I don't reckon. He'd be jealous. He's a bit possessive."

"He can possess me anytime," said Janie, smirking. "Speaking of which... did you say anything?"

"Me?" said Anjie, looking confused. "You wanted me to say something to our Arnold?" She was rewarded with a slap on the arm.

"Of course! You don't think I'm dressed up like this for any other reason."

"I don't know, Janie. Pete Vickers?"

"Oh come on!" Jane tipped her head back and roared with laughter.

"What's wrong with Pete?"

"Oh he's all right but he's a bit, um, straight ain't he?"

"You saying my brother's kinky?"

"Hope so!" Jane replied. The two girls burst out laughing again. "You know what I mean, though, don't you? Your Arnie has, well, he's got a spark... and those blue eyes... dreamy!"

"You perv!" This time it was Anjelica Dolan's turn to administer the slap. They giggled again. "For your information, Gaz has lovely blue eyes, too! If you must know I did slip your name into the conversation ... mentioned you might be interested in getting to know him better."

Janie put her hand to her mouth. "You didn't!" she gasped. "Really? Well, here's hoping... I ain't seen him around, though."

"Had a 'bit of business' to attend to, he said, whatever that's supposed to mean. It's got something to do with that little reprobate Mitchell Tiggs."

"Tigger? Oh I hope he's not involved with that toe-rag," said Janie, looking around and whispering to her friend. "You know he's a dealer?"

"I wouldn't expect Arnie to have much truck with drugs," said Anjie. "I heard he nearly took Tigger's head off for getting our Bruce involved, silly little git that he is."

"Hmm, oh well, here comes Gary. Let's get our drinks and have a mingle."

"You go," said Anjie. "I need a quick chat with the birthday boy."

"SIXTEEN, and never been kissed."

"I have!" protested Gary.

"Yeah," said Anjie with a grin. "By your mum." He screwed his bottom lip up, feigning hurt. "Oh diddums, I'm sowwy," she said in a silly voice. "Listen, I got you something. Hope you like it." She retrieved a small object wrapped in brightly coloured paper from her handbag.

"I'm guessing it's a book," said Gary, taking a sip of beer from a plastic cup.

"What else?" They laughed.

He ripped off the paper and stared at the cover. "Oh, Nick Hornby."

"Yeah, it's about football."

"It's about Arsenal!" he protested. "Couldn't you get me one about the Hammers?"

She punched him on the arm. "Ungrateful!".

"I'm teasing," he said. "Cheers. Fever Pitch. I've heard a lot about it."

"I've read it and it's really good... and I'm not even into football," she said.

"Oh, I see! You buy yourself a book and then give it to me second hand when you've read it. Charming."

"It's good to share, don't you think?" said Anjie. "By the way, where are the folks?"

"Down the local. Nothing special. Just said I could invite a few mates around for the evening. They'll be back soon enough I expect, to check the flat's still in one piece."

"You'll be lucky!" she said, looking out into the corridor. "The human wrecking ball just turned up." She indicated behind him and he swivelled to see Arnie walking through the door, waving to those gathered as if he had joined the ranks of royalty. Behind him trooped Chuck, Sly, Fancy Man, Vickers and, bringing up the rear, Mitchell Tiggs. "Wonder what they've been up to... without you, too," she said.

"I told Arnie I couldn't go because I had this thing to organise," Gary said unconvincingly. He didn't want to let on that he had no idea where Arnie had been. Normally they were in each other's pockets 24/7.

"You wouldn't turn my brother down for nothing! You two fallen out?"

"No!" he protested but wouldn't expand. "Listen, I've got to see him. You OK if I shoot off?"

"That's it... dump me as soon as your best buddy arrives," said Anjie. "Don't worry, I can look after myself: plenty of fit blokes around."

"Yeah and they're all qualified babysitters," he joked. She could see in his eyes, though, that her words had slightly got to him.

"Look, I'm joking," she said, patting his arm. "Think I'll go and see where my best mate has got to. I know she has to leave at 11pm otherwise her dad will turn her into a pumpkin!"

FIVE

"HONESTLY GARY, I don't know what's got into you these days. Stan, what you got to say to your boy? I hope he ain't going to lie and spin yarns, because we all know where he gets that from."

"Don't turn it around on me!" said Stan Marshall, fixing his wife with a glare. A burly man, he was standing in the front room wearing just a string vest and a pair of tracksuit bottoms that were an inch too short. Behind him was a life-size picture of Rick Parfitt, the guitarist with rock band Status Quo, all denim and flowing white hair. "Let me handle it Sheil. You go and get the tea sorted."

"God knows what they would say," she murmured as she left the room, her arm indicating the shelf above the artificial gas fire where the cream of British royalty stared out at them from behind cheap plastic photo frames. "You'd better come too Miss," she said to the girl with the light brown hair, cut short into a bob.

"Oh Mum!" protested the girl.

"You can peel some spuds for me, Lil. I don't want you hearing any of this. I hope you didn't see these... shenanighans." The teenager climbed reluctantly from the armchair in the corner of the room and followed her into the kitchen.

"Now then G-Man," said Gary's dad once the door had closed. He kept his voice low but clear. "We all get up to things when we're young and I can't expect you to be any different. It's all out there, isn't it? Girls, drink, drugs, sowing your wild oats – but I'm really surprised and concerned at the change in your behaviour over the last year or so. You've always been a good lad, never given us any trouble until now."

He allowed time for his words to sink in: "Firstly, we get a school report saying your grades have slipped and suggesting you're hanging around with the wrong crowd. You've been on report twice, once for bullying for heaven's sake, and your teachers are seriously worried you might not pass your exams. It's ridiculous. I know I'm no brain of Britain but you were doing really well. Take after your mother I guess because you were consistently getting A's in English and your teacher said you were the stand-out student in the class. They said they could see you working with words, til I pointed out you were gonna be a footballer. The last year or so, though, it's all gone downhill. Added to that we get a phone call accusing you of stealing petty cash from youth club which, quite frankly, just isn't on."

"They can't prove it was me," Gary protested.

"That's by the by," said Stan Marshall. "You should feel bad about it. Embarrassed. You don't want for much and that money goes to good causes. Hell, you're always moaning about the shocking state of the pool table down that club. That cash could have gone towards getting a new one and benefited everyone, not just you and your little mates. More to the point..." He put his hand in his pocket and pulled out a crumpled, cardboard packet. "I hope you didn't nick it just to pay for these. What the hell are you doing with cigars? I know me and your mum smoke..."

"Yeah, like chimneys," interrupted Gary.

"Well yeah, OK, we're not ideal role models but surely you know better. Don't make the same mistakes as us. I thought you wanted to make a go of this football thing and..."

"They're not mine," said Gary. "I'm looking after them. Anyway, Arnie said they ain't dangerous."

"Oh, he did, did he? Soddin' hell, it's Arnie this and Arnie that nowadays. Remind me of his medical qualifications? Bleedin' brain surgeon that Arnold. Do you think he's been on this earth long enough to know more than your parents? He doesn't strike me as the sharpest tool in the box, so why you take his word as gospel I've no idea. Jeez! You know his dad's a wrong 'un, don't you? His older brothers aren't squeaky clean either. Here's another thing. How come I found him leaving our bedroom on the night of your party? I specifically told you the bedrooms were out of bounds, apart from as a place to store the coats. When I got to our room there was a girl in there, tidying her clothes. She seemed a bit upset. We let you have the house as a treat for the night because it was your birthday. It wasn't supposed to be a brothel."

"I don't know anything about that, Dad."

"No, I bet... too busy smoking I wouldn't wonder and, while we are at it, I found these in the ashtray." He held up two small white objects. "If I'm not mistaken these are roaches... for spliffs. You'd better not be going down that route."

"Of course not!" protested Gary. "I would never touch drugs."

They sat there silently looking at each other. Gary loved his dad dearly and didn't want to upset him, but couldn't see what the fuss was about. He was young and enjoying himself while he could. It wasn't as if he had caused harm to anyone and the roaches had nothing to do with him, though he silently cursed Tigger, whom he suspected of bringing drugs to the party. He wasn't happy with Arnie, either, for throwing out the invitation. He always thought his mate felt the same way as he did towards dopeheads, but something had changed over recent weeks.

"Look, I'll pay the cash back to the youth club, out of my birthday money."

"OK," said his dad. "Glad to hear it. I hate being a nag son but sometimes it's the only way I can get through to you. You're only on this planet once and you can't always undo your mistakes. I appreciate it's nice to be popular but that doesn't mean you have to become an out-and-out little gangster."

In the hallway the phone rang. "Sorry, hon, can you get that?" Sheila Marshall shouted from the kitchen. "I'm up to my elbows here making your favourite, steak and kid."

"Wait there, because we haven't finished our chat," said Stan Marshall to Gary before stepping out into the hallway.

"HELLO? Mr Marshall? Hi there. Shankly Plumb. I'm one of the youth coaches at West Ham."

"Oh, uh, yes... Shankly?"

"Daft isn't it? Everyone raises their eyebrows at that. My old boy was from Liverpool – a huge Reds fan. Bill Shankly was his idol. Anyway, let's get to the point. We've been hearing some good things about your lad Gary. Like to invite him to a 12-week training camp with us so we can see how he fits into a top-flight football environment. There are plenty of talented kids around here as I'm sure you know. Some of the youth who came through here are on the way to the top: Frankie Lampard – that's the junior one, not the senior ha ha – Rio Ferdinand, Paul Ince. We've got a few good ones now, reckon they could win the Youth Cup – Joe Cole, very good talent, Jermain Defoe. It's the perfect place for your boy, he'll get all the encouragement he needs and if it doesn't work out he can set his sights lower. There's always Orient, ha ha. It's a good break, though, I'm sure you'll agree."

Bloody comedian, thought Stan Marshall. He was an Orient supporter. Still, this was the call he had been waiting for since he first took his boy to toddler practice on a cold Sunday morning when Gary was five. "Fantastic, Mr Plumb, fantastic," he said. "Wait there..." The football coach heard a rustle at the other end of the line and the distant shout of "Gary! Come here boy! You'll want to hear this."

There was a whispered conversation, then Stan Marshall was back on the line. "Excellent, excellent... sorry, hi Mr Plumb. When would you like to see us? Gary is keen to give it a go. He's studying for his mock exams at the moment but if it involves the summer and we can work around school I'm sure it will be fine."

"Ah, that's really good news Mr Marshall. We'd like him to come to our Chadwell Heath training ground at some stage this week so he can sign forms, etc. I'm sure he won't mind that. Then I'll fill you in on the full programme."

"Excellent, Mr Plumb. Just before you go… if it's not too rude of me to ask: is there any money involved? Travel expenses and the like? We're hardly a rich family and I tend to have to ferry the boy everywhere. I'm sure you understand…"

Receiving a non-committal answer, Stan Marshall returned to the front room. "Well done, son," he said. "I guess I can't stay mad at you for long. This is brilliant news. You certainly won't need these anymore."

Picking up the cigar packet he crushed it in his hand and deposited it in the bin.

SIX

"FUCK! Is that what I think it is?"

"What do you think it is, a cricket ball? Here, catch!"

The egg-shaped object flew across the small divide and Arnie juggled then grasped it in his fingers. It was heavier than it looked, dimpled, cold to the touch. He let the air escape from his lungs, only realising now that he'd been holding his breath.

"You fucker, Chuck. I know I said we needed to tool up, but..."

"Look," said the older boy. "What's your beef? I don't see a problem with bringing a grenade to a knife party." He chuckled. Turned to Fancy Man and offered a handshake. The other boy looked as shocked as Arnie, but couldn't turn down his closest friend. Arnie knew Chuck could be a bit random but this was way off the wall.

"He's gone in," shouted Vickers, leaning back from the front seat. "Shit, is that a...?"

"Yes, Pete. It's a real live grenade. Never one to go over the top, our Chuck."

"Fuck!"

"That's about the size of it. Anyway, you say he's in? Great! Let's just hope the little slimeball does the business, otherwise we're all in deep shit."

"I'm surprised you trusted him with this, Arnie," said Chuck, holding out his hand to retrieve his military piece of show and tell.

"Yeah... well he knows better than to upset me, Chuck. He fucks us over and I'll take that piece of hardware off ya and stuff it down his trousers. He'll be saying goodbye to his Alberts."

"Eh?" Vickers looked confused.

"Cockney slang, mate," said Fancy Man. "Albert Halls... Balls."

"Oh."

"He fucks us over and we'll be spending the rest of our lives in some shit tip like Mexico," pointed out Chuck.

Arnie lost it. "For fuck's sake, doesn't anyone trust me?"

"It's not you we don't trust. It's Tigger."

"Look, you suggesting I ain't thought this through? I might be younger than you, Chucky, but who came up with the idea in the first place? If it comes off I'm gonna make you all a shit load of money."

"If..."

"Look," said Arnie, pulling something out of his pocket. He handed it to Chuck. Fancy Man leaned over to take a look.

"Great, it's a fuckin' flyer for an old people's gaffe. You give me this by mistake?"

Arnie stared into his brother's eyes. The interior of the van had fallen eerily silent. "Shows what you know, don't it?" Arnie broke the spell. "That," he pointed at the flyer, "is where old Mrs Tiggs is comfortably living out the rest of her days. Gone a bit doollally she has and our friend Mitchell loves 'is old mum so has put her somewhere she can get proper care. Trouble is, proper care costs so he needs to get dosh from somewhere, so he..."

"Sells drugs." Vickers patted Arnie on the back. "I'm with you..."

"I ain't," said Chuck. "What's it got to do with his old dear, for fuck's sake."

"The point is," said Arnie. "I know where she lives."

"Yeah, we all do now."

"The point is not that you know, Chuck, or that Pete here knows, or that I know. The point is that Tigger knows we know, get me? He also knows that if he screws us over I can't guarantee the safety of his dear old mum."

There was another brief silence. "You bastard!" said Chuck, but despite the exclamation he was smiling. "I always thought you were an evil little fucker. Me and Sly used to call you Damien, after that kid in the Omen film."

"Cheers," said Arnie.

"It ain't meant as a compliment. Still, it's good thinking. You wouldn't really hurt the old dear, though, would you?"

Arnie locked eyes with his brother again and the silence returned.

"When do we move?" asked Fancy Man, breaking the spell.

"As soon as he is clear of the door," replied Arnie.

"Who are we expecting?"

"Jamaicans, mainly, I should think."

"Yardies?" asked Vickers. "They can be a bit nasty. Once we've done this thing, they'll come after us."

"Oh I don't know," interrupted Chuck, stroking his grenade.

"Fuck... oh, come on Chuck!" said Vickers, leaning further into the back of the van to address the oldest Dolan. "I know what you're thinking, and I know you're a crazy fuck, but there are gonna be an awful lot of civilians in there."

"Collateral damage," he said.

"Then we end up spending the rest of our lives in jail," said Arnie. "Not a good idea, Chuck. You haven't thought this through. I'm trying to build something here and it isn't a life behind bars. I don't wanna end up like our dad."

"What's wrong with our dad?" said Chuck, bristling. "I went to see him the other day and told him we were planning something big. He said you've got to create maximum chaos, put me in touch with these boys from Manchester, who got hold of this." He lifted the grenade. "They got plenty more, too. Do you think that would have happened without the old man? You should show him more respect."

"Whatever," Arnie tossed his head. "All I'm saying is I don't want to spend the rest of my life behind bars. If this comes off we'll be big time. You can buy one of them Scirocco's you're always going on about, or a Porsche. They don't let you drive fast sports cars in prison Chuck."

No response. Arnie took it as a small victory.

"Fuck! Here he comes," shouted Vickers.

"Masks?" said Arnie.

"Not yet," said Fancy Man. "We won't get past the bouncers."

"True, Fancy. But make sure you have them in place once you're inside," said Arnie. "In the meantime conceal your faces as best you can. With any luck there will be so many people queuing they won't be able to pick you out later."

"Let's take them bouncers out when we leave... just in case," said Chuck.

"OK, well you and Sly look after that."

Chuck couldn't resist another dig. "Who made you boss?" he said. "...and where's your big mucker. Why ain't he here in your hour of need."

"Gaz? Why ask that? You know he's playing football for West Ham," said Arnie, his temper rising, finger pointing in his brother's face. "You can't expect him to get involved at the moment. Maybe later. Anyway, you know why I'm in charge of this... it was my idea."

"And it was our money," said Chuck. "Me and Sly. If we hadn't done that post office you wouldn't have the cash to pull this off."

Arnie put his arm around the back of his brother's neck and pulled him forward so their heads were touching. "I know," he said. "I'm grateful. It's why we're a team, Chuck, but give me a break. Without a plan..."

"Come on, that's enough brotherly love. Let's go!" said Vickers. He pulled on his black leather jacket and took a latex mask from his pocket. He held it in front of his face. Kermit the Frog stared at the other inhabitants of the van. "It's time to put on a show, Muppets!" he said. "We'll see you later, Arnie. Good luck!"

Arnie slapped Vickers hand as the boy with the mask slipped from the passenger seat into the darkly lit street. Thudding bass beats invaded the van, the club over the road getting into full swing. Inside, Arnie imagined sweaty students off their faces, freaking out to the sounds. At that moment he could hear the haunting introduction of Fatboy Slim's "Right Here, Right Now" penetrating the night air.

"Don't forget. Maximum violence... but without that grenade!" Behind him, Fancy Man opened the back doors and exited the van, followed by Chuck and Sly. As the leader, he couldn't help but feel uneasy about the fact he wasn't joining them. Chuck was a bit like Stevo. You needed to keep a leash on him. Still, he knew it was more important for him to stay in place and welcome the guest than go out and join the fun.

As Fatboy Slim built to the big climax, Tigger turned up at the back entrance to the van, accompanied by a tall, dark-suited man. His skin was tanned, his face a portrait of confusion. "You better not have me here under false pretences, Mr Tiggs. You said there was big money involved. Well?"

Before Tigger could answer Arnie held his hand out, pulling the guest into the van.

"Sorry about this Mr Durak," he said. "I know this isn't the poshest gaffe in which to meet but my name is Arnie Dolan and I run a little operation called the Boxer Boys... you may have heard of us." The man gave no hint of acknowledgement, just folded himself over and took a seat on a wheel arch.

"Well, that's you," he said, finally. "Nah, ain't never heard of you. Me, on the other hand, you know. Not only that, but you know that my boys ain't far away. If you're trying to mess with me I'll have your entrails spread like a carpet from here to Dalston."

"Look, let's not fight," said Arnie. "I do, indeed, know who you are. That's why we are here. Tigger?"

The drug dealer climbed in and closed the doors, then squeezed through and lent into the front seat, returning with a suitcase. He placed it on the floor in front of the man named Durak and popped the catches. The visitor leaned backwards and eyed the contents, the brief silence sending Arnie's stomach churning. Eventually he spoke again. "Very impressive. That's a lot of money. Perhaps we do have something to talk about. What can I do for you?"

Arnie leaned forward and lifted out one of the bundles of £50 notes. "It's what we can do for you, Mr Durak. Let's just say this is a token of our respect and we hope it's the start of a long and prosperous relationship. You have the product we want and we want to be your exclusive business partner, helping you distribute it throughout the East End."

"And what if I said I already had an exclusive agreement with someone to do just that?"

Arnie leaned back. "Well, I think that deal is about to be terminated," he said.

As he offered a handshake, the world outside exploded.

SEVEN

"FANTASTIC HAT-TRICK, Gazza, mate. We've been treated to the Marshall magic tonight." Tony Aniwojo, a speedy winger from Hackney, put the high-five in the air and Gary accepted with a beaming smile. "Boys have got cash on you becoming the next Joe Cole, for real."

Gary aimed a playful punch at his team mate's arm. "Oh yeah, like that's going to happen."

"Serious," said Tony. "One of the lads overheard the coaches talking. You're nailed on for a YTS place next year, looks like. What about that?"

"Well, I guess anything can happen. Hopefully we'll be able to do it together. I wouldn't have scored two of those goals if you hadn't been distracting their central defenders to give me the space to run into."

"True dat!" Tony said, juggling a football with his feet. "It's the old Aniwojo magic... ask my dad."

"He was a pretty good player by all accounts."

"Yeah, the best, til some thug of a full back ended his career. That's why I got these twinkle toes... to avoid them big mutherfuckers!" The two boys carried on walking back to the dressing rooms. "Hey, terrible what happened to Jemal, wasn't it?" Jemal was one of their team mates, a promising young fullback of Turkish extraction.

"Eh, what?" asked Gary, realising that the boy had missed the game that day.

"He was in that thing the other week, the nightclub explosion? He didn't make it. One of them that was killed. People are saying it was terrorists, you know?"

"Really?" Gary nodded, suddenly feeling uneasy. He stopped walking and Tony turned to face him.

"Yeah, Ottoman Club down Hackney. Shit, I used to go there, man. They had an Under 16 night back in the day. No booze but great music. Three killed, two dozen injured at least they're saying. Massive explosion, then a fire. People were climbing the stairs and jumping out upstairs windows. Jammy was one of the kids that didn't make it. Many of them was muslims, no trouble. I can't see the terrorist thing, myself. Who would it be? Israelis or something? Maybe a right wing organisation, like the National Front. Sounds to me it's just crazy people. Lots of them about these days, man. The whole world is shit scary."

As he spoke, something tapped at Gary's memory bank. A conversation. Brief. Just out of hearing range. He'd had to strain to get the full jist. It had taken place a fortnight earlier between Arnie and Pete Vickers. His best mate had described Wednesday as D-Day and insisted everyone "tooled up". Gary didn't want to know. He had other things to worry about at the time, like the big cup semi-final on the horizon. He distinctly remembered one phrase that seemed out of context considering the topic of conversation, which obviously involved a ruck. In the midst of it all Vickers, more intelligent than most of the gang, had suggested that if all went well Arnie might find himself king of his own "Ottoman Empire".

"Look, I got to go," said Gary, suddenly keen to look at copies of the local paper his mum had stockpiled for recycling. He retrieved his bag from a locker in the changing rooms and said his farewells to players waiting to enter the shower. He could get washed and changed at home later. "Catch you all Sunday," he said, exiting and turning towards the car park.

Odd. He couldn't see his dad's car but Reg Philpott – one of Stan Marshall's mates from the market – was there in his shabby blue van.

He was waving in his direction, and Gary wondered what might have happened. It wasn't uncommon for his dad to be "held up" on market business but it was rare he missed him playing football, let alone not being there to collect him at the end. He would always conduct a full inquisition into the game, how Gary had played and whether he had been able to utilise any new skills the coaches had taught him.

Sometimes it seemed Stan was more committed to the cause than his son. The old man had told Gary that during his childhood he had harboured hopes of playing the game to a decent level. Truth was, though, he just wasn't very good. Having a son who could play was like he'd been given a second shot at the big time, and he intended to give it both barrels.

Gary said goodbye to his team mates and trotted over. "Hi uncle Reg, where's Dad?"

"Sorry son, couldn't make it. I'm here though and your mum is waiting for you at home so if you've got your stuff we'd better make tracks."

Heading off down the A13 towards Barking, Gary fished for more information. "Dad working late then, Uncle Reg?" Silence. Reg's face took on a pained expression. "What? Is something wrong? Was he in an accident or something?"

"No... no, nothing like that it's just... you'll have to wait for your mum to tell you. It's none of my business."

"Bloody hell! Oops, sorry Reg... I mean... well, the way you say it... it sounds serious."

Reg fiddled with the radio in front of him and changed the subject. "Ah listen, United are playing in the Champions League..." They didn't speak again until Reg dropped him in the Minter car park.

Ignoring the lifts which rarely worked, he ran up the stairs, screwing up his nose at familiar smells, stale urine and boiled cauliflower. Some kids were playing cards in the second-floor hallway and his foot brushed the deck as he charged upwards, keen to get to the bottom of the mystery. "Hey!" shouted one of the young teens, but he ignored them, pounding on, his bag swinging over his shoulder.

When he arrived the door to the flat was open and the scene inside was pure devastation. There were items strewn across the living room floor, picture frames and broken glass, and his sister Lily was rolled up on the sofa crying. Reaching the kitchen, a burning smell hit his nostrils and he saw his mum sitting trance-like at the table, her blonde peroxide hair falling randomly over her face, covering her eyes as steam billowed from a pan on the hob. He moved swiftly to turn off the ring. "Mum! Mum! What's happened?" he asked.

"He's gone, angel, gone…"

"Who's gone? Where?"

Suddenly, his mum sprang to her feet and wrapped him in a suffocating embrace, forcing him to drop his kitbag to the floor. "Your dad's gone. He's run off with his fancy woman and won't be coming back. I'm so sorry, son."

A jolt, like electricity, charged through Gary's body. His dad, Stan the man, the cheerful chappy they all loved, the man who had brought him up, taken him fishing, passed on to him an insatiable appetite for sport and was the blueprint for the way he wanted to be when he grew up, had left him when he needed him more than ever. He felt angry, betrayed, guilty and sick. It was like a bereavement but if his mum had said his dad had been killed in a car accident it couldn't have hurt this much. In that case it wouldn't have been a wilful decision on his father's part to trade in the family for… what? It didn't make sense, nor would it, possibly ever.

EIGHT

"WELL I FUCKIN' never! Where the hell have you been hiding?"

Gary Marshall recognised the voice instantly. He had been walking the streets of Barking aimlessly, something he found himself doing a lot as he tried to put things together in his head. He lived in a mental fug these days, searching for answers and coming up with nothing.

He raised his eyes from the paving slabs. "Hi Arnie, All right?"

"Pretty damn good," said the shaven-headed Arnie Dolan, proudly sporting a long green parka. It resembled an ordinary winter coat but Gary knew that with the retro scene in full cry, this kind of Mod gear was expensive. Underneath, Arnie wore a crisp white shirt and bootlace tie while on his feet were a stylish pair of Italian brogues poking out from beneath black sta-prest trousers. "I should be asking you that question though, Gaz. I hear your old man done a runner. Sorry an' all that. You guys were close."

"Yeah."

"Look, there's a do on tonight..."

"I can see that," said Gary. "You taking your Vespa?"

Arnie chuckled, but his expression was devoid of humour. "This?" he indicated his clothes. "It's for our Chuck's benefit. It's the old boy's birthday and you know how he loves the old Mod scene. Mind you, I'd love a scooter and one of me contacts says he might get his hands on one of those old classics – like that blue one Sting had in Quadrophenia? – but I'm still waiting to hear from him."

"One of your contacts?" said Gary, raising his eyebrows. "You sound like some high-flying businessman."

"So I am geez." Arnie draped his arm around his friend's shoulders. "You ought to kick that football nonsense into touch. Earn some real dosh with me. Know what I'm saying? Not many make it in your game. At West Ham it's about one every three years..."

"Yeah, but I've always wanted it, Arnie, and my dad..."

"I know. He was pushing you. We could all see it. Keeping us apart, shipping you off to football training. He didn't like me, your dad. I know. Still, he ain't here now, and there ain't no point pussy-footing around the truth. He's the male equivalent of a fuckin'..."

"Shut it!" Gary exploded, seizing Arnie Dolan by the hood of his coat, prompting a ripping sound. He brought his friend's nose to within an inch of his own. "Leave my Dad outta this, why don't ya? It's a bit fuckin' raw, mate. You're all right. Your dad..."

"...Is in fuckin' prison and has been most of my damn life. Tell you the truth I think he fuckin' hates me." Surprised at the outburst, Gary slowly released his grip.

"What do you mean? I thought you were close. You're always talking about him, how he gives you advice..."

"Yeah, if this is advice." He lifted his coat and pulled his shirt back. Faded scars and bruises were still evident on the skin. "You saw it ages ago. I don't know what you thought caused it. A bit of rough and tumble with me brothers? Fuck that. My dad used to put me in them boxing gloves then use me as punching practice."

"Sorry."

"Yeah well, we all got problems as far as fathers are concerned, don't we? You can defend yours all you want mate I'm just saying it's time you grew a pair. No one is going to do it for you. Look, we're your mates. We're the ones who will pull you through this at the end of the day. You shouldn't be moping about, you should get angry. You've every right. Come back to us, geez. I miss you and so do the rest of the boys. We had some good times, right? We're family. Remember that day we met?"

Gary nodded.

Arnie paused for a few seconds, then his eyes lit up. "Come to Brighton with us. Tonight. On the train. You know the 5.15, like in that Who song? There's a Secret Affair cover band gigging down there and we're all going along to help Chuck celebrate – Vickers is coming, Tigger, Fancy Man..."

"Well," said Gary thoughtfully, "I was..."

"Shit!" Suddenly Gary found himself hurtling towards the floor, his mate on top of him.

"What the fuck are you..?" The window behind them exploded, covering the two of them in chunks of flying glass. Gary looked up to see a figure on a motorcycle disappearing off into the distance, the rider replacing a metal object in his pocket. Around them the realisation of what had happened was hitting home. A girl screamed, while a shopkeeper ran out of the doorway shouting: "Young hooligans. Shooting up my shop. Call the police!"

Arnie pulled Gary to his feet. "Drive-by... at least an attempted one. Bloody Naj!"

"Hell," said Gary, brushing away loose glass. "Is this what your business is? Make loads of money but risk getting killed in the process."

"Probably just random. I expect they mistook us for someone else. Happens all the time. It's them Yardies I expect."

Something didn't seem right to Gary, though. He could feel his muscles twitching as fear sent adrenaline shooting around his body. "You said Naj, though, like you knew him. Hey, wasn't that the name of that little gangster you sorted out on the estate, the one you whipped with the dog chain? Shit, Arnie, what you into?"

"Nothing mate, nothing. Don't sweat it. Little fucker don't know who he's tangling with. I got connections now. Anyway, forget it. It ain't gonna spoil my day. How about it eh? Brighton with the boys."

"I would but..." Gary stopped himself. Something told him no good would come from letting Arnie know he was due to meet Anjie and go over some English homework notes.

"We'll pick you up at four," said Arnie, looking his mate up and down. "You could do better than jeans and a bloody Van Halen T-shirt though, mate."

Gary looked in a shop window, as if seeing his clothes for the first time. He'd spent so much time in limbo recently he wasn't even aware of what he had dressed in that morning. The shirt was one his dad had bought cheap from the market in the misguided belief every kid between the ages of 11 and 18 was into heavy metal. It stemmed from the fact that as a teenager Stan Marshall himself had been a bit of a rocker. When Gary reflected on it, Stan had always dictated what was fashionable, and his family went along with it as if he was the perfect role model. Well, that deception had been shown up for what it was, he thought, his resolve hardening.

"OK. Fuck it, Arnie, mate. Count me in," he said as sirens wailed in the distance.

HE WAS ACTUALLY enjoying himself for the first time since hearing the news that had turned his life upside down. Sitting on a train, swigging strong lager, cider and a mixture of spirits out of some dodgy bottle Tigger had produced from his pocket, they were having a proper laugh. Some of the business people in the carriage expressed their annoyance and found themselves baited mercilessly in response. Before the alarm was raised, though, they moved on to another carriage.

Gary took out his phone as they disembarked and headed for the Brighton Station exit. "Just got to call Mum," he told Arnie. "I'll catch you boys up."

"Hello?" The voice on the other end of the line wasn't his mother.

"Hey Anj. Listen, I'm sorry, can't revise tonight. I've been a bit stir crazy around the house, locked up revising in bedrooms. I needed to get out."

There was a moment's silence.

"You with Arnie and Chuck?"

"Well, yeah. Down Brighton. How did you know?"

"I heard them talking about giving you a good time to help you forget your troubles."

"Oh... right."

"Look, I think it's a good idea, really I do," said Anjie. "Be careful, though. You're vulnerable and with a few drinks in you well... I wouldn't want you to do something you might regret."

"Great!" said Gary, bolstered by alcohol bravado. "So basically, you are saying you don't trust me. Thanks Anj... you sound like my bloody mother."

"Look," said Anjelica Dolan softly. "I don't mean to, it's just..." She realised she was talking across empty airwaves.

ANOTHER FEW PINTS on the way into town and Gary Marshall was feeling light-headed. Pretty soon, though, his mood had slid into melancholy. Scanning one of the pubs in the fashionable Lanes area his eyes fixed on a well-dressed middle-aged man at the bar. The geezer obviously fancied himself as a lothario, leering all over an attractive blonde at least 15 years younger than him. When she kissed him, then climbed down from the stool and headed for the toilets the man turned his attention to a brunette on his other side. Gary noticed him take something from his wallet and slip it into her handbag, making the universal sign for "call me". Moving closer, Gary spotted the ring on the man's wedding finger and, without realising, he started muttering under his breath: *"Oh big man are you? Left the little wife at home and now you're out playing the field. How many kids I wonder? Yeah, probably got the whole brood all doting on their wonderful dad. God, people like you should get the snip at birth. Why do young girls fall for it? It's not charm it's smarm, and it's..."*

"Sorry, mate, can I help you with something?" The man stepped down from the stool and headed in his direction.

"Yeah," said Gary, "Maybe this?" The uppercut caught the stranger flush on the chin, sending him reeling back. People jumped out of the way as Gary leapt on him, punching him repeatedly in the face, mouthing as he did so: "Where's the wife, eh? Where's the kids? Think you're a right lad don't you..?" Blood smeared the man's face, his nose split open, his eyebrow badly cut. Now Gary was on his feet landing kick after kick, muttering obscenities, until hands grabbed him and tore him away and out of the door. The pub's token bouncer thought about giving pursuit but realised the odds were stacked against him and retreated inside. In the distance there was the wail of sirens. Suddenly, Arnie was in his face: "You fucking nutter! Haven't seen you in that sort of mood since that Chelsea game. Brilliant punch. Glad I taught ya something. Nice to have you back, bro, but let's not stand on ceremony. Better get out of here and clean you up."

NINE

GARY WASHED away the evidence in a nearby public toilet block, then the gang popped in to another pub for a drink before it was time to make their way to the venue, a ballroom nestling inside an old hotel on Brighton seafront. "Is that geezer you told me about gonna to be waiting for us?" Arnie Dolan asked Tigger. The dealer nodded vigorously, like a panting dog keen to get the approval of his master. "Yes, Doles, no problem. We're meeting him at one of them beach huts."

"Come on then, boys!" said Arnie, raising his voice above the hub-bub of noise in the pub, "I've got a nice little treat for you. Hope you've brought some money." They laughed and followed their leader onto the streets.

A brief walk later, the wind blowing in from the sea, they were crouched around Tigger as he knocked hesitantly on the door of one of the many gaily-painted beach huts along the promenade. No re-sponse. "Oh well done you little fucker!" said Pete Vickers. "I really don't know what you see in this little turd, Arnie. Messed up our plans again."

Gary, meanwhile, was struggling with both speech and coordi-nation. Wobbling from foot to foot, he was being held in place by Fancy Man. "Come on, son, bit of fresh air should do you good. If you want to chuck up let me know. Plenty of room on the sand there and doing so will give you a better chance of getting into the gig... help you sober up. Perhaps try putting your fingers down your throat." Gary nodded his head obediently, though half the words had passed him by.

"Hey, you lot!" The shout came from behind and the boys prepared to scarper, fearing the police. Instead they were confronted by a figure looking like a tramp, long straggly greying beard hiding a seriously creased face which was tucked into the collar of a long, tweed overcoat. Dirty hands were wrapped in fingerless gloves.

"Who the fuck do you think you are... Fagin?" Arnie said, laughing at his own joke. The crew around him joined in.

"Fagin eh? Clever sod are you? Well I might just leave you guys to it... go off and pick a few pockets."

"He was only joking, Mags, honest!" Tigger pleaded. "These boys are genuine buyers – I can vouch for them. Let's all calm down a bit. Who wants what?"

"Show us your wares first, Fagin," said Arnie, leering into the older man's face.

"You little..." Before he could complete the insult Arnie Dolan grabbed him by the throat, digging his fingers in and provoking a choking sound. From his pocket he drew a knife, poking the pointed edge into the pusher's chin. As hard as he tried to pull away the bloke called Mags couldn't release himself from Arnie's grip. Tigger, frantic at the prospect of losing one of his contacts, nudged Pete Vickers. "Pete," he whispered. "We aren't going to get the stuff this way and it's bad for business. Also, we don't want any cop attention, do we..?"

Pete, a seasoned negotiator even at his young age, stepped forward, talking calmly, his words meant for Arnie's ears. "Hey, come on guys, no need. This is just a little business transaction." He risked grabbing Arnie's knife hand and whispered into his friend's ear. Slowly the gang leader released his grip on the pusher's throat. Behind them Gary fell to his knees and threw up in the sand.

HIS SENSES RE-AWAKENING from a dull slumber, Gary felt marginally better. He could see the door to the hut was open and the character with the beard handing something out. Arnie retreated from the front of the queue and approached him. "Look at that old fucker!" he said. Gary studied the Fagin character, his mouth open wide in a leering smile which revealed a set of crooked, filthy teeth. Realising he was being watched the drug supplier's eyes locked on to Gary's. "Hey... you there! You look like you need something to perk you up."

Gary shook his head. He had never tried narcotics. His dad, despite his rock and roll past, was completely anti-drugs, though he swore by beer and nicotine.

"Go on, just the one," said Arnie, opening his palm to reveal he had taken possession of one of the tiny pills. "It'll make you feel a lot better." He coaxed Gary forward, his arm pushing gently at his back until he moved into Mags' sphere of influence. "Just hand over the readies and it's yours," the tramp-like character said, holding up one of the tiny pills. Gary studied it, thought of his dad's advice and the harm drugs could do, and out of sheer anger made his decision. He pulled a handful of crumpled notes from his pocket and the Fagin character licked his lips. "Yeah, that's it. Blue one. A score. Cheap at the price. What harm can it do?"

The transaction done, Arnie patted him on the back. "That's it mate. This will make you feel better... swallow these and we'll rule the world."

Gary felt numb. He could vaguely hear Anjelica's voice in his brain warning him to be careful. Arnie's powers of persuasion were undeniable, though, particularly when his own thoughts were distorted by drink. Gary's best friend was now waving his hands around like a conductor. "Do it! Do it! Do it!" he started chanting and the others joined in. He felt claustrophobic, peer pressure weighing heavily on his shoulders.

Finally, the chants pounding in his head, he shut his eyes, pictured his father's stern face, whispered "Fuck it!" and popped the stimulant into his mouth.

NOTHING. FIVE MINUTES in and there was no indication the drug had done anything to "alter" the state of his mind. Perhaps the pills were fakes, the crafty charlatan exchanging cash for cheap supermarket painkillers. There was a slight giddiness, but he put that down to the beer followed by the sickness, which had left him breathless and off balance, his head spinning. The voices around him were all talking at once but strangely he could keep track of the different conversations. It was only mundane stuff like Tigger whispering to Vickers "Thanks for getting me out of the shit, mate" and Fancy telling Chuck "I've got some cracking birds lined up. From south of the river. Met them a few months ago at a little rave near Tooting. Dare say I'll be able to fix you up..."

Suddenly Arnie was in his face again. "Feel it? Feel it? Probably needs a bit of help to kick in. Come on: Helicopters!"

His mate demonstrated by pushing his arms out and spinning down the boardwalk towards the pier, gathering pace as he went. Strolling tourists dodged out of the way with some odd glances and a degree of cursing but Arnie seemed oblivious to it all. Without being able to figure out why, Gary started doing the same, feeling light as air as he weaved circles and shouted "wee!" like a kid enjoying his own private game. The kaleidoscope effect provided by the lights made his head buzz, and for the first time in weeks he detected a smile affixed to his face. A wave of euphoria was building, as if he was celebrating the greatest piece of news in the history of the world. He felt impregnable, vital – that in the grand scheme of things he did matter.

For weeks he had considered himself insignificant, a loser, an unwanted product of his father's uncontrolled lust. All those times his father had heaped praise on him for a task well done or bigged him up as the most skilled young footballer of his generation had suddenly turned into empty words, lies. Then there was the biggest deception of all, the assertion he loved Gary and would sacrifice anything for him, the diatribe of deceit tripping off the tongue easily. How many times, too, had Gary heard him proudly announce to visitors that Sheila was his rock, the only woman who would ever matter to him?

There were grand gestures at Christmas, birthdays and anniversaries, his father lavishing his mum with gifts – most of them cheap knockoffs from the market – and joking that he didn't know how she put up with him. Wasn't that the truth? A man who spends his entire life putting his wife on a pedestal doesn't then knock her off with a big stick the moment younger, fresher talent comes along.

To hell with it, he decided. His dad was just a cheat who had subjected his family to a cruel form of mental abuse. Gary had spent weeks moping around, mourning as if he had been killed in some terrible accident while blaming himself for the catastrophe. He now saw clearly where the guilt should lie. He smiled again, eyes sparkling, and realised he could do whatever he wanted, be whoever he wanted to be, as long as he put his trust in himself and not others.

He caught up with Arnie and they walked the rest of the way down the promenade arm over arm, the rest of their small and extremely high entourage following behind. This little tribe – his tribe – had a bond, an understanding. Growing up in similar circumstances, each having been subjected to their own disappointments, their young lives having been spent either battling the system or their own kin. Through experience they had learned how to make things work in their favour, an approach developed through solidarity. Arnie's mantra was "stick together". If they could help fight each other's battles they would always have someone to turn to in their darkest moments. Boxer Boys Forever. BBF, just as Arnie had sprayed on an estate wall years earlier.

TEN

THEY SPLIT into pairs in case the bouncers were inclined to turn away gangs of males. Fancy Man and Chuck, fanatical Secret Affair fans dressed to mimic their idols, led the way, followed by Tigger and Pete Vickers. Arnie tucked his knife into his socks, then he and Gary took up the rear.

It was the stark contrasts that registered first when Gary stepped through the door. From brightly lit seafront he was submerged into nightclub darkness, the cold sea air being swapped for a warm interior heated by hundreds of bodies, wide-open spaces replaced by claustrophobic surroundings. The bouncers who patted him down made him feel tense and put him on a state of heightened alert.

Paying his tenner he stepped through deep purple velvet curtains to find himself surrounded by wall-to-wall mods, jumping and singing along to a song with which he was familiar. Guitars jangled, bass resonated and drums pounded, the singer on stage imploring him to recognise: "This is the time, the time for action". As he pushed further into the mass of bodies he felt his cheeks burning, not just hot but painfully so, his whole face ready to burst into flames. The heat was scorching, searing, combustible, like his head was inside an oven. He had the strange sensation of oil running down his hair and clinging to his face in gloopy lumps as if the inside of his head was emptying out or, worse, melting.

People were bashing into him, almost knocking him over, and behind he could hear Arnie urging: "Come on, son… right in the bloody middle. Give 'em a dig if they get in the way."

As the song built to a crescendo he pushed someone. His victim turned to have words then forgot his purpose when the music stopped, turning back to the stage and joining in the tidal wave of applause. All around were people cheering, shouting. They all felt too close to him and he started pushing them away.

"Hey, leave it out mate!" came a shout as Gary, hopelessly confined by human prison walls, lashed out and connected with someone's back. Arnie charged forward and planted his fist in the boy's mouth, blood instantaneously spurting out. Mayhem ensued as those in the vicinity tried to fathom what had happened. Desperate to get away from the clinging bodies, Gary searched for an exit. "Out of my way, out of my way."

He knew the voice was his but felt somehow disembodied from it. Those in front of him were like figures frozen in time, a painted tableau, their mouths open, faces contorted, bemusement evident in their petrified expressions. An ornate banister curved up the side of the ballroom and instinctively he made for the steps. Lifted by the sheer mass of people, at one stage his feet lost contact with the ground completely as the music pounded again. Before he knew it he was on the balcony looking down at a whirlpool of writhing bodies, climbing onto a table to see more clearly. "Are those ants below?" he asked no one in particular.

Up here the lights were dazzling and wave upon wave of cheers subsumed him. They seemed to be getting louder and louder and it dawned on him like a religious epiphany. The cheers were for him! It was as if he was expected to provide the entertainment now. He was standing on a ledge, high above the dance floor, a sea of awe-struck faces gazing up at him. As one they seemed to be communicating telepathically with him and he knew what they desired. They wanted him to do it, to replicate the moment in the film Quadrophenia when a mod dives from a balcony and is cushioned by a wave of people before crowd-surfing his way to safety. It made him feel important. He had their attention. He had limitless confidence. He had lost track of time, space, reality. "I can do this, I can do this," he whispered.

Out of the corner of his eye he saw Arnie approaching and illogically feared this boy, his best friend, was out to get him, to punish him, maybe for deserting him to play football or for leaving him on his own at a vulnerable time in life. That boy had a knife. That boy could take his life. "Gazza! Gary! Stop!" shouted Arnie.

No, you won't get me Doles, he thought. I have friends, so many friends, ready to cushion me, to rescue me, to cheer me in my moment of magnificence. I won't let you steal that moment. He stepped off the balcony rail...

"Oh mate. Fuck, noooo!!!" said Arnie, making a desperate grasp and coming away with a handful of nothing. As if waking from a coma Gary was suddenly aware.

At first he heard a deafening roar as people acclaimed his jump and he felt that he was soaring. But then... oh no, he wasn't soaring. He was falling. Falling very fast. Down, down...

Now he could see clearly below that they weren't ants but people, people getting bigger all the time so that he could see individual faces, looks of horror, the big picture below resembling a 60s billboard for one of those sci-fi B movies when aliens descended from the sky. People were panicking, moving away rapidly from the likely impact zone. He heard screams.

His lips were moving but the voice was confined to his mind. "Please don't go, not now..."

Too late, the people had gone. Instead he saw a tiled floor closing in – hard, hard floor.

Crash! Pain a thousand times worse than anything he had ever felt shuddered through his body as he made contact with the ground, feet first. He thought he screamed, a bone-freezing cry that only something in unimaginable agony could produce, but his mind was hazy on that point. As the faces crowded in above him he knew things would never be the same. He smiled. "Some performance eh, Dad?" he mumbled in his delirium before the black mists of unconsciousness wrapped themselves around him.

11

THE FIRST THING Gary sensed when he stumbled back into consciousness were bright, piercing lights. They passed rapidly above him.

Clack, clack, wobble; Clack, clack, wobble...

There were voices but he could barely make out what they were saying, the speech delivered backwards and making no sense. His eyes flickered in response to the lights and he was forced to shut them again. Without the sense of sight and unable to understand anything he was hearing, he had to rely on other senses. He wanted to touch, but that wasn't so easy either, his arms strapped to whatever the contraption was he was on. Smell? A strange mix...

Liniment and bleach, urine and boiled cabbage

He risked opening his eyes again, hoping things would become clearer. "He's waking up." A language he recognised. Human... English. Through his hazy vision he saw someone leaning over him, dark hair falling across an indistinct face. There were others, dressed the same... women all in white.

Angels?

Oh God, was this it? Death? Was the bright piercing light an ethereal entity looking down on him, assessing him before... before what? No, no... he couldn't be dead. He didn't want to die. Or did he? Confused. All he knew was he had to keep his eyes open, maintain his slender grip on reality. He was tired... drifting off. Just before he lost the fight, though, he thought he made out another figure, leaning over him, lifting his eyelids, trying to keep him from the comfort of oblivion...

Face beneath a blue mask, Talking, talking...Insistent voice

"What did he take? It's important... Drugs? High as a kite. Won't feel the pain for a while. Can you hear me? Can you hear me?"

Words, just words; Blurred words

"...Operation... Allergies? Anaesthetic."

Then he heard no more.

"HEY LOOK, HERE'S my boy. Oh my God... Gary? We're here for you, son." His mother's voice. He wasn't dead then. He could see her fuzzy shape next to him, smell her Chanel No 5 perfume, recognise the black and white pattern of her blouse, Cruella DeVil in 101 Dalmations.

"Mum?"

"That's right my lovely boy. It's your mother. Oh saints be praised, we've been so worried about you, me and your sister and Uncle Reg. Even... Well, you know. You've given us a nasty scare."

"Sorry... God, it hurts!" He felt a searing pain shooting up his legs.

"... it will do", said a man's voice. "What the hell were you thinking?"

"Leave him, Reg. Plenty of time for that. It's just good to see he's in one piece."

"Well..."

Gary noticed his mum quickly put her fingers to her lips, a signal for Reg to stop talking.

"What is it?" asked Gary. "My legs really hurt. What happened anyway? I don't remember."

"I'm not bloody surprised!" It was his sister Lily chiming in this time.

"Shhh!" said his mother again, lowering her voice to a whisper. "Language, Lily! He's only supposed to have two visitors anyway so we don't want to attract attention."

63

"Tell me," said Gary. "Don't talk as if I'm not here."

"Well..." said his mother, her voice breaking in the way it did when the royals made a special announcement. Tears were on the way. "... oh, you tell him, Reg."

There was a moment's silence and all Gary could think of was how this 'friend' of the family seemed to have assumed a more prominent role, one to which he was scarcely entitled. The father role. This realisation bought the truth rushing back in a flurry.

"You're in hospital, son," Reg began. "I'm afraid you had a nasty ... um, fall. You were at a rock concert, in Brighton, and apparently fell from the balcony. You're lucky to be alive if you ask me..."

"Reg!" said Gary's mother admonishingly.

"Sorry, Sheil."

"My leg's killing me," said Gary. "Both of them are."

"Yeah," said Reg. "You've done quite a bit of damage. According to the doctors, you broke both your heels."

Gary felt a wave of pain shoot from the bottom of his feet and reached down, but could only find thick layers of plaster on both legs. "Also, I'm afraid you've done some serious damage to your right knee ..."

Gary tried to translate the words into something meaningful. It was as if Reg was telling him a story about someone else. Then a thought broke through, followed by a hundred others in quick succession, like the breaching of a dam. "My football..?"

Silence. He saw Reg give his mother a knowing look as she wiped away a tear. "We're told the damage is pretty much... look, they think they'll be able to get you walking again, and with the right physio etc you'll be nearly as good as new. It's going to take a lot of hard work ..."

"I'm not going to play again, am I?" Gary felt a surge of pain as he tried to lever himself into a sitting position.

"No, son," said his mother, fighting back the tears. "I'm afraid your footballing days are over."

GARY SAT IN bed for ages mulling things over. Doctors came and went, nurses supplied a constant diet of painkillers and tried to boost his mood with their cheeriness, but his mind was intent on finding someone to blame, and kept coming back to one person. Stan the man. Stan the man with a plan. Stan the shagging, cheating, unfaithful sham. He muttered the words, seething, his hatred pouring out through clenched teeth, over and over, just fractions of sound escaping, but enough for the nurses to inquire now and again whether everything was all right. On occasion he would break away from his furious internal cursing, smile and assure them that, yes, everything was fine and dandy. When he wasn't muttering he was sleeping. This sequence of events repeated itself on and off until the day he came. The day Gary's hidden anger finally exploded.

He was just snoozing after lunch, the painkillers kicking in, when he heard a nurse called Rosie trying to grab his attention. He guessed it was to offer him a cup of tea and shook his head. "No, Mr Marshall," she said. "You have a visitor..." It was probably Arnie, come to check on his best mate, or maybe Fancy Man or Pete Vickers.

"Hello, G-man..."

The voice sent a shudder through his body. He almost choked, collapsing into a coughing fit. The nickname only one person in the world gave him. "Hey... hey, it's OK. Your old man's here." He felt two meaty arms lifting him and encasing him in a traitor's hug. Forcing his eyes open, he smelt stale booze and cigarettes and felt the rasp of an unshaven chin against his cheek. "Now, why the bloody hell did you go and do a stupid thing like that?" his dad asked in his usual know-it-all fashion.

Without warning, Gary wriggled violently out of his grip, grabbed the nearest thing to him – a full water jug – and threw it at his father. The direct hit sent liquid pouring over the bed, the impact of the glass container bringing a shocked look to Stan Marshall's face, one which would remain imprinted on his son's memory forever. As his dad jumped from the bed, Gary spotted a blonde woman lurking in the background. He knew she wasn't a nurse.

"What the hell, son...?"

Gary was furious and attempted to manoeuvre his legs over the edge of the bed. He threw the biggest haymaker he could muster at the O of surprise on his dad's face, connected with nothing and ended up sprawled on the floor. His father bent over. "Come on, son ... I know you're upset but..."

"Get him out of here!" shouted Gary, wriggling on the floor like a demented worm, his gown, soaked with water, riding up his body. "Someone... get this bastard out!"

"Sir, come with me, please, I'm afraid you're upsetting the patient. Let us get him back to bed. Please..." It was Rosie, gently coaxing Stan Marshall away.

"But I'm his dad!" he protested, weakly. Seeing Rosie's stern expression he relented. "OK, I'll, um, come back when he's a bit..."

"No! Don't ever come back," stormed Gary. "Take your fuckin' floozy with you and fuck off! I never want to see you again."

As he was lifted back onto the bed, he watched his dad's retreating back, saw the arm slip around Rosie as he whispered something to her, no doubt an apology for his son's behaviour when if she knew the truth she would see Gary had every right to react the way he did. The blonde in the black miniskirt and bright red blouse click-clacketed after them on high heels, his dad's bomber jacket draped over her arm, an excited puppy keen to earn its master's approval. Gary slumped back onto the bed and closed his eyes, willing the mental and physical pain to go away.

IT TOOK A visit the next day to finally bring a smile to his face. Gary had just finished a tasteless lunch of minced beef, carrots, lumpy mash and broccoli when she came through the door. The sun shone through the window onto her long black tresses and for a moment he had visions of angels in his head again. Then as she got closer he saw it was Anjelica, wearing her school uniform and swinging a book in her hand. She pulled a chair up beside the bed, leaned over and engaged his eyes.

"You absolute prat!" she said. "Didn't I warn you to be careful when you went off to Brighton? Eh?" He didn't know how to reply, but was just happy to see her and quite prepared to get ticked off for the privilege. "Well, you might have shunned me that day, but you can't run away now," she continued. "I'm going to keep a close eye on you. You obviously need a lot of looking after." Then she leaned over and kissed him. Just a brief peck on the lips, but it caused his temperature to soar and his cheeks to colour. "Oh, by the way," she said. "I brought you a present. I thought it was quite, um, appropriate in the circumstances."

She handed him a book. He read the cover. "The English Patient". For the first time in what seemed forever, he laughed.

12

"YEAH, GET THE fuck in!" Arnie Dolan punched the air, leaping almost as high as the striker who had just given West Ham a 2-0 lead in the FA Cup fourth-round tie against Cardiff City. He was dressed the part, wearing the claret and blue with pride, the number 10 adorning his retro football shirt. It was the number that Geoff Hurst famously wore, the Upton Park icon who scored a hat-trick for England in the 1966 World Cup final. Though too young to have watched him in action, Arnie had seen the goals plenty of times on video and been told tales of the great man's exploits by older members of the clan. He put his arm around Gary Marshall, who was dressed in an identical top, one that Arnie had bought him as a gift on his leaving hospital four years earlier. "Sorry," said Arnie. "Forgot about the leg. You OK?"

Gary waved his stick in the air. "You fuckin' bet! Get in there, Di Canio, you beauty," he shouted, stumbling about until his mates steadied him.

"Careful," chided Pete Vickers. "You'll have someone's eye out with that."

Arnie adopted a serious expression. "You sure you're OK?" he asked. "It's got to be tiring, standing on that leg. I know it's been a while now but I get the impression it still hurts pretty bad."

"Yeah," admitted Gary, "yeah, when I stand on it for any great length of time it aches like a bastard. It's getting better, though."

"Fuck it. I don't normally do this, but it might be a good idea to leave now – avoid the crowds, you know?" said Arnie. "Usually I'd be up for going out and hunting down Cardiff scum. They fancy themselves, but they ain't come up against us lot in the past. We'll bounce them all the way back to Paddington." He noticed Gary grimace. "No, mate, not today. You're our main priority, that's what mates are for, ain't it? I wouldn't want you being swept away… we might never get you back." Gary tapped him on the arm with the walking stick in mock anger. The others laughed. "Let's get you back to your mum," said Arnie, undeterred. "I don't want to be in her bad books again – she still blames me for that stupid balcony jump of yours."

"She'll come around, Doles," said Gary. "It's just raw, you know, what with dad leaving, then me doing something so stupid to wreck my football career."

"She's got plans for you, though, ain't she?"

"So she tells me," Gary said, laughing. "She's fixed me up to do some radio work with the local independent station – reporting on some of the minor league football games. Hayes and Yeading, or some such. Nothing big. Fair play, though, she isn't going to let me mope around. She persuaded me to go back to college and complete my English after my year out convalescing and now she's done this for me. She's a bit of a rock, to be honest."

"Sure. Still, I doubt there's much money in that reporting lark," said Arnie. "You could pack it in and come in with me. Who wants to work for someone else, when you can work for yourself?" As if to demonstrate the rewards Arnie took a £50 note from his pocket. "God I don't half fancy a smoke," he said. "Got a cigar, Pete?" Leaning forward from behind him, Vickers popped one into his friend's mouth. "Cheers." Reaching into his pocket he pulled out a match, ripped it across the zip on his jacket and protected the flame from the wind. When it had caught he lit the £50 note before touching the flame to the tip of the cigar.

"Hey!" shouted Gary, "Are you fuckin' mad? There are people on our estate who would kill for that sort of money, Doles."

"Nah," said Arnie. "They're too fuckin' lazy to kill. They'd rather scrounge off the State. At least I earned that money and I can spend it – or set it on fire – any way I like. There's plenty more where that came from, too. Enough for all of us. You're an intelligent bloke. I could use you pretty wisely. We could even go legit…"

"Forget it, Arnie. Honestly. Kind of you and all that, but I have to give this reporting lark a go. I owe it to Mum."

"Your loss. Best not to become a crime reporter though, eh?" Arnie said, laughing.

They walked out of the ground in high spirits, larking around on the way to the tube station. Arnie stole Fancy Man's state-of-the-art silk scarf and ran away from him down the street. Gary tried to trip Fancy Man with his stick but without luck. They heard the roar go up to signify that either West Ham had scored again or the game was over and they were into the next round. Happy days.

Turning the corner into the next street Arnie noticed a transit van parked up at the roadside. On closer inspection he said: "Well, well, well. Rhondda Van Hire. You don't see many round here hiring their bleedin' transport from the Rhondda Valley now, do ya? I smell sheepshaggers." He noticed a loose brick on a nearby garden wall and picked it up. "Right you bastards, you're journey home is gonna get a bit breezy."

Before he could throw the missile he was interrupted by a sound from behind. The Boxer Boys turned to see 20 thick-set men uniformly dressed in donkey jackets, jeans and heavy work boots. One of them turned to the others and raised his voice. "Oi, look at these fucking cockney scum, boys – they looks like they wanna smash our van up. Get 'em!"

The noise was deafening, the Welsh screaming like banshees as they charged the small group of Hammers fans. Arnie, realising they were outnumbered and fearing for Gary, grabbed his mate's arm and cajoled him towards the end of the street. "Quick!" he shouted.

"Quick? What do you mean fuckin' quick?" said Gary. "It's all right for you but I've only got one fuckin' leg!"

"Come on then, you cockney wankers. Thought you were supposed to be a top crew!" shouted one Welshman, smashing Vickers in the side of the head and sending him crashing to the ground. Others joined in the fun, shouting and swearing obscenities about the English as they kicked his prone form on the floor. "Fuck! fuck!" said Arnie, caught in two minds about whether to help Pete or facilitate Gary's escape. Reluctantly he chose the latter, veering through someone's gate and down a side passage.

The Cardiff fans were louder now. "Oi you fucking cockney rugmunchers, fucking come here," shouted the leader. "You want it? Looks like you do, mate, you were the one with the fuckin' brick." On closer inspection, Gary noticed the blood dripping from the Welshman's fists, the result of handing out an earlier beating. Gary had been in plenty of fights over the years, but couldn't recall feeling quite so vulnerable. He hated these attackers with a passion, particularly the foul-mouthed gang leader, and was certain he would come off second best in a fight. The trouble was his disability meant he was in no position to make a swift getaway.

Just as he made the decision to give it his best shot, the lane spat them out into another street. Hesitating for a moment in deciding which way to go, Arnie saw a large gang of Hammers boys approaching. They had emptied out of the ground moments earlier and been attracted by the noise of far-off battles. "All kicking off is it?" asked one. "We can't let them get away with it on our patch."

Arnie tugged at his wounded friend, urging him towards the safety of the pack but, frozen in the moment, Gary found the Cardiff City gang leader bearing down on him. He bent as a flailing right hook tried to decapitate him then smashed his stick into the man's gut. He took seconds to recover, though, and Gary wasn't prepared for the kick in the testicles that followed. As he collapsed to his knees, heaving, he felt the walking stick wrenched from his hand as the fighting erupted around him.

For what seemed like an age the sounds of a ferocious street battle consumed his senses and when Gary finally opened his eyes the first thing he saw was his stick crashing down on a prone figure on the floor next to him. From the direction of the stadium came whistles and the sound of horses' hooves, the police wading into the action belatedly. He looked up to see Arnie being swept away in a human tide as the crowd tried to escape.

Gary hobbled to his feet and retrieved his stick, realising as he did so that there was someone lying next to him in a pool of blood. He didn't recognise them but they weren't moving. With little time to think Gary focused on making his own escape, turning in the direction of the tube station. He didn't get any further. Rough hands jarred his arms behind his back and wrestled him to the floor, forcing him to drop the walking aid again. For a moment he feared it was a second wave of Cardiff fans, then realised the truth when his eye detected the blurred outline of a high-vis jacket.

"OK sonny, you're going nowhere but the station... and by that I don't mean the tube I mean the nick," said the arresting officer. "You've had your fun – now it's our turn."

13

GARY SAT ALONE in a cell. He could hear others shouting insults through the bars at each other, a mixture of Welsh and Cockney voices. The custody sergeant and one of the arresting officers had been swapping stories of how it had kicked off big time after the match, with fighting all the way from Upton Park to Paddington. Those arrested represented the tip of the iceberg.

Squeezed into a police van, Gary had been denied the return of his walking stick by the arresting officer, who just laughed. "So you can use it on me? Not likely mate, that's an offensive weapon, that is." At the station Gary was booked in by the custody sergeant, who made jibes about his "hardness" and asked him if he had anything to say. He was going to protest his innocence, but figured it would fall on deaf ears.

As time passed he sensed his situation was becoming more serious. Scenes of Crimes officers wandered around and he noticed one had his walking stick in a protective plastic covering. Bit late for that, he thought, remembering the way it had been manhandled from him by the cop at the scene. At one stage he heard a couple of thick Welsh accents shout a word that sent a chill through his bones. "Murderers!"

What could they mean? Had someone been killed? Who? Every week there were battles between warring fans but rarely were they fatal. Gary had always considering football rucks a laugh. You could end up with a few war wounds but they earned you extra kudos when you showed them off in the pub later. A life lost, though? A loved one not returning to their parents, wife or kids? That was going too far.

Finally a key rattled in the lock and two police officers came in, roughly hauled him up and dragged him, limping, to an interview room. A tall, stern-looking man with thick black hair was waiting, a tape recorder at his side. Gary was pushed down in the chair opposite and waited for the man to finish reading the papers in front of him. He felt edgy, as if he was being deliberately kept in the dark about something. He rubbed the troublesome knee, which had been throbbing constantly ever since the fight. The officer looked up. "You OK?"

"I've got a busted knee. It can be a bit painful."

"Perhaps you shouldn't be running around the streets of east London fighting Welshmen, then," suggested his interrogator. Gary ignored the jibe. "My name's Detective Inspector Ashley Wilburn. This initial interview is beginning at 8.30pm. Your name is?"

"Gary… uh, Gary Marshall. Do I need a solicitor?"

"We'll get to that. This is just a preliminary chat. You're one of the Boxer Boys?"

"Um, no. Not really."

"You don't seem sure. You live on the Boxers Estate though?"

"Well… yeah, but…"

"I think you qualify as a Boxer Boy then, don't you? Care to tell me what happened after the match today, Gary?"

"Hammers won 2-0."

"It was three actually, but I wouldn't expect you to know that. Too busy looking for trouble…"

"That's unfair," said Gary. "I was heading home with my mates when we were attacked and chased by Cardiff fans. I can't run because of the leg and they caught me and gave me a good kickin'. End of story."

"Hmmm," said Inspector Wilburn. He leafed again through the papers. "Wasn't quite the end of the story though, was it?" he said, removing a picture and placing it in front of Gary. "Recognise him?"

The face was battered and bruised and splattered with blood, a nasty gash spreading across the forehead. The eyes were closed. Their owner could have been asleep, resting peacefully, though the pillow was tarmac and the blanket made of black plastic.

"No," said Gary. "One of those Cardiff yobs I guess…"

"He's dead, Mr Marshall," interrupted the Inspector. From beneath the desk he lifted Gary's walking stick, still enshrined in the plastic evidence bag. Gary's heartbeat quickened, but he said nothing. "Your 'crutch', I do believe and, look here," his finger pointed at the bottom where a dark smear was clearly visible. "That, Mr Marshall, is blood; this man's blood," he tapped the picture. "Now I'm no Cluedo expert but I believe I've found the body and the murder weapon. All I need to do now is find out who our Professor Scum is. That shouldn't be a problem either because we've some pretty good CCTV footage from one of the local shops. They show a man in a West Ham shirt… come to think of it a shirt exactly like that one you're wearing – a No 10 on the back – bashing this poor bloke over the head with this stick. Refresh your memory, Mr Marshall?"

Gary looked back into the earnest, unblinking eyes. "Can I have a solicitor now?" he asked.

Part II

Present Day: Wales

14

"RIGHT SON, first things first, why do you want to work for the Sunday Tribune Despatch?" The wizened old man asked, swivelling his owl-like head and fixing him with an inquisitor's stare, his over-grown eyebrows meeting in the middle.

It had been the text book opening line and one he had planned for.

Exuding a confident air, he took his time, brushing something un-detectable to the naked eye from the sleeve of the bespoke silver-grey suit he'd bought from an upmarket West End store. After straight-ening his black pencil tie and crossing one expensive Italian loafer over the other he replied: "Well, being a sports writer on this paper has to be one of the most sought-after jobs in the profession. The Tribune Despatch has a huge reputation across the UK for nurturing young journalistic talent and sending people on to greater things. As a hungry and ambitious sports journalist myself I can think of no bet-ter way to further my career than joining an organisation that prides itself on excellence. If I am lucky enough to land the role I'll be able to learn my trade from seasoned professionals like yourself. Tell me, Mr Jackson, it must have been brilliant being here when the paper launched. How did you get from there to being the success you are now?"

"Call me Jacko young man," the interviewer had replied in his gravelly Welsh whisper, a good sign that the bonding was going well. "Now, let me see. That's an excellent question you've asked me there. Establishing the Sunday Tribune Despatch as a "must have" buy among the Welsh public is quite a story in itself..."

... And they were off! The inquisitor then ate up 15 minutes or so regaling the tale of how the newspaper came into existence; In other words 15 minutes he might otherwise have spent answering questions about himself. Whilst it might have seemed a lucky break, this was no accident but the result of two weeks meticulous planning. Perhaps he should use his skills to write the definitive manual: Blagging Your Way Into A Job, beginning with Tactic No.1: How to turn an interview around so that you ask the questions and the interviewer answers them.

It wasn't rocket science but you had to learn these things somewhere. The company he was with now had been only too happy to train up younger members of their staff on management techniques so they could groom them to replace older, better-paid executives and trim the budget in the process. One of the courses was selection/interviewing and the main thing he had learned was that wherever possible the candidate should do all the talking, not the interviewer. This enabled the company to ensure, through careful questioning, they had the person with the right skills for the job.

Turn that reasoning on its head, however, and you got the opposite result. As the candidate hoping to blag your way into a job you had to mould things in such a way that you said as little as possible and left it to the person conducting the interview to do all the talking. In that way they had less time to find out your faults.

"...you would be hard pressed to find any Welshman or woman worth their salt who would go without their Trib on a Sunday, particularly the award-winning sports section," the old man said in conclusion.

The devil in him wanted to ask, "Is that why you're selling a mere 30,000 copies a week?" but he kept his own counsel.

"So young man, I take it you know your rugby?" the sports editor asked, managing to lever in only his second question of the interview, the one for which he had carefully planned. No he didn't know rugby. He knew nothing about the sodding game.

"Yes of course, but I could never hope to rival you, Jacko," he replied. "I mean... four Lions tours and God only knows how many Wales internationals you've covered. You must have some great stories..." Tactic No.2: Feed the interviewer's ego so that he can't resist talking about himself. Having grasped the bait, the old codger was more than happy to speak for 20 uninterrupted minutes about his personal career as an international rugby writer of world renown, slipping in anecdotes of trips abroad with "the lads" where the paper was lucky to get any story filed due to the uproarious antics that happened "on tour". In a career spanning 40 years there were plenty of stories, each one more outrageous than the next. All he needed to do as the interviewee was prompt the sports editor occasionally and set him off on another tangent.

"Oh my gosh is that the time? We've been at it for nearly an hour and I'm supposed to be seeing another candidate." The interviewer said suddenly, looking up at the clock on the wall. "Is there anything you wanted to ask me?"

"I think you've just about covered it thanks, Jacko," he replied, smiling to himself at the accuracy of the statement and holding his hand out as an interview-terminating gesture. "It's been fascinating." It's been an easy ride was what he meant.

As they were about to conclude their business, though, the sports editor threw in the curve ball, the one question likely to trip him up more than any other. "Just before you go, there was one thing I was meaning to ask you," he said. "Why did you change your name?"

Damn. He thought he was going to get away with it. Perhaps the old duffer had some of his marbles left after all. Studying his college certificates and matching them up with the bylines on recent stories he had done, the sports editor had spotted the anomaly. It was time for Tactic No. 3: If you are anticipating a particularly difficult question, make sure you have practised the perfect riposte.

"Oh yeah, sorry about that Jacko," he replied. "It's a bit embarrassing to tell you the truth. There was this girl back around the time I was sitting my college exams. She had the real hots for me but she was a little bit, how would you say it, crazy? As soon as I realised her true nature I called it off but she wouldn't take no for an answer, tracking me down all over London, turning up on my doorstep at ridiculous times, following my girlfriends home, ringing my parents' house... you name it. Anyway, I thought the best thing to do to shake her off was to change my name. Haven't heard from her for years now, so I guess it worked." To the sports editor he hoped it would come across as amazingly candid. Infact, It was a total fabrication but the art was in selling it convincingly, just as his dad used to sell his wares on the market stall all those years ago.

"Oh you too?" said Jacko, laughing. "Hell, I could tell you some stories. During my younger days I'd get girls trying to contact me from as far afield as Christchurch, New Zealand, and Cape Town, South Africa. They liked a bit of Welsh, you know? Ha ha. Never got in the kind of hot water that required me to change my name though. Smart thinking, boy. 'What goes on tour, stays on tour' eh, Gareth? Or should that be Gary?" He tapped the side of his nose.

"I prefer Gareth now, thanks Jacko, It's grown on me."

"Splendid, then Gareth it is." Finally the handshake took place and he set off back to the train station, delighted with his day's work. His final gambit had worked out even better than he had hoped. Jacko now saw him as some sort of kindred spirit. What could possibly go wrong?

As he settled down in carriage B of the Friday afternoon Great Western Railway service from Cardiff Central to Paddington, he heard the ring tone, a tune etched in his brain and embedded on his heart. The metallic strains of "I'm Forever Blowing Bubbles" filled the carriage to the consternation of his fellow passengers, who were unable to disguise their disgusted looks. "Yes I know", he mumbled to himself, "It's the quiet carriage".

He pressed the button and whispered "Can you hold on a minute please?" into the phone. The girl next to him instinctively shuffled out of her seat to let him pass and he hobbled towards the sliding doors at the end of the carriage, almost tripping over a suitcase lying in the aisle. He sidestepped the booby trap just as the train rocked, landing him in someone's lap.

"Hey, you clumsy oaf!" protested a pompous voice and he looked up to see a balding man in frameless spectacles glaring at him.

"For fuck's sake, can't you see I'm disabled," he responded, grabbing the man's jacket lapel and pulling back his fist. He was about to strike when a hand grabbed his arm and he turned to see the one person with the power to disarm him at a time like this.

"So sorry," said the young woman, leaning over his shoulder and talking to the disgruntled passenger. "He's had a hard day and his bad leg is playing up. I do apologise." The man begrudgingly held his hand up, accepting the excuse.

Pulling him back she whispered: "Go on, take your call. This would be a silly time to get yourself in trouble now, wouldn't it?"

Realising his mistake he nodded and left carriage B to its grumblings. The phone had stopped ringing, but started up again almost immediately.

"Yes, how can I help?" He was forced to endure one of those annoying silences before a familiar voice came on the line and gave him the news.

When he returned to his seat he was smiling. He would be starting his new job in a month.

15

"*HELL'S TEETH! WHO comes up with these bloody things? I bet Barack bleedin' Obama didn't have to go through this when he arrived at the White House. 'Now, Mr Obama, being the new boy I wonder if you wouldn't mind filling out these forms pretty please? We need to know all your intimate details me old china, inside leg measurement, what you had for breakfast over the past year, how many times a week you and Mrs Obama do it'... No bloody chance! And, just for curiosity's sake, what's this doing for the planet? These companies are always banging on about being environmentally friendly, but there's half a bleedin' rainforest here. Why a questionnaire? People just lie. Give everyone a lie-detector test – much quicker and at least you might get facts, not fiction. Anyway, surely this form should have been presented to me before the interview, not weeks after I've got the bloody job.... Jesus Christ in a flamin' handbag, now the frigging pen's run out...*"

The entire diatribe was delivered with lips barely moving, a faint mumble escaping, words tumbling around inside his head like a washing machine going through a high-speed spin cycle. Though parts of his own CV read like the life and times of Walter Mitty, the irony was lost on him as he seized the opportunity to vent his frustrations. The venom directed at the pile of papers in front of him could just as easily be aimed at something else, the slightly burnt toast from the canteen, the temperature of the vending machine coffee or the time it took to load e-mails on his computer.

This inner fury grew and mutated like a hungry parasite, feeding off scraps of minor irritation. If he took long enough to think about it the anger had originally manifested itself in his teens, the by-product of a series of personal crises which had woven themselves into the fabric of his being. He had been a pretty happy-go-lucky kid before then – well, as far as he could remember.

"Fuck!" Having shaken the pen a splurge of ink clotted like a blue-blooded wound on the paper and simultaneously smeared itself haphazardly across the cuff of his brand new, clean white shirt. He'd only taken it out of the packaging that morning. All that time in front of the mirror wasted. Did these things only happen to him? He wondered sometimes.

At the top of the form was a simple four-letter word. *Name.* A relatively simple question with which to start. In bold capital letters he scrawled it down, realising as he did so that it sounded vaguely Welsh, not that he had planned it that way.

Gareth Prince.

As far as he knew, he had no taffy in him whatsoever. Prince was his mother's maiden name and she was as Cockney as Bow Bells, Vicky Park, the Rotherhithe tunnel and his beloved West Ham United. She hadn't used the name herself for decades and he'd never heard her mention any link to this miserable country, a place he was beginning to detest more and more the longer he was here, even though in effect this was his first day.

He had been born Gareth Steven Marshall but most people knew him as Gary or Gazza. Then five years ago, for reasons too complicated and personal to mention on the form, he had changed his name by deed poll to Gareth Prince, along with his driver's licence, bank account details and passport information. He'd thought about going the whole hog and altering his first name to Steven, but figured it was better to retain the original because he was more likely to acknowledge people if they addressed him as Gareth.

The name change idea had been cribbed from a former school friend called William Smith, who had entered the acting profession and been forced to adopt a new identity by the actors' union Equity. It wouldn't do for the film and stage industry to have two Will

Smiths. Gareth had seen the name Will Edge a number of times on his Facebook page – recommended to him as a mutual friend – and had failed to realise that William Smith and Will Edge were one and the same person until his sister had pointed it out.

He thought longingly now of that sister, his family and his past life as he peered out of one of the grimy windows. The rain was coming down in torrents, a grey and miserable day becoming drearier the longer it went on. With a sigh, he turned his attention back to the form.

Age: 32.

Date of birth: 26/05/83.

Birthplace: Barking, East London.

Reason for applying: An interesting question. The more he thought about his life the more paradoxical it became. Why had he turned his back on everything he knew in order to wholeheartedly commit to a place which raised his hackles? Even now he questioned his logic, wondering if the 'incident' all those years ago had somehow damaged the internal workings in his head. He had been asking himself the same question since waking that morning and peering at his surroundings through a fog of semi-consciousness.

Braving the persistent downpour he had walked to the office half a mile away and arrived dripping wet to be introduced to a stream of people with little hope of remembering their names. When they smiled at him he reciprocated with a cheery grin and a firm hand-shake while his cynical brain thumbed through an internal rolling index searching for ulterior motives for their hearty welcome. If he disliked and mistrusted the locals it was because he was convinced the feeling was mutual and that they were plotting the downfall of the English "invader" even now. Their animosity was betrayed in the way they were studying him from behind their computer screens, no doubt holding him personally responsible for everything from pit closures to the fact their international football team had spent so many years in the doldrums.

If there was a root to his irrational hatred, it had sprouted on a Saturday evening eight years earlier when he and his best mate had been chased through the East End streets by a gang of Cardiff City football thugs hell-bent on doing them harm. Horrible crew they were, spitting hatred and vile insults about the English, their values in stark contrast to everything he knew and cherished.

That initial impression, of a nationality with a large chip on its collective shoulder, had been reinforced by the country's comedians, musicians and actors, who seemed to spread like an epidemic through popular culture. He thought they represented the height of hypocrisy, telling jokes and singing about their dislike of the English, then moving to London when they got half a chance to further their careers and set up their own little enclave of Welshness in the heart of the capital. He was by no means a bigot but when it came to the Welsh, they did his head in.

His scattergun contempt for an entire nation had hardened during an argument with a toll-booth operator at the Severn Bridge the previous evening. Sneering at his presentation of a credit card, the tattooed blockhead insisted: "Cash only here, man, it's all about the spondooliks." He spoke and acted more like some bling-crazy rich boy rapper than a downtrodden employee of the highways department, provoking Gareth into labelling him a "Welsh jobsworth". The ensuing row did him no good and eventually he was escorted back into England by the police so that he could locate an ATM in Bristol. Unbelievable. This, of course, had made him more angry than usual as it delayed his arrival in Cardiff until just before midnight. He had completed the last leg of the M4 muttering under his breath, gripping the steering wheel of his Vauxhall Corsa so tightly that his knuckles turned white.

Reflecting on all this, he was stumped for something to write on the form but knew he couldn't tell the truth: That it was the last place anyone he knew would think to look for him. He settled for 'career advancement', explaining it was a golden opportunity to "build on the newspaper experience I have gleaned to date".

Job title: Sports reporter.

Publication: The Sunday Tribune Despatch.

Last employer: New Cross Advertiser.

Previous roles in support of the application: Apprentice professional footballer with... oh, forget it. It didn't matter. Water under the bridge, spilt milk, you could group the whole sorry episode under whichever cliché you wanted. He drew a thick line through the words with black felt tip, making further mess of the form. There could be no ghosts.

Skills in support of the application: He listed all the usual journalistic qualifications, embellishing some, but left off his biggest asset: he was an ace blagger. His ability to spin a yarn was unquestionable though he was starting to wonder whether he had done the right thing in talking his way into this job. He had certainly misjudged the scale of the Welsh nation's devotion to rugby. The clues were everywhere he looked in his new environment, walls festooned with posters of brawny men in red jerseys treading opponents into the mud and red scarves handily placed on computers as if the central heating system might break down at any moment. In the kitchen area he had noticed nearly every mug, plate and coaster bore the three feathers motif along with some reference or cartoon relating to the national rugby team.

That morning, of all the discussions which rumbled around the newsroom, none had been more animated than the one about the disappearance of a Welsh rugby hero known as The Legend. There were bouts of whispering, little asides swapped behind concealing hands, followed by an epidemic of giggling. Eventually one of the infected rose from his desk and sneaked across to a giant poster on the wall just opposite Gareth, attaching a piece of paper to the bottom of it before beating a hasty retreat. Not party as yet to office in-jokes, Gareth shrugged off the shenanigans, smiled half-heartedly and re-focused on his form-filling initiation. He popped another painkiller.

Married: No.

Children?

He felt a presence loom over him and raised his eyes to be greeted by the owlish face of Sports Editor Hugh Jackson. "Oh, hi Hugh," he said.

"Not Hugh, mun... Jacko, remember?" replied the owl in his slow-paced, breathless voice. "Everyone calls me Jacko, and I won't have it any different. I see you've got the forms, lucky you. Well, leave them for now. I've got a much more important assignment for you... Come over here, son." Gareth pushed himself up out of the seat and hobbled around the table. The sports editor was staring admiringly at a poster on the wall and his features screwed up in concern when he saw the scrawled note. The owl's head swivelled, eyes travelling the room in an attempt to establish who was responsible for the seditious act. As Gareth approached him, Jacko unpinned the note, screwed it up and tossed it in the bin. Not before the new recruit had spotted the treasonous message, though.

"Missing: Presumed Drunk".

Jacko tapped his finger against the restored poster, drawing Gareth's attention to a rugby player resplendent in red, diving to the ground with ball held out in front of him, people celebrating wildly in the background. "Meet The Legend, JW Owens, finest fly-half Wales has ever produced, in my humble opinion. You can take your Barry Johns, Phil Bennetts and the like, but none of them are on a par with the great JW. We need to find him, see?" Jacko's eyes took on a milky hue and watered up badly, as if he was having flashbacks to an affectionately remembered loved one recently departed. "As you are no doubt aware he bestrode the '70s like a colossus – think Godzilla on the streets of Manhattan in that film... what was it called?"

"Godzilla," prompted Gareth.

"Ah yes, that's it. Know your films, do you? Well, I'm proud to say I saw him in his pomp... The Legend, not Godzilla. I covered that memorable Lions tour to Australia back in 1978. JW was simply phenomenal. Really packed a punch – and only 5ft 10, too."

"Hardly a colossus then," muttered Gareth.

Jacko gave him a strange look. "Sorry?"

"Oh, uh, nothing Jacko, just got a bit of a frog in my throat." He manufactured a pathetic cough.

"Right. Well... it's like this," said Jacko. "JW was a regular columnist until recently. Unfortunately he was a bit... unpredictable. His
contract ran out about a month ago and some people had reservations
about renewing it, which was understandable I guess. Whatever,
I've decided we can't do without him. You see, with this World Cup
coming up we need all our big guns firing. Our circulation has been
falling steadily and this is our chance to stabilise, maybe even put on
a few sales. The Legend would be a fantastic addition to our overall
package. I can see it now in Sunday's paper: 'The Prince meets The
Legend'. You can interview him about who will win, who will crash
out early – England hopefully, no offence – and who the stand-out
performers will be. After that I'll discuss renewing his agreement
with us. Word on the street is he could do with a few extra shillin's."

Gareth felt a jolt in his stomach, nerves kicking in. He feared the
job in question might be beyond his skill set. He wasn't intimidated
by the idea of the search, but wondered what form the conversation
might take once he caught up with this rugby-playing god. "Hi, you
must be The Legend. Apparently you're the most famous person
around these parts but I'm embarrassed to admit that until today I
didn't have a clue you existed. You starred for the Lions, I'm told. I
know sod all about the Lions, Welsh rugby, the whole weird subject.
Care to fill me in?" No, this was a job more suited to a dedicated
rugby man.

Not wanting to expose his blagging pedigree, though, he merely
nodded. For all the holes in his knowledge, and these were giant
chasms rather than minor pin-pricks, he figured an hour or two spent
in the company of Google later would plaster over the cracks. Why
should investigating rugby be any different from other journalism research tasks? It stood to reason he would have to bolster his knowledge at some stage, with the world's biggest rugby event taking place
on these very shores in just a few weeks' time.

As Gareth gathered up pens, notebook, dictaphone and mobile
Jacko piped up again, waving his hand indiscriminately in front of

him, a finger poking out in the direction of a youngster with the red-cheeked complexion of a cherub and the physique of a body builder. "Take him with you," said Jacko. "It'll be a nice trip out for him."

"Fuckin' hell," Gareth muttered. He preferred to work alone and didn't want to hold anyone's hand or have to make pointless small-talk. He could only see this kid slowing him down, if that were possible in his current physical state.

Jacko gave him another inquisitive look. "Problem?"

"Oh no... no," Gareth lied again. "It's fine."

"Oi Jason!" shouted Jacko. No response. Gareth noticed a white lead running from the inside pocket of the kid's denim jacket to the vicinity of his right ear where it disappeared under oil-slick black hair. Registering this appendage, Jacko lent across the desk and unplugged him. "You with us, son?"

"Oh, s... sorry," the boy replied, startled.

"Fancy a trip out?"

He nodded.

"Right then. Your mission is to go with our new man here, Gareth Prince, and track down a missing person – JW..."

"JW Owens?" the boy's interest perked up considerably. All week his work experience duties had been restricted to re-writing small articles from local papers, dashing out to buy bacon sandwiches for the senior staff and making copious cups of coffee and tea. This was undoubtedly the high point of his week. "My dad will be so jealous, like," he said, beaming. "JW's his hero. Best rugby player there ever was."

Gareth noticed a theme developing. Just what I need, he thought, a star-struck fan in tow. "Come on then, pal," he prompted. "We'd better get moving."

16

GARETH SHIVERED, gazing up at the block of flats. A platoon of seagulls stood sentry on the roof, menacing in their stillness. It was as if they were monitoring every move, their off-white uniforms standing out against a gloomy tableau intensified by the wave of clouds which had gathered to airbrush out the sun. It might officially still be summer but, after a brief respite when the rain lifted and the skies cleared, an icy autumn chill had now settled, sweeping in from the direction of the bay and seemingly intent on staying for the duration.

The reporter felt overcome by an undefined sense of dread, as if something lay in wait behind the drab, mustard-yellow walls. His brain ran through equations, but kept coming up short. He couldn't work out how a sporting icon with such a massive reputation in these parts could be living in such a place.

The flats themselves had been constructed for upwardly mobile young office workers during the property boom of the 90s, but the yuppies had retreated long ago, the building's aesthetic appeal vacating with them. The individual units were now owned by a housing association and let out for a reasonable rent, none of which seemed to be reinvested back into the upkeep of the property if the crumbling walls and pathways were anything to go by.

Without warning a loud screech electrified the air, making Gareth flinch reflexively and spin around in alarm, only to witness a tawdry looking gull drop down beside him and vacuum up a castaway chip from the pavement. His heartbeat returning to equilibrium, the reporter stole a quick glance at his young sidekick, glad to discover his impromptu movement hadn't been noticed. The boy was focusing all his attention on the panel of numbers which bordered a steel security gate designed to prevent uninvited busybodies entering the grounds of the property. He pushed the button next to the pencil-scrawl which looked most like the name "Owens" and waited for a reply. Nothing happened.

"What now? Should we go back?" asked the workie.

"Fuck that, no!" Gareth snapped in whispered tones, his inner bully coming out. The kid looked hurt. Oops, there I go again, thought Gareth, silently cursing his ability to upset those who sought guidance from him. He instantly resolved to repair the damage. "Sorry kid, look... you want to be a journalist, right?" The boy shrugged. "Well, think of us as Woodward and Bernstein."

"What... Clive Woodward?"

Gareth was stunned into silence. Then it clicked. "You think I'm talking about the former England rugby coach?"

"He did win the World Cup," said Jason.

"He might well have done, son, but what has Clive bleedin' Woodward got to do with journalism?" asked Gareth, failing to rein in his temper. "Did he expose cash for questions in the House of Commons? Was he the one who established there were no Weapons of Mass Destruction in Iraq?" The workie looked blank. "...Bob Woodward, that's who I'm talking about... y'know? Woodward and Bernstein? Journos who uncovered Watergate? All the President's Men? Oh... Forget it. Christ! What I am trying to say is that sometimes you need to use your charm and, er, imagination to talk your way into places. It's called in-ves-ti-gating. Try ringing some of the neighbours' bells, come up with a story and get us in." He glanced over his shoulder to ensure no one had witnessed the rant. The boy just looked at him dumbly.

"You want me to lie?" he mumbled.

"Yes... no... look, never mind. Watch and learn..." Gareth pressed a button and a female voice responded almost straight away.

"Hello?"

"Hi, my name's Gareth, um, Owens. I'm a nephew of JW Owens. He lives in this block."

"I know him... the rugby player."

"That's the one. I'm a bit worried because I haven't been able to contact him, I've been pushing his buzzer but he doesn't answer. D'you think..?"

"He probably didn't hear you," said the woman stroppily. "He's been playing his TV a bit loud. My cats have gone all peculiar. If I let you in, do you think you might get him to turn it down a notch?"

Gareth agreed, winking at Jason, who looked back at him suspiciously. A buzzer sounded and they pushed their way through the gate. "Wow, man," said the workie. "I had no idea you were related to the great JW!"

Too dumbstruck to respond, Gareth commanded "ground floor" and walked through the small courtyard to the inner entry door. The work experience boy followed, clinging to the wall of the building, head arched backward, eyes darting left and right. My God, thought Gareth, he thinks he is in some computer game like Call of Duty. The reporter pushed the door open and waited in the corridor, hands on hips.

"Look, this isn't Helmand bloody Province and we're not in the special forces," he hissed when Jason joined him. "Can we just act normally from here on in? If someone sees you creeping around like that they'll call the police – think you're trying to con some old biddy out of their life savings, or rob a resident of their pension." Jason looked crestfallen, like a kid who had dropped his ice cream. Gareth felt bad, aware he was taking out his own personal grievances on someone ill-equipped to respond. "Sorry."

They crept along the corridor in the semi gloom, the grey walls presenting a fingerprint montage of those who had passed before. A feint murmur of voices could be detected amid the still, suffocating air. "This is the one," said Gareth, rapping loudly on the purple-stained door. Putting his ear to the wood, the voices were clearer now. The neighbour was right. The television was turned up loud, tuned to a lunchtime chat show for women, a strange choice of viewing for a former international rugby player.

He stood back, but there was no reply.

"You sure we've got the right number?" asked the workie.

"Five. Yes, Jase. That's what Jacko told me."

"Look, there's a spy hole!"

Putting his eye to it, Gareth tried to focus. Eventually, like staring into the depths of a murky goldfish bowl, shapes began to emerge. "No one's cleaned up for days," he whispered. "The TV's pretty loud and the place is a mess... there are papers all over the floor... Wait. I think I can see something on the sofa. It could be a person. They're lying very still."

He raised his fist and knocked loudly on the door again. "JW!" he shouted. "Hey, JW Owens, it's the Despatch. Are you OK? Can you open the door please?" Nothing.

Jason's face had drained of colour, as if he had been spooked by a particularly lurid ghost story. He tugged at the senior man's sleeve. "What!" Gareth hissed.

"Do you think we should go to the police? It's a bit..."

"Certainly not!"

"But..."

"No buts kid, we can handle it ourselves."

Gareth's mind was whirring now, his inner hack kicking in. A friend had once described it as the newspaper version of Stockholm Syndrome, as if he had been imprisoned for years and brainwashed into adopting behavioural patterns alien to normal human beings. He knew that to dial 999 would amount to alerting every TV and radio station in the civilised world to The Legend's demise – a whole day before the Tribune Despatch deadline. He wanted to put one over on the competition, not help them out. He checked again to confirm that what he was seeing was a body, then took the mobile from his pocket and punched in the numbers.

"Hey boss, It doesn't look good... I can see into his flat now," Gareth said. "I think The Legend is in there. There's a body sprawled across the sofa. We've tried his buzzer and rapped on the door. No response."

"Oh hell," replied Jacko. "The Legend? It's definitely him? I know he can be unstable, but..."

Gareth pressed on. "I don't want to alarm you unnecessarily Mr ... um, Jacko, but... yes I'm positive it's him and, well, not to beat around the bush, I've got a horrible feeling he's dead."

There was a sharp intake of breath, followed by what sounded like a profanity. Pushing aside the sentimentality, Gareth said: "The thing is... I was thinking... well, if things go our way, we could hold it for Sunday."

"Christ, boy!" exclaimed the sports editor, forcing Gareth to pull the phone away from his ear. "You haven't been here one whole day and yet it appears you've managed to kill off our greatest-living rugby player. Not only that, but you want the story as a soddin' exclusive! My God, we've only just had the Leveson Inquiry into journalistic ethics. What do you think the good Lord would make of that suggestion? Any other plans? Are you plotting a sticky end for the famous Pontypool front row?"

Gareth looked at the phone again. God, the Welsh windbag could talk. He tried to think up a suitable reply, the rugby 'joke' going well over his head.

"Hey, I'm pulling your plonker," said Jacko, no doubt sensing he had lost his audience. "I like it! Man after my own heart. Why do all the work for the other media outlets... they won't acknowledge our 'contribution'? Wish I'd sent you on your lonesome now though. Can you shut the workie up? We need a clear run, maybe through to sixish tomorrow night."

"Leave it with me." Gareth cut the connection and turned to Jason. "Listen, kid, don't say anything to anyone right? Not even your dad. It's our secret. Breaking silence is punishable by pain of death."

"But... but what if...?"

"You tell no one! Think of it as a game. You're a soldier, right, having been taken captive by the enemy. You're determined not to

reveal any plans, even under threat of torture. We don't know anything for certain yet. As far as we are aware The Legend has gone
away."

"Well… I don't know," the muscle-bound teen complained, flicking hair from his eyes. Just as Gareth was about to make him swear
on his mother's life, he chirped up: "Hey, we've got to know for sure,
though, right?"

"That's exactly what I'm saying, we don't know anything yet."

"What I mean is, I can get a better look if I go around the side
of the building. The windows are pretty high but, well, I'm over six
foot so I reckon I could see in …"

It sounded risky. Gareth feared someone might notice and blow
the "exclusive", but the kid was right, they simply had to know the
truth. "Go for it," he said and pushed open an emergency exit at
the far end of the corridor. Immediately they were buffeted by the
chill breeze, stronger on this side of the building as it blew in di-
rectly from the Bristol Channel. It penetrated their clothing, target-
ing their bones. Gareth clenched his teeth and rubbed his arms. His
feeling of unease was heightened, the hairs on the back of his neck
rising for reasons other than the weather. He'd seen a dead body once
before, and the sight was etched on his memory forever.

Heads down to make themselves a smaller target for the elements,
neither of them breathed a word as they trudged grimly around the
corner of the building and came to a window high in the wall. Jason
finally broke the silence.

"Give us a leg up."

"I thought you were tall enough… oh never mind." Gareth made
a step with his hands and said a silent prayer that he would be able
to support the bulky figure. Exercises less strenuous than this had
caused him trouble with his dodgy knee in the past, and the biting
wind wouldn't help. Jason put a black designer boot into the cradle
and hauled his full body-builder's form up to the window. He pressed
his nose against the glass and raised a hand to shield his eyes from
his own reflection.

"Oh bloody hell!" he exclaimed. "Yeah... it's a body all right. Fuck man."

"OK calm down," advised Gareth, frozen in position as if listening to the radio commentary of a particularly tense moment in a World Cup final penalty shootout. "What exactly can you see? Describe the scene as if you were a roving reporter at a live outside broadcast."

"I'm pretty sure it's him – the great JW," said Jason. "He's sprawled out on the sofa." His eyes raked over the prone figure, clad in shorts and a t-shirt, black hair liberally salted with grey falling randomly across a cushion. "Shit. He hasn't shaved for weeks, mun. His clothes are a mess and it looks like... oh no... there's a red stain on his white t-shirt, like... well... blood."

A loud caw broke the air again and Gareth wobbled in position, almost dropping the boy. One of the gulls had arrived to stage a watching vigil on the proceedings, swooping in to land on a windowsill two stories above them.

"Sorry, kid, what did you say?" He fought to regain his balance.

"I said... it could be murder." Jason drew the word out for maximum effect.

"Really? Bit dramatic, Jase." Gareth felt the thrill ripple through him. This was the story that kept on giving, the perfect scoop for your first day in a new job. It was a plot that could have come straight off one of those TV detective shows: Murder She Wrote or Poirot. It was Death of a Rugby Legend, and he'd somehow found himself centre stage.

Jason, meanwhile, studied the scene surrounding the body. "The place has been turned over good 'n' proper," he said. "The papers on the floor ... they all appear to be copies of the Sunday Tribune Despatch, open at The Legend's column. Could it be a message? You know, was he killed because of something he wrote? And the TV being on ... it's very loud... maybe... maybe someone was trying to hide his screams."

As Gareth pondered the question a metallic sound invaded his thoughts.

TAP... TAP... TAP.

"What's that?" Gareth whispered.

"Um, it's me. I knocked on the window," explained Jason. "Huu-uuh…"

Without warning, the workie lost his balance. Gareth tried to shift his weight, but his knee wasn't up to the task and he found himself clutching at air. The workie fell sideways, striking his head a glancing blow on the wall.

"Jase? Jase?" Gareth lent over the prone body, his voice coloured with urgency, his mind turning somersaults. Did he have two deaths on his hands? Were the company insured against the demise of workies on newspaper business? Could he personally be held responsible for the situation? Even if the boy recovered there might be a possibility he could sue for negligence. More to the point, what the hell had Jason seen?

From behind him came the sound of a door slamming and Gareth shot a glance over his shoulder, scanning the shadowed recesses of the building. He feared whoever had finished off The Legend might still be lurking there, but saw nothing. "Jase!" he said, more urgently this time, turning back to the patient and shaking him by the shoulders. "Fuck!"

Gradually the workie's eyes fluttered open, then slowly focused in on him. "… S… Sorry, boss," he croaked.

"Come on, kid, spit it out would you? What happened?"

"Well, I tapped the window…"

"I know. I heard. And…?"

"At first nothing. Then…"

"Yeah?"

"Then an eye sprang open and looked straight at me!"

"Shit!"

"After that he gave me the finger and told me to F off!"

"Who?"

"Him! The Legend!"

Gareth's great exclusive disappeared in front of his eyes. "So… not dead then?"

On cue, a crushing vice-like hand gripped Gareth's shoulder, making him leap to his feet in shock. "Dead?" thundered a Welsh voice as thick as anthracite. "Who's dead? Oh... you thought I was? Not on your life, buttie boy, not on your life. Fit as a fiddle, me. Now, who the hell are you and what do you want?"

Turning his head slowly, Gareth came face to face with the man they called The Legend.

17

THE SPECTRE OF death hung loosely around the former rugby player like a baggy old tracksuit. Though he was very much alive, and embraced life with boundless enthusiasm, little signs gave him away. There was a musty, slightly decaying smell he tried so hard to disguise with strong, manly after-shave; red, hairline splinter trails infringed at the corners of his eyes; veins and arteries pressed too close to the surface of the skin, giving the impression he might spontaneously combust at the onset of his next bout of laughter. Gareth had greeted this pale apparition with a proportionate amount of shock and fear, only to conclude pretty quickly that the 'second coming' was a cheap conjuring trick performed by someone who lived his life in thrall to alcohol.

"Sorry, boys, didn't know you were from the paper," explained The Legend, thumping Gareth on the back enthusiastically. "Gave you a bit of a scare did I?"

The question was followed by an impromptu attack of coughing, giving Gareth no opportunity to reply. When The Legend recovered, he put his key in the lock and threw open the door. The smell hit Gareth the second they crossed the threshold. It was as if something rodent-like had died under the floorboards after smoking a forest of tobacco and drinking a bathtub of stale beer. Gareth rubbed his stinging eyes and held his hand over his face like a medic entering a contaminated zone.

Jason appeared oblivious to it all. He was staring open-mouthed at the collection of giant photographs on the corridor wall. Encased in nicotine-varnished frames and hidden behind glass stained with watermarks, they showed a dark, wavy haired character brought to life in monochrome. In one he was being held aloft, his face caked in mud, by other similarly attired characters looking up at him with broad grins on their faces. The hairstyle lengths and preference for sideburns and beards told tales of a bygone era when sportsmen imitated rock stars. In another picture the same character was pushing a rigid arm into the face of an opponent, his hand fanned open as if determined to leave an impression of fingerprints on a human canvas, ball tucked protectively under the other armpit.

"Wow!" said Jase.

"Like 'em boy? Got them presented to me by the paper way back in the day. Not the Despatch, one of them London papers, the Express I think. I was a hero even in England then, eh?"

"Second Test, Melbourne, 1978," said Jason, studying the picture. "That was taken in the lead up to the second try. You received a pass from the Scottish scrum half Malky Murdoch, sidestepped their second row Colin Gumstead then handed off Peter Bacharach there before charging towards the line and giving a perfect inside pass to the centre Willie McTravis. Paul Alun Williams, the full back, was supposed to be taking the kicks but he had a dead leg and was off the pitch so you slotted the penalty between the posts from wide on the right touchline. That made it 15-12 to the Lions and it was a backs-to-the-wall effort that enabled you guys to hang on and win the game. Awesome man! Then this one was after the third Test when you..."

"...Yeah, very good son. Are you a psychic or something? You remember it better than I do! How do you know all that?"

"Seen the whole thing many times on video. My dad's got a recording of nearly every game you played and has noted all the salient moments down in a book, with all the newspaper cuttings – he's a real fan. I guess I'm just a chip off the old block."

"Hmm, well I tell you what... um... what's your name again?"

"Jason, sir, but everyone calls me Jase."

"OK Jase, how would you like to do me a favour?"

"Would I!" said the work experience boy. "You name it Mr Owens, sir, and…"

"Call me JW." A bony elbow struck Gareth a painful blow in the ribs and he momentarily lost his grip on his nose, breathed out rapidly and suffered a coughing spasm. "Ah, that's a nasty cough you got there," said The Legend. "I know the feeling. That's what I've been laid low with, the lurgy. Bit of flu I reckon." He indicated in the direction of the front room where a low mist hovered over various bits of mismatched furniture. "Haven't moved off that sofa for days. Got a couple of quid on you, butt?"

The Legend held out his hand patiently. Bringing his airways under control, Gareth found himself pinned by the same earnest, soul-searching and slightly disconcerting stare which had greeted him in their initial encounter. "Um, yeah, think so," he said, fiddling in pockets.

"It's for light bulbs," said The Legend, grabbing a fistful of coins from Gareth's hand and taking a £5 note for good measure. "I'll give it back to you when I manage to get to a cashpoint. A bulb blew last night and I was too unwell to do anything about it."

"Oh yeah… the flu," said Gareth with a hint of sarcasm.

If The Legend noticed, he showed no sign. "Yeah, that's it, butt. Knocked me out it did. There I was trying to fight it off when to make matters worse I'm plunged into darkness. Here you go, son." The Legend dropped his freshly acquired wealth into the hands of the workie. "Shop's just out the front, turn left and it's on the corner there. Get about four, would you? 60 watt, large screw-ins – and don't think I'm being smutty. Ha ha, there's a good lad." As Jason went to leave The Legend grabbed him around the bicep. "Bit of muscle on you, boy. Hard as marble. Play rugby do you? Listen, don't go spending the change on them girlie mags, I know you kids. I want it, right? Better still, get me half an ounce of shag." Jason looked at him, tongue-tied, a devout follower being read the commandments by his deity. "It's rolling tobacco," The Legend explained, assisting him to the door with a shove. Gareth felt a smirk forming, amazed at how The Legend had swiftly adopted the borrowed currency as his own.

Jason gone, the former rugby star quickly revisited the story of his lost week. "Yeah, I've been meaning to replace some of them bulbs for ages," he said. "You know, they go 'pop' and you think, 'Oh it's all right, no rush, I can make do with the other light'. Then at the worst moment that one goes too and you've got no back-up. You're in total darkness. Luckily I had candles." He indicated to a table in the front room where a thick tube of red melted wax sat next to an overflowing ashtray, throwing other-worldly shapes across a grimy wall.

"Aaaah," said Gareth, a light switch going on inside his own head.

"What's that... sorry, what did you say your name was... Geraint?"

"No, it's Gary... uh, Gareth. Oh, nothing really. I've just twigged. We thought it was blood."

There was a brief pause, "Ohhhh! You mean this!" The Legend pointed to the broad red mark on his shirt. "Some of the wax dripped on me. Couldn't really see what was happening in the dark and then didn't have the energy to get changed. Wasn't expecting visitors, anyway. Jacko sent you, did he?"

Gareth nodded.

"Great guy, Jacko. Brilliant sports editor. Known him years. Did he tell you..?"

"... That he covered the Lions trip to Australia? Yeah, he might have mentioned it."

"He wants me back doesn't he? Wondered how long it would take, what with the World Cup coming to Wales. Couldn't do without my invaluable insight, I guess. I'll have a look in my diary... make sure I haven't got a lot on. The after-dinner speaking circuit gets busy around this time, you know, particularly with such a big event on the horizon. I'm very much in demand."

"Oh, right," said Gareth, trying to figure out who would want this ramshackle character delivering speeches to the glitterati.

"Anyway Geraint, let's 'ave a cup of tea shall we?" said The Legend. "Kettle's in the kitchen. Feeling a bit weary after all the excitement,

I am. Think I need a sit down. Later we can go out and get a swift beer. No point in moping around here any longer. What d'you say?"

Gareth thought about correcting him over the name again, but decided it wasn't worth the hassle. Instead he nodded and went in the direction indicated, hand fixed firmly back over his nose. He had no idea what he was going to find in the kitchen, but prepared himself for the worst. Behind him he heard the voice of a well-known TV chef explaining how to make pancakes, his recipe punctuated by a rhythmic, deep-throated snore.

18

THE LAMB AND FLAG was one of those popular city centre pubs which fill up rapidly on Friday nights. Gareth, Jason and The Legend squeezed into the crammed interior and manoeuvred their way towards the bar. An elbow caught Gareth in the ribs and he lost his balance, his dodgy knee buckling. Muttering "twat!" he jabbed back with force. Mistake. Someone shouted "Oi!" and he was grabbed painfully by the forearm. He turned to find Cardiff's version of the Incredible Hulk glaring down at him, a pint glass nestling like an egg cup in his huge, hairy fist. Thick, black eyebrows connected in the middle of a cinderblock head which was split unevenly in two by a zig-zag nose. His hair was shaven to within a millimetre of his skull. The reporter realised he was in trouble.

"Did you say something mate?"

Gareth shook his head.

"You gone and spilt my pint down my best trousers. What I want to know is: what are you going to do about it?"

What I would like to do is grab that glass and break it over your big buffoon head, thought Gareth. Instead he gave the meathead his most amiable look as he considered whether he could get away with a head butt, just to get him to release the arm. "Umm, let me get you another," he offered. "What would you like?"

"Oh English are you?" deduced Cinderblock. "Well what I would really like is the money to pay my dry cleaning bill. About 15 quid I reckon." He turned and smirked to a couple of fellow steroid-injecting monoliths, relishing the act of humiliating someone smaller and less physically threatening than himself. Gareth felt his fists tightening. He was ready to explode with rage, but a sensible voice in his head told him he was vastly outnumbered and any retaliatory action would only end badly. Frozen in the moment and trying to think of a suitable response to take the heat out of the situation, he was grateful when the cavalry arrived.

"Excuse me, butt, what's the problem here?"

"Oh... my... God," exclaimed Cinderblock, his eyes widening. "Hey boys, look, it's The Legend! The great JW. Wow man." His paw released Gareth and his crooked face took on a more accommodating expression. "Let me shake your hand, sir. This is truly an honour. I've seen all your best moments – on DVD, wasn't really old enough to see you live – magician you were, sir, particularly when you were giving it to the Saes."

"English, that means," The Legend whispered to Gareth before squeezing Cinderblock's hand fiercely and giving him his full attention. "No problem, boys. I apologise for my friend here," he placed a protective arm around Gareth's shoulders. "Old Geraint here doesn't really know where he is at the moment. You know how it is? Been out on the lash all day – stag weekend." He winked. "Half bloody English, Bit of a lightweight."

"Oh yeah, sure JW, sir," said Cinderblock reverentially. "We know what you mean. We're on a stag do, too. We're all members of the Pontyprenis Club, up the valleys, innit. Our scrum half is getting himself hitched tomorrow... poor bloke. Hey, you wouldn't mind signing his shirt, would you, and a couple of other things? Let me get you guys a drink. Oh, silly me, I imagine he's had enough... but what would you like JW?"

"Very kind, boy, very kind. I'll have a small pint of lager with you."

As Cinderblock turned away The Legend indicated with his head that it might be a good time for Gareth to move to a less testosterone-fuelled area of the pub. Happy to put distance between himself and Cinderblock, the reporter carefully squeezed his way through to the far end of the bar. His plan to remain incognito didn't last long, though.

"Hey you!" At first he tried to ignore the shout but when it was repeated he reluctantly turned to face the figure desperately trying to attract his attention. A man in a full cream suit, orange shirt and yellow patterned cravat was sitting at a table in a corner of the room waving his hands in Gareth's direction. He had perfectly white, candyfloss hair and was raising a glass of red wine as if in a toast. The drink matched his complexion. Another nutter, thought Gareth, and started to turn away. "You're the new chap aren't you?"

Gareth muttered "Go away", but couldn't take the risk of infuriating another local. He limped closer so he could hear better above the constant thrum of the crowd. "Sorry?"

"You're the new sports writer on the paper... the Despatch. Sorry, let me introduce myself. Tucker-Green. Quinten. At your service." He bowed and indicated the chair opposite.

"You're on the paper too?" Gareth asked warily.

"Oh yeah, been there forever. Well... after my spell on the nationals, of course. Chief Feature Writer. Really can't wait for the World Cup. I imagine that's why you're here, too?"

Gareth hadn't realised how close the event was until earlier that day. Very few people in London seemed to be talking about it. Still, he wasn't prepared to give up his big secret to a stranger. "Yeah, well ..."

"Splendid. And to whom am I speaking?"

"Oh... it's Gareth. Gareth Prince."

"Good Welsh name. Splendid. We can call you Prince of Wales ... Like the pub on the corner. Excellent." He chuckled. "The others will be here soon. Can I offer you a cheeky glass?" He pointed to the bottle of wine on the table. "Chateauneuf Du Pape. Forty five quid a bottle. Luckily..." he tapped his nose. "I know the landlady so I get a bit of a, um, discount."

"No, I'm fine, thanks," said Gareth. "I'll stick to beer."

"Philistine!" said Tucker-Green in mock horror. "You're just like all the rest. Ah well, no educating the proletariat, I guess. Still, the other pint of lager and packet of crisps merchants will be here soon. You'll feel at home then. And this is...?"

He pointed to a spot beyond Gareth's shoulder. The sports reporter swivelled to see Jason looming over him, holding two pints of beer in his hand. The work experience boy didn't seem to register that his actions had taken Gareth by surprise. "Here you go, boss," he said, handing over one of the drinks. "Figured you might need it. It's the local brew... people swear by it..."

"But you're..." Gareth was about to give away the workie's age, but quickly reined himself in. It wasn't as if he'd avoided pubs when he was officially too young to drink. "Thanks. Jason, um... what's your second name?"

"Shakespeare."

"Oh... right. Well, Jason Shakespeare meet Quinten Tucker-Green. He's the paper's feature writer." Quinten leaned forward and shook the boy by the hand.

"Pleased to meet you, son. Good name for a journo, eh, Shakespeare? Now... let me guess... work experience?"

Jason nodded.

"Good boy. I hope the Prince of Wales here is looking after you."

"Yeah," said Jason enthusiastically. "I've 'ad a fannnnnntastic day. Met the great JW Owens. In fact, he's just over there, having a pint with a few of the boys from my rugby club."

Gareth couldn't hide his shock. "Your rugby club?"

"That's right. Valleys boy me... Pontyprenis is my team. I play for the Under-18s. Flanker. The coach says I'm pretty good. I model myself on Sam Warburton."

Gareth had no idea who that was, but nodded nonetheless. "They're a bit... um, intimidating," he said, indicating Cinderblock, who was now in earnest conversation with The Legend.

"Ah, they're all right. Just got a bit of booze in them. Any trouble, though, and my dad would sort them out... with a little help from me, of course. We're quite a team."

"Y-e-a-h," said Gareth slowly, failing to see how a child, even as well-built as Jason, would be able to tangle with full-grown men.

"Anyway," said Jason, taking a seat beside him and focussing on Quinten. "He's great, isn't he? The Legend? Just got Gareth out of big trouble."

"Really?" said Quinten. "Oh yeah, he's a sweetheart is The Ledge. Me and him go way back. He seems to be enjoying himself." He indicated across as the former rugby star emptied three quarters of a pint down his throat in what appeared to be one gulp. Suddenly Gareth remembered the hi-jinks in the office that morning, all the talk about the great JW "mystery".

"Now I remember," he said. "You're the one who put that note under the picture!"

Quinten either chose to ignore the accusation, or had far more important things on his mind. "Ah, and here come the second wave ..." he announced.

Gareth turned to see a group of people pushing through the crowd. A woman led the way across to their table, curly red hair bouncing on her shoulders. Her hand stretched out. "You're Gareth, I was hoping you might be here," she said. "Nice to meet the newbies. I'm Monica... Monica Matthews, news editor." She turned to the other five members of her team and announced: "This is the new sports reporter Gareth Prince. Let's give him a true Welsh welcome."

"Don't forget it's publication day tomorrow, Mon!" came a voice hidden in the crowd. "It better not be 'too' warm a welcome." Her entourage laughed.

"Good point. Mustn't go over the top on a school night," she said, turning back to Gareth. "And on that note, let me introduce you to the team."

19

THE LEGEND WAS in his element. He wasn't sure whether the warm glow he was feeling came from the two double whiskies he'd just consumed or the radiated affection of the crowd around him. These were his people: They loved him, idolised him, revered him. On any given night he could walk into a pub like this and not have to put his hand in his pocket. Magic.

It wasn't one-way traffic though, even if the financial transactions seemed that way. He worshipped them, too. His people. Only in Wales could you get such a depth of passion, an intimate bond between sportsman and fan. They might provide the fuel that drove his engine, but they got a glorious switchback ride in return as he regaled them with wondrous stories they were too young to recall. A raconteur extraordinaire, he was courteous and charming, the bon viveur. For them, this chance audience with The Legend would go down as the thing that made their Friday night extra special, something to be cherished for years to come, immortalised by a blurry photograph on a smartphone or a spidery scrawl on a flimsy piece of spare tissue paper.

The light in the corner of his eye was playing tricks and he couldn't focus too clearly on who was speaking to him now, but no matter. More arms went around his shoulders, he smelt the strong allure of an exotic scent in his nostrils and felt the delicate brush of fly-away hair against each cheek. He could just make out silky strands of blondeness through the mishmash of imagery on either side of him as another camera phone snapped into action, a kiss simultaneously planted teasingly just below each ear. He guessed the girls to be in their early 20s and bathed in the pure innocence of the brief encounter.

Another voice, one from earlier, spoke above the others. "Ah Ledge, mate, we've got to go. Hit the clubs, you know how it is. The totty can't wait for us much longer. Oh, one last thing though. Can you sign this for us? It would be great if you could. Super memento for me to take away."

A pen was pressed into his hand and a finger pointed at something wobbling in his peripheral vision. Perhaps it's time I got glasses, he thought, leaning over to make contact with the object. He put his hand on the side of the table to steady himself and scraped the pen across the paper, concluding with an elaborate flourish of a hand once capable of passing a rugby ball quicker than the blink of an eye. "There you go, butt. Hope you enjoy!" he said, hugging Cinderblock affectionately and waving goodbye as the group pushed their way from the premises.

"Why did he ask you to sign that?" inquired a voice from behind him. He pirouetted slowly to find the new reporter standing there.

"When you're as famous as me, son, people quite often ask you to sign their books," he explained proudly. "They snap up every little bit of memorabilia they can about you: magazine interviews, programmes..."

"I get that bit," said Gareth. "But that book wasn't about you. It was Ian Rush's autobiography."

The Legend smiled crookedly, threw his hands in the air as if to indicate the point was of no consequence, then toppled forward across the table, sending glasses flying in every direction.

GARETH HAULED THE Legend back to his feet with the help of Quinten and Jason. Monica arrived with sympathy and tissues, a token gesture in trying to remove the beer stains from the rugby hero's faded and worn blue blazer, which boasted a crest on the pocket and had been a stock item in his wardrobe for more than 40 years. The group formed a huddle to protect him from anyone who had been offended by his actions and might be inclined towards physical retribution. They guided him to the door while whispering platitudes to the bar staff, explaining how sorry they were and how the fallen idol had been ill all week and had probably keeled over due to rampant flu.

Unfortunately this kind of incident was a regular occurrence in the life of faded rugby legend JW Owens. Landlords and bar staff passed on the stories from pub to social club to nightclub. They were dispersed with a disrespectful chuckle in the manner of a stand-up comedian railing at the wife. It meant the group's excuses, intended to placate those who had been pressed into service to clean up the mess, fell on deaf ears.

"JW, you're barred!" shouted a well-dressed woman who had slapped on liberal amounts of garish make-up. The Legend, perplexed at first by the splurge of colours that in his skewed concept of the surroundings made her face resemble a child's painting, waved his hand in the air in a show of defiance. "Good riddance you old crone!" he slurred. "This boozer's bollocksh anyway. You should thank me. People came in jussht to meet me, not drink your foul beer and queue for days for the privilege!"

It was a gutsy display which would have been slightly more effective if he hadn't fallen face first over the doorstep and landed like a discarded mannequin in the street. While Jason and Quinten helped him up, Gareth walked into the road to flag down a taxi. When one pulled up beside them he withdrew his wallet from his pocket and leaned through the window.

"Hi mate, can you do us a big favour," he said. "Our friend here is not at his best. He has been suffering from flu all week and has had a bit of a relapse…"

"So… he's been drinking, sir," said the Asian driver in a melodic Welsh accent, looking over Gareth's shoulder. "Nothing unusual for a Friday night. That's how I make my living, taking people home who are incapable of driving or walking." His mood changed quickly, though, as his eyes focused fully on his potential fare. "Oh, it's him," he said. "Well, that will be £25... in advance."

"What?" Gareth exploded, thrown by the extortionate amount. "You know who this is, do you? He only lives down the Bay, you robbing..."

"Yes, that's right sir," agreed the driver, attempting to defuse Gareth's anger. "But, you see, I've taken Mr Owens home on a couple of occasions and when we arrive he always seems to have misplaced his money. I let him off because... well... he is The Legend. But I made a vow to my wife and kids that I wouldn't take him again until he paid me what he owed."

Gareth brought himself under control. He couldn't really argue with the logic. He looked through his wallet and came out with a £20 note. He shouted over his shoulder. "Hey Quinten, got a fiver? It's for a good cause."

"I'm not some kind of philanthropist you know, dear boy!" the feature writer complained, pulling up alongside him. The Legend was tucked under his arm and weaving from side to side.

"Look, I'll give it back as soon as I get to a cashpoint, OK?"

The feature writer sighed. "Oh very well then." He left The Legend leaning against the car and went through his pockets, coming up with a mangled £5 note. "Here..." Turning back to reclaim the patient, Quinten realised too late that the formerly immoveable object was on the move again. The two men watched as The Legend slid slowly along the length of the taxi and disappeared behind the boot. When Quinten went to retrieve him, he was on his knees, decorating the road surface with a spray of vomit that matched the colour of the restricted parking lines. "Oh lor'," said Quinten. "He's just upchucked. Give us a hand will you, old chap?"

"Hey!" shouted the taxi driver. "If he throws up in the taxi that's another 50 bucks, you know. It'll put me out of action on a Friday night when I should be doing my best business. You'd better give me your card, sir, in case I need to get in touch."

Gareth moved one way then the other, not quite sure which emergency demanded his attention most. Having been in the job for less than 24 hours he didn't yet possess business cards. He felt his hackles rising. "Oh for fuck's sake, fella, I'm new to this soddin' place, can't you..."

Fortunately Monica came to the rescue, putting her hand on his arm and pulling him away before passing a slip of paper through the window. "We're with the newspaper, the Sunday Tribune Despatch," she explained. "Give us a call and we'll sort it out – but please make sure he gets home safely."

"Thank you, miss," said the driver. "I will make sure Mr Legend gets back to his flat. No problem."

Freed of the responsibility, Gareth bent over and put his hand under The Legend's armpit. As he lifted he felt a jolt pass through his knee. He knew he was going to suffer over the next few days. Damn pisshead, he thought to himself. "Let's get him in the cab then," he said to Quinten, who was dabbing at a yellow patch on the lapel of his jacket.

"Bloody hell, that's another trip to the dry cleaners and a small fortune gone," Quinten complained, replacing his handkerchief in the top pocket of his jacket and bending over to take the strain once more. "How much more is this bugger going to cost me?"

Having levered the patient to his feet they managed to pour him into the back of the taxi as Monica held open the door. He sprawled face down across the seat. Breathing heavily, sweat forming on his brow, Gareth asked: "What now?"

"Well, the night is young and there are some rather decent late night establishments in the vicinity," said Quinten. "It's your first day so you should be initiated in the time-honoured fashion. Let's go get a nightcap."

"That'd be great butt," chimed in Jason, who had been a passive observer until now. "I'm really enjoying myself. Don't often get into the big city."

Gareth looked at him sternly. "I think Mr Tucker-Green was addressing me, not you," he said peevishly. "Don't you have a home to go to, son? Won't your parents be worried?"

"Nah, don't sweat it," Jason replied. "I rang my dad earlier. He's a bouncer round at the Token Pole, said he'll give me a lift home when he knocks off work. All I've got to do is turn up there later."

"Token Pole eh?" said Quinten. "Mighty fine establishment. If it wasn't for young Monica here, I would suggest we pop along for a bit of, um, exotic entertainment."

Monica tutted then explained to Gareth, who was feeling cast adrift from the conversation. "Lap dancing club. Just down there on the right. Quinten is a member, no doubt."

By now the rest of her entourage had arrived. She turned around to address them. "Well, Quinten, you can do what you like," she told him. "I fancy going to Kiwis for a bit of a dance. Any takers?" There were howls of approval.

Their attention distracted, no one noticed the bedraggled figure slip out of the far side of the taxi and weave down the street, as if attempting to reproduce the famous sidestep of his youth.

20

KIWIS WAS A lively establishment at the entrance to one of Cardiff's proliferation of small arcades. Popular chart music from four decades pounded out from within as people at various stages of sobriety formed a queue outside and fashioned ways of talking their way past the bouncers. For Monica Matthews and her gang it was no problem. They had an understanding with the establishment that they could enter free of charge any time they liked. In return the owner quite often saw his club mentioned favourably in articles about nights out in Cardiff.

Gareth returned to a low table with a tray of drinks. He realised that he was getting short of cash, but felt it only right to make the gesture, aware that it would accelerate the bonding process.

"Where are you staying?" asked Monica as he settled down next to her and took a sip of his drink.

"There's a small B&B on the Newport Road which I'm using as a base," explained Gareth. "It's £25 a night though, so I've got to find something a bit more permanent pretty quickly. I'm using my savings up and I don't get paid for a couple of weeks."

"Bummer. If we had a spare room you'd be welcome, but me and the fella have two kids and not enough room to swing a cat. Oh yeah, we have a cat too." She chuckled.

"We could put you up, butt."

Gareth swivelled on his seat to see Jason beaming at him.

"How the hell do you do that?" demanded Gareth. "You're like creeping Jesus, sneaking up on people."

"Sorry, don't mean to," the boy said, crestfallen.

"It's all right," said Gareth, once again feeling guilty for snapping. "I've just had a bit of a day of it, is all." He considered the offer. "I don't know. You live in the Valleys, don't you?"

"Yeah, but it's not far, and it's only me and dad. Gran does some cooking for us, too. She makes lovely Welsh cakes, and cawl, and her Welsh gravy is fantastic, butt."

"Butt what?"

"Eh, oh no," The workie sniggered. "Sorry, it's a Welsh term. Better get used to it. It's short for butty... means mate, like."

"Oh, right," said Gareth. "I wondered what that was all about. The Legend kept using it. By the way, those things you listed, Cowell was it? Welsh cakes? You do realise I haven't a clue what those things are?"

Jason looked bemused. "Never heard of cawl? You don't know what you're missing, butt. It's a kind of soup. Anyway. Serious like. Dad could do with a bit of extra cash and it's cheaper living in the valleys than in the big city. Public transport's not bad either, but if you have a car, all the better. You've got one of them, haven't you?"

"Yeah, sure," said Gareth, mulling things over in his head. "I don't know. I don't want to impose..."

"No trouble. Consider it a done deal."

Gareth wasn't sure the conversation had gone quite the way he wanted. Young Jason irritated him at the best of times and he felt uncomfortable about the prospect of spending time outside work in his company. The financial situation was critical, though, so he figured he could give it a few days to see how it panned out. There was nothing to stop him leaving if the situation didn't suit. "Very kind of you, Jason. Thanks."

"Great," said the boy, chuffed with his powers of persuasion. "I'll let Dad know tonight and you can move in tomorrow. How does that sound?"

"Let's see what he says first," said Gareth, pleased that the boy's spirits had lifted.

"A toast then!" said Quinten. "To Gareth, our new Prince of Wales, and his faithful sidekick Jason. A match made in heaven." They raised their glasses and drank.

GARETH reached the front door of his bed and breakfast just after 1am. He had twice stumbled up paths previously only to realise he was in the wrong place. He had drunk far more of the local brew than he intended but he didn't consider this solely the reason for getting the directions mixed up. He had arrived late the previous evening following his Severn Bridge problems and that morning had been far too hyped to take note of his bearings. The fact it was raining so hard that he could barely see a hand in front of his face was another contributory factor, and this particular B&B didn't stand out on a street chock-full of similar establishments.

Fumbling with his keys he located the lock and whispered "shhh!" to himself as he pushed open the door, the rattle of a chain sounding extra loud in the silence. The absurdity of his situation prompted him to chuckle. Once the giggles started it was hard to contain them and he prayed the sound wouldn't wake the prickly landlady he had met on his arrival.

Staggering up the stairs he navigated the narrow corridor, located room 4 and let himself in. The trek to find an available taxi on Cardiff's main street, coupled with the tour of the Newport Road and the journey up the stairs, had really taken it out on his knee, so he grabbed a glass of water from the tiny bathroom in what was generously described as his "en suite", popped a painkiller and studied his complexion in the mirror. Vacant eyes stared out from below a head of black hair and, even though his girlfriend had dyed it a while ago, the transformation still took him by surprise. Having supped more than his fair share of alcohol he wondered if it was wise to add his medication to the mix but knew he would struggle to sleep without it and had a busy day tomorrow – his first deadline.

Flopping flat out on the bed, he looked around the room and felt a strange urge to cry. God, had his life really come to this? The beige wallpaper and the flowery car-boot curtains screamed tempo-rary not permanent, while the plaque with three feathers on the wall just polarised his despair. It was like being in one of those halfway houses set up for those who spent time behind bars and he won-dered whether he would ever be Gary Marshall again, able to enjoy the same creature comforts Gary Marshall had.

He thought of his mum back in her flat, surrounded by a bizarre mixture of the royals and Status Quo, the woman who had been there for him when all his other support groups had collapsed. He won-dered what Lily was doing. He had been so close with his sister, but she was now living far away in the wilds of Scotland with her hus-band, having also traded in an old life for a new one and changed her name, though the circumstances were entirely different. Finally, he thought about the girl of his dreams, and the kid, and wondered whether there would ever be a scenario where they could live out their lives happily together.

In a concerted effort to break the drink-induced blues he levered himself up again and opened a drawer, pulling out his laptop and placing it on top of the dresser. Dragging across the only chair in the room, he settled in front of it, lifting the lid and booting up. Inputting the wifi code given to him on his arrival, a screen saver of the girl and the kid greeted him and he immediately felt much better. If he couldn't be Gary Marshall any more at least he could pretend to be him.

Gareth had bought a new laptop and phone shortly after changing his name, altering all his email log-ins and passwords, together with his Twitter handle. He had then set up an entirely new Facebook page under his assumed identity, choosing only to add acquaintances he had met since the name change. It gave his work colleagues in south London quite a laugh when they saw he had a meagre 23 friends on the social media site but he shrugged it off, explaining he had been an unpopular geek at school and his mother had insisted on moving him at regular times to extricate him from bullies. Embracing his new life, he had even gone as far as to change his car so that there was no paper trail by way of log books, insurance and vehicle tax. To the Driver and Vehicle Licensing Agency Gary Marshall no longer owned a car.

All these precautions would look sinister to a special branch investigator, GCHQ spy or MI5 operative, but there was no real hidden agenda. He had just reached a point in his life where he needed to find a way to halt the run of misfortune that had plagued him. To remain Gary Marshall would mean someone from his troubled past was always likely to pop up and entice him back to the old ways – something that would inevitably lead to more trouble. He was desperate to avoid one person, in particular, even though he loved that person like a brother.

In a way it was a shame that he had to ostracise himself from those with whom he had grown up, but he knew that to maintain contact with them would jeopardise the future goals he had set himself. He had a second chance to make good and intended to go as far in his adopted profession as possible, as a thank you to his mother if nothing else. By doing so he hoped he would be able to cancel out a myriad of regrets.

In some ways, he guessed, it was tantamount to punishing himself. After all, he couldn't revisit the old haunts. Perhaps the biggest loss was the fact he wouldn't be able to return to Upton Park to watch his beloved team, even though in truth he'd become a 'lapsed' Hammer some time ago and suspected he might even be on the banned-for-life list. Of course, his mum had bleated about the way he was cutting his ties but she knew deep down she had set him along this path in the first place.

It was she who had warned him his friends would cause him nothing but trouble and she who had smoothed the way for him to reach his current profession. As for his girlfriend, she'd been hands on in constructing his new persona, knowing deep down he was making the right move. She couldn't grumble when she saw it was working out. She knew where he was and hopefully when things settled...

He decided it was enough self reflection for one night. It was time to get back to the charade and play the game of smoke and mirrors. He might as well enjoy it.

He logged on to his Facebook page, not the one he had set up five years ago as Gareth Prince but the original he still ran under the name Gary Marshall. He had kept his old account and his previous Twitter sign-in so that he could lay a false trail of breadcrumbs, knowing the information would soon get passed around his old gang. He clicked on status update and began typing, warming to the task like any blagger would. "A great opportunity has arisen in Dubai. Sun, sea, sand. Good money and all tax free. I'm going out there for a couple of weeks to see the lay of the land. Could be the start of a whole new life."

21

AN UGLY FACE spitting venomous words,

A flying fist, tattooed knuckles connecting with brittle bones. Crack.

Prone on the floor, unable to move.

Drip, drip of blood from a broken nose.

Eyes closed, waiting for the end.

Then nothing.

Around him, chaos.

Feet pounding, punches landing, sirens wailing, voices swapping insults in different accents.

One noise louder than the others. A dull, repetitive thud. A squeal. Pleading.

"Stop! No..." Thud.

Then a more familiar voice. "You want me to stop? You started it, you bastards!"

Eyes sprang open, expecting to see the walking stick beating its morbid rhythm... but there's only sunlight breaking through the drab curtains, casting its beam on the bedside clock.

6.50am. Damn.

The man now known as Gareth Prince realised he had a full bladder, a consequence of his eventful first night out with the Cardiff crew. There was little chance of him getting back to sleep so he lifted his troublesome leg over the side of the bed and pushed up agonisingly into a standing position. Then he remembered. It was production day, his first on the Despatch.

A STRANGE SENSE of déjà vu gripped him as soon as the lift doors opened. He'd been here only yesterday, of course, but it wasn't the decor jarring his memory banks, it was the smell. His stomach almost jettisoned the sausage, egg and bacon he had devoured at the cafe he'd found in the city centre as a quick-fix for nagging hangover pains. It wasn't an odour you could forget easily: the unmistakable fragrance of dead rat under floorboards, combined with a certain *je ne sais quoi* of stale hops, alcohol and tobacco and topped off with a delicate touch of eau de fly half.

Against his better judgment Gareth took another sniff of the air and tried to establish where the stench was coming from. At the far end of the room he could see the glass-fronted office which belonged to the editor. Surely not there, he thought, but hobbled in that direction hoping his senses were leading him down a false trail.

As he closed in on the target, though, the smell grew stronger. Then, without warning, his leg bumped up against something and he sprawled forward, just regaining his balance as a metal filing cabinet loomed in his sights.

"What the bluddyell?" The voice was instantly recognisable. It belonged with the smell. Peering behind a desk Gareth came across a brain-freezing sight. It was as if a mangled, rabid bear was emerging from hibernation from under a moth-eaten, tea-stained sleeping bag. Brushing fur from its eyes with grimy, dirt-encrusted nails the creature peered at Gareth through sunken sockets. It rubbed at them to make sure it wasn't hallucinating, then uttered a barely decipherable grunt. "Oh…S'you."

"JW? What the hell are you doing here?" Gareth exclaimed. "We sent you home in a taxi eight hours ago!"

The Legend hauled himself into a sitting position. "Uhhh… do us a favour, would you? Tone it down a bit and, uh, get us a coffee, there's a good boy. Machine's over there." A gnarled finger pointed in the general direction of the lifts. Gareth was half way to the vending area before he asked himself what the hell he was doing. Realising he was unlikely to get any sense out of his visitor until he completed the task, though, he put change into the machine and ordered two black coffees with extra sugar. He watched a weak stream of grim-looking liquid squirt into two plastic cups until they were half full, then picked them up and went to see if the monster had risen.

JW Owens had taken the time to fold his beloved blazer neatly across the back of a chair, but was still wearing the same creased white shirt, which now seemed to be embellished with a large splodge of something hideously orange. He followed the direction of Gareth's gaze. "Oh, uh… steak bolognaise," he explained. "Must have been to Horns."

"Horns? What's Horns? We put you in a taxi and sent you home. You were, um, pretty much the worse for wear. Care to enlighten me?"

His rheumy eyes stared at Gareth. For a second they lit up as if he was about to provide an answer, then they went dead again and he leaned back against a desk. "Yeah well…" he said. "Horns is a steak house. Opens late. It was a bit of a night, like. I remember us having a few in The Lamb, but after that…" he paused, looking to the ceiling for inspiration, then muttered: "No, it's gone… just give me 24 hours and I'll piece it together." With that he rose from the sleeping bag like a macabre butterfly emerging from a chrysalis. Gareth just gawped.

Following the direction of the reporter's gaze The Legend exclaimed "Ah, fuck…" then pulled the filthy bedding back around his midriff. For some reason he was naked from the waist down. "Had a bit of an accident to tell you the truth, boy. Came in here on the way home because I was dying to, um, use the facilities. I know the blokes on security, see. I told them I was dropping something off… not really a lie. Ha. Didn't quite make it though. Oh, damn…" He started shuffling towards Gareth, his eyes mimicking the reporter's in their alarm. "My, uh, trousers…" he cried. "I washed them out in the toilets then put them on the radiator in the editor's office…"

The pimply backside shuffled off through the glass partition and Gareth slowly sipped his coffee. He had expected his introduction to

Wales to be a bit alien at first, but his mind could never have conjured up this turn of events. Leaving The Legend to sort out his wardrobe malfunction, the reporter was wandering towards the batch of work stations that collectively made up the sports desk when he heard the lift ping. "Shit!" he exclaimed, heading back quickly in the direction he'd come. "JW! JW! Quick, for fuck's sake, get out of there!"

The Welsh rugby hero emerged, one leg inside his pants. "What's up, butt?"

"Someone's coming... quick!" Gareth lent over to help him on with the other pants leg. He was on his knees when a schoolma'amly voice froze him to the spot. He twisted his head to see a tall, willowy blonde, power-dressed in a pin-striped navy blue suit jacket with huge shoulder pads and a pencil skirt that finished inches above her black-stockinged knees. Her arms were crossed above an ample bosom encased snugly in a pleated white blouse.

"What on earth is going on here?" she demanded, her voice tinged with the hint of a Scottish accent. "Hell, is that you, JW?"

"Ah, hello Lana, my lovely!" said The Legend. "How are things?"

"I could ask you the same thing," she said. "Isn't that Mr Prince with you? I hope there's a reasonable excuse for this, ah, behaviour."

Gareth's stomach hit his boots. Not only was The Legend running amok on the editorial floor of the Sunday Tribune Despatch, but the editor Lana Desmund had just turned up to find him in what appeared to be a compromising position. He sensed authority exuding from her with the same potency as the powerful, expensive perfume she was wearing. Tall for a woman, she exacerbated the anomaly by wearing heels.

"Don't be stupid, mun, Lana!" boomed The Legend, as he went on the offensive in his deepest, most masculine Welsh voice. "Surely you don't think there's something sexual going on here? I think you've known me long enough to know that I prefer the ladies! Young Geraint's not sucking my willy, see, he's just helping to tie my laces. They came undone and I've got a bit of a bad back. All entirely innocent. See?"

"Hmm, well... On your feet Mr Prince, we've got a conference in an hour and I'd like you to come along to see how we do things. Gosh, there's a smell in here. Awful. I'll get the cleaners up to see if they can squirt something around to make it a bit more bearable." She walked on towards her office then turned back in their direction. "Anyway... JW... John... What are you doing here? I thought your contract was up."

"Yes, Lana, that's true, but Jacko wants me to help out with the World Cup."

"Hmm. I'm not sure if we need your brand of 'help'. I'll have to see Jacko about that." She continued on to her office.

"Fuck!" Gareth said, letting out the breath he had been holding.

"Aah, she's all right," said The Legend. "All naggin' no noggin' I'd say. Shall we get on?" He turned and picked up the sleeping bag which had been hidden out of the editor's view.

"What are you going to do with that?" Gareth asked, wrinkling his nose.

"Oh, I keep it here," said The Legend, tucking the mouldy-looking article under Gareth's desk.

"You can't do that!" the reporter said, horrified.

"Why not, butt? No one's ever complained."

"Really? Well I am. It stinks! And it ain't very hygienic."

"Oh come on, butt," he argued. "I need it. It's always here in case of emergencies, see."

"Yeah? Well I think we'll get a bleedin' flea infestation – and that would be a Health and Safety emergency."

The Legend had lost interest. He was fiddling around under the desk. Eventually he emerged with an equally badly creased yellow shirt. It was cleaner than the one he was wearing, though with his current complexion it would make him look like a bowl of weak custard. Kneeling beside the desk, he stripped off the old shirt and pulled the new one over heavy set shoulders. A musty dampness still hung in the air, enhanced by stale beer. "Shouldn't you freshen up?" Gareth suggested.

"Not a bad idea, butt." The Legend opened a filing cabinet drawer and Gareth snatched a glimpse inside. It had contents similar to that of a bathroom cupboard: mouthwash, toothpaste, deodorants and after-shave balm. Scooping the toiletries into his arms The Legend headed off in the direction of the facilities – a man well practised in the art of damage limitation.

Gareth turned his attention to his computer and logged in. At least he would be able to get The Legend's World Cup column out of the way. He fleshed out some questions in his mind, but it was difficult to concentrate after all that had taken place. With the raw material on offer he suspected he might have bitten off more than he could chew.

He needn't have worried. Once The Legend had returned from his ablutions things went well. Gareth took down the rugby star's words, transcribed them and checked anything he didn't fully understand on the internet. Something was finally going right on what had begun as a frenetic day. Gareth had just completed his article when a petite, fresh-faced blonde stepped out from behind the glass partition of the editor's office and belied her diminutive stature by bellowing "conference" at the top of her voice.

"Mr Prince, I understand you will be joining us," said Jacko, who had arrived a short while earlier. Gareth paused to gather up his notebook, then spotted Jason heading in his direction. "All right, Jase?" he asked.

The work experience boy, looking surprisingly fresh despite his late night, nodded. "Yes, sir!"

"Do me a favour, would you? Don't call me sir. Listen, you know how to send stories through to the sports editor, don't you? I've left my interview with JW on screen. If you could do the honours it would be a great help."

"Leave it to me," agreed Jase. Gareth started moving away. "Oh, Gar?" He turned back. "You're still moving in with us tonight, yeah?"

"That was the plan."

"Great. Well, we got a bit of a 'do' on at the rugby club, so best if you come there first. I'll give you the directions later?"

22

JACKO'S VOICE BOOMED across the desk. "Just read your piece, son. Excellent. You have The Legend's voice off to a tee, see. I'm putting it on the centre spread and our artists are gathering some decent pictures from the library. We need a shot of you for the paper. In fact, the best picture would be of you and The Legend together. I'll try to arrange something. Is he still in the building?"

"To be totally honest, boss, I don't know," said Gareth, slightly taken aback. "I expect Jason was the last to see him."

"Oh yes, sure. Where is the young 'genius'?"

Gareth detected a note of facetiousness in Jacko's voice and felt instantly protective. Though he had to admit he found Jason tiring, the boy had thrown out the hand of friendship to him, a stranger and an English one at that, something Gareth hadn't been expecting. The workie had offered him a cheap roof over his head and even vowed to protect him if any enemies cut up rough. If this was a godsend or a curse he had yet to decide, but the youngster merited the benefit of the doubt. "Probably nipped out for lunch," Gareth told Jacko. "I'll have a word when he gets back."

Jacko pushed himself up and came around the desk. "Listen, son, I meant what I said, it was an excellent piece and just what I need right now," he grunted, nodding his head in the direction of the editor's domain. "You heard what she said in there? She hasn't got much time for The Legend, can't handle his, umm, eccentricities. That's why we've got to play it a bit careful, like. You know?"

Gareth nodded. He couldn't have failed to note Lana's reaction when Jacko had outlined his World Cup plans in conference. "This tournament can be huge for the newspaper, particularly if Wales progress," Jacko had told an assortment of journalists, ad reps and marketing men. "We know things haven't been going too well of late. Newspapers the country over have seen circulations shrinking. I believe we have to do a number of eye-catching big name features and get some famous Welsh rugby characters on board. That's why I want to give JW Owens another chance. Whatever you think, Lana, The Legend is the biggest name the sport has to offer and I don't see where in the whole of Wales we are going to find a bigger name for the kind of money we have on offer. We might have to put up with the odd idiosyncrasy, but..."

The editor had cut him short. "He's a drunk and a nuisance," she stormed, "and quite capable of embarrassing us in this situation. Be it on your own head Jacko. I know you two go way back and, of course, I am grateful to you for keeping an eye on the budget, but when all is said and done he is a loose cannon. Make sure he doesn't sink us."

Jacko's voice brought Gareth back to the present. "What d'you reckon? Can we keep him on the straight and narrow? The Legend?"

The reporter knew he should air his doubts, but something stopped him. Perhaps it was the sports editor's earnest belief in his own personal hero, or maybe it was the sympathy he felt for the ex rugby player, who had little money to speak of and no close family. Memories of The Legend stepping in to help him ward off some thuggish bullies in the pub the previous night gatecrashed his thoughts, and he replied before he'd really considered the consequences.

"It's certainly worth a try," said the reporter. "He knows his stuff, as I've learned from speaking to him today. Plus, you are right about him being revered. In the pub last night he couldn't move for people wanting to be photographed with him or seeking his autograph. I got the impression they lap up anything he says or does, so I imagine his World Cup column would be pretty popular."

"Aye, you know what I'm feeling then son," said Jacko. "That's good... that's very good in the circumstances." His eyes honed in on Gareth from beneath the bushy grey eyebrows, and the reporter felt a shiver run through him. "I've decided he can be your little project. It's your job to interview him every week, find out what makes him tick and give his column the true Legend's voice. You seem to have a knack for doing that... I wasn't peeing up your back and telling you it was raining when I said it was a good piece. Of course, your new responsibilities will include keeping him on the straight and narrow, it goes without saying."

Not for the first time Gareth succumbed to an involuntary motion in his throat. Having just swallowed a mouthful of hot, tasteless coffee from the vending machine he sent it spraying out over his workstation, leaving dark splodges dripping down his computer screen like one of those artistic screensavers. "Hang on..." he squeaked, but Jacko had already walked off.

Gareth considered his predicament. It was like being an addicted gambler who had just been dealt the hand from hell. How was he supposed to keep this whirling dervish of a life force under control? It would be like capturing a sunbeam or imprisoning air. From his brief experience of The Legend he had established that the man was oblivious to accepted conventions. He lived in his own vortex, repelling contrary viewpoints as a magnet rejects polar opposites. He would no more toe the line of normalcy than turn down a lifetime offer of free booze.

Gareth reflected on his ill fortune as he watched his boss settle back behind his work station and lift the phone. He supposed that's what good managers did – delegate out the tough stuff. In the final analysis, Jacko's whole credibility with the editor Lana Desmund was hanging by a thread so he in turn was loading the pressure onto his newest recruit. At least Jacko had shown appreciation of Gareth's work, which had to be a good thing, particularly as the reporter felt he had been flying by the seat of his pants when writing the article – one based on memories of JW's most successful trip Down Under.

Hoping for some pointers to what he'd done right, Gareth decided to revisit the article he'd written. He clicked on the sports basket and brought his story up on screen, and as he read it again an eerie feeling came over him. The sports editor was right. The article was written with great authority. It gave the impression it had been composed by someone with their finger on the pulse of the sport. The author had done his homework with a diligence bordering on the obsessive and had set the tone perfectly. It was just a pity that hardly a word remained of what Gareth had written.

Sure, the chronology of events was the same, but little things stood out: Facts here and there that hadn't been mentioned in the interview. There was a passage, for instance, about the outnumbered but thrilled Welsh contingent among the Lions fans striking up a pulse-quickening rendition of Hymns and Arias at the end of the third Test in Sydney and how it had caused The Legend to well up with pride and shed tears on the running track. Then there was the little girl in Welsh dress who was passed over the barrier to present him with a bouquet of daffodils as a thank you, and the impromptu jig he had joined in with the Irish players, a Riverdance ahead of its time. All this had taken place on the outfield as the Aussies sank to their knees in despair. Colour infused the piece. It was vibrant and alive, as if it had taken place yesterday and not 40 years ago.

Who on earth could have tinkered with his stuff and to what end? Gareth looked around furtively. If one of the more senior members of the writing team had intervened – Quinten Tucker-Green, say, or the chief rugby writer, Barri Michaels, whom he had yet to meet – surely they would have told him about it or, at least, flagged up the anomalies to the sports editor.

His eyes fell on the news desk. The attractive redhead Monica was in a huddle with her reporters, outlining their duties for the day. None of them, he assumed, would find the time or inclination to alter his copy. Further on was the picture desk, but there was only one person there, an old guy to whom he had yet to be introduced. His previous knowledge of photographers suggested it was highly unlikely they would possess the enthusiasm or grammatical knowhow to completely rewrite a story. The whole episode was a mystery.

By mere process of elimination there seemed to be just two alternatives: Either The Legend had altered the article himself, or...

"Hi, boss... Gar. Sorry... Just nipped out for some chips. Want one?" A polystyrene tray was thrust under his nose containing pale looking potato strips covered in a brown congealing substance. "Curry sauce," explained Jason. "Lush it is. Had a half n' half down chip alley but ate the rice with my saveloy." The reporter shook his head, then beckoned the work experience boy closer. "Jase, could I have a word, mate? In private. Bring your chips... we'll go to the canteen."

SO THE TRUTH came out. Jason said at first he had only meant to read through the article. After all, the words had been dictated by The Legend, each one carefully chosen to give the reader a forensic insight into what it was like to compete on the biggest of sporting stages. As someone who had been brought up to love everything about the game of rugby it was an opportunity not to be missed. To expect him to just press a button and send the article on its way was like putting a nice juicy steak in front of a starving rottweiler and expecting it to turn its nose up and wait for its portion of dog food.

Rugby was in Jason's genes, passed down by his sports-mad father, his grandfather, who swapped fighting the Africa Korps for locking horns on a rugby field with those he'd stood shoulder to shoulder with among the Desert Rats, and his great grandfather, who had toiled down the local pit all week before spending free afternoons brawling in muddy fields with 29 like-minded individuals. If it was possible to study the subject at school, Jason was a cert to register an A-plus in Rugby Union history.

In the string of villages that spread like an oriental carnival dragon along the foot of his valley, half the population spent a disproportionate amount of time talking about, planning, saving up for and travelling on trips to Ireland, France, Italy, Scotland or London – depending on which places the Wales team were visiting in the Six Nations that winter. The rest of the time they were making feasibility studies into the possibility of a summer trip Down Under, or perhaps venturing further afield to wear the red jersey in obscure locations like Argentina, Japan or Canada.

The rugby clubs were the hives where all plans were formulated and Jason wished that one day he would be doing well enough financially to join in a valleys' mass exodus. So far a trip to see England v Wales at Twickenham was the height of his adventures.

"I'm sorry, Gar, it was just... well, some of it was wrong," he said. Gareth opened his palms and invited him to expand on the statement. "For instance, like, there was the bit about him jumping into the crowd after the second Test... it just didn't happen. If you look at the DVD – and I had the box set for Christmas and have watched it thousands of times – it was in fact Maurice McCluskey, the Scottish No 8, who did that. JW seems to have forgotten but he was out cold at the time, having taken a left hook from a giant Aussie prop called Mac Lyons. I'll show you on the DVD if you like... I altered it, then realised there weren't enough words any more so had to add a few things here and there. The Legend was still here, so I pointed out what had happened and 'reminded' him of a few things. Then he agreed to a few amendments and, well, that's what happened. He was quite happy all in all but I can see why you're upset. I guess I got carried away. Sorry, like, I should have told you. I expect you'll want me to leave now, so I'll just get my things..."

"Sit... down!" The force of the words made the workie drop into his seat instantly. "Look, Jason, I admit when I first realised what had happened I was pretty bloody angry," said Gareth. "You could have made me look a right clown. You're not a writer, hell you're just a kid playing with the grown-ups for a few weeks during the school holidays. Have you any idea what shit you could have caused for me?" Jason nodded his head. "No, I don't think you've got a clue. It was a silly, reckless thing to do. I've only been in the job for a couple of days and I'm trying to make a good impression. If this got out it would have the opposite effect."

"S.. sor..."

"I don't want your apologies. Look... you don't work here so you are entitled to walk away whenever you like but, well, it seems like I might need you."

Jason's mouth dropped open. "Really?"

"Well, you've pointed out what happened quite neatly," said Gareth. "If by reading my piece you came to the conclusion I know nothing about rugby then you would be damn right. I haven't got a scooby."

"Eh?"

"Sorry, it's cockney slang. Haven't got a Scooby Doo... clue."

"Oh."

"Anyway, where was I? Oh yes. Rugby ain't a game they play in inner-city schools in the heart of London. The playgrounds are too hard to be diving all over the place, bringing people to their knees, unless the plan is to bash their heads in and take their pocket money. No, rugby's a wealthy, country landowners' game across the border, mostly played by the rich, farmers and public schoolboys. Therefore I know precisely zilch. You, on the other hand, possess what I need. Insider knowledge. To be entirely truthful with you, I blagged my way onto the paper and never in a thousand years did I expect to be handed the job of ghostwriting a column by a top rugby name. I did it because I really needed this job."

Gareth went silent and Jason wasn't sure whether he was supposed to fill the void. He held on for a couple of seconds and was about to speak when the reporter started up again. "I told Jacko I'd covered a fair bit of rugby in my time and he didn't dig too deeply, thank God. Now he's made me responsible for The Legend. From what you're telling me his memory is a bit flaky and in my position I can't afford to get caught out. So you help me and I'll return the favour, maybe get you tickets to World Cup matches." Jason's jaw dropped open, but Gareth was on a roll. "Hell, I'll even help you out with your journalism if you feel this is what you would like to do, and in return I need you to read my stories and make sure there are no glaring errors. I saw you turn your nose up when I mentioned journalism but from what I read this morning you have all the ingredients it takes. You're alert, your written English is excellent and you know how to write. Perhaps it's because it's rugby, a subject dear to your heart, but you pride yourself on accuracy too..."

"Well, thanks boss," Jason said.

"Don't call me that, I'm not your boss. I'll ask you a favour, though ... from one mate to another. Don't breathe a word of this to anyone. If we get found out, it's my head on the chopping block." The workie nodded. "Good. By the way, what happened to The Legend?"

"Ah, well, strange story see..." said Jason. "We had our brief chat and I showed him the piece like. Then I asked him if he fancied a drink. When he said 'Yes' I nipped over to get some water from the cooler, like. When I got back he'd gone."

It might have been strange to Jason but to Gareth what had happened was all too clear. He had an idea where he might find The Legend, but there were an awful lot of boozers in Cardiff.

23

GARETH STOPPED THE car and swore. He was stuck in a country lane hemmed in by overgrown hedgerows. The small white Corsa, one of the older automatic models, was packed to the roof, piles of boxes and bin bags hindering his visibility in the rear view mirror. Continuing forward would probably make matters worse, resulting in him having to dump the car and walk back to civilisation. There were no turning spaces, and reversing seemed fraught with danger. He feared crashing the car into a gatepost or something. Damn sat-nav. He wished he had just stuck to the simple instructions the work experience boy had given him.

Instead, he had parked his brain in neutral and put faith in technology. The sat-nav had insisted the country road was a "short cut" to the valleys town of Pontyprenis but in truth it was little more than a dirt track. The sky was filling ominously with bloated, tea-stained clouds and he feared a heavy downfall would leave him marooned.

"Bloody Wales," he muttered, slamming his hands full force against the steering wheel. A chorus of sheep bleated somewhere off to his right. With no alternative, he stuck the car in reverse. It travelled unimpeded for 50 yards but his vision was impaired by the dim light and he didn't see the danger. Before he knew what was happening the wheels were spinning and he was going nowhere. He put the car into drive, but that didn't work either and with his bad leg he didn't think pushing was an option. The situation was hopeless. He would have to abandon the vehicle and get help. He could call the roadside recovery company which held his membership, but what would he tell them and how long would it take for them to get to him? He hadn't the foggiest idea where he was.

His predicament reminded him of one of those old werewolf flicks where the potential victim had to yomp across fog-drenched moors after a mysterious object in the road forced them to swerve and crash. His feverish mind ticked over. Perhaps he could put forward the idea to a film studio: Cockney Werewolf in the Valleys. He chuckled, a laugh of despair rather than amusement.

Jason's simple-to-follow instructions had been designed to get him to the Pontyprenis rugby club. It was going to be a good night there, the youngster had told him. There was a bit of a do planned, one the boy's dad had helped organise, and afterwards Gareth could move into his new home.

He didn't feel up for a heavy session. His head was still tender from the local beer he had been force-fed the night before. It was only after his fifth pint that the loquacious Quinten had leaned over and told him: "I'd be careful with that old chap, you know its nicknamed Skull Attack, don't you?" Well it had certainly lived up to its reputation. Gareth wasn't an accomplished drinker and the headache had kicked in early, getting incrementally worse throughout the day.

For the umpteenth time he asked himself: "What am I doing here?" He was a city boy, had spent all his life living among the high rises, hustle and bustle of a busy metropolis. Cardiff had been a slight step down, but this? He cursed himself for not thinking things through. Another problem with the beer, it was as if the locals had plied him with some kind of drug that made him acquiesce to their most outrageous demands.

"Come and live with me in the valleys, Gar?"

"Of course, work experience lad I don't know from Adam. Why not?"

Too late, he realised he was actually talking to himself. It was something he did in moments of extreme stress, transforming his frustrations into words and muttering them through clenched teeth and almost frozen lips. He had even attempted a Welsh accent, though it sounded more like he was a resident of Delhi when he played it back in his mind. Oh God. He banged the steering wheel with his fists again, hollering like a banshee before lowering his head and butting it in an attempt to bring his brain back to a state of logical thought. It's a conundrum, Gary. Solve it. You're supposed to be a bright lad... Damn, now he was sounding like his old maths teacher back at Barking High.

He tried to open the driver's side door. It moved about a foot, then stuck rigid. It had hit some kind of barrier, a fence or a hedge. Gary Marshall, back in his days of supreme fitness, might have just squeezed through but fat Gareth Prince didn't stand a chance. He pulled the door shut as the first raindrops hit the windscreen. Leaning over into the back seat he looked for his coat but soon gave it up as a hopeless task. It would be buried beneath DVDs he would never watch again and CDs by bands he had grown out of years ago. He would just have to risk the wrath of the weather gods.

Crawling across the seat he pushed at the passenger door. It gave a little further, not far but just enough. He dragged himself across on his belly and fell through the opening, landing horizontally on a rutted grassy verge. Clambering to his feet in an undignified manner, he brushed himself down and looked back the way he had come. It was completely dark now, the rain getting heavier. He could see a dim halo of light in the distance but not much more. Perhaps a farmhouse. Someone there might be able to help him out of his predicament.

The pathway was slick from the rain already, its hardened, caked-on crust dissolving like a Rich Tea biscuit dunked too long. It was terrain better suited to hiking boots than slip-on Italian loafers, and the increased suction of the reconstituted surface threatened to rob him of his expensive footwear. After a quarter of a mile his hopes of an early solution were dashed. A bolted, padlocked fence loomed up in his path. So, despite the sat-nav's insistence it was a through road, the useless technology had somehow neglected to indicate there might be immoveable barriers in the way.

Having come this far though, lured like a drifting ship's captain to the lights on the horizon, he muttered "In for a penny" and climbed the fence. Dropping down on the other side he immediately felt he had made a mistake. One foot sank up to the ankle in a substance he feared wasn't mud. As if to confirm his worst suspicions the loud bellow of a cow came from nearby, possibly one with a bad case of tummy ache. The sucking sound as he lifted his foot acted on his teeth like chalk to a blackboard. Jeez! He removed the now un-recognisable object of footwear and scraped it as best he could across the grass. A rumble of thunder accompanied the action and the rain began to fall heavier still.

He was starting to think the decision to leave the car behind was foolhardy. "Bloody great, you English idiot... nice idea this, 'Let's go for a ramble in the lovely hillsides, butty'," he shouted out loud in the Indian accent. As if in answer the cow raised its voice again, and this time it sounded a lot closer. Turning slowly, he saw it no more than 100 yards away. It breathed steam from its nostrils and looked pretty annoyed about the intruder on its patch. Its dark eyes seemed focused on him and its solid neck and block-shaped head made him illogically think of the boxer Mike Tyson. Old Iron Mike. The heavyweight champion of cows. With horns. Not a cow then...

A bull! The animal was circling now and in his musings he hadn't realised he had wandered from the gate. Like a good boxer stalking his opponent, the bull had cut off his escape route and the only way out was across the field. Gareth put his hands out to ward off the animal, but his stalker didn't look the type to take no for an answer. He started cutting down the distance between them, forcing Gareth to retreat further into the unknown. Although the voices in his head told him running was probably the worst course of action, he was reluctant to listen to them anymore. There were those who would have told him to look the animal straight in the eye and stare it down. Or, better still, punch it on the nose. Or was that sharks? Gareth feared if he attempted such brinkmanship he would be in serious danger of injury. Pausing long enough to remove his other loafer and his socks, while at no stage taking his eyes off his adversary, he stood upright, feinted to run one way then dashed in the opposite direction, his knee screaming in pain due to the sudden activity.

If he had checked over his shoulder, Gareth would have seen Tyson the bull take three steps forward, snort through his nostrils again, consider giving chase, then resume nibbling the grass. By now, though, the reporter was half way to the other side of the field, his hair matted through a combination of rain and sweat, his suit soaked through and his shoes unrecognisable from the ones he bought from an exclusive West End store shortly before leaving London.

AT LAST another fence appeared on the horizon. The lights were that much closer now and Gareth saw two large white posts materialising out of the mist. He clambered into the next field, noticing the grass was much shorter and neatly bordered by a white line. A rugby pitch.

"Hey, you!" came a shout from his left. "What d'you think you're doing?" A character in green Wellington boots and a flat cap strode towards him.

"Oh, uh... sorry. My..."

"Never mind that. Don't cross that whitewash, we got a game tomorrow and I don't want anyone churning up the pitch. You'll have to go around."

"Of course... sorry."

"Where did you come from anyway? Nothing but fields over there."

Gareth shortened the distance between them, his shoes and socks still in his hands, his feet caked in mud. "I drove down a lane over there and got stuck. The sat-nav..."

"Bloody sat-navs. It happens all the time here. That's Wyn Bagwell's farm. Number of times he's had to call for help because a bloody great artic has got stuck down there... it doesn't bear thinking about. Don't know how they thought it was a main road. Yeah, you used to be able to drive through there to get to the village but Wyn got peed off with it. Disturbed the animals. One of his cows got knocked down once. Terrible mess... As are you, boy. What do you plan to do now then?"

"Well, I'm a bit stuck and was hoping someone might help. Is this Pontyprenis Rugby Club?"

"That's right, boy. This is it. Home of the greatest rugby club in the Valleys."

"Ah... I'm supposed to be meeting some people here. I heard there's a bit of a 'show'."

"Show is it? You're not from around here, are you? Sounds like London talk... This aint the West End. Hey, you're not that Gareth fella by any chance?"

Gareth nodded. "That's right, Gareth Prince. You're..?

"My boy's told me all about you. Don't quite match your description, though," he laughed. "Name's Will... Will Shakespeare. I'm Jason's dad. I hear you'll be staying with us. Trust you won't be turning up like this every night."

"Oh," said Gareth, laughing. "No, um, of course not. Nice to meet you... did you say Will?"

"I know, Will Shakespeare. Everyone has a good laugh about it, but it hasn't done me any harm." The two men shook hands. "I've had a bit of a hand in, um, arranging the entertainment. I certainly wouldn't call it a show, though... it ain't Les Miserables, or anything like that. There's bingo, chicken in a basket... just a bit of fun on a Saturday night. All for charity, too. Mind you," he looked Gareth up and down slowly... "You don't really look dressed for a night out. Probably in need of a bit of charity yourself."

Gareth peered at his sodden suit and his methane-enhanced shoes. "No, I guess I'm not. I've got a change of clothes in the car but..."

"Yeah, I know. The car is marooned way back there. Maybe I can help you out. I'm the groundsman here in my spare time, you see. Hey, we've got an Under-14 academy quarter-final against Tumble tomorrow. Big game for our youngsters... why don't you come along to report it?"

"Um... can't really."

Will looked crestfallen. "Not big enough for you lot?"

Gareth acted quickly to keep his new landlord onside. "No, it's not that. Of course I'm interested. It's just that our paper has already gone to press. It will be on sale tomorrow so the big quarter-final is too late for us. I might come along as a spectator, though."

"Really?" His inquisitor looked genuinely excited. "That would be great. A bit of celebrity interest. We haven't had anyone famous in our midst since Ivor Northern, played for Wales in the 60s. Then there was Charlie Blenkstone..."

"That rings a bell, actually," said Gareth, searching his sporting databanks.

"Serial killer," said Will. "Back in the 30s. Known as the Pontyprenis Poisoner. Got rid of his wife and his mam. Made them Welsh cawl laced with arsenic, he did."

"Ah," said Gareth, finding the conversation had taken a turn for the strange.

"Anyway, look. You're very wet, you can't really go back to your car... come with me. I've got to get ready soon, too. We'll find you something, I'm sure. Meanwhile, give me your keys and I'll get someone to rescue the motor."

Gareth hesitated, then patted his pockets. No keys. He remembered hearing something drop as he left the car. Hell. "I must have dropped them back there," he admitted. "Damn!"

"Never mind," said Will, "I'll send some of the boys out to find them. Meanwhile, come this way." He followed the groundsman to a small wooden hut not unlike one of those used to house prisoners in the Second World War.

"Changing rooms," announced Will, turning the key. "We keep the lost property here."

24

GARETH FELT LIKE a refugee. He was wearing a tight-fitting black and white hooped rugby top over baggy tracksuit pants and a pair of ill-fitting but comfy pink crocs. Following Will's instructions, he told the well-built bouncer at the entrance to the main building that he was on the guest list and, after producing the press pass from his wallet to prove his identity, he was allowed to move into the main hall.

It resembled a school dining room, long benches pushed up against trestle tables all symmetrically lined up around a central point. In the middle was an elevated area of canvas, surrounded by three ropes spread around four corner posts. A boxing ring. A buzz of excited chatter rose from the large gathering settled in the hall. Trying to get a glimpse of Jason he grimaced as he pushed up onto his toes to scan the ocean of heads bobbing around the bar. There were just too many bodies.

Gareth joined the queue at the bar, desperate for a drink after the traumas of the evening. He was cold, ill dressed, out of place and his bad leg ached. After waiting for some considerable time a blonde in a floral dress with bright butterfly tattoos on each of her upper arms came across. "Yes babes, what can I do you for?"

"Ah, right, um, pint of bitter please," he said.

"SA?"

He shook his head.

"Oh, well normal bitter's off, so it's SA, lager or Guinness."

He settled for a pint of Guinness and looked for a seat. Eventually he plonked himself down at the end of one of the tables, scanning again for Jason and his father. "Hey, butt, that's my seat," said a voice behind him. Gareth's memory gave him a nudge. He twisted on the bench. "Oh, don't I know you from somewhere?" demanded Cinderblock.

Gareth opted to play dumb. He had used the technique with police interrogators and in showdowns with school headmasters, and though he'd only had limited success he knew that as soon as he opened his mouth the game would be up. Vaguely shaking his head in the questioner's direction, he reached over to take a sip of the Guinness. "Yeah, yeah, you look familiar, butt," continued Cinderblock. "Maybe in here, yeah? You a regular? I would guess third teamer. Prop? Hmm, probably not big enough. Maybe a hooker or an out-of-shape scrum half. Been on the injury list? Well, whatever, if you're a member of this club you must be aware that Matt Warinski, first-team vice-captain, always sits here. That's me, by the way, so if you wouldn't mind moving..."

"Is that really necessary, Matt?" came a voice from behind him. Gareth tried to see around the block of muscle and lard. He was in no doubt it was Jason who had intervened, though he sounded altogether more confident and purposeful in his home environment. "Look," continued the disembodied voice. "A load of your mates are over there, Matt. They've got a much better view of the action. This bloke's with me. I told him to wait for me here. You don't mind, do you? A one-off?"

"Well, I don't know," said Cinderblock, his face creasing as if he was dealing with the toughest trigonometry problem ever. "If I let someone just come in and take my seat now, who's to say it won't happen next week? It becomes open season, like. Anyone can take Warinski's seat. Next thing you know my opponents get to hear about it and start giving me grief on the rugby field. Winding me up. You know?"

"It won't come to that Matt," insisted Jason. "It'll be our secret. You let people know you chose to move and I don't think anyone will raise the matter again."

"I hope you're right Shakespeare. Looking forward to it, by the way. Break a leg, as they say."

Cinderblock turned to Gareth. "See you mate. No hard feelings eh? Best of luck with the thirds, or whatever." Gareth simply nodded. "If you're his mate then that's fine by me." He wandered off in the direction of his friends.

"All right, Gareth? Told you I could handle him." The sports reporter was rendered speechless, though. In his sphere of vision now stood a figure in white tights, knee-length boots, a red velvet cape and a curly orange wig stretching down past his shoulders. An ornate red wine coloured velveteen flat cap sat perched on his head, a quill attached to it with velcro. The face was plastered in foundation, a touch of rouge added to both cheeks.

"What the hell are you wearing?" asked Jason.

"Oh sorry, What...?" The reporter finally found his voice. "Did you say, what the hell am I..? you can talk! Have you looked in a mirror?"

"Had to, butt, it's got to look exactly right," replied Jason. "It's my professional gear, didn't I tell you? Oh yeah, this is a job I actually get paid for. Not bad, to be honest. I get £15 per gig plus as many beers as I can sup."

"What's the play?"

"Oh, no, not a play mun, Gareth, no," he replied. "No, ha ha, a play? I can see where you're coming from but, no." He lowered his voice as if confiding a secret. "Wrestling, it is. Thought some of the lads in the office might have heard of me and passed it on. Just assumed you knew. I'm fighting in a minute. For charity. Get a bet on..." he winked. "We won't lose to these lads."

Gareth had numerous questions spinning in his head, but before he could open his mouth the lights dimmed and a man in a black tuxedo entered the ring, arm in arm with a glamorous, blonde assistant. The room filled with cheers, hoots and catcalls. "Got to go," said Jason, tapping him on the shoulder. When Gareth turned around there was no one there.

"Ahhhhhh Laydeeez and genl'men," said the man in the tux, shouting into a hand-held microphone, intent on copying the approach of the WWF wrestling and boxing MC's he'd seen on TV. "For your pleasure now, the first bout on our card is a tag-team contest between the Green Gremlins from over the hill in Tonicraigau." Two bulky bald characters wearing what appeared to be hand-me-down superhero costumes jumped into the ring to boos and heckles. They wore luminous green costumes with a lightning strike in gold zig-zagging down the front. Gareth was reminded of an annoying advert for kitchen cleaner. The atmosphere was hostile and Gareth scanned for emergency exits in case a quick getaway was needed. "And, in the red corner, that famous father and son team, the boys whose every performance is pure poetry and will leave you shouting for more, it's Pontyprenis' very own dynamic duo..." the boos had turned to ear-shattering cheers and wails, "... the Bard Guys!"

Two figures sprang into action from the opposite side of the ring, leaping the rope and landing in perfect symmetry on the canvas. They were both over 6ft tall and wore similar attire, the only difference between them being the colour scheme. Rather than his groundsman's uniform, Jason's dad Will now wore a brown wig while his robes and hat were in various shades of green. His bright yellow wrestler's boots reached the top of his calves and he sprang around from foot to foot, doffing his cap to the audience on all sides.

Without warning he grabbed the mic from the MC and addressed the crowd. "If you haven't heard of us, my name's Will, and this is my son Romeo," he lied. "We are the bardest tag team on the planet." To deafening cheers and thunderous applause they jettisoned their hats and wigs into the corner. "Friends, Welshmen and rugby men, lend me your ears! I come to bury these Green Gremlins, not to praise them; The evil that men do lives after them, the good is oft interred with their bones, so let it be with these damn Gremlins."

Gareth recognised it was a modified version of Mark Antony's speech from Shakespeare's Julius Caesar, delivered in a theatrical way to bring the audience to their feet hollering their approval. Warming to his task, the rugby-loving bard in tights dipped into the Merchant of Venice. "If you prick us, do we not bleed? If you tickle us, do we not laugh? If you poison us, do we not die? And if you wrong us..." he pointed a menacing black-gloved finger at the two opponents in the corner, "...shall we not revenge?"

The audience were on their feet, surrounding the raised canvas, pointing at the two neighbouring villagers in their green capes, threatening all manner of harm to them and chanting "Bards, Bards, Bards". It wasn't a play but for pure theatre it was difficult to beat. Shakespeare Senior turned and threw the mic back to the MC, then stripped off his cape to reveal an all-in-one wrestling suit and a giant rose tattoo on one arm with the word Mary scrawled underneath. He leapt over the top rope and out of the ring, leaving Jason on his own with the two green-clad bruisers who were at least ten years older than him. As Jason stripped down to his fighting gear one of his opponents pointed and shouted a few insults which, because of the frenzy of the crowd, were indecipherable. He climbed out of the ring on the other side.

The MC reminded the wrestlers there were rules that needed to be followed and explained the point-scoring system, then left the ring. A referee in white shirt and black trousers, who stood only as tall as the two wrestlers' chests, held them apart as the blonde paraded around the ring holding a white placard high above her head which announced Round One was about to begin. The bell sounded and the ref moved nimbly to his left to avoid being crushed in the ensuing collision.

Wrestling was another sport about which Gareth knew little, and in the opening moments it was difficult to see who had the upper hand. The tall, muscly work experience kid pulled his opponent to and fro, trying to knock him off balance. The other man was having none of it, though, locking Jason around the back of the neck with an iron grip. Not to be denied, Gareth's young colleague suddenly switched tack, moving backwards and pulling his nemesis with him.

As he reached the ropes he held out a hand and his father touched it, leapt the rope and delivered a forearm smash which sent the Green Gremlin staggering backwards.

Marching across the canvas Will Shakespeare followed up with a kick to the solar plexus which doubled up his opponent, before smashing two fists down on his exposed neck. The Gremlin sank to his knees as the chant resumed: "Bards, bards, bards".

Rather than finish off his opponent, though, the elder Shakespeare walked back across the ring and tagged Jason, who was now standing on the top rope. "Oh my God," shouted one of the enthralled audience, "he's going to attempt the Shakespeare Sonnet!" The two wrestlers tapped hands and Jason took off, spread-eagling himself as he leapt towards the prone victim. Just before he landed, though, his intended target reached out a hand and was dragged clear by his tag mate, leaving the youngster to belly flop spectacularly onto the canvas. A loud "Oooooh" escaped from the crowd. Jason lay still and Gareth feared he'd been knocked unconscious. The Gremlins weren't alarmed, though, and the second fighter leapt into the ring to flatten himself across his indisposed opponent. His arms and legs pinned to the canvas, the referee lent over Jason and counted: "One ...ah, two... ah..."

Just as he was about to declare a "fall", though, the body underneath writhed and bucked, sending the attacker flying. Jason then crawled across to his father, who tagged him and jumped over the ropes. He looked genuinely angry at the Gremlins' treatment of his offspring and stormed across, shouting threats at the man in the green suit. A forearm smash hit home, then another, as the atmosphere reached boiling point.

Jason's dad seemed to have lost all control as he rained down blows while, behind him, the referee attempted to intervene. He tapped the berserk wrestler on the shoulder and tried to pull him aside, only to receive a crunching elbow to the nose which sent him crashing to the canvas, too. Some bystanders leapt forward to pull him clear of the ring.

With no ref, the second Gremlin leapt onto Will's back. It was two against one and his team mate took full advantage, crawling out from underneath the unseemly scrimmage. As one Gremlin held Will's arms behind his back, the other pummelled him with illegal punches to the gut. The crowd's boos rang around the room, engrossed as they were in what now resembled a no-rules bar room brawl. Just as it seemed the victim of the assault would lose consciousness, Jason joined the fray, bringing a wooden footstool crashing down across the back of Will's attacker. It shattered as the victim fell to the floor, seemingly out for the count. Jason then turned his attention to the Gremlin holding his dad, slamming his fist into the man's lower back with such force that he slid to the ground. As the noise threatened to take the roof off the building, dad and son clambered to the top of the ropes and, in perfect synchronisation, threw themselves off, landing square on top of the prostrate Gremlins. "Oh my God," came another voice, "It's a double sonnet!"

Returning to the ring, the referee knelt between the two flattened Gremlins and thumped the canvas, the crowd helping to deliver the count. When he reached three and spread his arms wide the whoops and cheers poured down as if a major sporting feat had been achieved, a cup final won or a league title snatched.

The Bard Guys stood, bowed regally to all four corners of the room, gave each other a hug then exited the ring and made straight for the bar. Bruised and battered, the Gremlins waited until the coast was clear before crawling out from under the bottom rope and making their escape, the hubbub around the room providing the perfect distraction.

25

WILL SHAKESPEARE thrust a can into Gareth's hand. They were sitting at a large oak table in the kitchen of the country cottage the Shakespeare family called home. There was a small archway into the working area and large wooden Welsh dressers lined two walls, boasting all manner of trinkets and souvenirs, together with a plethora of photos of a smiling child at various ages. The more recent ones showed just the boy and his father, but there were pictures of a fitter, tanned dad and an attractive brunette with a Hollywood smile who, Gareth guessed, was the woman of the household. On the top shelf of one of the dressers was a collection of silver trophies.

Switching his attention to the can in his hand, the reporter realised it was the brew the Welsh referred to as Skull Attack. At first he considered handing it back, but he had the taste for alcohol after recovering from what began as a traumatic evening and he didn't want to reject his new landlord's hospitality.

"Get your mush around that, boy! Proper stuff," said Jason's dad. "Brains, see, that's what you've got there. Appropriate name really. Brewed in God's own country. It took brains to come up with a beer like this."

Gareth didn't want to appear disrespectful, though his previous experience of the beverage was that it made his frontal lobe ache. "I thought they made faggots," he said, taking a tentative sip.

"Aah, faggots, aye," said Jason's dad. "Dare say they're Welsh as well. Don't think it's the same company though. You get faggots in that London?"

"Dad, don't be silly, course they do," said Jason interrupting. "You're embarrassing me."

"Sorry Jase," said his father, patting him on the head. "Anyway, Gareth butt. How did you enjoy the Welsh hospitality? Hope you had a good time."

"Oh yes, thanks," said Gareth. "I thought it was an excellent night. And you two… what a show you put on. How did that come about?"

"It all dates back to when my Mary died, I guess," said Will, indicating the photograph on the sideboard. "Me and the boy had to find a few things in common to help us bond. He was always with his mum as a kid, really. I was working a lot of the time and Mary brought up the boy. Then three years ago she died. Cancer, poor baby. Now my angel's with the angels. We had to deal with it the best way we could." Will rolled up his sleeve to show off the rose tattoo. "Had this done in her memory," he said. "Jason says he's going to get one but I told him to wait, just to make sure it's something he really wants." He gave his son a meaningful look. "Anyway, after that trauma in our lives I had to make a few adjustments and he started going everywhere with me. His Gran helped out on occasion, but I knew life couldn't go on the way it had… still, it helped me to understand my boy much better, and one of the things I learned was that he was mad on that wrestling malarkey they show on the TV. Wanted to be a John Senior or…"

"Cena, dad… the name's John Cena," said Jason grumpily.

"Sorry son, anyway… Cut a long story short I enrolled Jason in a martial arts course. I wanted to toughen him up a bit. It's survival of the fittest around here and if someone senses a weakness in you…"

"I can imagine. I've already met a few blockheads who wanted a pop at me."

"Warinski?" said Will. "I heard about that. He's a pussycat. You know what I'm talking about though. Anyway, I went to pick Jason up from one of his classes and his coach said he was really coming on well, ready to go for his brown belt in karate. During the conversation he told me he was putting on these professional wrestling shows and had even got the Welsh language TV channel interested. He took one look at us, clocked the name and said, 'you two would be dynamite'. Jase was only 15 at the time but, of course, he had shot up and looked much older than he was. After that meeting he begged me to have a go. I told him if he worked hard at school we would look into it. Well, he got an excellent report so I contacted this bloke again and he invited us to train at his gym."

Will went back to the kitchen to retrieve more cans. Gareth was feeling pretty woozy by now but urged Will to continue the story. "Well, that's it really. Jason's still doing well at school…"

"I imagine he is," said Gareth. "He's a bright lad. He helped me out today and did a brilliant job. I seriously think with some hard work he could make a fine journalist."

"Really? I'm not sure I want him raking around in other people's garbage, like."

"Look, Will, it's not like that…"

"So you say, Gareth, but he tells me you wanted him to make up stories to get into The Legend's building yesterday and that you didn't want anyone to be informed when you thought The Legend was dead. Not very above board, that, boy, is it?"

"Leave it, Dad. I guess he has a right – he IS The Legend's nephew."

"Um, actually Jase, I made that up, too," confessed Gareth, feeling acutely embarrassed. Will laughed. "Look, OK, maybe you're right Will, but… hell… it's a pretty good job, it pays quite well and it needs talented people. Imagine: your boy could one day be covering the Rugby World Cup final for the Sunday Tribune Despatch."

"Really?" Jason's eyes lit up. "You think so?"

"Someone has to do it and you've got an encyclopaedic knowledge of the sport. Why not?"

"Wow! What about that Dad?"

"Yeah, uh Jason, there's a lot to talk about there. You mustn't get carried away just because you're star-struck after meeting The Legend," interrupted Will. "Anyway, Gareth, tell us about yourself. How did you end up here?"

Gareth took a deep breath, summoning the strength to recount a tale that was particularly painful to him. He wasn't going to tell the whole story, but saw no harm in letting a little of the real Gary Marshall out. "It wasn't always my first desire to become a journalist, I wanted to be a professional footballer," he said. "Had my chance, too, before fate took a hand."

"How so?"

"I had trials with West Ham," the reporter revealed, "and was even offered a footballing apprenticeship by the club. I had a few months to go and all the signs were they were going to take me on full-time."

"What position?"

"Well, I had a pretty good eye for a pass to be honest, and I used to play either in the centre of midfield or as an overlapping left back."

"So what went wrong?"

"Well," Gareth gathered his thoughts. "I messed up. I went off the rails a bit and picked up this..." he rolled up his trouser leg to reveal an ugly pink scar stretching 12 inches up his knee. "That was the end of my football career."

"Sorry to hear that son," said Will. "A similar thing happened to me to be honest. Maybe when you know us better we'll swap our stories. We don't want to embarrass you, though. How about another beer?"

"To be honest, Will. It's been a long day," said Gareth. "I'd like to acquaint myself with my new room, if that's all right with you."

"Fair enough," said Will. "By the way, we managed to find your car keys. A couple of the young lads from the under-16s recovered them. I'll pop around with Jase and we'll retrieve the motor in a minute. Tell me, though, before you hit the hay... How did you get into this game?"

"Luck, I guess," admitted Gareth. "My mum pushed me at school, even though my dad insisted I was going to be a football star. After the injury she fixed me up with part-time work on one of the local radio stations, my insider knowledge of football helped and from there I wangled my way onto a journalism course at Portsmouth.

Later I got my first job on a local London paper covering Millwall and Charlton. From there my fate was pretty much sealed."

Will was impressed. "Long way from London now though, son. What brought you to this neck of the woods?"

Gareth left an interval before answering, saying more in the silence than he did when he finally spoke. "Oh, you know," he said. "Change is as good as a rest they say. I fancied getting away from London and forging a path on my own."

"Well, we're pleased to have you, son," said Will, his eyes suggesting he hadn't swallowed the explanation. "You deserve praise for finding another career path. It's not easy when you set your heart on something and it all goes tits up. Things haven't worked out too badly, have they?"

"Not at all," Gareth agreed. He'd stayed awake past 1am for the second night in a row and felt shattered. Rising from the table he felt his phone vibrate in his pocket and a shiver passed down his spine. He only knew a few people who would consider ringing him at this time of night and he had only trusted a couple of them with this number. He thought about leaving the call unanswered but was worried something might be wrong at home. His mum wasn't getting any younger and had spent a while in the local hospital a couple of years earlier. He pressed the answer button. "Hello?"

"Geraint Prince?"

"No... um, not Geraint. The name's Gareth."

"Ahh, I've been fed a bit of false information. It is Mr Prince, though?"

"Who's calling?"

"Ah, sorry. It's the police, sir. Don't want to ruin your Saturday night but..."

Gareth zoned out, his heart skipping a beat. He wondered if his anonymity had been compromised. Then it struck him. Only one person he knew called him Geraint. "...We're outside the block of flats where he lives. It's a bit of an emergency and we wondered whether you might help. He's asked for you, JW... claims he knows you well."

If two days, most of them spent in an alcoholic stupor, constituted knowing someone well, that was true, thought Gareth. Not hearing a reply the policeman continued. "It would be really great if you could come down here, sir. It wouldn't be putting too fine a point on it to suggest it's a matter of life or death."

26

"WE'RE SERIOUSLY considering taking him in front of the magistrates and requesting an ASBO."

"You what?" Gareth looked incredulous. "Aren't ASBO's for teenage hoodlums? Surely ex-Wales and Lions rugby stars don't fit into that category?"

"They can be for anyone and anything we want, mate," said the constable. "It stands for Anti-Social Behaviour Order. Some old granny up the valleys has a string of them to her name. She's the worst neighbour you could possibly imagine. Mind you, the way our friend JW is going, he can't be far from challenging her. Duck!"

Without warning the well-built PC wrapped a protective arm around Gareth and brought all his weight to bear, pushing the reporter to his knees and making him cry out in pain. Simultaneously something black, round and flat flew over his head. Without the policeman's intervention it would have caused him a nasty injury. The object crashed against a wall and fell to the floor, shattering into pieces. Gareth carefully rose alongside the PC and leant over to study the offensive weapon, which had been thrown like a ninja assassin might despatch a lethal spinning star. He stared at the label. "Bloody hell!" he exclaimed involuntarily. He had nearly been taken out by "Help Yourself", a Tom Jones 45rpm vinyl record.

"See, he's a law unto himself," said the PC. Their conversation was interrupted by a loud crackle before a metallic voice shattered the Sunday morning peace.

'MR OWENS, THIS IS THE POLICE AGAIN... PLEASE COULD YOU PUT THE RECORDS DOWN AND MOVE AWAY FROM THE LEDGE. WE ARE WORRIED FOR YOUR SAFETY. DO YOU UNDERSTAND? I REPEAT, MOVE AWAY FROM THE LEDGE. WE HAVE DONE AS YOU'VE REQUESTED AND HE IS HERE NOW... GERAINT FROM THE TRIB IS HERE NOW. SO YOU CAN CALL OFF THIS... PROTEST.'

THE POLICEMAN with the megaphone seemed awfully small from where JW Owens stood, legs apart, wobbling in the early morning breeze five storeys up on the roof terrace of his block of flats in Cardiff Bay. He was doing his best to bring his legs under control. They seemed have been crafted out of a child's modelling clay or perishable rubber. Under his left arm a stack of vinyl nestled, covers removed, and he wondered what it was doing there. Looking down he realised some of it must have slipped from his hands, because there were small black shapes dotted around the courtyard. He tried to focus on them more clearly but his rapt attention just made his legs shake more, like a rookie centre facing a rampaging back-row forward.

'WATCH OUT JW!" the policeman cried.

With nothing to break his fall, The Legend arched backwards and dropped to the ground, flat out. God, he felt tired. He didn't think he could move again. He was not only worn out from the exploits of the evening, he was drained of purpose. Maybe here, at last, he would be able to sleep, to put behind him the traumas that invaded his protective outer shell on nights like these. He shut his eyes and let his mind wander. The day had started so simply. He had been at the Trib, and after exhausting his library of recollections he felt himself flagging, only for the young valleys kid to come to his rescue by suggesting he go for a drink.

A hair of the dog was exactly what he needed so he'd wandered down St Mary Street to a little hostelry opposite Cardiff market where his buddies were already ensconsed, browsing the racing pages and deciding on how to gamble their hard-earned cash. After that his day trod a familiar path. He enjoyed a couple of pints as he and his mates revisited simple times gone by when the English were only put on rugby fields to make the Welsh look good, and when a pint of bitter could be bought for 14p. Scraping together a couple of quid from friends who could always be relied upon to pull a man over a temporary fiscal speed bump, he disseminated some to the bookies, feasted on a pack of pork scratchings and relieved a city centre off licence of half an ounce of rolling tobacco and one of its cheaper bottles of vodka. It fitted conveniently into the lining of the knee-length greatcoat he had somehow acquired from his mate Archie.

Archie, Iwan, Hector and Willie Ap were the sort of blokes you heard described as salt of the earth. He would stick by these lads, as they had stuck by him. He'd known them forever and they loved him like family. Some people who weren't in possession of the full facts suggested the relationship was one sided and urged him to kick them into touch. People like Jacko at the Trib, whose enduring theme was that they would bring him down for good eventually. The sports editor harped on and on about them being users, whose only specific goal in life was to piggyback on his fame, fortune and good name in order to line their pockets and legitimise their crazy schemes.

Sure it was true that at times he lent them a hand, meeting a bank manager here or speaking to a licensing magistrate there, in an effort to smooth the way for certain projects they had on the go, but that was what friends did for each other. They had been there for him too, hadn't they? When the family split apart and there was the trauma over the boy. Yes, on a couple of occasions he had been left seriously out of pocket, having to sell his house and some of his possessions, but everyone knew that business was a gamble and the cards didn't always fall right. What were possessions anyway? It was people that mattered. Friendship. Camaraderie. Hell, if they weren't his friends, then who was? No one else gave a toss.

He'd lost his family, the people he most cared about, but others had it worse and he couldn't complain. Sob stories were for losers, as his father once told him when he was dumped by the school beauty queen in his home village in the wilds of West Wales. You didn't hear sob stories down the pit, or in the steelworks, and people lost far more than their girlfriend, or a few quid, in those days. They lost eyes, limbs, even lives, and bore it all with stoic bravery, so his dad said. Even now he missed his dad, a strong spirit who wore his integrity as a badge and was taken well ahead of his time by that most unforgiving of diseases, emphysema.

His mates were his 'surrogate' family, the ones who listened to his woes and bought him a pint, played dominoes with him and fed his ego. They hadn't for one minute considered deserting him. Salt of the earth. True enough.

Strange then, that when he left them at around 8pm with the light fading and the youngsters hitting the streets in search of a good time, he felt particularly maudlin. Hadn't they laughed and joked, shared uplifting stories and drank till their faces were beaming and their pockets empty? Hadn't they rolled about on the floor in a bizarre effort to replicate the last act of defiance from a Lions test match in South Africa a few years ago, leaving them flushed with joy until the killjoy of a barman suggested they drink up and leave before his posher clientele arrived for the evening. Strewth, how much had they put behind that bar over the years? He swore it would be the last time he honoured the establishment with his presence then staggered out into the evening.

Returning to his flat, he realised he still had the greatcoat and the vodka. They had been topping up their beer with it throughout the afternoon, but there was still a good half bottle left for company.

From then until now everything was a blur, though he was sure he could piece it together, like muscle memory in a rodent. Having followed the same paths again and again the pattern had become ingrained in his psyche. At some stage the bright lights must have come. He wondered at times if they were akin to visions, his father trying to give him messages from beyond the grave, but he knew the old man wouldn't have sanctioned the excruciating pain in his frontal lobe which accompanied them.

To cope with his infirmity he would have lain on the sofa and drifted off, giving his body time to fight the debilitating condition. Later, waking disorientated, he would have taken himself to bed and hoped by the morning his ailment was a distant memory.

Why, then, was he on the roof? And why did he have a pile of 12-inch records under his arm? Still lying flat he shuffled them now like a card dealer with a case of the yips. He tried to focus his blurred vision on the labels: Tom Jones "She's a Lady", The Beatles "Sgt Pepper's Lonely Hearts Club Band", Engelbert Humperdinck "After the Lovin'". They were signposts from another time, prizes from his collection which helped him travel back decades to a period in his life when it seemed impossible anything could go wrong. If these were in his hands, then which anthems of his youth lay in pieces on the concrete below?

At least the records were a clue. They painted a picture of a night spent reminiscing, and finally he could connect the remaining dots. There would have been the projector, the films, the photo albums, a kaleidoscope of happy times in stark contrast to the miserable emptiness he felt now. Yes, there could be no sob stories in public, but when sharing a worn down flat with ghosts it was easy to buckle. He knew the exact segment of black and white celluloid that would have brought on the melancholy and prompted a leaking in the corner of his eye, like the gradual breaching of a rain cloud. Next there would have been the heavy droplets running down his cheek and eventually the irreversible stream pouring over his chin and soaking his neck and shirt collar. He felt his cheeks now, and noticed the residue still there, a combination of salt and water that had marked a segment of his skin.

"Mr Owens, Mr Owens, sir. Don't move. Are you OK?" He looked up at wispy blond hair and uplifted eyebrows. His inquisitor wore a green uniform. "I'm a paramedic, sir. Name's Richard. I'm a big fan of yours. Please don't be nervous. I'm here to help. Yeah, I've heard all of your stories sir. Don't move will you? We just need to do a few tests, ascertain everything is as it should be. All right with you? Great!"

Behind the medic a blue peaked cap shadowed a stern facial expression. "We've had complaints," said the officer. "We'll have to take him in as a danger to the community. He's put other people at risk with his behaviour. I know he's a popular figure, but he was lobbing records off the roof at his neighbours. Completely out of control…"

"Sod 'em!" bellowed The Legend, trying to get to his feet. "They're just bloody busybodies. Should mind their own business."

"OK, OK," said the paramedic calmly, turning to the officer. "Look, I realise your position but you must appreciate mine. He's hardly in any state to do anyone harm now, is he?"

The officer shrugged and moved back a couple of steps. The paramedic rolled The Legend's sleeve up and wrapped the blood pressure cuff around his arm. "Just a couple of tests, sir. How is your back? You took a bit of a fall."

"I think it's OK, butt," said The Legend, calming down. "Look, I think I'm sorted now. Just need to rest. Can you get me to bed?"

"I'll sort it," said a new voice and for the first time The Legend got a glimpse of the newspaper lad, what was his name? He felt himself relax. He didn't know why but he could relate to the English boy as if an invisible bond connected them. He peered up at the man attending him and put on his best disarming smile. "Honestly, I'll be all right from here, I'm sure," he said, pointing his finger at Gareth. "Geraint will look after me now. Geraint from the Trib." The man shrugged, helped The Legend to his feet and handed him over to Gareth's custody.

27

"HOW ARE YOU, Geraint butt?" The Legend perched on the edge of his unmade bed and looked up at the reporter through rheumy eyes.

"Jeez, for the last time, it's Gareth. And I would be a lot better if I didn't have to come out here in the early hours of Sunday morning to get you out of the shit... butt." Gareth's mood had darkened at seeing the patient none the worse for his ordeal.

"I'm sorry, mun, truly I am. Don't know what got into me. One minute I was walking back after a couple of bevvies with the lads, like, the next it's as if I had a blackout, see. A light went off in my head and I am standing on a roof destroying my record collection."

"Well, sometimes alcohol can cause amnesia," suggested Gareth peevishly. "I somehow expect the two things are inter-related."

"Eh?" The Legend looked genuinely perplexed.

"Never mind... listen. I've had a bit of a night of it, and this doesn't help. I got driven here by a bloke who decided it was a good idea to break the speed limit, even though he'd had a few beers at home before he 'volunteered' to give me a lift. It was a pretty scary experience."

"Really?" asked The Legend.

"Will Shakespeare his name is. He is our work experience boy's dad and I'm lodging with them out in Pontyprenis."

"Well I never. You mean Will the Drive, or Great Shakes as they used to call him." The Legend's face lit up. "You're well and truly honoured. Top man. Do you know in his heyday he won some of the greatest driving prizes known to man? The Le Mans 24-hour race, for instance. Fantastic achievement for a boy from the valleys and, of course, he learned all his skills driving around here, tearing around on Caerphilly mountain and such."

"That explains his confidence behind the wheel," said Gareth. "I was worried. He agreed to drive my car and I was clinging on for grim life. In fact, when I said where I needed to go he was keen to help out... said you knew each other from way back and he's your biggest fan."

"The feeling's mutual," said The Legend. "He was a true global star, Shakes. Sure we were good – you know, the rugby players – but he fought off challengers from all over the planet. Haven't seen him in, ooh, 18 years. Pretty sure he wouldn't be drinking though. After the accident and his first marriage collapsing I recall he gave up the beer for good. Sounds like he was putting on an act for your benefit, to make you think you weren't drinking alone."

"What accident?"

"He was in Monaco practising for a big race and got a puncture in a tunnel," explained The Legend. "Shakes claimed that if his reactions had been better he might have avoided the wall and squeezed out the other side but I'm not sure it's true. It's what he believes though. He'd had a late night out galavantin' with film stars and such and felt his powers of concentration weren't what they should have been. He'd spent a lot of time all over the world, away from family and friends, and he says in his own words he got seduced by fame. What with champagne parties and lost nights, beautiful women...to cut a long story short, the docs had to operate on his spine and that was the end of his career. He thought it was a punishment from above and cleaned up his act."

"I had no idea," said Gareth. "What a terrible thing to happen."

"It gets worse. His wife Dorothy was an actress, got wind of his philandering – there was a story in one of the tabloid rags, no offence – and she left him. They shared a house in London but with the collapse of the marriage he returned to the Valleys, where he eventually married again. The last thing I heard he had been blessed with a child."

"You've met the boy," said Gareth. "Jason, the work experience lad who has been tagging along with me. For his part, Will is groundsman at Pontyprenis Rugby Club."

"Oh," said The Legend, looking crestfallen. "I guess when you lose it..."

"Don't worry. He seems happy as Larry. His second wife Mary died, sadly, but he and his son have a fantastic relationship and the injury doesn't seem to restrict him. In his spare time he is a bouncer and a wrestler! He's very active and wouldn't expect you to feel sorry for him. If anything..."

Concern furrowed The Legend's brow and Gareth realised he was treading on dangerous ground. "You should try to get some rest. I'll take the sofa and stay the rest of the night."

"If you really don't mind. You don't have to. I just needed you to vouch for me so they wouldn't cart me off to the hospital. I reckon I'll be fine from here on in... just got a bit of a fuzzy head."

GARETH SPOKE briefly to Will on the mobile, thanking him for his help and explaining there had been a "bit of a misunderstanding". The former rally driver clucked as if he knew all about The Legend's misunderstandings, then offered to pick him up. Gareth assured him he would be fine making his own way back to the cottage. "By the way, I didn't realise you knew The Legend so well. He tells me you don't drink."

"Completely teetotal," Will agreed.

"But, back at the house..."

"Non-alcoholic beverages I assure you. Don't worry, son, your car is safe in my hands."

"Yet Jase..."

"Is old enough to make his own mistakes. I figure that if he drinks in front of me he won't be going around behind my back with his mates, getting out of control and into trouble."

Fair point, Gareth thought. He said goodbye to Will and hung up the phone. Taking stock of his surroundings, the first thing he noted was the vodka bottle, a quarter full, standing on the living room table. A pile of cigarette ends erupted from the ashtray, but he wasn't sure it had been emptied since his last visit. New to the scene, though, was a large white screen hanging from a tripod, a projector on the table throwing a spartan white glow onto it. Puzzled, Gareth went back to check on The Legend. He found him sleeping soundlessly in the bedroom.

The reporter put the kettle on. He figured the patient would sleep for hours now. Searching the cupboards he found a few ruptured tea bags at the bottom of a cylindrical china pot. Rather than give up on the idea he discovered a strainer in one of the drawers and a quirky hand-painted teapot in another cupboard. Looking closer, the figure immortalised in paint bore a striking resemblance to the teapot's owner. Inserting two of the broken bags into the pot, Gareth applied hot water and covered it with a tea towel, itself embroidered with a rugby scene. He wondered if there was anything in the apartment that didn't pay homage to the sport and past glories.

He poured the tea through a strainer into a mug bearing the three feathers and the rather tired catchphrase Keep Calm and Support Wales, then warily took a bottle of milk from the fridge and was pleasantly surprised when he sniffed it to find nothing untoward. Though dog tired, his mind was ticking over too much to sleep. He considered putting on the television but his eyes kept straying to the projector. Could he? Should he?

Perhaps just a quick look. After all, it was almost a prerequisite of being a journalist to have an inquiring mind, so why disappoint? Putting his tea on the table, he studied the contraption. Long before the days of video this, he guessed, was how people recorded things. He noted the spools and the fact the entire tape was wrapped around one of them. Bending at the knees to take a closer look he winced at the pain, but didn't dwell on it, his mind pre-occupied.

Finding a loose end to the spool, he tugged it until it unravelled and ran it across to the other one. Clipping it in place, he turned the spool until it wound itself around. Satisfied they were connected, Gareth felt a sense of achievement as he moved on to study the projector. There were a series of buttons just like on a VCR: Stop, play, rewind, fast forward. He pressed the play button and the tape began to wind through. Knowing he was intruding into another person's private life, his guilt was assuaged by the fact he had a mystery to unravel. The truth behind The Legend. He had gone too far to stop himself now.

28

IT WAS a portal into the past. Gareth felt as if he was squinting through one of those What The Butler Saw telescopes you found at the end of a disintegrating seaside pier. The scene was a beach. A young man with jet black hair, tight swimming trunks and an impressive six-pack on a healthy, caramel-skinned body was throwing a rugby ball high in the air for a young boy to scamper after it. A little girl of around five, her mane of long blonde hair caught in a gust of summer breeze, followed in his wake as they clambered across a sand dune. Retrieving the ball the boy, looking like a miniature version of the man, turned and swerved around his sister. Returning to the man his reward was to be lifted high in the air and placed on broad shoulders. The girl stood below them, hands reaching up in an effort to share his attention.

Gareth looked at the side of the projector to see if there was a volume or sound button, but could find none. He resumed his seat, like a cinema punter having been afforded a private viewing of an old silent movie. Now, from the right corner of the screen, a blonde woman in a lipstick-red, all-in-one bathing suit began sneaking up on the happy family gathering. As the man concentrated on keeping the boy balanced, the woman whipped the rugby ball from under his arm and careered away down the beach, the little girl giving chase again.

Aware too late what had happened, the man put down the boy and swiftly made ground behind the woman, bringing her crashing down with a rugby tackle just as she entered a dune. Jokingly, she tossed sand in his face. Feigning blindness, he appeared to scream, then brought his knees up to sit astride the woman, his legs pinning her arms to the sand. As he bent forward for a kiss the two children appeared from nowhere, jumping on his back and sharing the happy scene.

"What the fuck do you think you're doing?!" The deep Welsh voice resonated through the flat and Gareth leapt to his feet in front of the projector, his body becoming part of the visual tableau.

"Sorry, um, JW... I thought you were asleep."

"Evidently," said The Legend, moving towards him, fists balled at his sides. "I let you into my home, befriend you and this is how you repay me... to go through my things while I'm incapacitated?" There was no longer any sign of alcohol affecting his speech. His annunciation was perfect, his message clear, his voice displaying a hint of menace that Gareth hadn't previously encountered.

"Look," he said, holding his palms out in a defensive gesture to indicate he had nothing to hide.

"I think you're the one who has been doing the looking – at my personal things," said The Legend. "You may think I'm an old man, English, but there's fight left in me yet, I tell you. I can't believe you would... go through my private stuff like that. Then again, you're a bloody journalist aren't you? I should have known. Serves me right. I've always been open with the press and they've tended to confer some respect on me, at least around these parts. But my friends warned me, hundreds of times, I shouldn't trust your type and it seems they were right."

As The Legend advanced, Gareth realised he was cut off from the exit. The only way out was past the figure with the vicious stare blocking his path. He would need all his powers of persuasion to bring this human ball of fury under control. Though he wasn't convinced it was the right move, his instincts told him that the best way to counter this assault was to fight fire with fire. He had to regain some kind of respect and cowering away wasn't the answer.

Staring into The Legend's bloodshot eyes he said: "I'm sorry, but I was just curious. I wanted to find out more about you... I hardly know you, for Christ's sake, and yet you're demanding I come and rescue you from the police at some ridiculous time on a bloody Sunday morning. I've done you a favour, pal, even if you can't see it because the bloody booze has clouded…"

He didn't see the punch coming. It connected perfectly on the right side of his jaw, sending him reeling back into the screen, ripping the canvas and bringing the whole lot crashing down. He tried to gather his scrambled thoughts, to put them into a coherent and logical order. Then the lights went out and it had nothing to do with a blown bulb.

"AH, THE SNOOP'S coming around," said a gravelly, disembodied voice. Gareth felt like he had been struck with an iron bar as he tried to piece together the scrambled jigsaw of his brain. He flinched jerkily into a sitting position as a loud knocking and shouting came from off to his left. Stars flooded his consciousness and he flopped backwards. He could make out the voice now and it was angry.

"Hey, you starting up again?" demanded a male voice from the other side of the door. "Listen Owens, if we have to call the Old Bill again they're going to lock you up. Alice is probably on the phone this minute. We ain't slept a wink because of your shenanigans. You should have more respect for your neighbours."

Now Gareth could see The Legend standing over him, the bottle of vodka in his hand, minus its top. "Shit, hang on JW – look we don't want any more trouble tonight, do we? I'd better sort this…"

"You make it out as if this scenario is my fault, boy," he said, trying to muster his anger again. Gareth could tell, though, that his heart wasn't really in it any more. "Ah, might as well let the police come. I'm tired. Let them have their way."

"No mate, can't do that I'm afraid," said Gareth. "I know you don't like it, but I've got a job to do. Jacko told me to look after you – keep you out of trouble – so just you wait there."

"Jacko thinks I need a baby sitter? Bloody hell, I'm old enough to look after myself."

Gareth didn't have time to argue. He struggled to his feet and grabbed for the arm of the sofa as he felt his troublesome knee collapse under him. "Shit, didn't think I hit you that hard," said The Legend.

"Oh, you did a pretty good job," said Gareth. It was as if a balloon of tension had burst in the room. They both chuckled.

"Oi, Owens, come on, what excuse is it this time? You going to shut the racket up or what?"

Gareth looked through the keyhole to see a bulky figure with a wispy comb-over in lime green boxer shorts and a string vest, his chest hair sprouting unruly out of the top. He waited a few seconds, then flung the door open. A smell of B.O hit him full in the face. "Hello there, sorry, can I help you?"

The unfamiliar face took the neighbour by surprise. "Oh, er, who are you? I want to speak to Owens."

"Ah, well, Mr Owens is asleep right now. I'm his nephew. I'm sorry but it may have been me you heard. I was just tidying up the flat and knocked something over. I'm terribly sorry, it was loud, wasn't it?"

"Bloody woke me up actually, son. Can't believe Owens would have slept through it." He tried to look over Gareth's shoulder, but the reporter shifted to block his eye line.

"He has had a long night as I am sure you can appreciate. As I say, it was an accident. It won't happen again. Now anything else I can help you with?"

Gareth maintained eye contact until the other man grunted and looked away. "No, er... you're all right. Just keep the noise down in future, eh? Oh, and you're bleeding, mate. Did you know? Just there..." He pointed to his own cheek. Gareth put up his hand and brought his finger back down. There was, indeed, blood. "Oh, thanks. I bumped myself when I was trying to prevent the... thing falling over. I better get a plaster on this. See you around." He closed the door and lay back against it, trying to get his breath back. Then he leaned down and rubbed his knee.

"I've been meaning to ask you, what's wrong with the leg, Geraint?" said The Legend from behind him.

"Oh, an old injury. Not to worry, I'm used to it."

"I'm sorry," said The Legend, "For over-reacting I mean."

"No need, honestly, it was my fault. You're right, I'm a snoop, but it wasn't as if I was going to use anything I found and put it in the paper. I just wanted to know more about you. It's my inquisitive nature. I've been thrown together with this huge Welsh sporting star and, through my own ignorance it's true, I know little about you. My mum always said my nosy nature would get me into trouble." Gareth chuckled. "Strange thing is I get it from her!"

"That was totally out of character for me," said The Legend. "Hell, I can't remember the last time I punched someone in anger. It was a good punch though, butt, wasn't it?" Gareth rubbed his jaw in response. "The thing is there are some things you just need to keep secret, right? I mean, at the end of the day it was why I gave up the game."

Gareth knew better than most what The Legend meant about keeping secrets. He only had to look at his current state of affairs. "Yeah?"

"I couldn't stand the attention to be honest, butt," The Legend admitted. "One minute there I was, working in a steel foundry, a nobody, playing rugby as a hobby... a time-consuming one I'll grant you, but remember it was all amateur back in the day, not like these guys who get paid a pretty penny for pulling on a shirt. Before I knew it I was touring thousands of miles away, playing pretty well with these other lads from other countries, enjoying it like a bit of a holiday away from work. When I come back, though, flying into London there is this huge crowd waiting. Completely bananas. I thought there was some rock band arriving at the terminal but they were there to greet us, The Lions. I get through the customs and am swamped by reporters, fans, the lot. There are no police in sight. To be honest, it was scary. Hell, a couple of women actually took off their undies and threw them at me. Tom Jones, sure, but me?

Can you imagine? Life wasn't the same after that. I was never very good at saying no and ended up touring around the country, opening fetes, speaking at sports award dinners, you name it. All expenses only, too, and still trying to hold down the day job. The bosses were getting sick of my absence. It couldn't go on... it was one or the other."

"So you went back to the foundry?"

"Oh no," said The Legend, shaking his head. "That's what I should have done perhaps, but I decided instead to cash in on my fame. They say you get only 15 minutes, don't they? Well, I knew mates who had been forced to give up the game with injuries and the like, a couple in particular confined to wheelchairs, so I signed some promotional agreements with popular products at the time, did some TV work, agreed a deal for a couple of books that Jacko ghost wrote for me, then put my name to videos and the like. Of course, being an amateur I wasn't allowed to make money while I was playing, so as the deals rolled in I took the big decision... packed up the game."

"How old were you?"

"Twenty eight. Still had a few good years left in me, I guess."

"That's no age," Gareth agreed. "You must be envious of those who play now."

"Ah, there's no point looking back... and I did have a whale of a time. Fell in with some of the superstars from other sports. I was a personal friend of the big football stars at the time and we went to champagne parties, all sorts. Of course, there was temptation, women just throwing themselves at your feet, but it was as if I had just stepped off the planet into another world. Unfortunately, it was the beginning of the end for the marriage."

"You strayed?"

"Never. No, I was always faithful to Brenda. She was my child-hood sweetheart and we had grown up together. She knew me better than anyone. We got married, had my boy Martin and girl Ellie, and everything was great. The trouble was I lost sight of all that. Actually, I think she would have forgiven me for straying. It was the other stuff, the way I was frittering money away on things, putting the family at risk. We were from poor families in west Wales, most of the time we had to pinch the pennies to make ends meet. I saw the fame as an escape, she saw it as a massive millstone. Looking back, she was right."

Gareth looked at the screen, crumpled on the floor. "That was them I take it?"

"Happier times. A holiday away from it all down Rhossili Bay in west Wales while I was still playing. A wonderful few days with the family. Probably one of the last times I can remember when I was naturally happy."

"Well, you know what they say – a problem shared is a problem halved," said Gareth. "Well, my mum does anyway."

"These are problems I'd rather forget altogether."

"No chance of reconciliation?"

"Hey, she eventually ran off with one of my best pals, a flanker for the Scarlets, um, Llanelli. Iolo Ap Gwyllyn. We had all known each other for years. When I was away so much I guess he became a shoulder to cry on. It all got a bit nasty when it came out in the open, messy divorce etc. They eventually emigrated to Oz."

"You don't see the kids?"

The Legend went silent, and Gareth detected his eyes watering up. "Look," said The Legend. "Let's leave it there. It's almost five in the morning and I reckon we both need some sleep." Without another word he turned and headed for bed.

"Shit," muttered Gareth. He thought he was making a break-through, only for The Legend to clam up suddenly. Still, he was right. It was late and it had been one hell of a day. He would just have to delve deeper into the mystery of JW Owens on another occasion.

29

WHEN GARETH ENTERED the office on Wednesday morning, Jason was already busy at the computer. "All right, mate?" the work experience boy said by way of greeting.

Improvement on boss, thought Gareth. Slightly. "Fine, son. What are you up to?"

"I thought I would just open a file of useful information you might need as a background to the Argentina game – you know, the World Cup warm-up match in Dubai? I've given you a rundown of both sides, who are the leading points scorers, try scorers, the amount of caps each player has and past results between the two nations. You can think of it as your homework." He chuckled.

"Good idea," said Gareth distractedly. "Listen, while you're here I wanted to run something past you, a ... challenge if you like."

Jason's eyes lit up. "Anything you want boss, uh, Gareth. To do with the rugby is it?"

"Well, kind of," said Gareth. "It's a bit of background research. I want you to see if you can get in touch with JW's children. His wife Brenda emigrated to Australia back in the late 80s as far as I understand it, taking them with her. I would probably try to avoid the wife if you can, I imagine it's still delicate even now, but use your nous and see what you can find out about the kids."

"You mean kid," said Jason. "Only his daughter went out to Oz... think her name was Eleanor."

"Well, no... he had a boy as well. Martin," corrected Gareth. "I saw film of him..."

"He died," said Jason. "The way I understand it he stuck with his father and refused to go abroad. He was living here with JW when something went horribly wrong. He was attacked by muggers or something, as far as I can recall. I was only really young at the time though, butt, so I've only heard bits and pieces of the story. I'm pretty sure JW has never talked about it in public."

"How horrible!" said Gareth. "Must be awful when a child dies before you do. Poor JW. It makes sense now. He got pretty upset when he was telling me about the family on Saturday night. OK, see what you can find out, anyway, about Eleanor."

"Sure thing," said Jason. "By the way, what's happening about the game in Dubai? Are you going out there?"

"He isn't... but I am," announced a voice from behind them. Quinten was standing there, resplendent in red jacket and black trousers, his cheeks so shiny he might have applied rouge to them. He was beaming like the magician who had just revealed, untouched, the £50 he had appeared to rip up a few minutes earlier. Confident he had their attention he explained: "I've got a few strings I've been able to pull – an airline owes me a favour for a little piece I did for them a while back and I've good contacts with the Dubai tourist board who have fixed me up with a hotel. I'll tie it in with a travel feature and kill two birds with one stone, as it were. The whole thing's sorted and Lana's agreed."

"I guess you, me and JW will be watching it on the TV then," Gareth told Jason.

"Oh well... good luck with that," said Quinten. "Anyway, what were you saying about The Legend? Got into another fix or some-thing?"

"Oh no, nothing," said Gareth.

"Fair enough," said Quinten, though his facial expression indi-cated he wasn't happy about being denied another juicy bit of gossip. "Can't stand around chatting all day... au revoir," he waved his hand behind him as he walked off back to his work station.

Once he had gone, Jason gave Gareth a quizzical look. "I want to keep this family reunion plan under my hat," the reporter explained.

"Only me and you can know about it. It would make a great newspaper exclusive, no doubt, and my normal attitude would be to jump all over a story like this, but I kind of owe The Legend and am sure he doesn't want his private life blasted all over the papers – particularly with what you've just told me about his son. Some things should stay private and some people's privacy should be respected."

Jason raised his eyebrows, surprised at the response. Have I really got such a bad reputation already with the locals? Gareth thought. He ploughed on. "Anyway, start with the cuts in the library. See the chief librarian and tell him you want anything he's got on Brenda and Eleanor Owens – I bet they've done a few stories on her in the past. With any luck we might be able to pull it off."

"Sure boss, will do." Jason flicked a salute at him and wandered off in the direction of the library. As Gareth watched him go he heard a pinging noise: He was being alerted to an incoming e-mail. He shook the mouse to refresh the screen and saw that he'd received a new message. In the contact line was the name Hana. He felt a shudder go through him as he clicked the mouse. When the message sprang open it contained just three words, but the impact they had on him was huge. His face went pale and he detected the onset of a headache.

The message simply read: "He's home today."

Part III

London & Cardiff

30

"MYYYYY VICKERS OLD lad, you are getting a big boy!" Arnie Dolan tucked the brown parcel under one arm and put his other around the shoulders of the slightly overweight young man standing on the pavement.

"Oh come on, Doles, I only saw you a couple of months ago," protested Pete Vickers. "I ain't going to do much growing now – I'm 32!"

Without warning he was rocked back by a punch to the gut so fierce it nearly sent him falling into the passing traffic. He involuntarily let out a sound as the air escaped his body. "Didn't mean your height, you fat bastard," sneered Arnie, with a mean chuckle. "I meant this fackin' pillow you're keeping up your jumper. You're out of condition, boy, we'll have to do somethin' about that."

He put the offending fist to his chin and adopted a pose, as if having a philosophical debate with himself about the meaning of life. Eventually he asked: "What does 'Oof' mean anyway? Bizarre isn't it, how people say oof when they take one in the derby? Rhymes with poof. Not very manly that is it, Vickers old son?" The chuckle stopped as abruptly as it started.

Vickers didn't respond. Face contorted, he coughed then began to wretch, doubled over. "Hey! Watch the fackin' shoes! New they are," said Arnie in mock horror. "First really new thing I've had for seven years. Course, our Anj bought us a few things inside, you know? She's a good girl. But it ain't the same. I got these off that internet. Amazing what you can do on it these days. They let me use the computer as part of my 're-ha-bili-tation'. Wankers. Look," he lifted his boot to the level of his doubled-up mate's nose. "Real leather, smell it?"

Vickers flinched, fearing he was about to become too familiar with the steel toe-capped brogues, then nodded vigorously. "Very nice, Doles." He slowly bent his body back into shape and looked pleadingly into the eyes of his old school friend. "What did you do that for, though? I mean, I been here for you all this time, visited on regular occasions, bought you some snout and, y'know, some of the other stuff and the first thing you do is wallop me in the bread basket. Not nice."

"Yeah, well..." said Arnie, "it ain't nice in there either. Toughens you up, know what I mean? Every day. Bloody jiggaboos trying it on, them fackin' Muslim brotherhood characters wantin' a pop. You find you have to act first and ask questions later."

"But I'm your best mate, Doles. Stuck by you through all this. Where are the others eh? Can't see them queuing up to meet you."

"I only asked for you, didn't I?" said Arnie, his face softening into a grin. Then, as if a switch had been flicked inside him, he grabbed Vickers around the neck again and squeezed hard, the muscles bulging under his clean white shirt. Using the knuckles of his other hand he rubbed vigorously on his captive's head. "You're me bestie, ain't ya? Me right-hand man. I'll see the others later, but you ... well I had to have my bestie here to meet me when I came out of clink, didn't I?"

As quickly as he had attacked he relaxed his grip, leaving Vickers coughing and spluttering and desperate to avoid puking. "Yeah," he croaked. "Course, thanks Doles. Great to see you. We all missed you."

"All?"

"Well..." Vickers quickly changed the subject. "Look, I've arranged a home-coming party back in the old 'hood. Sent out messages on Twitter, Facebook and everything. You get me? Some of the..." The last words of the sentence were squeezed out of him as Arnie increased the pressure on his neck once again.

"Mate... mate," said Arnie. "Don't start with all this 'black' talk. You ain't no rapper on the streets of Noo Yawk, you're an Englishman. 'You get me?' – what's that mean? I'll tell you what it means: It means if I hear any of that shit coming out of your mouth again I will 'get you'. Comprende?"

"S... sorry mate," spluttered Vickers, trying to work out what he had done wrong and how to avoid another indiscriminate assault from the man who claimed to be his closest friend.

"And Twitter... what the hell is that? Sounds like what it says, something a twit would use. Facebook? Some of the guys inside kept going on about that. 'Are you on Facebook'? Load of bollocks, if you ask me. Why have people knowing your private business? Don't make sense, that."

Arnie was off on another rant. He seemed to fill his sentences with questions that he didn't expect to be answered. He'd had a relatively short fuse in all the time Vickers had known him, but it now seemed minuscule and he was likely to go off at any moment. The spark, it seemed, could be anything.

As quickly as he attacked though, Arnie could become amiable and calm. "Ah... never mind, you big slug... come on," he said. "What car are you driving these days?"

"I got a nice little Focus, you know, family car. Me and Janie got the two kids now and..."

"Ah, yeah. Good old Janie. Done all right there, mate. Great tits. Sorry I couldn't get to your wedding. Couldn't get the time off, y'know? Her Majesty wasn't very accommodating." He grinned again, though while the humour registered in dimples on his cheeks it never quite reached his eyes. "Come on then, let's get the family wagon and get the merry fuck out of here."

As Vickers led the way, Arnie took one last look at the old grey stone building where he had spent the past eight years. He took in the imposing gate with the metal latticework above it giving the appearance of an old castle drawbridge, the uneven walls which seemed to be punctuated with turrets out of medieval times, the arch windows which were barred and imposing.

He noted with a sense of warmth the royal ensign floating in the cooling breeze. Then, slowly and deliberately, he raised two fingers in a v-shape in its direction.

"Goodbye Wano... you cunts!" he shouted.

31

"COME 'ERE MY lovely bird!" Arnie threw his arms open and the young dark-haired woman ran into them, her red nails digging into his back. Anjelica's slender frame was emphasised by a tight-fitting blue T-shirt bearing the slogan "My other brother's a jailbird" and jeans which cut off just below the knee to reveal freckled, sunbed-stained calves. He hugged her so tightly she imagined her bones rubbing together and feared something might snap. "Missed you so much, chicken," he said, finally releasing his grip and standing back to admire the shirt. "Hey, is this a dig at me?"

She gave him a mischievous grin that showed off pretty dimples in her cheeks. They were framed by a shining bob which gave the impression of a hip chick, like one of those 60s models: Jean Shrimpton or Twiggy. "Do you think I would take the Mickey out of my big brother on his first day of freedom?" she asked, a finger dangling coyly from the corner of her mouth. He shook his head, but his eyes said yes. They both collapsed into giggles.

"Is that him? Is that my big boy?" came a voice from the kitchen.

"Sure is, Mum," said Anjelica. "In the flesh. You gonna come and say hello?" There was a shuffling sound and she moved aside.

Mrs Dolan had aged terribly in the eight years since her middle son had been sent away. The slender, attractive figure she had once boasted had long gone. She was now squat and broad-shouldered, decked out in a leopardskin onesie. On her feet were Mickey and Minnie Mouse comedy slippers. "Hello, son," she said as he came forward and lifted her into the air. "Great to 'ave you back. It seems such a long time. What a travesty of justice! This legal system we got in this country… it's all wrong."

"Never mind that, Mum," said Arnie. "I'm out now and we can make up for lost time. Where is he anyway? Where's my boy? Where's Stevo?"

The two women gave each other knowing looks. "Oh honey!" The older woman said, breaking the brief silence and hugging him to her shoulder again. This time he pulled away.

"What?" he demanded, detecting a change in the atmosphere. "What's happened to my dog?"

"We didn't want to upset you, darlin'," his mum said. "Stevo had to be put down a few months back."

"What? He was fighting fit that dog when I went away. What the hell..?"

"He was getting older, angel, and unfortunately he went a bit loopy," she explained. "Your dad had to take him to the vets for an injection. All very peaceful, it was."

"Dad? He's out?"

"Just a flying visit. He was allowed out on licence for a bit, but he's back inside now. When he came home though, Stevo went for him. Gave him a nasty bite in the cheek... there was blood and everythin'. Your dad said he couldn't have him around with your sister having a young child in the house, so he muzzled him and a couple of mates helped him take Stevo away. I'm so sorry, but we had the little one to think of, you understand?"

Arnie didn't understand. He was beside himself with fury. Unlike humans, Stevo had been loyal to him through and through. He was truly man's best friend. "It wouldn't have bloody happened if I had been here – none of it!" he said.

"I know, bubs," she agreed, "but you wasn't here was you darlin' and, well, someone had to make a decision about what was best for the people who were here, particularly Max. Don't you want to meet him, by the way? You are his uncle, after all."

There was a moment's silence as the women tried to gauge how Arnie would react. His glacial blue eyes peered out from under a corrugated forehead, looking past his mother and pinning his sister to the spot. "Where is he then?" he said softly. "Where's this nephew I've heard so much about?"

"I'll go get him," she said, happy that the tension had lifted.

"Max... I like that," said Arnie, allowing his anger to slowly disperse. "Reminds me of Mad Max. Another film title, mum?"

"They're not film titles, they're the names of action heroes. You are my little action men," replied the older woman, pushing her hands through a steel-grey perm. "Not this one, though, this is all your sister's work. Anyway, are you suggestin' there was something wrong with the way I chose your names? They were your dad's idea." She clouted him on the forearm and he threw his hands up in mock surrender.

"Nah, mum, how could I? I think our names are great. Fair play to you. Nothing to be ashamed of when we walk down the street, is there? I hope we live up to them, and I think most of us do... apart from that poof Bruce."

"Leave him alone," said his mother, bashing him in the forearm again. "Well, you live up to yours, for sure. I didn't mean for you to take it so literally and become some kind of East London Terminator."

"Aww, that's not fair, mum, now is it? Those coppers fitted me up. And some grass…"

"Water under the bridge, honey. You can't dwell on it. Look, here he is… here's my little soldier." As Anjelica came back down the hall a little face poked out from behind her leg, gripping tightly to her jeans pocket.

"Don't be bashful, son, let's have a look at you," he said. "Come to your Uncle Arnie. Hey, can't wait to take you down the Hammers. It'll be peachy." He dropped to his haunches and his sister stepped aside, holding the boy in place, though it seemed to be against his wishes. Finally, she gave him a nudge and his momentum carried him into the embrace of the stranger, who whisked him instantly into the air and in one swift movement placed him on his shoulders.

"Careful with him," said Anjelica. "He's only little."

"Yeah, right… it's OK sis," said Arnie. "He's a big tough fella ain't you? Mad Max. How old are you now? Five is it? Probably take after your dad… if any of us knew who that was!"

"Oh, don't… please," begged Arnie's mum, slapping him again on the shoulder. "You've just got home, we don't want to go over old ground."

"I'm just saying," argued Arnie. "Boy should know who his dad is, that's all." He gave his mother a long, poignant look, a grin still fixed on his face though the humour had long since gone.

BEFORE THAT EVENING'S party there was a gathering of the Dolan clan. Squeezed into the small front room, the men were catching up while their women gossiped in the kitchen and the kids played upstairs in one of the bedrooms. Standing by the big ornate mirror over the mantelpiece, the eldest boy Chuck, who was in his late 30s now, raised a glass and put his arm around the ex-prisoner. "Here's to our beloved brother. Great to have you back, pal. We all missed you a ton." He gave Arnie a squeeze. "Glad you stayed out of trouble long enough to come home. I had a vision of you stabbing a screw and staying inside forever. Don't worry, though, we've been taking care of business."

Sitting on the arm of a sagging brown chair, another of the men murmured something.

"What's that Sly? Somethin' you would like to share?" asked Chuck, fixing his young lookalike with a stare. Both men had shaved heads and were wearing designer jackets with polo shirts and black trousers. There was six years between them, otherwise they could have been twins. The man called Sly had a quieter voice, betraying a shyness in company, even though he was now among those closest to him.

"Just agreeing with you, Chuck. It's great to have him back."

"What about you Bruce? You glad to see me?" Asked Arnie of a younger man with blond, shoulder-length hair who was slumped casually in the chair.

"Fuck off, you'll want that car back now. I've grown quite attached to it. And your old girlfriends. Had every one of your birds since you've been 'doing bird'." Bruce cracked a smile. "Ha ha, had you there! Everyone knows you ain't got any girlfriends anyway. Boyfriends after your time inside, I suspect. I imagine they gave you a right..."

Without warning Arnie leapt at him, grabbing the chair and tilting it backwards so that Bruce flew over the back and Sly bounced off the arm, flipping over a table containing a lamp and a beer glass. Chuck quickly grabbed Arnie and pulled him up straight. "Oh fuck, you mad clown, I hope Mum didn't hear that!"

They set about righting the room as best they could. "How long are we going to be, guys?" said Vickers from the sofa. "I told Phil down The Hope I'd be there to set up around 7."

"Can't go yet," said Arnie, brushing down the suit he had borrowed from Sly, a shiny silver affair with a black bootlace tie. "He ain't here, is he?"

The others looked at each other, not sure who should give the explanation. As always it was left to Vickers. "I don't think the Crip's coming, mate," he said, watching Arnie's face carefully to gauge the reaction.

"Don't call him that!" said Arnie, his expression betraying his confusion. "You know I hate that nickname... and what do you mean, not coming? He knows I'm out, don't he? You did tell him?"

"Tell him?" chimed in Sly. "Chance would be a fine thing. We can't even bloody find him."

"What? One of my closest mates? Disappeared off the face of the earth?" Arnie studied the faces. He knew something wasn't right, but couldn't put his finger on what. He suspected he wasn't getting the whole truth. "That Hackney lot ain't done for him, have they? You have searched for him I take it? God, if those cheeky muthafuckers ..."

"It's nothing like that." Chuck spoke quickly to ease the tension. "I'm sure he's fine. He's just moved on I guess. I don't know exactly where he's moved on to, but he got a job south of the river and I can only imagine it's been keeping him pretty busy. We haven't seen him around. He hasn't been in The Hope..."

Arnie added things up in his head. "... Well, the bugger never came to see me inside, which I thought was a bit off. I know his mum wasn't well for a time and she had a downer on me, but eight bleeding years? You'd think he might have made a bit of an effort, seeing as I took the rap for us all but hey, ho."

"To be fair, Doles, it was you that gave that guy a beating, mate," pointed out Vickers.

"Shut it!" Arnie stormed, quickly lowering his voice. "Are you fuckin' mad? I don't want our mum to hear that sort of thing. For Christ sake she thinks I was fitted up. I don't want to, um, disillusion her with the truth."

Vickers' face showed genuine fear. "N... no, of course not Doles."

"So," said Arnie, considering the evidence like an Agatha Christie detective addressing a room full of suspects. "I knew my boy was taking some sort of course and doing work experience at a radio station – ever since his football got kicked into touch. So he got a job eh? Still, it was in London. Not far enough away that he couldn't come and visit his old mate or at least pop in to see the old gang and inquire about me. He never was the same really, though... after the incident I mean. And his mum was on his case all the time. Bit rich, though, not showing your face when your closest mate comes out of nick."

He looked at Vickers, who was rapidly realising that all the "best mate" talk directed at him earlier in the day had been a distortion of the truth. "What about Anj?" he said. "They used to be quite close."

The other men looked back at him blankly. "You'll have to ask her," offered Bruce, finally getting comfortable again after putting his chair back into the upright position.

"Oh don't worry, I will," said Arnie. "Because it's all a bit fucking strange if you ask me."

32

IT WAS A typical East End boozer serving the roughest estate in the area and though it was putting on airs and graces for the day it had changed very little in the eight years since one of its most loyal customers went away. Beneath the sparkly decorations a closer look revealed peeling paint, dilapidated wood and upholstery which was spewing its insides out onto the stained, tiled floor.

A huge customised 'Welcome Home Arnie' banner stretched across the wooden apron above the bar as part of the disguise, book-ended by balloons of various shapes and colours. The man to whom it referred was now the centre of attention for the 20 or so invited guests, other locals keeping their heads down and supping their ales discreetly in the nooks and crannies around the expansive room. No one in East London would want to inadvertently attract the attention of the Dolans if they could avoid it.

To say the family had a reputation for trouble was like saying King Henry VIII was partial to wedding cake. It went all the way back to grandad Billy, who had been part of the Brink's-MATT gang that got away with three tonnes of gold bullion and £26m worth of gold, diamonds and cash from a warehouse at Heathrow in 1983. Fleeing the country, he ended up in the criminal's playground of the Costa del Sol in Spain, where he was regularly visited by his grandchildren. Chuck and Sly had spent a year there after the Hackney nightclub bombing and though there was no evidence to connect them to the incident, the rumour factory had regularly tossed out their names over the ensuing months.

Dad Maurice, or big Mo as his mates called him, was back in Belmarsh for an armed robbery at a Kent post office having spent a large proportion of his adult life in a collection of high-security prisons throughout the UK. The grapevine had it that he was currently leading white inmates in a war with a large number of incarcerated Islamic terror suspects. No one was in doubt that it was mum Beryl who held the family together, no mean feat under the circumstances.

Chuck was definitely a chip off the old block. He had a violent streak which had got him in plenty of trouble in the past and many suspected Arnie knew exactly how to pull his strings, using the older brother and his mates as enforcers as he set about building his empire.

Sylvester lived up to the nickname Sly because he was more con-artist than muscle and among his more lucrative and highly illegal schemes was one in which he attached a hidden camera to a local cashpoint and managed to obtain the bank details of 160 users in one morning, prompting a series of identity thefts that netted him a small fortune.

Anjelica, the only girl, was the second youngest. Despite the family pressures she had resisted temptation and kept her nose clean. She had qualified as a nurse through determination and hard graft and now worked long hours at the Royal London Hospital in Whitechapel. Bruce was the youngest and lived in the shade of his infamous brothers. Few knew exactly what he was capable of as yet.

As for Arnie, the middle Dolan child had street nous and brains, virtues that had quickly seen him assume his place as the leader of the infamous Boxer Boys. Even at a relatively tender age Arnie had earned a fearful reputation for his dexterity with his weapon of choice, a knife, and those who upset him had the livid scars to prove it. With help from the gang he had put together a powerful protection network and a number of local drug pushers, illegal bookies and market traders handed over a "cut" of their profits to keep him on their side. Unfortunately for him, the spell behind bars had come at just the wrong time. He was poised to expand the business into other areas of London when disaster struck. How the police had tracked him down he still didn't know, but it was something he aimed to find out.

"Well, thanks a lot for coming, you mugs!" he shouted, raising his pint glass in a toast. "Shame more of you couldn't find it as easy to get to Wano, but I don't suppose you'd get a free pint for making that journey." The audience chuckled politely at the barb. "Anyhow, now I'm out let's tell you a story. When they first banged me up in that shithole I can't tell you how bad it was. I remember sitting there on me bunk and watching this rat running around. D'you know, it got me thinking about the rat who put me in there. If that rat is here, let me tell you... Arnie's out and he's coming to get you." He glared at each face, making them feel uneasy. He wanted to unsettle them. "That's right. If you lot thought I was going to sit around on my backside enjoying my freedom, you're wrong. I shall be out and about, meetin' and greetin' my old customers, pledging to help them with any, ah, problems they might have... you listening, Tiggs?"

His eyes fell on the long-haired, skinny bloke with the acne-speckled face. He wore grubby jeans and a greasy white T-shirt with tattoos stretching up his arms. "Sure thing, Arnie!" Mitchell Tiggs piped up with false bonhomie. He'd really wanted to be a long way away when Arnold Dolan got out of stir and it was only pure cowardice that had dictated otherwise.

"Good, cos my pal Vickers will be poppin' around to see you, you cunt." There was a lot of polite laughter but no one was going too far, fearing the Dolan stare might fall on them next. "Anyway," continued the honoured guest having sucked the joy out of the occasion, "drink up cos I'm told there is another half hour of the free bar then all you freeloaders can start buying me beers." His eyes focused on his mother, who was standing a little way back from the huddle, chatting with a friend. "Mum!" he shouted, to get her attention. "Make sure you're first in the queue. They've got some pretty good barley wine, I understand, and I want you dancin' on them tables by closing." She interrupted her conversation to raise her glass and bestow on him a proud, beaming smile.

As people drifted away from the centre of attention Arnie gave Vickers a nod, indicating a corner table. It was the signal to get the gang lieutenants together for a business meeting. One by one they drifted across, accepted a firm handshake from their leader and took a seat. The old Jam song Going Underground was belting out from the jukebox and Arnie drummed his fingers on the table to the beat.

"Hey, Fancy, how's it goin'? Remember this one?" he said to the curly-haired blond man with a paisley cravat tied at the throat. He was dapper as always, his collared white shirt ironed to within an inch of its life, his trousers pressed so sharply you could cut yourself on the crease.

"Sure do, mate. Used to love all them Mod bands – The Jam, Secret Affair – back in the day. Christ, remember Brighton?"

"Hardly goin' to forget it, am I?" admitted Arnie with a smile. "That was a hell of a weekend. Shame it was brought to a close so early, for some of us anyway."

They both laughed. "Yeah," agreed Fancy. "Didn't alter our plans too much, though. I laughed so much I nearly pissed myself for real."

"Yeah, yeah," Arnie looked around and waved a shaven-headed straggler to his seat. "You seen him, lately?"

"The Crip? Not for, well, years," said Fancy. "Once that thing happened he tended to avoid us and do his own thing – I guess you getting banged up was the last straw. I heard he was working out at New Cross, but there are rumours he's moving to the Middle East, would you credit it? It sounds like good money, though. I put a message on Facebook saying to get in touch, that we should have one last night out before he leaves for the sun and sand. Not heard anything. I asked his mum about him once when I saw her in the street. She sent me packing. Told me he had moved out but wouldn't tell me where he'd gone... nothing. Just said he was better out of it. She blames us, you know?"

"I'm fully aware. Silly bitch," said Arnie. "She thinks I'm the biggest offender, too. Apparently it was my fault he decided to do what he did, as if he didn't have a mind of his own. Had a right go at me when I went round to see him after he came out of hospital. Batted me around the ear, she did."

"Yeah, well, she told me he'd made a 'grown-up decision'," continued Fancy. "That was exactly how she put it. He'd been given a second chance, she said, and he was determined to make it work, and that meant leaving the gang behind. She even had the cheek to tell me never to call at the flat again."

"These old folk eh? No fucking manners. Does she think she owns the estate? I knew some old lags like that in prison. They learnt soon enough they couldn't boss me about. Anyway, he wasn't in the gang, not really. Lord knows, I tried to get him involved, but he always had loftier ideas. A pity."

"Hey, those old lags – bet you taught them a proper lesson, Doles," chipped in a late arrival.

"Aaaaaaaah!" said Arnie, smiling. "Tigger, you little prick. How are you?"

The drug dealer pulled a chair up to the table. The tattoo was clearer to Arnie now: a swastika which leaked out of his forearm.

"I'm good... and it's great to see you, boss."

"That new art work on your arm? Nice touch," said Arnie. "Mind you, don't get yourself sent down any time soon. In Wandsworth you would be pinned down and they would saw off that arm with a rusty scalpel. When they had it in for you, you were toast. Mind you, I had a few top boys looking after my interests. If they attempted to take one of us out, we would take two of them. It was pretty bad and, of course, they targeted me when I was the new guy, but I blinded this big fucker in one eye – bit off his ear, too – and they left me alone after that."

"Nice work," said the tattooed newcomer.

"Thinkin' about it, what happened to you when that trouble kicked off?" said Arnie, switching on the Dolan stare. "Didn't see you for dust and don't remember you being in here afterwards. Brave old Mitchell Tiggs eh? Everywhere the trouble isn't." Without warning he leapt to his feet, smashed his glass on the side of the table, grabbed a shard and with his other arm pulled the man called Tigger across the table by his red braces. Slamming the jagged edge into the tattooed forearm, he brought a howl from his victim. "Going to say sorry, are you, Tigger?" he demanded, looking him in the eye.

"Aaaaagh, s... sorry Doles. Really I am. If I could have done your time..."

"You're a big, brain-dead wuss, that's what you are Tigger," said Arnie, flinging him back into his seat. "In fact, I wouldn't put it past you to have grassed me up. You do that, Tigger? You the rat? You looks like a rat. One minute I was in here celebrating a result, next thing I'm being dragged out of me pit at 6am in the morning by the fuckin' Sweeney, wearing just me keks."

Tigger was now exaggeratedly shaking his head from side to side. He knew once Arnie Dolan had an idea in his head it was difficult to shake him out of it.

"Hey, hey," intervened Vickers. "Tigger's straight, Doles. Honest. I'm sure of it. He was with me when it all started. They gave us both a kickin'."

"So?" said Arnie. "You telling me the Old Bill didn't pick him up afterwards? Grill him and show him some pictures? You can't, can you? Like me, you don't know where he was that evening."

"It ain't Tigger's style boss."

Arnie waved him away. "His style? He ain't got no style. He's a fuckin' drug dealer. Not only that but he 'samples' his own product. Look, he's high as a fucking kite even now. How am I supposed to trust someone like that." He cast his eyes around the table. "I'm gonna look into this anyway, because one of you bastards did for me ... and, when I find out who, they're gonna wish they'd stuck their lips together with superglue."

33

WHEN Gareth turned up for work on Saturday morning Jacko was charging around the newsroom ranting like a banshee. It was the first time he had seen his boss lose his cool. Normally the veteran sports journalist took everything in his stride, the stereotypical laid-back Welshman. Something had happened to sorely test his patience.

His ire was directed at two men dressed casually in jeans and Welsh rugby jerseys who were looking anywhere but in his direction. They shrugged their shoulders, cast helpless glances at each other, shrugged their shoulders again then gazed forlornly at a television monitor hanging above the sports desk.

"Can you believe it?" Jacko demanded. "One of the biggest days of the year for this bloody newspaper and look!" He pointed at the screen. A sign glowed ominously from it. *'You do not have access to this channel. Please contact your satellite administrator for more information'.*

"It looks like we haven't got anywhere to watch the game," said Jacko, lowering his voice to a level where he intended for just Gareth to hear. "I don't know what we can do at this late stage. I've asked these boys to fix it, but they're about as useful as a chocolate teapot." Despite his attempt at subterfuge he earned a dark look from one of the men, who boasted a comb-over of Bobby Charlton proportions and wore his rugby jersey tight across a substantial beer gut. "It's typical of this place, I tell you boy! Sounds like someone cancelled our bloody subscription. Who in their right mind..?"

"That would be the MD," chimed in comb-over. "Said we were spending too much money and wanted to cut back a bit. His reasoning was that the rugby was on terrestrial channels anyway."

"All the rugby bar this warm-up game," pointed out Jacko. "Christ, you couldn't make it up. Here we are, supposed to be the biggest regional Sunday newspaper in the country, and we can't afford a few bob for the meter. Since when did the MD know the ins and outs of TV sport scheduling anyway? He doesn't brush his teeth without first taking advice from elsewhere. Does he realise what we do here? Mental, it is. I mean, for heaven's sake, he doesn't give us a budget to go out and cover these games ourselves then cuts off our only access to them."

Gareth was impressed. The rant was in the realms of something he might come up with on one of his better days. "Well... is there anything you can do?" asked Jacko, fixing the men with an icy glare. Comb-over was in Don't-shoot-the-messenger mode, feeling seriously put out by Jacko's verbal assault which he figured was directed at the entire IT department. Gareth thought the other IT rep might be dumb, until he chimed in: "Only with the MD's say so I'm afraid – and he's on holiday."

Unhelpful. Gareth had experience of IT departments in the past and once suggested to one of their number that the nickname stood for Ignorant Twats. The next time his computer broke down his plethora of messages went straight to answer phone, his calls never returned.

"What's all the fuss?" inquired a female voice. Lana Desmund came striding across the office.

"Ah, man, it's the rugby, Lana," said Jacko. "Looks like we won't be able to watch it – some wally has ended our satellite subscription without telling anyone and the big game starts in a couple of hours."

"Oh, I see," she said. "Hmm. That is a problem."

Looking at her, comprehension flickered across Jacko's face. "Oh, I don't believe it! You knew about this, didn't you? Bloody hell! I would have thought the bloody editor would be on our side."

"Jacko!" she stormed. "Can I have a word? My office... now!"

Moaning to himself the sports editor set off in her wake.

"She's gonna have his guts for garters, butt!" chimed in a voice from behind Gareth. The phrase tugged at one of Gareth's deepest childhood memories and for a second he was transported back to his teen days as plain Gary Marshall. He turned to find The Legend, resplendent in his blue blazer, coffee in one hand and notepad in the other. "What's the problem?"

"Oh," said Gareth, his mind returning to the present. "Some clever clogs decided to cancel the satellite subscription."

"Bummer! Still, it's not like we haven't got alternatives, is it?"

"Oh?"

"Yeah, they're setting up a special screening at The Leek. It's a great little pub. We can watch it there."

Gareth considered The Legend's proposal. The plan was inviting disaster. Still, what alternative did they have? "OK," he said. "When Jacko comes back I'll suggest it."

The phone rang on the sports desk and Gareth answered.

"Who is that?" said a crackly voice down the line. "It's not Jacko is it? Hang on, it's the new chappie – our very own Prince of Wales. Am I right?"

"Hi Quinten, how are you?" asked Gareth. "There's a bit of a delay on the line. Is Dubai treating you OK?"

"Dear boy, it's sweltering out here don't you know," replied the feature writer. "It must be 100 degrees. I can't quite see how this will be good preparation for September in rain-saturated Wales, but I'm hardly complaining. Gives me a chance to top up the old tan. Marvellous. I was hoping to speak to Jacko."

Gareth told him about the problem with the TV subscription and Quinten laughed. "Only on the Despatch," he said. "So what are you going to do?"

"I don't know yet," admitted Gareth. "Looks like it could be the pub."

"Ahh. Brave man, brave man."

"Yeah, Quinten, thanks for the moral support," said Gareth. "Enjoy the holiday... I'll let Jacko know you rang."

"Cheeky beggar... holiday? I'll have you know..." The feature writer didn't finish the statement. With a couple of beeps and whistles the line went dead.

THE LEEK was some way out of the city centre so Gareth, Jason and The Legend jumped into a taxi. By a strange quirk of fate the squat Asian dressed in a red Welsh rugby shirt was the same cab driver who had promised to get The Legend home safely on Gareth's first night out in Cardiff.

"Ah Mr Legend, good to see you," he said. "I wondered what had happened to you. You were in my cab and then disappeared into thin air. Off to see the game is it? It's going to be a good one. I fancy our chances against the Argentinians, even though they have a strong pack and a great team spirit."

Gareth couldn't help wondering if everyone in Wales was a rugby expert, even those born nearer Madras than Merthyr.

"So where are we going?" asked the driver.

"Ah, we're off to the Leek, mun, Ravi," chimed in The Legend.

"Oh, good stuff. It'll be heaving, mind. Bet the atmosphere is bril-lliiiaant! So, you all work on the paper? Why aren't you out there? I would have thought you blokes would have front row seats – catching the rays in the Middle East."

"Someone has to stay at mission control," explained Gareth, look-ing out of the window and daydreaming for a moment about what it might be like if his false Facebook life actually came true. Certainly the weather would be better.

The car splashed and swerved at speed through the backstreets. The sky was a gloomy grey, the hidden sun being filtered through a gauze of ominous, dark clouds. Passing through the city centre Gareth became aware of how many people were out and about. There was a steady stream of humanity pouring down towards a central pool where they were gathering in one giant puddle of Welshness. They all wore some form of red – shirts, scarves, beanie hats. The girls tended to be a bit more creative. There were mini-skirts, boots, home-made headwear and even colour-coordinated bras on display. One group in particular looked like they had been consumed by giant daffodils, like something out of that musical Little Shop of Horrors, their yellow painted faces poking through artificial foliage. They were laughing and joking, splashing water at each other from puddles that had formed overnight.

In the hub of the city, Gareth was astonished to see orderly lines of fans queuing patiently outside pubs. He checked his watch. It was barely 11.30. For a moment he imagined valleys' job centres might have looked similar when the pits closed down, then gave himself a mental slap on the wrist for stereotyping. There was no doubting, though, this was one of those special days when the Welsh could freely indulge their two favourite pastimes – rugby and drinking. He guessed they went hand in hand, like pie and mash on the Old Kent Road.

The taxi turned right at a roundabout then sharp left until, with a screech of brakes, it pulled up outside a pub with a giant vegetable hanging outside. The Leek. Mounted on a metal pole on the pavement was an inflatable sheep, a message taped to it. "Enjoy a pre-World Cup breakfast and watch Wales devour the Argentinians in style," it said. An arrow was pointing to a rear door.

Paying the taxi driver and following directions they arrived at a set of double doors patrolled by two bouncers resplendent in full dinner jackets and bow-ties. Gareth needed a double take. "Hi Dad!" said Jason as he approached one of the bouncers and gave him a high five.

"All right lads, come on in," said Will Shakespeare. As Jason stepped aside his father came face to face with The Legend. "Well, well, as I live and breathe... JW Owens!"

He put his arms out and the ex-rugby player moved in for a man-hug. The two old friends stood like that for a while. "Christ, Will the Drive... the great Shakes!" said The Legend, finally pulling away. "Fantastic to see you again. This is your boy?"

"That it is," said Will, shaking The Legend's hand again. "He has told me you've been very good to him this week... it's been an absolute joy for him."

"Hey, the pleasure's all mine butt," said The Legend. "He's a good lad, Jason, bet he's pretty good at rugby too. He's got the build."

"Oh aye, he's getting better. Look, you'll have to come to Pontyprenis and watch him some time. You can be my guest. Anyway, welcome to The Leek. Go in and find yourselves a seat. Jason rang ahead so I've reserved you a table right near the big screen."

As Gareth went to follow them in, an arm shot out. "Sorry, not you, son," said the other bouncer, extending a firm hand like a cop halting traffic.

"I'm sorry?"

"Yewer, bloody English!" he shouted before collapsing in laughter.

"Oh, ha ha," said Gareth.

"Sorry about that, Gar," said Will. "No hard feelings but it was hard to resist a little joke. Set Vince up for it... should have seen your face ... in you go, mate."

34

JANE VICKERS stood at the kitchen sink of her three-bedroomed former council house and stared out of the window at the small patch of overgrown lawn which dropped hints at a normal family life. There was a kids' paddling pool, left out from the day before, a skateboard lying on its side with one wheel missing and a variety of footballs at various stages of inflation. None of the things were registering, though, and it was only when next door's tabby came into view through the hole in the garden fence that she shook herself back to reality, tapped the window and made angry, arm-waving gestures in a vain effort to prevent it using her precious flowerbeds as an open-all-hours feline toilet. Looking up with a dismissive air, its vacant stare reminding her of the root cause of her melancholy.

Scraping the remnants of her young daughter's breakfast into the recycling bin – boiled eggs and toasted soldiers – she was struck by the poignancy of the act. She felt as brittle as an egg this morning. Though she showed her husband Pete and two children Diane and Simon a tough shell on the outside, she knew she wasn't far from cracking. From the moment she had woken at 6am to Pete's relentless snoring, just about everything had contributed to her irritable mood.

Mind lost in reflection again, the sleeve of her dressing gown flicked a drinking glass from the draining board and it smashed at her feet on the floor. Cursing, she bent down to fetch the dustpan from the cupboard underneath the sink, only to be attacked by cleaning products stored there higgledy piggledy. Sinking to the floor, she felt tears coming but knew he couldn't see her in such a vulnerable state.

It wasn't Pete she was concerned about, but his mate, Arnie Dolan, sleeping on the sofa in the next room though probably awake now thanks to the sound of shattering glass. She still projected her anger onto her husband, though, because it was easier and, let's face it, it was his bloody fault. For all his caring ways and willingness to take on the responsibilities of a husband and father, for all his cheerful morning greetings and faultless generosity, Pete had a blind spot when it came to his old pal and, not to put too fine a point on it, boss. She tried to object when he said good old Doles would be staying "just until he got himself straight" but it was one subject on which he was immoveable.

He made it out as if his relationship with Arnie was a two-way thing and that there was an unbreakable cord between them, but she suspected her husband's loyalty was based purely on fear. What he had failed to put into the equation when he had offered their hospitality so freely was how the house guest's arrival impacted on her personally.

The two men had arrived back from the "Welcome Home" party in the early hours of the morning, Pete reeking of booze as he clambered into bed next to her, while she had yet to encounter the new arrival. The anticipation chilled her, because at some stage they would see each other and she was curious about what he would be like after all this time. The worst thing was their reunion was likely to happen this morning while Pete, shaking off his hangover, was taking three-year-old Diana to pre-school before doing the weekly shop. His itinerary was as predictable as the ticking of the damned kitchen clock and she cursed him for not sensing her unease. A more receptive husband would have latched onto her inner thoughts and broken the mould just this once, perhaps suggesting she do the chores while he played host to his friend. Was a little diversity too much to ask?

She suspected the truth was more simple than that, though, guessing that Pete would grasp any chance to put distance between himself and Arnie to escape his bullying for a couple of hours. He had no qualms about leaving his wife in the firing line, though. Bastard. As she swept up the broken glass and stood to deposit it in the bin the familiar earthy voice tore through her flimsy defences.

"Hello Janie."

She shuddered, nervously brushing a strand of dyed blonde hair behind her ear and subconsciously straightening her dressing gown. She could feel the silk of the nightie beneath it holding tight to her natural curves. She had never possessed a model's figure, and having two kids had hardly helped in the constant battle with her weight. The men in her life didn't seem to mind though. Pete always said it was nice to have something to get hold of, and described her as a real woman. She shouldn't really care what Arnie thought, but felt vulnerable and exposed and inwardly cussed herself for not having dressed sooner. Reluctantly she turned to face him.

"Arnie," she said evenly, tasting his name on her lips for the first time in an age.

"You're looking good, doll. Very bleedin' good." He advanced into the room, his arms wide as if giving a group hug to the claustrophobic surroundings. "You and Pete got hitched then? Got yourself a nice little family life together, kids, the whole kit and caboodle. I'm very pleased for you. Genuinely. Sorry I couldn't make the wedding and all that, but, well, you know..."

She felt uneasy and tried to pull back, but he was encroaching on her personal space like a spider advancing down its web on a captured fly, or an expert boxer narrowing the angles in the ring on a vulnerable opponent trapped on the ropes. She felt the cold metal of the draining board beneath her wrinkled, dishwater-worn hands, becoming conscious of her age and the time that had passed since she'd last seen him. She went to put the offending hands into her dressing gown pockets but he grasped them and held her arms out wide, taking in her entire being with those blue, piercing eyes. She wanted to resist but felt her limbs had been constructed from putty and might break away if she tried.

He'd always been a good-looking bastard, but there was a harder edge to the pretty-boy features he once possessed. There was still some strange charisma there, though, and her mind flashed for a moment to the evil wizard Voldemort in the Harry Potter books she had bought second hand for her seven-year-old son, only to find herself captivated by them herself. The undeniable power of his dimpled smile, the firm line of his jaw and the light brown hair that drifted like a gentle wave across his forehead – they all drew her to him as if a spell had been cast. She sensed there was something missing, though, from the Arnie she had known, a sliver of humanity that existed before he was put inside.

Her eyes focused on his face and she noticed the new scar, the one that spelt danger, jaggedly exiting his thin, understated eyebrows and heading towards the deeper grooves of his ridged forehead. Picking up on her interest, he sneered: "You should see the other bloke." Coming from someone else it might have drawn a chuckle, but in her mind's eye she dreamt up the image of a man with terrible injuries and knew somehow Arnie meant every word. God this man, this deceitful, hateful, arrogant man. Once she had thought she loved him, and had lusted after him for most of her teen years.

"I was hoping you might have saved this for me doll," he said accusingly, and before she could mount any kind of defence she felt something cold run up from her belly to her cleavage. She grabbed for the dressing gown belt to repair his handiwork but pieces of material fell to the floor and it was only when her eyes followed them that she saw the knife in his hand, the large one that Pete used to carve up the Sunday roast and had only recently sharpened. How had she not seen him take it from the draining board?

Swallowing her fear she edged away from him defiantly, a surge of resistance building up. "Oh come on!" she protested. "I was never your first choice, Arnie, and you know it. There were plenty of birds who came higher up the pecking order than me. I was just your bit on the side, your last resort if one of the others failed to show."

He moved quickly again, grasping her by the arm and pinching her skin as he lifted her onto her toes. She knew instantly it was going to create a bruise and tried to pull away again as electric messages sparked across the nerves in her belly.

"Don't!" she implored, seeing the bulge in his boxers and doubting she was strong enough to repel him. His warm breath tickled her neck as he spoke into her ear through gritted teeth. "Hey girl, I always fucking came back to you. You know that. Yeah, there were others, course there were. A man has his needs and some girls just put it out there, like an all-you-can-eat fucking buffet, but you and me had something special didn't we? We were great together. I can remember the first time, on that pile of coats, at that party. Whose was it? Oh that's right, Gary's. I walked in on you..."

As he spoke her mind was already flashing back. Gary's 16th birthday party. When the clock had ticked past 11 she set about retrieving her coat, a blue puffer jacket, from the main bedroom, having no wish to upset her dad. She wasn't aware quite when she had sensed his presence behind her. Suddenly his arms had locked around her, tight, pinning her to his body, as rigid and unyielding as a brick wall. He had whispered something about fancying the pants off her and she had then felt his lips paint circles over the hot spot on her neck. He stank of booze, cigars and something distinctly Arnie and as he lent his full man-child body forward, her legs buckled. His hands had moved fast, stiff fingers probing harshly while with his other hand he had turned her over, kissed her fiercely, the two of them wrapped in a straitjacket of abandoned coats.

At first she tried to pull away, but when his tongue broke through the barrier of her lips she felt she had no alternative than to go with it, share the experience. Perhaps this was what she had asked for, though for a long time afterwards she did wonder whether what he had done was legal. She was young, though, and had put the signals out so genuinely felt that if anyone was to blame it was her. The pain had been excruciating at the time but her girlfriends had told her it got better after your first time so she bit her lip and put up with it. When it was over, he looked down at her and smiled. Then, without a word being exchanged, he got up, pulled up his zip and walked out of the door, leaving her lying there wondering exactly what had happened. She had stayed for a while, remaining in that position, until the door had swung open and Gary's dad had appeared. Obviously stunned by what he had unwittingly stumbled across he had backed out apologetically and after that she had hurriedly straightened her clothes and run downstairs, feeling as if every eye was watching her knowingly.

"I fucking remember all right... bastard!" she shouted now, once again attempting to place a fist on him, aiming for his muscular chest, enveloped in a skin-tight T-shirt. Before she made contact, though, he grabbed it and his lips collided with hers. She felt her teeth rattle, before his tongue went so deep it was as if he intended licking every ounce of self-respect from her. Almost as soon as it had started, he pulled his mouth away again, then twisted her around. She cursed under her breath as his arms enveloped her and his fingers pinched her nipples. "No!" she shouted, trying to find some leverage to pull away. The punch to the kidneys ended her meagre resistance.

It was over in barely a minute, and she looked at herself in the reflection of the kitchen window. What a mess. Hair dishevelled, mascara smeared, one breast exposed to the unwelcoming grey gaze of the outside world. In the blink of an eye on an ordinary Monday morning her whole resolve had crumbled, like a smoker turning back to the fags after a long period of abstinence. Again here she was: the easy lay, the slag, the slapper. However much you tried to change, some things stayed the same.

Tears sprang from the corner of her eyes as she watched the reflection of his retreating back. "See ya later, Janie," he said cheerfully as he went. "What you givin' Pete for tea? He don't like sloppy seconds."

Just then, the doorbell went.

"YOU'RE NOT dressed yet? I thought we had a date." Anjelica Dolan stood on the doorstep, hands on hips.

"Sorry, love, just got held up. You know. Routine things. Getting Pete and Di out the house, doing the washing..."

"Yeah, I know babe. Probably spoiling my brother, too, I wouldn't doubt."

Janie hoped the shocking jolt she felt from the question hadn't found its way to her face. She disguised it behind a smile. "Oh, er, no, not really, no. Haven't seen him this morning, to be honest."

"Not surprised," Anjelica Dolan said with a chuckle, switching little Max from one arm to the other. "He's been making up for lost time. Probably been out reintroducing himself to his harem and partying like it's 1999 all over again."

"Oh yeah." The voice came from behind Janie. She twisted, dropping the tea towel from her hands. Arnie stood there, wiping his hair as if he had taken a shower, though Janie knew he couldn't have done so that quickly. "I must say the Vickers family have shown me wonderful hospitality, Anjie babe. Janie here has been catering for my every need." He winked at her as she got up from retrieving the towel. "You girls off out on the town then?"

"Come if you like," Anjie said. "It will really cheer you up, having your nails done and lying on a sunbed." She laughed.

"Nah, you're all right. Things to do, people to see." He retreated back into the darkness of the hall.

"Come on in, Anj," said Janie, not wanting to be left alone with him again. "I'll just get ready. Freshen up the make up and throw on a few clothes, won't be long."

For the first time Anjie saw the red marks around her friend's eyes. "You OK, hon? You look like you been crying."

"Eh?" Janie turned away. For a fleeting moment she felt like owning up, telling the sister who was so dedicated to Arnie Dolan: "Your wonderful brother's just raped me in the kitchen". It was easier to lie, though. After all, who would Anj believe, the brother she doted on or her drama-queen best friend?

"Nah. Peeled a few onions for our tea. Everything is hunky dory."

"In that case, hurry up. We've got an appointment for 12.15 at that new American nail bar. They do all sorts – stars and stripes, Nike swoosh logos, you name it. Should be a right laugh."

THE TWO YOUNG mums were strolling through the concrete labyrinth of Westfield Shopping Mall at Stratford when Janie spotted a familiar face. "Hey look... over there!" she said, nudging Anjie in the arm.

"What?"

"Isn't that...? It is, you know."

"I can't see anyone, just old biddies pushing trollies and..."

Janie stopped and put a hand on both sides of her friend's face, angling it in a certain direction. "There! It's Gary's mum, isn't it? Looks like it to me. Sheila Marshall. She's a good old laugh. Wonder what happened to her boy. Him and your Arnie were thick as thieves. Come to think of it, I always thought you had a bit of a soft spot for him. Let's find out where he's been hiding."

"Oh come on, Janie, we've got plenty to do, haven't we? There's no time to..."

"This won't take a minute. You didn't fall out with him did you? I've not seen him for ages, but we weren't that close. You on the other hand..."

"No," said Anjie, resigned. "No we didn't fall out, just drifted apart. He's probably got an entirely new life now. He went away with work I think..."

"I always thought you'd make a good couple. You'd like to see him again, though, for old time's sake, I bet. It's not like you been inundated with boyfriends is it?"

"No," Anjie snapped. "That's all water under the bridge. I could ask you the same about my brother."

Seeing her friend's face take on a pained expression, she immediately regretted it. "Sorry Janie, didn't mean anything by it. You're a happily married woman now, and I know he always treated you a bit rotten."

"It's nothing." Janie hoped her watering eyes wouldn't give her away. "Look, hang on, she's going. Sheila! Sheila!"

A woman with dyed black hair scraped into a ponytail on top of her head, and dressed in a leather jacket and skirt over what looked like heavy biker boots, turned and scanned the crowd. "Yoohoo!" shouted Janie, waving her hands wildly, ignoring Anjie's protests. Running across the concourse, Janie grabbed the woman in question under the armpit, leading her back to Anjie and Max.

"Told you!" said Janie. "Look, it's Sheila, good old Sheila. Great to see you Mrs Marshall, you remember Anje, don't you?"

"Um, it's Philpott now," said the woman who, close up, looked every bit of her 60-odd years, despite wearing clothes meant for people a third her age. "And yeah, of course I remember Anjelica. How are you dear?" The two women looked at each other in a strange way that indicated to Janie they knew each other better than they were letting on. What's more Max was hopping about excitedly.

"Am I missing something here?" asked Janie.

"No, no, course not," said Anjie. "Sheila just pops in to see Mum sometimes, don't you Sheil? How are you, anyway? It's great to see you again."

A lie, thought Janie. She had never seen the two mothers exchange a single word. In fact she got the distinct feeling they disliked each other. She recalled years ago there had been a chill in the air whenever the two women were in close proximity. "I've got an idea," said Janie, determined to probe a bit further. "I'm simply gagging. Let's hit the coffee shop over there and catch up, it will only take a few minutes."

Before the other women could register an objection, she was charging off in the direction of a sign advertising Coffee Empire, dragging Max along with her. "I want a drink!" he shouted excitedly.

"Exactly, Max," said Janie. "We could all do with a nice drinkie."

IT WASN'T UNTIL Janie had finished her coffee and a couple of indulgent cream cakes and disappeared to the toilets that the two other women threw off the shackles. "Thank God for that," said Sheila. "She doesn't half ask a lot of questions."

"You handled it well, Sheil, telling her you hadn't heard from Gar since he went out for that interview in Dubai."

"I hate telling porkies though," the older woman said. "Can I have a cuddle?"

"Look, better not," said Anjie. "We don't want her to get more suspicious than she already is, do we?"

"You heard from him, Anjie?"

"Just a couple of e-mails is all," volunteered the younger woman. "I think he's been pretty busy, what with the new job and everything."

"Yeah, yeah. You ain't told her anything, have you?" Sheila Philpott indicated towards the toilets.

"I haven't said nothing. It's difficult, mind, she's my best friend."

"They're your rules babe," Sheila pointed out, her voice rising beyond a whisper. "You and my boy decided on this. Strictly no talking. Christ, it's like I imagine it was in the bloody war, loose talk costs lives and all that. What are you so worried about? Once it's out in the open..."

"You know he's out, don't you? Came out on Friday. He's staying at hers and all."

"Really?" Sheila looked surprised. "They had a bit of a thing, didn't they?"

"Yeah, though neither will admit it. Still, she's got two kids now and is married to his best mate. Remember Pete Vickers? I can't see after eight years she and our Arnie are going to be that close."

"Hmm," said the older woman, looking doubtful. "He can be pretty persuasive that brother of yours. Aah, look at him!" Max was smiling at the sight of a small dog tugging his owner across the square. "So... talking of dogs – how is Arnold?"

"Oh, leave him, Sheil!" Anjie's raised voice attracted the attention of some of the other customers. She instantly switched back to whispering. "I know you never liked him but it wasn't all his doing you know? Your son was thick as thieves with him. Easily led from the front as they say..."

"True," agreed Sheila. "Mind you, a lot of skeletons in the cupboard now. I'd hate any of them to get loose for all our... Christ sakes is that the time! I got to go get Reg his lunch. Take care, both of you." She leant over and kissed Max on the top of his head, then picked up her shopping bags, pushed away from the table and hobbled for the exit in her heavy boots.

"What skeletons?" asked Janie.

Anjie wondered how long her friend had been standing there. "Oh, nothing. We were just discussing Hallowe'en," she replied.

"Right," said Janie, "a bloody event that don't take place for another month or so. Why do I feel like I'm being treated like a bloody mushroom? Kept in the dark and fed a load of old horse shit."

35

THE LEEK resembled a giant Christmas grotto, but instead of a jolly, smiling Santa there was a life-sized cardboard cut-out of the Welsh rugby coach, a dour-looking Kiwi called Martin Misry, just inside the entrance. He held a scarf above his head with the words: "Come to Wales for a World Cup experience to remember". A couple of lads stood either side of it, like guardsmen on royal protection duty, while their mate captured the moment on his smart phone.

All manner of Welsh regalia hung from the beams – scarves, dragons and inflatable sheep, some of which had been painted red. The hubbub of noise was overpowering, as loud as a city centre pub anywhere in Britain on a Saturday night, the queue for the bar five deep though the clock had only just passed 12.

"Over here Gar!" The reporter saw Jason waving to him from a table just in front of the big screen. "No need to bother with the bar, I've got you a pint, man."

Gareth pushed his way through the crowd and sat down. "Listen, Jason," he whispered through gritted teeth. "It's all well and good getting the beers in, but we're not fans enjoying an afternoon on the lash. We've got a job of work to do here. We can't act as if it's a jolly boys outing." He nodded in the direction of The Legend. "The last thing we need is to give him ideas as well. You know what he's like."

The youngster adopted his sulking puppy look. Gareth couldn't fault his willingness to please but still found it irritating. "I just thought you would want to fit in boss," said Jason, "get the sense of a real Welsh atmosphere. Feel part of it all... sorry." He took a sip from a pint which looked suspiciously like Skull Attack.

"Do us a favour, Jase," said Gareth. "Go and rescue JW would you? Bring him back here. After all, he's the reason we're here in the first place. The match can't be far from kick-off." The workie trotted off and emerged a minute later, his arm draped around The Legend. Pointing at the screen, Jason said: "Here they come, boys, look at them! That's a team, all right. The perfect blend of youth and experience. Better than your lot." He waved a taunting finger in Gareth's direction.

"My lot?" Gareth felt irked by the teenager's new-found confidence. "Don't know who you're on about. West Ham?"

"You're English, aren't you?"

"Oh sure," agreed Gareth, "but I've as much in common with those bleedin' public schoolboy hooray henrys as I have with the flippin' Welsh."

"Whatever... I'm telling you, you've had your chips," said Jase, warming to his theme. "If we meet you in the World Cup semis I reckon there can be only one winner. God, did you see your team of old has-beens the other day?"

Those around them were belting out the Welsh national anthem. On the screen rugged men in red shirts were mouthing the words with gusto... "Gwlad, glwad..." In the stands at the ground, too, the camera panned across a large contingent of fans standing and singing. Gareth, though, was smarting at what he perceived to be an unwarranted attack.

"So it comes to a game of rugby over here and it's suddenly 'pick on the English' day," he said. "Well, fuck you very much. Anyway, remind me how many World Cups Wales have won? Oh, is that a big fat zero? I seem to recall England have at least managed one."

Jason fell silent for a moment. "Yeah, well, that was the worst World Cup ever," he retorted eventually. "Everyone agrees on that."

"Everyone over here, you mean. And, anyway, how many finals have Wales reached? How many near misses? I seem to recall England have been in three."

Huge hands suddenly grasped Gareth under the armpits, lifting him up and swinging him around. For the third time in just over a week he came face to face with Cinderblock. "Oi you patronising English wanker!" Beer-infused phlegm rinsed Gareth's face. "If you want to watch your beloved England why don't you fuck off back over the bridge? Here, I'll lend you the money. Hey, don't I recognise you from somewhere?"

Before the situation escalated, two mighty arms came between them and pushed them apart. Cinderblock looked momentarily shocked. "Hey!"

"All right, Matt, butt?"

"Oh, it's you, Jase. Saw your dad on the door. You OK?"

"Yeah, sound. What seems to be the trouble?"

"This little Saes is having a pop..."

"Mate, it was banter. I was winding him up to be fair. He's a pal of mine. Moved in with us, actually."

"Well, keep him out of my way. Bloke's got a death wish if you ask me."

"Forget it man. Enjoy the match. They're about to kick off. Come on Wales!" Jason put his arm around Cinderblock and they began to chant loudly as a wave of noise rolled around the pub. "Wales! Wales!"

Regaining his seat, Gareth gratefully watched Cinderblock disappear to join some of his mates in another area of the pub. "Sorry boss," said Jason, sitting down. "It was my fault. I got carried away with the occasion."

"No harm done," said Gareth, using a finger to loosen his neck from his shirt. The atmosphere felt claustrophobic. He wasn't keen on enclosed spaces and big crowds, a side effect of the incident.

He looked around and a feeling of dread consumed him. "Hey, where's The Legend?"

"GREAT TO SEE you out. What brings you here anyway? You're normally working on match day." The man with the grizzled face wore a badly fitting toupee that closely resembled a bird's nest. While he thought it made him look younger he failed to notice others around him were admiring it purely for its comedy value.

"Ah, TV doesn't work in the office apparently, Willie Ap," replied JW Owens. "That's why they brought me down here. Look, it's great to see you and all but I should be getting back."

"Hey, not so hasty, JW, we haven't been out together for the rugby in, what, must be nearly a year. It can't hurt to have a few pints with your buddies, can it? If you are worried about them newspaper people we can sneak out to the Feathers down the road. I'm meeting Archie, Iwan and Hector there. It'll be like old times. What do you say?"

The Legend knew in his heart that it was a mistake but he'd been feeling melancholy of late. Martin's birthday had been around this time of year and he always dreamed about spending match day in the pub with his boy. A couple of drinks and the company of his good friends was probably just the tonic he needed. "OK, I'll just tell..."

"Better not," said Willie Ap, grabbing his arm and straightening the bird's nest with his other hand. "Can't fight your way through that lot, there'll be trouble. Look, the door's only here. I'll make sure you get back in plenty of time. You can explain to the paper boys you got split up from them by the crowd. They're not going to miss you for half an hour, not with all these people around."

The Legend shrugged. "Guess not, Willie Ap. Anyway, you're a good pal. I can bank on you to do right by me."

The two mates threw their arms around each other and pushed their way towards the exit.

"THIS IS A disaster!" said Gareth, "Jacko's going to kill me!"

"Don't panic, man," said Jason. "Let's go and see my dad – he might have seen him."

As they pushed their way through the crowd there were complaints of "Watch it" and "That's my foot butt" before one huge groan took over. Gareth turned to see a big Argentinian forward diving over the line having shrugged off two Welsh tacklers. Five minutes gone and Wales were 5-0 down. He felt like laughing out loud, going to find his nemesis and shouting "In your face" at him. His temper was rising but he needed to bring it under control and think things through logically. The Legend had been with them a few minutes ago. He couldn't have gone far.

A search of the pub, the toilets and questions to the bouncers and bar staff yielded nothing and by half time they had given up hope. "He just can't be here," he said to Jason, rubbing his leg which was now giving him serious grief, as it did in times of stress.

"Well, it's a big pub and it's packed," the workie responded. "I'm sure he'll turn up. Look, we'd better watch the rest of the match hadn't we? Just in case..."

"Yeah, you're right. Someone has to know what the bloody hell happened."

They settled back into their seats, Gareth's mind ticking over about how he was going to explain this one away to Jacko. It would register a black mark against him, no question.

On the pitch Wales were struggling. Midway through the second half they found themselves trailing 16-10 before breaking away to score a try and conversion that enabled them to win by the tightest of margins, 17-16. A deafening rendition of *Bread of Heaven* rolled around the pub. It was an intoxicating atmosphere, even though Gareth hadn't touched a drop. Hoping to catch a glimpse of the missing Legend, he scanned the delirious fans who, high on the mixture of a win and a vast quantity of alcohol, were patting each other on the back and distributing hugs to anyone who wanted one. Below the screen Cinderblock was waving a sheep above his head and leading his boneheaded minions in a deafening chorus of "Wales, Wales, Wales". The Legend, though, was nowhere to be seen. Turning to Jason, Gareth couldn't resist a sly dig. "Anyone would think you'd beaten the All Blacks," he said. "Come on, it's time we faced the music."

"SO WHERE'S OUR star columnist?" asked Jacko as they entered the office.

"Uuuh, slight problem there," Gareth replied. "We were all right during the first half. He gave us his thoughts and I got them all down here." He raised his notebook hoping like crazy Jacko wouldn't ask to inspect it. Gareth had scrawled down some notes in the taxi back, but they wouldn't survive close scrutiny. If Jacko wanted to see them the blag was over. "Then he went off to the loo and… disappeared."

"Disappeared?" said Jacko with irritation. "What did he do, fall down the pan?"

"Boss, it was teeming in there. One minute he was at my side and the next… gone. You can't expect me to follow him to the loo as well."

"Follow him? I expect you to undo his trousers, get his todger out, hold it to the porcelain, even wipe his arse if he needs it… I told you that we had to keep him sober, mun. What bit of that didn't you understand?"

Gareth was simmering, his face red with a mixture of embarrassment and anger. Inside he was ranting, telling himself he hadn't gone through journalism school, slaved over 100 words per minute shorthand, revised long hours to bag an A in his law exam then endured the whole proficiency test fallacy just to be a nursemaid to a drunken old Welshman. He was starting to like some people on this side of the border, thought he could understand better what made them tick, but this latest experience was persuading him to return to his original diagnosis.

"OK, OK… he knows the score," Gareth argued. "I'm sure he'll turn up."

He didn't realise he had raised his voice until there was a chuckle from across the room. Evidently the sports sub-editors found his assurance amusing. He imagined they had seen it all before and felt the butterflies gather in his stomach.

"Well, I hope you watched the match," said Jacko. "We're having trouble with our link to Quinten. It may be a question of flamming both the match report, the quote pieces and The Legend's column. I've got Barri Michaels looking at the quotes, but if you could scrawl down a bit of a report, say 26 paragraphs or so, we'll make do with that." Dismissing Gareth, he strode off in the direction of the picture desk.

"Fuck!" Gareth shouted. He kicked the desk so hard with his good leg he felt the impact bounce around to his bad knee. "Jesus!"

"Hey, Gar mate, no sweat," said Jason. "I took some notes. I'll tap them out on the computer, then you can knock them into some kind of shape."

Gareth was doubtful. "How quickly do you type?"

"I wouldn't say I was the fastest," admitted the teenager. "I'm pretty good on them computer games but it's just pushing one or two buttons, you know, fire and move, fire and move..."

"Shit!" Gareth removed the bottle of painkillers from his pocket and popped one into his mouth. His wound ached and he only had himself to blame. Suddenly he had a brainwave. "Mate, go and find yourself somewhere quiet and take this." He thrust a device the size of a pocket torch into Jason's hand.

"What is it?"

"It's a dictaphone. Go to the canteen, maybe, hold this button down and speak your match report into it, then bring it back here and I'll transcribe it. It will be a lot quicker."

"OK boss, no problem." Jason took the device and headed for the exit.

THE SONG ON the jukebox summed up The Legend's mood perfectly. He was in *Strictly Come Dancing* pose, one hand holding that of his great friend Willie Ap Jones and the other nestling against his back as they dragged each other around the 60s-style illuminated dance floor. Singer Morrissey droned bleakly about being happy in an alcoholic haze.

"You're my best friend, Willie Ap," slurred The Legend to his dance partner, "you know that? You, and Archie and Hywel and ... well... I don't know what I'd do without you."

The man he was pledging undying love to was suddenly wrenched from his grasp. The Legend wobbled backwards, landing on his backside on the dance floor, his head colliding with a pillar as he fell. "Oi, wasshit!" he shouted. "Jewnohooiyam?"

"Course, I know who you are," said the bouncer. "You're a drunken nuisance: JW Owens, the old pisshead banned from every decent boozer in the city. Apparently you were famous a long time ago, but you're not now. It's time you left. Hop off." The bouncer grabbed Wales' greatest-living rugby player by the scruff of the neck, carried him to the door and ejected him onto the street. His vision blurred, he had difficulty weighing up what was so different about Cardiff today. Then he realised. It was dark. In fact, it was positively black and the streetlights were on. He didn't understand. It seemed like minutes ago that he, Geraint and Jason...

"Shit!" He suddenly had a moment of clarity. He was supposed to be writing his column for the newspaper. He patted the pockets of his jacket, decorated in dust and detritus from the dance floor, and staggered to his feet as Willie Ap came flying through the same door. "Ahhh, Ledge...." he said, opening his arms for a hug.

"Fuck that, butt." The Legend brushed him aside. "I'm supposed to be bloody working. You said you would get me back. What the hell time is it?"

Willie Ap made a strange face which translated into "how the hell should I know?" then fell to the pavement. The Legend had only one thing on his mind – getting to the Sunday Tribune Despatch offices. He ran towards an approaching taxi, flailing his arms above his head as he trod a path through his mate's vomit.

"IN THE FINAL minutes Paul Wyn Cooper headed off down the wing, switched the ball inside to Iolo Williams, who barged his way over from close in. Leigh Davies converted the try to enable Wales to snatch victory from the jaws of defeat." Jason sighed, clicked off the tape recorder and got up from the seat. He was in a toilet cubicle on the ground floor, a last resort once he found the canteen shut. He pulled the chain, opened the door and walked out. A smattering of applause greeted him. "Oh hell!" he said with embarrassment. He recognised one of the three men as chief rugby writer Barri Michaels. "Well, well, well, young workie," said Michaels. "...And who will benefit from those wise words I wonder?"

GARETH LOOKED AT his watch. Just gone 9pm: an hour to deadline and no sign of The Legend. He had done what he could as best he could. Jason, looking slightly perturbed, had handed over the dictaphone and as Gareth transcribed it he realised it only needed a tickle here and there, a word changed, a paragraph switched, and the reader could be persuaded the writer had been pitchside watching the action. When he asked the youngster if he was all right, Jason said he felt a bit sick. Gareth wondered if the three pints of Skull Attack he had downed were to blame.

"Not a bad match report, Prince," said Jacko begrudgingly. "We've managed to get a colour piece and a back page story from Quinten, and Barri's come up with the quotes. Now all we need is our 'expert' to add his expansive rugby knowledge and unquestionable gravitas to the product. Where the hell is he? Please don't make me go into the editor's office cap in hand..." He was interrupted by a loud ping and the room went silent as everyone focused on the elevator doors.

Sliding open, they revealed JW Owens in all his glory.

A man who was revered up and down the country.

A man who had a sidestep and weave in his playing days that people still spoke about in whispered tones.

The man simply known as The Legend.

In fact, he was doing a sidestep now. He stumbled out of the lift and swayed one way, then the other. Unfortunately he hadn't managed to fool the static desks in his path, crashing over one and falling headlong into another. Gareth, Jason and Jacko raced to attend his prone body. In different corners of the office, people turned to converse with their co-workers, smiles creeping across faces as they revelled in the latest calamitous fall from grace of a great rugby star.

Letting him feel the full force of his seething resentment towards The Legend at that moment, Gareth administered a slap to his right cheek so hard people physically ducked as if a cannon had gone off. "Come on, JW, hey!" he shouted. A glob of spittle dropped to the floor from the corner of The Legend's mouth. He was trying to speak! Those gathered around leaned over, desperate to hear the morsel of wisdom he was about to impart. "Notebook!" Gareth urged Jason, who reached up to a nearby desk and passed him some paper and a pen. The Legend breathed in deeply, slurred some incomprehensible words which sounded remarkably like "extra time", then collapsed to the floor in a heap.

"Look!" shouted Jason from over Gareth's shoulder. "He's got a piece of paper in his hand. That'll be his notes! He was going to scrawl them down during the game."

Gareth tried to wrestle them from him but, in the manner of an old rugby hero determined to retain possession, The Legend wouldn't relinquish them, the grip reminding Gareth of the first time he shook the old man's hand. Eventually, the vital piece of paper came free with a mighty tug. At least, half of it did. The other half remained stubbornly buried deep inside the former rugby star's fist. "Fuck!" shouted Gareth.

"Never mind," piped in Jacko, "Maybe it's only the first-half notes. We won't need them, you said you already had some."

"Don't be a dipstick," Gareth chastised his boss, unable to contain his fury. "It's split down the middle! I need the other half."

Jason leapt forward and pushed him out of the way. "I know a technique," he said. "It's from my martial arts training." He grabbed The Legend's wrist. Gareth couldn't quite see what miracle he performed but the hand suddenly fell open. Retrieving the vital piece of paper, Jason passed it to Gareth. "Here you go," he said. "Do what you can with that."

Gareth looked at it closely. "Bloody hell!" he groaned, "it's illegible. It looks like a snail's taken a walk through some ink and crawled across it. No way can I read this…"

Jason snatched it back. "No, you can't but I can... most of it's in Welsh! Let me go and..."

The lift door pinged again. "Shite!" said Jacko. "That'll be Lana. She's been out watching the game and having drinks with rugby's top brass. She'll go mental if she sees him. Help me, quick!" He started rolling the body under a nearby desk, Gareth and Jason lending a hand. "Stay here!" ordered Jacko, forcing Gareth down onto a seat, obscuring from sight the spreadeagled body under the work station.

The sports editor reached the lift just as the doors opened. "Lana!" he said, opening his arms in an extravagant gesture. "What do you make of that? Fantastic performance I think you'll agree."

The editor, dressed in a pinstripe jacket and black pencil skirt with a split in the side, wrinkled her nose. "Hello, Jacko, um, yeah not bad. It was only Argentina though. Has any of your team been ill? There's an awful smell in the lift as if, well, someone has thrown up in there."

"Thrown up? My boys? Not likely, Lana!" His tone made the suggestion sound preposterous. "They haven't touched a drop as far as I know. Take Gareth over there. Been in the pub all day but sober as a lord and, I can tell you, he's been working like nobody's business, what with our link between here and bloody Dubai crashing. Anyway, how should we handle it? Your office?"

Without waiting for a reply he set off for the far end of the room, Lana Desmund following.

"Quick!" Gareth turned to see Monica Matthews pushing a wheelchair. "Pour him in!" urged the news editor. "We've got to get him out of the office before Lana finds him. Otherwise Jacko is for the firing squad and so, my dear, are you."

Gareth jumped to his feet and Monica helped him roll The Legend from his resting place. His eyes fluttered, but he didn't wake. Lifting a deadweight wasn't easy and in the end they had to call Jason in to help. The muscle-bound teenager put his hands underneath the ex-rugby star's armpits and hoisted him into the chair. "Cheers, Jase, now crack on with his column. I'm going to try to get him home," said Gareth. "Any help you need, I'm sure Jacko can tidy it up."

Monica pressed the lift button and the doors opened. "Quickly Gareth," she urged. "And keep your head down, it looks like Jacko and Lana may have finished their chat."

He manoeuvred the wheelchair into the lift and pressed the button for the ground floor. Just as the doors closed he saw Jacko heading back towards the sports desk, Lana in hot pursuit. He wiped his sweaty brow. What the fuck was this madhouse he had joined, he asked himself as the lift descended.

36

HE WAS JUST wondering how he would get the patient through the gates of his block of flats when The Legend once again rose from the dead. "Where... where are we, butt?" he asked.

"On the way back to your place," revealed Gareth.

The Legend started fumbling in his pockets. "But... my notes. Where are my notes? I've got a column to write."

"All taken care of." Gareth felt his temper rising. The Legend had spent half the day in a drunken coma and now had the cheek to suggest he was ready for work. He had no idea of the headaches he had caused. "Jason should be typing them up as we speak. You've got a lot to thank us for. What the hell do you think you were playing at, getting into this almighty mess? I can't keep making excuses for you. Lana will dump you like a shot again if she ever finds out what's gone on."

"Ahh, you're angry, butt," said The Legend. "Fair do's. Guess I had one too many. It was just... well, I bumped into some mates. They said they would get me back in time to write my column and I guess I believed them." He looked crestfallen. "Sorry."

"Ah, what the hell," said Gareth, mellowing slightly. "I can't do anything about it if you aren't prepared to go some way to helping yourself. You've got to cut out the booze mate, seriously."

"Yeah... yeah." The taxi arrived at their destination and Gareth paid the driver before helping The Legend out of the back seat. "Shit, couldn't half do with a livener," said the ex-rugby star. "You know, just to make me feel a bit human again. I got a nasty pain in my head and can't think straight. Nothing a pint of SA wouldn't..."

"Have you listened to a word I've said?" demanded Gareth, his anger re-igniting. "For fuck's sake, drink is going to be the death of you... you hear me? It's going to bloody kill you. One day you just won't wake up. Christ – what the hell would your Ellie think if she could see you?" He pushed The Legend towards the security gate. "Now put your code in and let's get inside. We need a chat, you and I."

"What was that about Ellie?" The Legend's face registered alarm. "She isn't likely to see me is she? It's a bit pointless bringing her up. Painful, too. I thought better of you. I thought you were my mate."

Gareth realised he'd gone too far. "Yeah, OK, sorry. It's just, well, I'm trying to help you and you throw it back in my face. There has to be more give and take, specifically a bit more give on your part."

The Legend fell silent, making three attempts at entering his security code before finally landing on the right one. The gate swung open and they walked through to his flat. Once inside Gareth put the kettle on while The Legend went into the front room and lit a cigarette. He flicked on the television. The local news was updating the sport stories of the day. Gareth heard an expletive from the front room and ran in to see what the trouble was. "Well I never," said The Legend, watching the highlights of the winning Wales try. "We bloody won!"

"What?" exclaimed Gareth. "Are you trying to tell me you didn't even know the result?"

"Last thing I remember we were trailing 16-10. I'd written a piece knocking the whole team, the coach, the lot. Well, well, well… The boys said we wouldn't come back from that and that we might as well move on. After that it's all a bit of a blank."

"You see? This is what I'm talking about!" railed Gareth. "You've missed the entire crux of the story. I mean, whatever you do in this business, you can't get the bloody result wrong. It's ridiculous!" He handed The Legend his cup of tea.

"Ahh, I know butt. Look, sorry... again. I can't keep saying it. It was just... I was feeling a wee bit anxious, you know?"

"Anxious? So your answer is to sink Cardiff's entire supply of Skull Attack? Ever thought of perhaps popping a valium instead?"

"I don't do drugs," said The Legend, straight-faced. "I know I went a bit over the top, but the boys..."

"Look, fuck the boys, John, they wouldn't piss on you if you were on fire. They just like the idea of being in the company of a legend. They think it gives them kudos." He paused for thought. "You don't mind me calling you John, do you, as we're being 'friends'?"

"No, butt, course not."

"Which reminds me... what does the W stand for?"

The Legend looked perplexed for a moment.

"You know, your name. What does the W stand for?" Gareth repeated.

"Oh that!" said The Legend. "It stands for Wayne, boy."

Gareth thought about it for a minute. "Your name is John Wayne?"

"Uh huh. John Wayne Owens. My old man was a huge fan of his films." The Legend tried to pull off the film star's look and drawled: "Get off your horse and drink your milk."

"Yeah, um, I don't think he ever said that."

"No, really? Ah, I don't suppose he did, butt. Got to say you're the first person I've told about that in some time. Everyone just took to calling me JW – from a very young age in fact – makes you somehow forget your identity. I even sign autographs, cheques, you name it, with simple JW Owens. How about that? Now you know, I don't mind you calling me John Wayne, if you like. Seeing all the faces looking surprised will be a laugh."

Gareth lifted his eyes to the ceiling. "Really? Maybe. On one condition. We cut down on the sauce. It's important to me and it's important for you. I don't want to tell you this, but it's the truth and I figure you need to be given some honesty around here. Everyone treats you like this big star, but they lie to you constantly because they are only telling you things you want to hear."

The Legend looked baffled. "What do you mean, son?" he said. "Who lies?"

"Well, I know I haven't been here long but it's an impression I've got. Those supposed mates you saw the rugby with, for instance. They said they would get you back in plenty of time, didn't they?"

"Well, Willie Ap did, yeah."

"And he didn't. He could have cost you your contract and probably your whole credibility with Lana and the Trib. That's not the actions of a friend, is it? And look at the other night. You signed a book for a fan... Ian Rush's autobiography?"

"Oh yeah, I remember. Bloke was thrilled to meet me, he said. I hate to let down my fans."

"Yeah?" said Gareth. "Well guess what? I looked on EBay today and there it was. That 'fan' was selling it for £100 or nearest offer, an Ian Rush biography with your signature scratched on it. Collectors' item, I guess."

"EBay?"

"Yeah, it's a computer auction site. Surely... oh never mind. The point is he didn't want that book for himself, or a mate, or a sick brother or sister, or fawning mum or dad. He wanted it for the simple reason he could make some money out of you. Get it? And, looking around, there are an awful lot of people who would cash in the same way if they could."

"Oh, I don't think that's true," argued The Legend. "See, that's the trouble with you. You can have a go at me, but at least I can see the good in people. You're different – always finding fault with them, you are. Take that boy, the one who tried selling that book I autographed. How do you know he hasn't got a sick mum or sister or something and desperately needs cash to get them the right treatment?" Before Gareth could respond, he added: "The answer is: you don't. God, if you gave me the choice I would rather my attitude than yours."

The Legend fell silent, realising he had said enough. There was a small part of Gareth's brain which nagged away quietly at him all the time, telling him roughly the same thing. He now wished he hadn't been so blunt and wondered if it was his inner anger coming out, seizing on the opportunity to take the moral high ground and hurt a fellow human being. He'd done it before, though this didn't feel the same. He felt he had done the right thing, believing the power of truth to be the only weapon that might shock the former rugby star into adjusting his lifestyle.

Finally, The Legend broke his silence. "Hell, I never knew that," he said.

"What's that, John Wayne?"

"That you could sell things on the internet. Simple when you think about it, but who came up with the idea? The modern world's a very strange place at times." He took a sip of his tea. "Anyway, Geraint…"

"Listen John, I'll say this for the last time. It's Gareth…"

"OK, look… you have seen all there is to see of me. You have snooped on my private life and read me like an open book. But if we're to be true friends, isn't it time you told me a bit about yourself? I mean, what are you running away from?"

"Running, I'm… how..?"

"It's obvious boy. It really is. I've seen it before, even done it myself… and I can tell you, you don't want to be running all your life. You have to make a stand at some point or, well, you could end up like me… losing everything."

Gareth thought about it. What the hell? The Legend had a memory like a sieve and would probably forget the whole story by tomorrow. It might be cathartic to reveal some of himself if it helped develop the bond between them. "Well, for starters my name isn't Geraint."

"OK, I get it."

"No you don't… not really. Because it might as well be. A little while ago – about five years to be precise – I changed my name by deed poll. People where I come from call me Gary Marshall…"

37

A FAMILIAR sound broke into Gareth's dreams. For a moment he lay there, believing it part of his subconscious. I'm Forever Blowing Bubbles. The West Ham theme tune. A traditional favourite. His ringtone. Shit! He sprang upright in bed and reached for the phone on the dressing table, making a quick reconnaissance of his surroundings. Small room, boxes and bags in a corner, clothes on a chair. Curtains featuring cartoon character Fireman Sam.

Ah yes. Back in the valleys.

Chez Shakespeare.

He'd stumbled in at around 8pm the previous evening having spent the day with The Legend. They had talked into the early hours of Sunday morning, Gareth telling him all about the incident that had ruined his football career and how he was trying to place a barrier between himself and the past. The old rugby hero was sympathetic and seemed to understand his reasoning, remaining remarkably focused for someone who had been comatosed just a few hours earlier. When Gareth had imparted as much information about himself as he was comfortable with the two of them grabbed a few hours sleep, then enjoyed a fry up at a local cafe before returning to the flat to watch a couple of live sporting events on TV. Later, Gareth walked back to the bus station and took the Number 54 to Pontyprenis, being dropped off virtually at the door of his new home. After a brief conversation with Will and Jason he had cried off to bed early, desperate to catch up on sleep. Even so, it was a restless night, the dreams coming thick and fast, the leg aching, punishment for revisiting his past.

He looked at the caller ID on the phone. "Hi Mum... what time is it?" He registered a sour taste in his dry mouth, reached over and picked up the glass of water standing by the bed.

"Never mind that. He's gone! Toe-rag's gone and bloody left me. And taken my tickets with him," she announced. "Oh sorry, sweetie pie, it's your mother... I am fumin'. I guess enough people warned me about him."

"We're talking about Reg?"

"Who else, lover? Look I ain't seen you in yonks. You getting too high and mighty for your dear old mum?"

"Of course not, Mum. You know the situation."

"I know, love, but it's hard. You're all I've got. She, your sister, gallivanted off with that bloke of hers and now... well, that's the thing... you won't even tell me where you are. South Wales is as much as I know. That can't be right."

"Look, I'm sorry. When I feel things have settled down a bit we can arrange to meet up. How about that?"

"Sure, sure... I saw Anj the other day you know... and Max."

Gareth felt a twinge of longing, mixed with guilt. "Yeah?"

"He's getting very big... looks..." Her voice trailed off as her mind wandered.

"OK, Mum," the voice came out haltingly. "What was the purpose of the call again?"

"Listen to him," said the woman, her pure East London accent suddenly taking command of her telephone voice. "Think he'd be glad to hear from his old mum but, oh no, has to be a reason for the call... Here I am, stuck all alone on this bloody housing estate in the middle of a ghetto and you're deserting me. First it was your sister, now you. What on earth did I ever do to deserve this?"

The one thing Gareth could guarantee about his mother – and he loved her dearly – was that she would repeat everything, over and over, but rarely completed a sentence before another idea took hold. "Look, it's not about you, mum, honestly," he argued. "It's about me, my career and, well..."

"Oh, your bloody career, is it? Well, let's face it, there wouldn't be a career if it wasn't for me! Then, once I've served my purpose you go swanning off, leaving your dear old mum suffering from a broken heart." He thought he heard a sob, then a noise which sounded like someone blowing into a tissue.

"Please don't cry, mum."

"Oh don't you worry. I wouldn't cry over you. I just got a bit of hay fever. That Tommy Scrivens would never have deserted his mother like this. He's a good boy."

"He's in jail for armed robbery, Mum."

"Yeah, but at least she knows he is only at the Scrubs and she can visit him when she wants."

"He was arrested trying to flee the country for the Costas."

"He would have sent for her, I'm sure."

The tit-for-tat could have gone on forever. "OK, Mum, you've laid the guilt trip on me. Fine. Now what's this about Reg?"

"That no good..." she stormed. "It was the drink again. Bugger was supposed to be back... I did his favourite pie and mash – but he didn't drag his sorry arse in here till 9. Playing pool, apparently... then claims there was a riot. I mean... round here?"

"Mum, you haven't seen the news?" Gareth protested. "They've been rioting everywhere in London again. Christ, it's been a war zone since that kid got shot by police. Turn on the telly and you'll see what I mean. A foreign student had his jaw broken, mugged in broad daylight and his Xbox stolen by yobs pretending to help him. And that was just around the corner from you... It's all on YouTube..."

"YouTube, shmutube... He was bloody lying!" she insisted. "Could hardly stand, let alone hit a ball with a stick or rob a store and carry a telly. The only riot going on was when he got back here. He thought it was a big joke. Well, I lost it, didn't I? Threw his ruined dinner straight at him, best casserole dish 'n all. Broke it too, the swine!" As if it was Reg who was responsible for the damage. "He ducked and it ended up plastered on the kitchen wall. Well, I went for him, I did – you know what I'm like – and he bloody well held them up, didn't he? My Quo tickets. Right in front of me face. He was shouting, 'one more step and they gets it!' I don't know what Rick would have thought..."

Gareth nodded to himself. His mother had been obsessed with the rock band Status Quo since before he was born. Every year she saw them perform at their annual Christmas concert in the East End. The world might have moved on rapidly from the days when they graced Top of the Pops, but to Sheila Philpott it was like a comfort blanket – as long as there was the Quo everything was right with the world. The Rick to whom she referred was guitarist Rick Parfitt, whose framed photograph still took pride of place on her lounge wall. He was right up there with the Queen and the Royal family in her personal pecking order of those meriting the utmost respect. He doubted, though, Rick would spend too many nights worrying about the whereabouts of Sheila Philpott's Christmas concert tickets.

While Gareth was reflecting on the situation, his mother was still talking. "...Then he backed away, down the hall and out the door – probably to his fancy woman."

"Oh come on, Mum! Fancy woman? Reg isn't like that. He might be a bit of a bloke's bloke but he's not a womaniser, not like da…"

His sentence came to an abrupt halt and he cursed under his breath. He had come perilously close to committing one of the cardinal sins in the world according to Sheila Philpott. It was fine for her to mention his father but if either of her children did there was big trouble. "Anyway," Gareth hurried on, attempting to cover up the momentary lapse. "...He'll be back, Reg. You know he will … and he'll bring your Quo tickets with him, I'm sure. After all, his stuff's there."

His mother snorted.

"Oh Mum, you haven't…"

"In the dumpster out the back… Rubbish deserves rubbish, darlin'… Oh, and talking of rubbish, Anjie told me that no good brother of hers is out… Your 'best' mate. Shame really. Can't you sort it out with him? I know it's partly my fault. I thought he was a bad influence and gave him a piece of my mind after your accident, but, well, I'm sure we could get past that. Things are different now. He's probably learned his lesson."

"Mum, I told you and so did Anjie. Arnie won't understand. Anyway, there's a bit more to it than that..."

"I know but I'd love to see more of him."

For a moment Gareth thought she was talking about Arnie. Then his brain made sense of the mish-mash of broken threads. "Yeah, Mum, I know... so would I."

REG PHILPOTT SAT at the bar of The Hope and Anchor staring into his pint of London Pride. Sheila had always been a no-nonsense girl, a bit of a tough cookie, and he guessed her unforgiving nature was a by-product of her failed first marriage. If it was possible, she seemed to have become even feistier since the kids left: Lily now north of the border with her Scottish husband and Gary... well, who knew? Not him, that's for certain. Business in that family was conducted on a need-to-know basis and there was rarely anything Reg needed to know.

It was unfair. Had he not rescued Sheila when that scumbag left, picked her up and put all the pieces back together? She would take any amount of grief from those kids and Gary, in particular, had got away with murder over the years, almost literally. Reg was the one who got it in the neck. He had taken on a lot, too, more than most blokes. He'd always had a soft spot for Sheila. He'd known her bloke for what he was and felt sorry for her, though he suspected deep down she had always been aware of Stan's 'weakness'.

When Reg stepped in she had little money, two teenagers on the verge of leaving school and a terrible lack of self-esteem. Slowly, he'd built her confidence up, treated her like a lady and done all he could to cushion the blow, including playing taxi driver to the kids and bailing them out of the odd scrape. All things considered, he felt he'd earned a modicum of respect and trust, but when he had turned up slightly late for dinner the previous night through no fault of his own he had received the mother of all bollockings and been forced to sleep in the van.

"Cheer up, son, it may never happen." Reg lifted his drooping, bloodshot eyes to focus on the man in front of him. Well, perhaps overgrown boy was a better description. The person who had referred to him as "son" was the kind of age his own son would be now, if he'd had children with his first wife.

"Oh... all right, Phil. How are things?"

"Could ask you the same question, Reg. You've been sat there with a face like a slapped arse nursing that pint for 30 minutes."

"Oh, you know..."

"Women trouble? Bet it is, it all starts with them."

Reg looked at the young man in front of him, the son of the elderly landlady who had run The Hope since before decimalisation. He wondered when the Talking Blob had ever suffered woman trouble, unless it involved a spat with the matriarch in question. He was at least five stone overweight and had a haircut which reminded Reg of the stories his own dad had told him about back in the day when women placed a bowl on the head of their offspring and cut around the rim to ensure the length remained even all the way round. A basin cut, that was it. Irish Phil had so much to offer the young females of the area.

Even though the audience wasn't ideal it was the only one Reg had and he needed to offload to a sympathetic listener. "Had a row with Sheila if you must know," he volunteered.

"Told you," said Phil, basking in his new man-of-the-world status. "Why don't you have another drink and tell me all about it?"

For the next 40 minutes he listened intermittently as Reg raked over the bones of the previous evening. He'd been enjoying a game of pool when he suddenly remembered Sheila was making his favourite dish for supper. He left the pub in plenty of time, although he'd probably drunk slightly more than he intended. Walking back to the Boxers he'd come to a halt at a police barrier which was preventing his progress. When he tried to talk the officious little prick of a cop into letting him through because he only lived a few hundred yards away the bloke had threatened him with arrest. From what he could glean, there had been a riot and the local rank of shops had been looted. Police were under strict instructions to deter all potential troublemakers from entering the area.

"I mean, do I look like a looter to you?" Reg asked Irish Phil as he took a cigarette from the packet on the bar and played with it, considering going outside for a smoke.

"Course not," said Phil, warming to the role of confidante.

Reg put the cigarette back on the bar and continued his story. The upshot of the riot was he had to take the long way around and arrived a few minutes late to find Sheila standing, arms crossed, in the kitchen, silently fuming. "Threw my dinner at my head, she did," said Reg, pointing to the exact spot the culinary delight would have hit. "Lucky she didn't break my skull I tell you. Fortunately I'm good at ducking – had plenty of practice." He bobbed and weaved on his barstool like a modern-day Muhammed Ali.

"Bit out of order that," said Phil. "What did you do?"

Reg told him about the Quo tickets, his get-out-of-jail card.

"That worked?"

"Of course! She loves the Quo. Wouldn't do anything to jeopardise her chances of seeing them this Crimbo."

Irish Phil looked at Reg with a new respect. "Sounds like you shouldn't have gone home at all, mind you, buddy. Hey, you missed a bit of a do in here Saturday."

"I was down the snooker hall. I saw the posters, though. Young Arnold's back?"

"Good as new, the nasty little bastard. Surprised your Sheila's boy wasn't here mind."

"Oh, come on Phil, when was the last time you saw our Gary in here?"

Phil screwed up his mouth, a third chin materialising to help support his podgy, bloated head. After a moment's thought he conceded: "Must be a couple of years."

"Right. He doesn't even live around here now, though God knows where he's gone. He was over at New Cross for a while, working on the local paper there, but his mum tells me he's moved on... not that they ever put me in the picture."

"Strange. Wasn't he going to be a footballer until that nasty incident? You would have been rolling in it then, son."

"Sure, sure... No doubt Sheila would have kicked me into touch though, her 'boy' being in the big time and all. Anyway I guess that was the start of it, why he and Arnold aren't the bosom buddies they once were."

"How so?"

"Well, I think if there was a good thing to come out of that, um, accident it was that it helped Gary wise up to him, y'know? I don't know the full story but I think Gary somehow blamed Arnold for what happened, and I wouldn't be surprised if he was behind it in some way, y'know? Perhaps he arranged for Gary to take those drugs. Look, I know those two were as bad as each other at times, but our Gary was never a bad kid, just ended up in the wrong crowd."

"Maybe it did him a favour. I mean, he wasn't involved when Arnie got banged up, y'know?"

"Funny you should say that," Reg countered, his face screwing up in concentration as he tried to refresh a faded memory. "Earlier that day Gary bumped into Arnold in one of the pubs near the Hammers ground. They went to the game and later all hell broke loose. Not many people know this but Gary was taken in for the offence originally, then the police made their inquiries and discovered it was Arnold who'd caved that kid's head in. I picked Gary up from the cop shop when they released him. I remember him telling me bits about it, though to be honest he was pretty sheepish. Blamed that dodgy leg for letting him down. He couldn't get away as quickly as the others. I don't know if it was an excuse he was giving me to keep me and his mum sweet and I don't think I've ever heard the entire truth about that incident. All I know is that one of the other lot bought it, and Gary's walking stick was the murder weapon."

"Manslaughter wasn't it?"

"Same as murder in my eyes. A man had his life taken from him. No worse crime than that. To this day we're all so grateful Gary wasn't charged. He was just setting out on the newspaper road. I can't even hazard a guess as to what his mother would have done if he'd have gone down."

Phil moved along the bar to serve another customer.

"Hi Phil, how's it going?" asked the new arrival.

"Hi, Tigger, how are you son? What happened to your arm? Looks nasty. Did..?"

"Ah it's nothing man," said the drug dealer, looking down at the bandage covering the area. "Just a bit of a misunderstanding. Lager top and the pool cues please." He looked across to where Reg was nursing his pint. "All right, Reg? How are things? Hey, you were playing pretty well last night. Pity you had to shoot off. Did I hear you mention your boy, Gazza? How's he doing these days? Good lad, Gar, liked him a lot. Bloody good pool player too. Someone told me he was in the Middle East somewhere, making himself rich with Arab money."

"Can't help you there, Tigger, haven't seen or heard from him for ages," said Reg, lifting his glass to salute Mitchell Tigger. "I'm not sure about going abroad. Sometimes it's as if he and his sister have stumbled off the face of the earth." He climbed off his stool and walked towards the pool table, searching his pockets for shrapnel. "OK if I take on the winner?" He placed two coins on the side of the table and cast his eye over the jukebox for a second. Then he returned his attention to the pool table so he could assess his potential opponents.

38

ANJELICA DOLAN could barely conceal her excitement. She re-read the e-mail like a naughty schoolgirl indulging in a raunchy novel: 50 Shades Of Gary. She giggled.

"Dear Hana, I can't spend another moment without seeing your lovely face or feeling your arms around me. I miss you so much and realise perhaps I've been a bit selfish. It's unfair that Max should be deprived of seeing his dad any longer. I don't want to be erased from his life completely and fail to see how a quick visit would jeopardise anything provided we are careful. I was chatting to Mum this morning and she gave me the guilt trip. Babe, why don't you visit this weekend and stay for a couple of days? It's going to be a massive occasion, what with the Rugby World Cup starting, and there are lots of events planned. I'm sure we can find plenty to occupy the two of you. I have to work on the Saturday – but we can plan around that. I could meet you at the station and book you guys into a hotel. You can get to know the place while I get my work done then on Sunday we can spend the day together. What do you think? Please say that it's OK, all my love, Laszlo."

OK? God, it was more than OK. She bent over the keyboard and tapped out a quick reply. When she had finished she read it through again and chuckled. The nicknames had been her idea, one which he seized upon with relish. It would probably sound silly to others but it was a confirmation of their shared love of literature, signifying a certain moment in time when their friendship started to metamorphosis into something much deeper.

A knock at the door interrupted her thoughts and she sneaked a quick look at the clock on the screen. Hell, was that the time? She sent the message and lowered the lid on the computer. "Come on in!" she shouted. "I'm decent."

"Hmm, not what I heard," said Arnie, chuckling as he opened the door.

"I'll just get my stuff and then I'll be out of your hair," she said. "It is all right to keep an eye on Max isn't it, babe? I'm not going to be long, but I've just got to get a few bits down the shops. Then we can spend the rest of the morning together, take him down the park and stuff, before lunch. I bet you miss that, eh, Mum's Sunday dinner?"

"You don't know how much," said Arnie, looking down at the dark-haired boy who was playing with some Lego figures on the carpet. "Hey, Max, what d'you wanna do, play Star Wars?" He picked up a miniature Darth Vader. "I'll be on the dark side and you can be Luke and all his poofy mates."

Anjie bashed him playfully on the arm. "Don't tease," she said, "And let him win now and again. I know what you're like. Won't lose at anything, even to a five-year-old. It's lovely to see my two favourite boys getting along, though." She gave Max a squeeze, then turned to her brother on the bed, hugged him and pecked him on the cheek. "Won't be long."

"Take as long as you like," said Arnie. "Hey, you got any computer games for this thing?" he pointed to the laptop, which was sitting on the desk by the bed.

"Um, yeah, he's got some somewhere," said Anjie distractedly as she hustled around for the things she needed to take with her. "Have a look. I think there's a Smurfs game in the bottom drawer over there. See what you can find."

Arnie turned his nose up. "Smurfs? I was hoping for Grand Theft Auto."

She punched him again. "Arnie, he's five. I don't want him picking up your bad habits: stealing cars and acting badly with ho's." She laughed.

"Ho's, ho's," chimed in Max.

"Oh, look... see what you've done now?"

"That was you, not me!" said Arnie indignantly.

"Naughty word, Max, don't say it again please or I won't buy you any sweeties."

"OK Mum. I want sweets," said Max. "No ho's. Bad word."

"Good." She gave him another kiss, picked up the designer hand-bag Arnie had bought her as a thank you gift for all she did for him while he was in prison, waved her hand and left.

Arnie bent down to Max's level, looked him in the eyes and, to the boy's clear delight, winked. "Let's see what we can find, eh?" he said. "I bet there's a Call of Duty somewhere around here..."

Rummaging through the drawer, he settled for a game called Angry Birds where you hurled feathered friends at various constructions, creating havoc. Arnie was partial to a bit of mindless demolition, and found it amazing how computer geeks pocketed a fortune simply by coming up with wacky ideas. Perhaps he was in the wrong line of work. He was about to turn on Anjie's computer when he realised it was already booted up. Moving the mouse so that he could get access to the slot which took discs, he was aware of the screen springing to life and a list of correspondence appearing in front of him. Anjie's e-mails. He was about to close down the application when one in particular caught his eye. It was a message to a bloke called Laszlo, a name he didn't recall.

He might have felt awkward reading Anjie's private things if it wasn't for the fact that embarrassment, guilt and shame didn't figure highly among his personality traits. When people suggested he was a psychopath they may have thought they were paying him a compliment, but to a certain degree it was a medical fact. He did possess 'some' genuine emotions, like the love for his sister which, he was pretty sure, was real, but not many. The name Laszlo had raised his hackles.

What was Anjie doing communicating with one of those eastern European scroungers? They had arrived in the country thanks to lax EU laws, flooding not only the legitimate jobs market but the criminal one, too. Christ, when he was inside he had to organise swift counter measures when a gang of Bulgarians tried to muscle in on his business. Fortunately eldest brother Chuck and his crew sent them packing south of the river.

So let's see, he thought. Who's Laszlo? He double clicked on the message and a few lines appeared on the screen...

'Dear Laszlo, what a fantastic idea. I know the boy will just love it, seeing you again. It's a shame you had to leave the way you did. I'm sure it's not easy settling down in a new country. I doubt you've had time to learn the language yet ha ha! I think Max missed you, you know? Just a feeling I get. Please make the arrangements. Got to fly, the errant brother is due to pay me a visit and it wouldn't do for him to walk in on me when I'm writing to you. Keep me informed and I'll ring when I can. I'll give him a big hug from you. Max that is, not Arnie. Anyway, love you xxxx'

What the hell? Max was hanging from his leg now. "Angry Birds, Angry Birds, please uncle Arnie, Angry..."

"Shut up!" he shouted, regretting his response as soon as it had passed his lips. The boy began to snivel, a prelude to full-scale tears. "Sorry Max, sorry... look, uncle's just trying to fix it now," he said, holding him at arms' length and looking into his eyes. "Tell you what: if you're a good little munchkin and stop crying we'll go and get some ice cream from the freezer. OK?"

The boy sniffed back his whimpers. "Ice cream? Mummy says 'no ice cream before lunch'."

"Yeah, well Mummy isn't here, is she?" said Arnie, conspiratorially. "Uncle Arnie's in charge now and what he says goes. Sounds like Mummy's silly little ice cream rule was made to be broken, anyway. It will be fine as long as we make it our little secret."

Max put his finger to his lips, mimicking an adult's call for quiet. "Shhhhh!" he said.

"That's right, our little secret," said Arnie. "Just like your mummy has a little secret." He decided he had to keep the information he had gleaned from Anjie's e-mails under wraps, too. He certainly couldn't confront her with what he had learned for fear that a rift might develop between them. He was a firm believer that knowledge was power and, now armed with a name, a few discreet inquiries would be the order of the day. He looked at the little boy and wondered: Was it a possibility that Max was the offspring of some bloody foreigner? God, he hoped not. He clicked off the e-mail and closed the application. He wasn't so sure about Angry Birds now. He was a pretty angry bloke.

39

JACKO WAS WAITING for Gareth when he arrived in the office on Tuesday morning. By the look on the veteran sports editor's face he wasn't putting out the welcome mat. "Bloody hell, mun, she must know something, Gareth!" were his first anxious words.

"Sorry?" replied the reporter. He wasn't playing ignorant it was just that so much had gone on over the weekend he didn't know where to start.

"Lana. I'm sure she suspects something… about The Legend and his, um, little performance," said Jacko.

"She saw it?"

"I don't know but most of the people on this floor did. It only takes one tittle-tattler chasing brownie points and we're up shit creek without a soddin' paddle."

Gareth didn't see why he should protest his innocence. Looking after drunken rugby players wasn't in his job description. When Jacko's phone buzzed the sports editor leapt on it as if the noise would wake sleeping dragons from the depths of the office basement. "Hello… yes Lana… certainly… right away, Lana."

"Three bags bloody full Lana," muttered Gareth.

Jacko looked at him quizzically before jerking his head in the direction of the editor's office. Gareth headed off, colleagues watching him like religious freaks preparing to issue the last rites to a dead man walking on death row. Editor's secretary Ffion waved him straight into the inner sanctum. Lana's head was buried in a national newspaper, her nails peeling the pages as clinically as they might remove the skin from an orange. Today they were red, the three feathers pattern somehow displayed in the middle of each one. She was acting as if she hadn't even noticed his presence, though he was sure she was just following procedure as laid down in the manager's rulebook. Point one: make junior staff feel uneasy by keeping them guessing for as long as possible. He decided to wait her out, rather than force the conversation.

Slowly her head rose. "Why Mr Prince, there you are," she said. "This won't take long. Grab a pew."

The only other chair in the room had seen better days and put him below Lana's eyeline. As he sank down into it a squeak emerged and he felt an uncomfortable pinprick in his backside, judging it to be a loose spring. His imagination was already running wild about the nature of the summons and he started dreaming up a scenario whereby the inconspicuous weapon had been secreted beneath the upholstery for just such an occasion. A punishment. He held back the desire to jump up and shout out.

"I was looking for you on Saturday night," said Lana. "You'd, um, disappeared. No one seemed to know where you were. Care to explain?"

"I'd been there most of the evening to be fair," he replied. "I'd filed my copy so I wasn't really needed any more. I had my mobile in case anyone needed to check anything. I left because I promised to do an errand for JW."

"Ah, and where was the 'great' JW on such a busy night? I was looking for him, too. I suppose he was enjoying some of the local hospitality... Wales winning and all." Gareth decided it was safer to keep his mouth shut until the whole mystery unfolded. "Anyway ..." She picked up the paper again as if there was a speech inside written particularly for her benefit. "I just wanted to say that the piece he did for us on Sunday was, well, I can only describe it as quite extraordinary."

A feeling of impending doom flooded Gareth's body. He had been so busy instigating The Legend's escape he hadn't had a chance to read the article Jason had put together. "Oh yes, extraordinary…" she continued. "It was, quite simply, the best I've ever read from him. It was the most clicked article on our website. It was intelligent, humorous and informative and the writing was, well, astonishing for someone who I have had the dubious pleasure to read for more years than I care to remember."

Gareth couldn't take his eyes off the editor. He wondered when the sucker punch was coming. "My only question is why?"

There it was.

"Why, Lana?"

"Yes, why is he suddenly able to articulate his feelings so eloquently? To be honest, I can only draw one conclusion…" Here we go, thought Gareth, waiting for the axe to fall. "… It's you."

"Me?"

"Yes, Mr Prince. I must admit I had my doubts when we took you on. I tend to invest in local talent… you know where you're going with the Welsh. They are in tune with our rugby patriotism, our loves and loathes, and for the life of me I failed to see how an Englishman could relate to that. Normally, they just don't 'get it'. But Jacko was convinced, said you had interviewed really well and gave the impression you knew your stuff, so all I can say is: well done! Keep up the good work and you're going places. No doubt about it."

"BRILLIANT JOB deciphering The Legend's hieroglyphics, Jase," said Gareth, grabbing a quiet moment in the canteen with the work experience boy.

"I didn't," said Jason.

Gareth wondered whether his confused brain had managed to scramble Jason's response. "What?"

"I had to blag it, butt. I'm sorry, Gar, but it seemed to be the best thing to do."

"Right," said Gareth slowly, quite unable to understand what Jason was trying to tell him. The workie flicked a strand of his jet-black hair from his eyes.

"It was like this, see. I knew you might be in trouble for what had happened with The Legend. Jacko wasn't happy about you letting him get drunk..."

"Letting him get...?"

Jason saw a Prince explosion building and acted quickly to defuse it. "Well, that's the way he was interpreting it, anyway. I thought our only hope of getting out of the shit was to make sure The Legend filed... and on time. So, yeah, I blagged it."

"How?"

"Well, when I saw those scrawled squiggles on the paper I thought we were fucked, like. Sorry. Then it came to me. Pretend it's in Welsh! I doubted anyone would know the difference. Barely anyone speaks it in these parts. So that's what I did. No one was any the wiser so, basically, I made it up. Sorry."

Gareth was silent for a minute, then his face lit up and he began to chuckle, a reaction which soon turned into a full-on belly laugh. He couldn't remember the last time he'd found something which made him laugh out loud or feel such unbridled joy. The knotted ball of pent-up frustration which had lodged deep within his stomach was untangling at a rapid rate. He jumped up, completely failing to register the pain in his leg, grabbed Jason by the ears and planted a big kiss on his forehead. "Brilliant!" he said, savouring the word so much he had to repeat it. "Simply brilliant! Well, well, well..." He pointed at his eyes and Jason gave him a quizzical look. "Look at me, son," he said. "You, boy, have the makings of a brilliant journalist. Thinking on your feet, blagging, improvising... and, damn it all, writing like a true pro too. My God even the great Hugh McIlvanney..."

"Is he the bloke on the evening news?"

"What? Oh no, no. That's Huw Edwards. McIlvanney is one of the greatest sports journalists... oh what the hell, who cares? You saved us, and I am eternally grateful to you. We'll go out tonight, down the rugby club perhaps, celebrate. Hell, I'm going to pull up every tree to get you on the first rung of the journalism ladder. I've got a few decent contacts..."

"Sorry, very nice of you and all, but can't make it tonight. Me and Dad are supposed to be training. We've got a big charity wrestling match at the Millennium Stadium. It's being staged right after the opening World Cup game against South Africa, can you imagine? It's all part of the big international weekend so we got to get it right. Another time?"

"Of course."

"Why all this praise, though? What's happened?"

Gareth told him about the meeting with the editor, his fears followed by his utter relief when she lavished praise on The Legend's column.

Jason nodded. "OK," he said uncertainly. "My main concern, though, is that he likes it… the great JW."

Gareth beamed. "Mate, he'll love it, I assure you. You've saved his bacon."

"Ah that's good." Suddenly Jason's eyes lit up. "Shit, that reminds me…" He dug into his denim jacket pocket and Gareth thought for a moment he was going for his earphones, but instead he pulled out a slip of paper. Unfolding it, he smoothed it out on the table. "Look! I got it this morning."

Gareth started reading and the smile on his face expanded. The day was just getting better and better.

40

"HOW.. UM, HOW...?" The Legend's mouth fell open, unable to articulate his reaction to what he was seeing.

"I got Jason to look into it," explained Gareth. "I thought you needed a special incentive to help you kick the booze and get your life back on track."

The Legend looked at him in such a way the reporter feared there might be a repeat of the assault that followed the projector moment. Then the ex-rugby star's face softened. "You're sure... I mean, it's definitely from her? How do you know, butt? Could be someone just pulling my plonker, you know, some kind of sick joke. Or maybe it's someone with the same name. Owens is pretty common, isn't it?"

"Ahhh, but it's not Owens is it? She's married now and her name is Clifton. Jason found an article about her on the internet, from the Sydney Morning Herald. It was about her netball abilities – apparently she is a bit of a star, playing for Manley or someone."

"Well, she was pretty good as a kid. That makes sense."

"The article mentioned her famous father, the great JW Owens, and quoted her as saying she owed all her sporting prowess to him and how she missed him... I mean you... very much."

"OK, but..."

"Jason rang the paper and they gave him an e-mail address. He sent her a message explaining how you missed her and would love to get back in touch... this is what we got back."

The Legend read the words again.

"Dear Jason,

Thanks so much for getting in touch. If there was a chance I could see my father again it would be absolutely wonderful. We lost contact over the years after Martin's funeral. He disappeared off the radar. I have been living with a bloke called Charlie and about a year ago we got married. Very quiet affair. I did send Dad an invite because I wanted him to give me away but I got no reply. Anyway, we had a son and guess what? We called him John after Dad. It's actually perfect timing that you should contact me now. Charlie is a massive rugby fan and wants to come to see the Wallabies in the World Cup. I think they are playing in London so we'll be arriving on the Wednesday or Thursday after the tournament starts. Can't quite remember the times to be honest, but I'll let you know. I wondered about making contact with Dad while I was over, but I thought he was trying to avoid me, that I was a reminder of what happened in the past, you know, with Martin and that. I didn't realise it might be something as simple as him moving flats. Gosh, I hope this works out, I'd love Dad to meet John. I think of him every day and sometimes sit here and show his grandson old pictures and tell him stories of how Grandad was this great rugby player revered around the world. He'll be delighted to meet him in the flesh, as will Charlie I'm sure.

All the best,

Eleanor 'Ellie' Clifton (nee Owens)

The Legend brushed at his face, as if a stray cobweb had latched onto his cheek. Then it happened. Gareth noticed the eyes filling up and at first thought it might be his response to a lack of sleep or another heavy night on the town. Then, though the old man tried to fight it, a tear was left with nowhere to go so wound a path through his bottom eyelashes and onto a ruddy, vein-marbled cheek. No sooner had he brushed it away than there came another, and another, until the dam broke and the flood began. He stumbled back, his face in his hands, and fell into the old armchair. Gareth felt awkward, unsure what to do, stretching out a hand tentatively and dropping it on the ex-rugby player's back. He rubbed gently, but could find nothing to say. It was as if a friendly giant from a fairy story had been brought crashing to its knees. The bravado, chirpiness and bullish veneer which was an integral part of this man's visible make-up had been chipped away in an instant to expose a vulnerable, mortal human being underneath.

The venting seemed to go on for hours, but in reality lasted just a couple of minutes. Gareth retreated to the kitchen to gather his thoughts and put on the kettle. It's what his mother would have done. "Come on, love, dry those peepers and let's have a lovely cup of tea," she used to say. He could hear her voice in his head, providing the sympathy and solace to go with the brew. He recalled one such 'tea' moment happening a couple of days after his dad left. His mother found him wrapped in his duvet bawling his eyes out, brought him a cuppa and then teased out his woes. "Who has he gone away with Mum? What did we do?"

She didn't hold back, giving it to him straight and true. It was the way his mother was. She preached honesty as the best policy and wasn't going to change even in these trying circumstances. "It's nothing to do with us, or you... don't ever think that, darlin'," she had said. "It's all about him and his selfish attitude. You know he went to Amsterdam a couple of months ago? On a business trip? Well, it was really to bring in some dodgy gear you can't get in this country to sell on a mate's market stall. Anyway, the way I understand it he met some bloody little northern tart out there who batted her eyelashes at him and, well, your dad's not getting any younger and it must have made him feel special somehow, so instead of thinking about all the wonderful things he has got here, his ego took over. I don't know how many times he saw her but he's made his bed now. In bloody Bolton. Don't worry though, love, it won't last. She'll get bored soon enough. Still I won't have him running back here, you understand? He's hurt me enough times. I'm sorry. I know he's your hero – like all fathers should be to their sons – but I can't sugarcoat the pill. It is what it is. He's a philandering ratbag who's only interested in himself. We'll get through it: you, me and Lily. I promise you. It's important now to do well at school."

"And at football, Mum," he had reminded her, wiping the tears away.

"Yeah, sure..." Even at that stage, though, there had been something in her voice, a slight hesitation, which told him she wasn't convinced.

Putting the painful thoughts out of his mind, Gareth found a tray in the cupboard, typically depicting Welsh rugby players in old-fashioned kit. JW himself was in the middle of the panorama and Gareth couldn't help wondering if there was anything in the flat which didn't hint at his former glories. If it was anyone else's house he would have thought the owner a big-headed egotist, but with The Legend it was somehow sad, as if he was clinging on to the memorabilia to remind him who he was, and what his past had been about. More simply, they were probably freebies and all he could afford after his business schemes failed.

Gareth loaded up the cups, added some biscuits on a plate, then returned to the front room. What greeted him shouldn't have been a surprise considering the company he was keeping, but it was. The Legend was down on all fours in the corner of the room, removing a bottle of vodka from a sideboard. On the table were three similar bottles, each with a small amount of clear liquid nestling in the bottom. "Ah, you're back!" The Legend said looking over his shoulder, as if Gareth had gone to the shops, not just the kitchen.

He looked different already. The tears had gone, the puffy cheeks were fixed in an expression of grim determination. "Grab these, would you?"

"John Wayne, let's not do this. I've made tea, look. Don't you think..?"

"Stop there, Geraint, I'm warning you. I'm on a roll and it's got to be done."

"Yeah, but surely this isn't the time for drinking."

The Legend raised himself slowly to his feet, peering into the clear liquid at the bottom of the bottle in his hand as if the answer to everything was floating there. Lifting his head, he looked Gareth in the eye. "Drinking? No, you got it all wrong, butt," he said, smiling. "No drinking now I've got a mission." He indicated the array of bottles on the table. "These have to go. Perhaps you could give me a hand, find a black bin liner or something, and we can clear away this filth. I need to have all my wits about me now, because my daughter and my grandson are coming to see me."

41

AS THE LEGEND walked through the gate of his block of flats, a bin bag full of nearly empty vodka bottles in his hand, a familiar figure was waiting to greet him. "Well," he said, "if it isn't the great Shakes."

"Hi old timer, figured you might need some moral support," said Will Shakespeare. "You know... been there, done that."

"Oh, you needn't worry about me, man," protested The Legend. "I'll be fine. I think I know where I'm heading now."

The former rally driver walked towards his old friend and put his hands out, grabbing the ex-rugby player by the forearms and forcing him to put down his burden. "Look, I know how tough it can be to do this on your own and when Jason told me about your good news I just thought you needed a helping hand. Listen, I'm not sure this place is good for you. The neighbours can get on your case a bit and I think perhaps you need to get away from the memories and that miserable flat."

"Hey, what do you mean miserable?" protested The Legend. "It's my home that is, butt. Don't worry about me. It's got everything I need."

Will stood back and looked his old friend in the eye. "Really? Because I think there are a bunch of broken old memories inside which you could do without. Hell, your daughter and your grandson are coming over. It's a new beginning. You want them to see you like this? In that place? I reckon you should come with us. My friend

Gwynfor at the Vicarage is offering you, um, what would you call it, sanctuary? That's a good word."

"You mean rehab," said The Legend. "I'm not sure I need treatment."

"Really?" asked Will, raising an eyebrow. "You can't kid a kidder, old man. You remember I had all those problems, when I was trying to live the Monte Carlo lifestyle? Lost everything? Well, it only got better when I admitted I had a problem. Look at you, JW. The other day you watched a whole rugby match and knew nothing about it... not even the score! And that is supposed to be your job."

"The English boy told you that, did he?"

For the moment there was tension as the two old sportsmen glared intently at each other. Then The Legend broke the stand-off as he burst out laughing, Will joining in. "Yeah, I guess that's some kind of achievement," acknowledged the former rugby star. "Can't recall a bloody thing! Would you credit it?"

"I know. Ridiculous! Look, stay in Ponty for a while, at least for the duration of the World Cup. Jase has promised to give your place a lick of paint, brighten it up a bit while you're taking what we can call a holiday. The people of Pontyprenis love you. They'll be delighted to have a legend living among them and it will be good for you and I to recall old times. I can set you up with an office in the rugby club and a TV on which to watch the matches. It will be a home from home, I assure you."

AN HOUR LATER they were in the main hall of Pontyprenis Rugby Club. JW had swiftly packed a bag before climbing into Gareth's Corsa alongside Will, the reporter confined to the back seat of his own car. Then, for old time's sake, Will had driven at break-neck speeds across Caerphilly Mountain in a small detour ahead of their arrival in the valleys.

Gareth was grateful for help in attempting to "fix" the old rugby hero. He had found himself backed into a corner by the newspaper and felt it almost impossible to juggle his own work with watching

The Legend, so Will's offer was too good to turn down. Not only would it get JW away from his depressing flat, but it would keep him away from his dodgy mates.

Though Gareth had arrived in the country wary of the Welsh his stance had altered greatly over the short time he had been there. He now felt some of his new acquaintances to be more trustworthy than, well, the entire population of the Boxers Estate. He still wasn't 100 per cent convinced his work colleagues weren't conspiring behind his back, but since staying in Pontyprenis he had forged bonds that would hopefully last a lifetime. Will and Jason Shakespeare had a father-son relationship he admired and envied. It reminded him painfully of how things had been with his father before the whole thing was ripped apart. In moments of self-analysis Gareth could trace all his pent-up anger, his dark moods, his prejudices and acts of bullying back to that single reference point, the moment his dad gave up his right to be called a parent.

He was disturbed from his reminiscences when Jason turned up in his peripheral vision, can of Coke in hand and earphones in place as always, pieces of equipment as essential to him as a life-support machine to a coma victim. Sometimes, when Gareth let his mind wander, he could imagine pulling the attachments clear from the side of the work experience boy's head, then watching him deflate to a crumpled heap of empty skin on the floor.

To be fair the workie was never short of ideas and it had been his suggestion they secrete The Legend away in Pontyprenis. Gareth immediately bought into the idea while Will had been typically ebullient and happy to help. Now here they were, discussing the next step.

"I'm afraid we're not much for secrets around here," said Will. "Too small a place, see. Everyone finds out everything about everyone else all the time, you know? Still, we've a place for JW as long as he wants it."

"Will, you're a true friend," said The Legend, stepping forward and giving him a hug. The two aging men stood there for a long time, entwined in the same way their lives had been linked together over many years. Though they hadn't kept in touch for long periods, the connection was solid, unbreakable, the kind of bond two men form when they have lived through good times and bad, sharing a lifetime of extreme highs and unfathomable lows.

"Right, boys, sorry to break up the grand reunion, but there's work to be done," announced Gareth. "Jase what are you planning now? I've got to go back to the office if you'd like to come with me."

"To be honest, Gar, I was hoping for the afternoon off," said the workie. "Me and dad were planning to work on some new moves. We're fighting some Aussies – well, they're a couple of barmen from Splott, tell you the truth, but still…"

"You've got a fight coming up? I'd love to see that!" said The Legend. "Do I get an invite?"

"Hell, yeah," said Jason. "The Legend seeing me fight? It would be the greatest honour ever!"

"Bloody hell, JW!" exploded Gareth, all eyes turning to him. "Here I am trying to keep you away from temptation and you want to attend what will undoubtedly be a boozy occasion at a rugby stadium where every bloody Welshman for miles around will want a piece of you."

Jason's smile was replaced by a frown.

"Never mind Jase," said Will, giving his shoulder a consoling pat. Then another thought clicked in. "Hey, I'm sure we can find some way of disguising him, know what I mean?"

Jason's face brightened. "Yeah, our wrestling props box. We got loads of stuff in there!"

Without another word, Gareth shook his head and slipped away, the full insanity of what was going on here suddenly dawning on him. The two old sportsmen were arguably the most open and honest people Gareth had ever met but while Will had shunned the limelight since his motor racing days, The Legend still couldn't resist the lure of the crowd and the big occasion. The idea that he could go incognito was preposterous in his eyes.

"Bloody Welshies!" Gareth mumbled under his breath as he left them to it. This time, though, the words were accompanied by a smile rather than a sneer of hatred.

42

JANIE VICKERS WAS upstairs putting laundry away when she heard the front door slam. "That you love?" she shouted, a note of trepidation creeping into her voice. She wasn't expecting Pete back so soon. He had chores to complete and was then taking the kids to the park. There had even been the promise of a trip to the cinema to see the latest Walt Disney epic in 3D if they behaved themselves. Her feeling of unease grew with the sound of a light tread on the stairs. It was him.

It wasn't that his walking pattern varied significantly from anyone else's, rather it was down to a sixth sense Janie possessed without having a clue as to where it came from and what caused it. She was pretty sure she didn't possess any 'special powers' but it was the same when the telephone rang. Pete and the kids often poked fun at her when she immediately said, "That'll be Mum", or "That's Anjie's ring" when the home phone trilled.

"Don't be silly Mummy!" her eldest, Simon, had said only the previous night, "the phone ring is the same whoever is on the other end of the line." His expression had morphed into one of complete astonishment when his mother picked up the phone, put it to her ear and said: "Oh hi, Anj, how are you? We were just talking about you."

True, she didn't actually know that many people so it was roughly a one in four chance, but then again it could have been for Pete, business or pleasure, and that multiplied the odds dramatically. There were the kids, too, and though their mother discouraged them from using the phone at such a young age there was nothing she could do if other parents weren't so strict and allowed little Johnny to grab the receiver and punch in the number of his bestest friend.

On occasion she used her 'powers' for her own benefit, to get the kids to bed on time, or persuade them to eat their broccoli. She would wave her hands mystically in the air and talk about using "Mummy's Magic" to punish them if they didn't do as she asked. They would scream then do what she had ordered.

The footsteps were nearly upon her now and she dropped clothes to the bed in a heap, unconcerned as to whether they were folded properly or not. She turned towards the door and her heart beat a rapid tattoo in her chest as his grinning face appeared around the corner. "Knock, knock!" Arnie Dolan said. Subconsciously she pulled her blouse around her. She had only thrown on some rags this morning, knowing that her plans did not involve stepping out of the house at any time and aware no one was scheduled to call. She brushed down her grey sweatpants with the frayed bottoms. "I thought you were at your mum's for dinner today," she said.

"Change of plan," he replied, strolling uninvited into the marital bedroom. In her scattergun train of thought her mind conjured images of Vikings and Romans, invading places where they had no right to be.

"Can I get you anything?" She hoisted up a basket containing dirty linen and walked towards the door, aiming to force him back out of the room as quickly as possible. This space was sacrosanct, the place where she lay with her husband and where her two children had been conceived, and again her mind silently repeated the mantra: "You've no right, Arnie Dolan, no right at all to be here".

As if interpreting her thoughts, he leaned out and rested his arm against the frame, blocking her exit. "You can just answer me one question, Janie," he said, his eyes like glass, reflecting her face back to her but failing to let her see inside him or work out his intentions. "After that, I'll leave you to your wifely chores."

"Oh?"

"Yeah. One teeny question and I'll be out of your hair... promise." He paused for effect and the breath caught in her throat. "Who's Laszlo?"

Of everything she had imagined him asking her: if she would give him a blow job for old time's sake, if he could borrow her damn car or even if she could rustle him up a three-course meal, this was the last thing she was expecting. Warning shots ping-ponged around her brain as if a gunman had got loose in her head and was shooting up her synapses. Arnie's face registered no emotion but the manner in which he had asked the question filled her with dread. What made it worse was that she had no single clue as to what he was talking about. She rifled through the recesses of her memory to obtain a suitable response but all her searches came back empty.

"I'm sorry Arnie," she said, battling to bring her nerves under control. "I have no idea who you mean."

The slap was from the shoulder, directed to cause the maximum pain to her cheek. Her knees held her up for a short while, but crumpled when the painful message reached her brain and demanded a response. She felt like one of those bendy dolls with pipe-cleaner legs her daughter spent so much time playing with in her bedroom, cheap things made popular by a TV programme on the kids channel. That's it. She felt cheap. For all her so-called Mummy Magic she had been unable to conjure up any defence against this invader, to keep at arm's length a man who was capable of wrecking her happy family unit.

Now she had let her guard down he was going to treat her like his sex slave, a whore to satisfy his every whim. When he grabbed her by the forearms she knew the punishment wasn't over. He pulled her from the bed where she had fallen and looked down on her with hypnotic, shining eyes, probing for a weakness. "Don't give me that shit!" he said, "You're her best friend. I suspected you two might try to keep something like this from me. I can't fucking believe it!" Genuine anger. She was actually surprised. For someone who tended to only pay lip service to emotions this was a departure from the usual Arnie.

"Arnie, please, you're hurting!" she said. "Let's sit down and try to work out..." Slap! He hit her again, but held on to her this time so she couldn't feel the comforting respite of the mattress. She felt blood trickling from her nose down to her lip and over her teeth as her face fixed in a grimace.

"Laszlo, Laszlo," he chanted. "Come on! How many people do you know with that name? I'd say it's probably one. It's not like you go out to the pub and say, 'I'll have a vodka and orange Laszlo, can you bring it over please, I'll be sitting over there with Laszlo, Laszlo and fucking Laszlo', now is it? So tell me: Who... Is... Laszlo?" She just stared at him. She'd seen films of torturers trying to get the truth out of people who didn't possess the answer, scenes like that one in the Tarantino movie where the guy cut off the cop's ear to that upbeat little song Stuck In The Middle With You. It was an impasse. She didn't have an answer, he wouldn't take no for an answer. Result: more torture. A vicious circle. She had to choose her next words carefully - couldn't cope with another fearsome slap.

"I'll find out for you, Arnie," she blurted out. "It must be someone Anjie hasn't introduced me to, but I promise I will find out. You trust me don't you?"

His features softened. "Of course I trust you, Janie," he said. "You deserted me to marry my mate then cheated on him with me. I can't think of any bird more trustworthy than you, darlin'. For that reason, just this once I'll show you some mercy. I want to know who Laszlo is. If Anj hasn't told you, quite honestly I'm flabbergasted. I could carry on beating it out of you but, hell, life's too short and I've more important things to do. Reading between the lines it appears Laszlo is the father of my poor bastard nephew, Max. I want to find out why he's deserted my sister and her little boy and then give him a jolly good piece of my mind." The last bit was delivered in a mock posh accent, designed for laughs. She tried to oblige, but her lips stung and she wasn't sure she had the ability to pull off the deceit.

Finally, he guided her back to the bed, gentle now as if none of the violence had taken place and the only thing that had passed between them was a reasoned adult conversation. She looked at him through the tears, a red welt forming on either cheek giving her the appearance of a gaily painted doll from a bygone era. "Please Arnie, listen," she said, "Anj has never told me about Max's dad. Honest. She's kept him to herself like some life-or-death secret." Thinking about it, that was pretty much what it had to be she mused as the phrase escaped her lips. Life or death for this Laszlo bloke, anyway. She hoped for his sake he lived up to his name and was staying in another country far away. "I've asked her... of course I have, many times. But she just puts her finger to her nose, which is as good as telling me to butt out."

"So you do? I've never thought of you as the sort of shrinking violet who lets things rest just because someone says so, Janie. Still, I'll play fair with you, you being my first love and all. You've got four days. Apparently they are due to meet up and I need you to find out where and when. No biggie."

"What? No, you can't..."

"Oh Janie, Janie," he said, looking into her eyes with utmost sincerity. "You surely aren't suggesting I can't do something? You know me better than that. I wonder what Pete would say if he ever found out his wife had screwed his bosom buddy behind his back. I don't think he would be very forgiving."

"Screwed?" she said, finally summoning up reserves of courage and raising her voice. "That was rape, Arnie! Tell Pete that and it would really land you in it."

"Yeah, well maybe I would just have to deal with the 'wrath' of Pete. What's he gonna do anyway, the fat lump? Sit on me? Steal my Mars bar? Eat my dinner if I'm not home early enough? Come on Janie, don't be so fucking stupid. Yes, he might confront me, and I think that's a pretty big might seeing as he knows he will come off second best. More likely he will just ask me if it's true. What will I say? Rape? She's lying Pete. You know your minx of a wife has always had the hots for me. She waited for you to go out and take the kids to school and she jumped on me. I didn't have a prayer, guv, honest. Once her 'passions' are up there is no stopping her."

He leaned towards her as if he was going to kiss her but finally she summoned up all her mummy powers and took the attack back to him, slapping him across the face. Shrinking back, she expected to get the same in return, twice as hard.

Instead his face slowly formed into a smile and he broke into a laugh. "You see?" he said. "You can be a pretty formidable woman when you've got your mind set on something. I didn't stand a chance in hell. Now why don't we kiss and make up... what do they say? In for a penny, in for a pounding?"

43

THE DRUG DEALER leaned against one of the estate garages and skinned up, out of sight from prying eyes. He was excited, so excited in fact that only a doobie could calm him. Arnie Dolan wouldn't approve but fuck him. Doles always insisted the dealers shouldn't smoke their own product, but indirectly he was responsible for Tigger's mood, so he could hardly be surprised. Tigger needed something to help him think through the right way to approach the situation.

He sparked up and sifted through the information he had come across purely by chance in The Hope the previous evening. If he played his hand right this newly acquired knowledge could get him right out of the shit. His arm stung, reminding him of his predicament. Once you were in Dolan's bad books, it was difficult to extricate yourself from them. He had seen other poor saps fall victim to the merciless little gangster. Mind you, he couldn't recall him being as vicious and unhinged as he appeared to be right now. Prison life had done nothing to calm him, quite the opposite. Tigger had spent a night in A and E having a dozen stitches inserted into his arm as testimony to that.

The dilemma he had now was how to use the information. It was like being in possession of a top trump but not being sure when to play it. What made things difficult was the close bond between Arnie and the Crip. Certainly, before Arnie was sent down you wouldn't have been able to say a word about his closest friend without booking yourself a long stay in hospital. Tigger detected, though, that Gary Marshall's disappearance had somehow weakened that bond.

The Crip's absence had been a topic of much discussion in The Hope. People speculated where he might have gone, and the reasons for his departure, as gossips do when there is little else to talk about. There were those who claimed to be his Facebook and Twitter 'friends' who told a variety of conflicting stories about his whereabouts, that he was living the life of a hotshot reporter everywhere from the north of Scotland to the Middle Eastern Emirates. Even so, many of those same people had expected him to turn up like a bad penny for Dolan's release party, the terrible twins re-united.

The story of their unusual partnership was legend in these parts, two boys from similar backgrounds but with vastly differing outlooks on life thrown together over a barney on the estate and inseparable ever since. Marshall, the more than useful schoolboy footballer with a dad pushing him to make the most of his talents and a mum insistent that he studied hard at school, and Dolan, the son of a career criminal, the estate wild child who cared little about education and future ambitions, doing his best to get by day-to-day despite a lack of parental guidance. He was smart, though, having learned more vital lessons on the streets than any of his peers could glean from the local inner-city secondary school they now laughingly labelled an Academy, as if it was a production line for a wide diversity of talents rather than a breeding ground for gangsters.

When Arnie had been banged up there had been plenty of questions asked but few answers forthcoming. At first it seemed the gang leader had got away scot free only for him to be dragged off in handcuffs after a dawn raid at his house. He had given a couple of coppers something to think about, one in particular limping away from the premises, his hand covering a nasty swelling around his right eye. The family dog hadn't exactly helped the police with their inquiries either, showing solidarity with its owners by attacking the first officer through the door and occupying him while the others searched for their quarry.

It was all very dramatic, the whole estate emptying out onto the street as the streaky figure of a half-clad Arnie Dolan was dragged kicking and punching to a waiting van. The mother followed him out, lending her own brand of abuse to proceedings, then the brothers. The family were close, and if you took on one you had to take them all on. Neighbours had all sorts of theories as to what was in the evidence bags one of the forensics people was carrying when they left the house. Everything from a stash of cash to a victim's missing limb.

One thing the gossips were sure about, though.

"Doles isn't happy."

"Doles says he was grassed up."

"Heaven help the person who decided to dob Arnie Dolan in. When he comes out he'll turn over every stone to find the culprit."

Understandable really, but why the hell did he think Tigger was involved? Everyone knew what a coward the drug dealer was and how he wouldn't dare risk upsetting the bully who had hounded him through his teens. If they were looking for motive, they might have suspected he wanted to take more control of the drug business for himself, but that blatantly hadn't happened. Every month Tigger had religiously handed over Dolan's share of the profits to his right-hand man Vickers, never scrimping, never cheating. Tigger felt miffed the cloud of suspicion should hover over him, knowing full well that he could have made significant personal gains if he had sold Dolan down the river. His motivation for staying loyal might have been pure fear, but even so...

It was the general suspicion of all drug dealers that had put him in such a spot. He felt like he was in a discriminated-against minority. Who said people who dealt in class A's were not to be trusted? It wound him up sometimes. Still, now was the time he could prove he was a good soldier. He crushed the spliff under his foot, put away his baccy tin and walked around the corner to the street on which Dolan lived these days, a guest of the Vickers family. He had it straight in his mind how to tackle the situation, reminding himself that this was his one chance to prove his loyalty to the boss.

"WELL, IF it isn't old Tony Montana!" said Vickers with a big smile on his face. Tigger gave him a blank look. "Scarface, you know? Pacino in that film? Instead of Scarface though, it looks like Scar arm. Nasty cut you got there boy. To be honest..." he lowered his voice and leaned out of the front door, "you're taking a bit of a risk popping around here. Arnie's got it in for you. Don't ask why, I told him you'd popped up right as rain with his money every month, but he still holds a bit of a grudge. I reckon it was over that thing, you know, with the Crip? That dodgy gear?"

"He can't blame me for that!" protested Tigger. "He asked me to source something that would give us an exceptional high and that's what I did. How the hell was I to know the bloke was going to chuck himself off a balcony? Jeez!"

"OK, OK. Keep your voice down."

"Why, what's the little druggie been saying?" Arnie Dolan appeared in the hallway behind Vickers, thumping his hand into a child's boxing glove. "Didn't think he'd have the nerve to show up around here after the other night. You sure you haven't lost your marbles, Tigger? Perhaps my warning wasn't strong enough for you, eh? Well, maybe I can make it a little less subtle." His arm shot out, pushing Vickers out of the way. Blue eyes bore into Tigger's; ice cold, no compromise.

"P... please, Doles, listen mate..."

A fist connected with his throat, immediately cutting off his windpipe. He fell to the floor, gagging in the hallway. "Not on the bloody carpet, Tiggs," he heard Vickers exclaim, "the missus will bloody kill me!" The drug dealer was desperate to get his words out to prevent the beating escalating, but all he could release was a series of coughs and splutters. Arnie sank to his knees in front of him and Tigger felt excruciating agony as a steely hand gripped him by the face, fingers digging in until he thought his cheekbones might snap.

"What you trying to say then, Tig? What little excuse can you come up with to stop me from finishing you off here and now? My God, son, you think you can crawl out of your little sewer and come around here, eh? Eh? When I bet..."

"It was the Crip!" croaked Tigger through clenched teeth.

His head catapulted into the door post, knocking him dizzy. As he focused he saw the merciless eyes staring at him from inches away. "Don't ever call him that!" stormed Arnie.

Tigger knew he was dead and buried. In his mind's eye he saw his body floating in the Thames having been unceremoniously dumped there at dead of night. He knew his only chance was to get the next bit right. Trying to free his head from the buzzing and prevent himself from choking over the words, he managed to squeeze it out. He had to say it fast and in one hit to save his skin.

"Gazza... Gary Marshall grassed you up Doles... I'm sure of it. And I ... I reckon I can prove it."

44

"WELL HELLO REG, how are you, mate?" Arnie Dolan draped his arm around the older man and leaned into his personal space, blue eyes studying his face as if trying to interpret a confusing roadmap. Eventually they latched on to Reg Philpott's own bloodshot eyes. For Reg, it felt like a silent interrogation rather than an attempt at conversation. He plucked up false bravado and attempted to answer the question.

"Hey, Arnold, I'm great! Fantastic... and you're out. Brilliant. Irish Phil told me as much. Sorry I missed your homecoming..."

"Yeah, well, never mind that, Reg, it's not a problem. You weren't the only one. Much closer friends than you missed it, too." He turned to his sidekick. "Hey, why don't we get old Reg here a drink, Vickers, and we can play catch up? How you keeping, Reg? I've been a bit, um, out of the loop, you could say. How's that stepson of yours? Now, there's a friend who was otherwise engaged for my homecoming party."

"Well, he isn't really..."

"What? Your stepson? Course he is, course he is. You've been more of a dad to him than, well, his proper old man, haven't you? You did near enough everything for that boy after you winkled your way into his family. Word has it..." he lowered his voice, "...that you even got him out of the odd scrape with the Old Bill. Am I right? I'm right. A little bird told me. You know. Even when you're locked away in clink you get to hear things. Amazing how the old 'network' functions. Come on Vickers, where's that drink? What'll it be, Reg? Pride?"

Tongue tied and disorientated by the scattergun form Arnie Dolan's words were taking, the older man just nodded in response. "Great, great. Pint of Pride for Reg and, I know, get him a little chaser to go with it. Vodka. Make it a double." All the while his eyes were boring into Reg's, daring him to protest. A murmur from the old man brought a sharp response. "What's that, Reg? Speak up…"

"Look, I really shouldn't," he said, summoning up the courage. "Our Sheila is waiting for me to…"

"Not what I heard, Reg. I'm told she booted you out. That right?"

"Umm, we're fine now, we made up. But I don't want to upset her again. You know women." He chuckled, but it came out like the last desperate squawk of a bird with its neck caught in a discarded piece of plastic packaging. With his arm applying more pressure to Reg's shoulders, Arnie turned again to his sidekick. "Oh, I know women, don't I, Vickers?" His mate nodded. "Yeah, and the way with women is to show them who's boss, Pete, isn't it? You don't want to be letting them run the show all the time, keeping secrets from you and the like, or the next thing is they are running around shagging every geezer in sight and making you look a right Muppet, with everyone knowing what the fuck's going on but you. Look, come on Reg. We won't keep you long. How about a game of pool? I just wanted to find out how my old mate was doing? Good old Gazza. My best friend. Sorry Vickers, of course you're my mate too, but you know how it is: I'm missing him greatly. I thought you might be able to shed some light, Reg, being his surrogate Dad and all."

"On my life, son, I know fuck all. She won't tell me… I dunno why."

Arnie exerted more pressure on his neck and started walking away from the bar, forcing Reg to leave his stool and accompany him across to the pool table. "Vickers, load up the balls would you? There's a good boy. Me and Reg here is gonna have a little game. I remember you were pretty good back in the day, Reg. You still got it?"

"Well, I hope…"

"Yeah, you've still got it. The thing is, you never lose a talent once you got it. You've got a talent for pool and I've got a talent for other things like, ah, finding stuff out. Like one of them detectives: Sherlock or maybe Poirot. Or what is it those Canadian coppers on horseback are called?"

"Mounties?"

"That's right, the Mounties. You know what they say about them Reg?" The older man shook his head. "No? Well they say they always get their man. That's a bit of a reputation to live up to, isn't it? Well, I reckon I'm a bit of a Mountie, because I always get my man. Heads or tails?"

Arnie Dolan produced a coin from his pocket and tossed it in the air. Reg mumbled "Heads" and it came down as tails. "Ahhh, you can break then," said Arnie. "Vickers, set up the balls would you?"

As his friend placed the triangle on the green baize, the gang leader walked to the wall and picked up a cue. When he returned he retrieved a small square of blue chalk from the table and flicked it across the end of the wooden implement. He handed it to Reg Philpott. "There you go, Reg. Show us how it's done."

Reg could feel his cue arm shaking as he bent down to address the ball. He sensed impending danger but didn't have a clue how to avert it. Making contact with the white it veered off the side of the pack, spreading the balls across the baize.

"Oh, look at that Vickers, you daft sod… you left a bloody ball off."

"Eh?"

Without warning Arnie grabbed Reg around the head and marched him to the far end of the table. "This big fucking ball here should go on the end there, just against the cushion, like this." He thrust the old man's head against the table. "It's a new game I learnt in prison called 'Killer' and the rules are this…" He lifted Reg by the hair and bent down to stare into his frightened eyes. "I play a shot and continue playing shots until you tell me everything you know about where my old mate Gary is right now and what he has been getting up to. Got it?"

"But I don't know…"

"Now you see, Reg, that's the wrong answer. Hold him Vickers…"

Arnie's accomplice looked reluctant. "Isn't there…"

"Fuckin' hold him, you cunt!"

Shocked at how quickly the situation had escalated, Vickers moved forward and held Reg's head hard against the cushion as Arnie moved to the other end of the table, chalked his cue, then walked back to address the white ball. He took two practice swings, sliding the cue effortlessly up to the white ball, then smashed it as hard as he could into a red that had escaped from the back of the pack. It collided with Reg's nose. There was a sickening crunch and a scream. "Lift him up!" commanded the pool player.

Vickers grabbed Reg by his straggly, greying hair. His nose was bleeding, a large lump appearing in the middle. Red marks stained the baize. "Here," said Arnie. "That might have hurt a bit so we probably need to apply the anaesthetic." He lifted Reg's pint of bitter from a nearby table, drank a sip from the top then poured in the double vodka. Walking over to Reg, he roughly poured the beer in the direction of his blood-stained mouth, alcohol dripping onto the pool table as he did so. "Now, a direct hit means I get another go. Before that, care to tell me the little tale of the night at the police station?"

"Gnumph." Reg found it difficult to talk through his broken nose.

"I'll start you off," offered Arnie. "Gary was arrested after our little spot of bother, am I right?"

"Phnuh."

"He was taken to the police station and the Old Bill called you, good old Reg, the stepdad. You went along to sort the problem out and…"

"… an' I dunno, s'honest truth, Arnold, you gotha…"

"Believe you? But Reg, you're a lying bastard. I don't have to believe anything you say. In fact, you're interrupting my game of Killer with this nonsense… Vickers!"

Vickers stepped forward again and pushed Reg's battered head against the baize. Arnie shaped up behind the white and sent a yellow ball crashing into Reg's ear. He howled with pain. "Ahh, you ruined my shot," said Arnie. "Your fucking big head got in the way of the pocket. Vickers, sit him down there and give him another fuckin' drink."

Reg looked like he had been a round with the world heavyweight champion. One of his eyes had swollen, his nose leaked blood and his teeth were covered in it. His ear was turning a dark shade of purple.

"Hey, you all right? Fuck, Reg, what's happened?" Irish Phil waddled around the corner into the pool area.

"Mind your own business you Irish gimp and fuck off back to the bar. Nothing's happening here, right?" One look at Arnie Dolan's face and the aggressive manner in which he was pointing the pool cue brooked no argument. The barman nodded and disappeared. "Right, Reg, have another drink and let's think this through logically," said Arnie, now totally calm. "Gary was arrested after some bloke ended up with his brains splattered in the street. He was taken to a police station and interrogated. You turned up and they let him go. Now what am I missing? I know, why DID they let him go?"

"I really don't…"

"How about," said Arnie, putting his finger to his bottom lip, "…and this is just a theory, you understand, an educated guess… how about he told them that he wasn't to blame but that he knew someone who was. Yes, and how about that someone being… oh, I don't know… for argument's sake, me… could that have happened?"

"Look, I washn't there, for the in'erviews. I dunno. Sh'poshible."

"Poshible?" said Arnie, imitating his victim. "I would say it was highly fuckin' probable… that would certainly explain why he scarpers when I come out of nick. Wouldn't it?"

Reg could do nothing but nod. "And if that's the case my next question… and this is the million dollar one, folks …" He lent down to whisper in Reg's injured ear, raising his voice at the last moment, "…WHERE THE FUCK IS HE?"

The old man started shaking his head vehemently. "Give him another drink, Vickers... help him loosen up." Vickers poured more of the pint down their prisoner's throat and over his badly soiled clothes. "Damn, we didn't finish our game of Killer." Grabbing Reg by the hair he dragged him towards the pool table again.

"No, no, shtop!" shouted the victim. "Look, Gash had to go, it was nuffin' to do wif you Arnold, honesht. His mother sesh he made a mishtake, got shum girl up the duff, needed to get away because he didn't want, you know, to pay no maintenansh. It wasn't anythin' to do with dobbin' you in." Dolan pushed Reg's head hard against the green baize.

"Who's the girl then? Maybe she can help me track him down."

"I... I dunno. If she knowsh, Sheils won't say. He would never 'ave turned you in, though, mate. Shay what you like about Gash, and I know he changed after his dad left and the ashident, but he was no grash. Never. I'll tell you shumfin' else, too. I think he changed his name... goesh by hish full name, Gareth, now. I heard the mishus on the phone..."

"At last! Something interesting," said Arnie, letting Reg go. Vickers moved forward to force their victim's head to the baize again, but Arnie had grown bored of the game. "Ah, fuck it, Reg. You're such a streak of cowardly piss you would've cracked by now if you knew more," Dolan poked at the broken nose with the cue, making his victim wince with the pain. "Fuck off out of it, before I change my mind."

Part IV

Reunions

45

"COME ON YOU silly mare, you're going to miss it!" Anjelica Dolan was leaning out of the door of the First Great Western train waving her hands in a circular motion. Out on the platform Jane Vickers hopped along, trying to reunite the high-heeled Manolo Blahnik with her foot. The expensive item of footwear had some-how become lodged in a drain cover in the platform and parted company with its owner, who had cursed loudly and retraced her steps to retrieve it. After performing a not inconsiderable feat of contortionism, she reached the carriage just as a guard emerged to give the all-clear to the driver. Anjie helped her up and they collapsed gig-gling into their seats – Max sitting in a corner by the window looking on in bemusement.

"Well," said Anjie, "That was a good start to our magical mystery tour wasn't it? You dumb-dumb! Why do you always have to make a drama into a crisis?"

"Ah, you know me Anj," said Jane, gulping in air. "Bloody shoes. They cost a fortune. The least I should expect is for them to stay on my bleedin' feet for longer than two minutes. Not that I bought them, mind. A gift from my wonderful hubby." The statement may have been made with tongue firmly inside cheek but Anjelica took it at face value.

"He's a good bloke your Pete. A real keeper. Always thought he would do right by you."

"Talking of blokes, where are we off to at this short notice then? Come on, let me in on the secret. It said Swansea on the board, are we going to Taffyland?"

"That's about the size of it."

"Don't tell me: You've met some muscle-bound rugby player or maybe a dirty, sexy coalminer." Her cackle ripped through the carriage. Snooty faces edged around magazines and newspapers trying to work out how this uncouth woman was allowed to share a carriage with them.

"Bloody hell, love, what year do you think this is, 1960? I don't think there are any mines left in Wales and where the hell am I going to meet a rugby player on the Boxers?"

"You never know."

"Oh come on, think about it. What with working all those hours at the hospital…"

"There! There!" Jane screamed, waving her hands around excitedly. "The hospital! Maybe, I don't know, some Welsh team had been playing up here at Twickenham and one of them got injured and…"

"Your imagination is running away with you, Janie," Anjie told her oldest friend. "Look, it's nothing like that. I will let you in on a secret though… it's going to be a real treat for him." She nodded in Max's direction. He was staring out of the window admiring the engines lying idle in sidings outside Paddington. It was the first time he had been on a train and the little boy had been beside himself with excitement when told of their mystery trip. He had travelled on the London Underground often enough but this was a proper locomotive, like Thomas the Tank, running on outside lines and everything.

"Oh you can't… you don't mean… really?" Jane was red in the face now and could hardly get her words out, her hands flapping like an excited teen at a boy band concert. "His D..A..D?"

Anjie nodded.

"Well… about time, I can tell you," continued Jane. "One of the biggest mysteries of the universe about to be revealed. It's like… I don't know… how they built the pyramids."

"I think they worked that out ages ago," pointed out Anjie who was, nevertheless, delighted to have brought such a look of happiness to her best friend's face. She had sensed for a while Jane wasn't in the best of spirits. She guessed her and Pete had hit a rocky patch or that the children were having problems at school. Normally Jane confided in her so she feared it might be more serious, maybe something to do with her best friend's health, heaven forbid. She didn't want to pry but thought a few days away might help her get to the bottom of the matter. There were two reasons for the trip, therefore, even though the main one was to see her bloke, Gary Marshall, the father of her child and the love of her life.

Gary had been very uneasy about the situation at first. They hadn't gone through all this just to give up the secret so easily. It had taken a lot of persuasion on Anjie's part for him to agree that her best friend could tag along. He pointed out that Janie had been quite close to Anjie's brother Arnie at one stage, but she assured him that was no longer the case. Janie was devoted to Pete and had been sworn to secrecy about their little trip. Anjie confessed that she felt Janie was pretty close to the truth anyway, her suspicions raised when they had met Gary's mum during one of their shopping trips. Just to make sure there were no accidental slip ups, Anjie hadn't even told Janie where they were heading or who they were going to meet but once the secret was out of the bag she was sure Janie would guard it with her life.

The excuse they had conjured up for Janie's family and anyone else who was curious was that they had been invited up north by one of Anjie's old nursing college mates for a hen weekend. The girl now worked in Manchester and was due to marry in a fortnight.

The final argument that swung the deal with Gary was that Janie would be able to look after Max if they needed some privacy.

TWO HOURS LATER Anjie was scanning the Cardiff Central station concourse, standing on tip-toe to see above the heads. There were hundreds of people milling around the station area and she guessed more visitors than normal had come into the Welsh capital in advance of tomorrow's rugby. Gareth had warned her that Wales' first game of the World Cup was taking place on Sunday afternoon against South Africa and that the locals would be flooding into Cardiff for a pre-match booze up. It would be like the Welsh equivalent of the Notting Hill Carnival, people donning fancy dress and planning to make a whole weekend of it, even if they hadn't managed to secure one of the 73,000 tickets which had been like gold dust to obtain.

Janie Vickers was twisting her head this way and that, stunned by the clothing of the women in this strange place. Anjie wasn't surprised. Janie wouldn't dream of leaving the house for a day out without being dressed top-to-toe in designer gear, yet the women around them were draped in all sorts of weird and wonderful garb. One girl waddled past dressed like some giant vegetable while another had her whole head transformed into a daffodil, yellow tinged face poking through the petals. Others just looked like cheap hookers in long red Welsh rugby jerseys and little else, as if they had forgotten to put on trousers that morning. Add to that a reasonable contingent wearing the familiar green of South Africa who had just got off the same train and you had an interesting mix.

Suddenly Janie spotted someone in the crowd and nudged Anjie sharply in the ribs."Oww!" her friend howled.

"Hey, isn't that…? It has to be. Oh hang on," a flicker of understanding washed across Jane Vickers' face. "Oh, you gotta be kidding me. You didn't? Really?"

"Yep, that's about the size of it."

Janie indicated to young Max. "And he's…?"

"Very clever Janie, you should be on Mastermind. Specialist subject: The bleedin' obvious."

The figure in question spotted them and pushed his way through the crowd, almost bowling over a Welsh rugby fan in a dragon costume. He looked completely different these days, his strawberry-blond hair now jet black and a lot longer than when she last saw him. There was something about him that was unmistakable, though: the limp.

When he got to within a few feet he flung himself at Anjie, giving her the tightest hug he could manage. Then he kissed her full on the lips.

"Oh, bloody hell, get a room!" said Janie, laughing.

Anjie broke away. "Well Janie, meet Laszlo," she laughed, not noticing the strange look of comprehension that had crossed her friend's face.

"Explain," asked Janie. "The Laszlo thing, I mean."

"Oh, it's just a little 'code' Gary, sorry Gareth, and I came up with. Bit silly really... I call him Laszlo and he calls me Hana. It's from that book The English Patient by Michael Ondaatje. It's a story about how an injured pilot called Laszlo crashes in Italy during the war and is nursed by a Canadian girl named Hana. It kind of reminds me of the story of our relationship."

"Really?" said Janie. "I'm afraid I don't think it's that dramatic. If you ask me it's more like a spy story... all these secrets. You call him Gareth now?"

"We have our reasons." Anjie turned to Gareth. "Now, I think there's someone you haven't seen for ages and would like to meet." She pulled Max around from where he was hiding behind her leg and, oblivious to the crowds, Gareth knelt down in front of his son. "Well, look at you," he said. "It feels like I haven't seen you for absolutely ages! Do you remember me, Max?"

The little boy looked at him doubtfully. "Are you a knight?"

Gareth was perplexed. "Um, no, not really. Would you like me to be a knight?"

"I just thought you were," the boy explained. "You just fighted that dragon."

Gareth looked in the direction Max was pointing. The bloke in the Dragon suit he had pushed past was veering through the crowds towards the exit.

"No, he's not a knight, Max," said Anjie, ruffling the little boy's hair. "He is far more important than that. This is your daddy."

THE THREE ADULTS chatted happily as Gareth led the way into the McDonalds on the High Street. It was busy but the two girls squeezed into a window seat with Max while the reporter went to the counter to order their meals. "Make sure he gets a Happy Meal," said Anjie. "He will want the T-o-y."

"Yes I want a toy… Daddy," said Max, cleverly working out the word. The adults fell around laughing and his bottom lip dropped. Anjie leaned over to reassure him. "Hey, big fella, don't cry," she said, "we're not laughing at you we're laughing at that man's balloon!" she pointed out of the window and the little boy's face brightened as he saw a character dressed head to toe in Wales gear, including shorts and rugby boots, holding an inflatable sheep by a string.

Gareth delivered their meals then squeezed in beside Anjie and sipped from a cup of coffee. "Listen," he said. "I can't stop long. Sorry and all that, but it's a bit busy for us today… press day and all. We have to do a preview to the big rugby game tomorrow. Still, I'll be all yours then. I had to pull a few strings because a lot of hotels were booked. To be honest it cost me an arm and a leg but, well, I haven't had much else to spend my money on since I got paid. I booked two nights, if that's OK."

"You'd better believe it," said Anjie. "I booked Monday off. It was hardly worth coming down here for one day and I knew you would be working. It's OK, though. We can find plenty of things to do, can't we, Janie?"

"Oh yeah, no problem," agreed her friend, looking out at the busy Cardiff streets with a smile playing across her lips. "I would quite like to do a bit of 'window' shopping to be honest. There are some mighty fit blokes around here!"

"Hey, not in front of the boy!" said Anjie with a big grin on her face. "Remember your wonderful husband, sat at home pining for you."

"Oh, God, Pete… I nearly forgot," said Janie. "Excuse me you two, I'm going to take this to go. He'll be wondering where I am so I'll check into the hotel and give him a call. Coming Max? Let's leave the grown-ups to have a little chat with each other. Hey, with any luck you may get the chance to talk to Simon. I'm sure he'll be back from football training now."

"Yay!" said Max happily. He was very fond of Janie's son who, though three years older, was good natured and happy to spend time with the little boy.

"Thanks Janie," said Anjie. "You're a treasure."

They both gave the boy a cuddle and a kiss, then watched them leave. Anjie put her hand on Gareth's and looked into his eyes. "You know, it's such a crying shame that things have to be like this," she said. "It's not fair you can't see your son."

"I miss him and I miss you, but what choice did we have?"

Her eyes fell to the table. "None I suppose. You know what Arnie's like. He'd only think his best friend and his beloved sister had been sneaking around behind his back – he can be so paranoid."

"It's not as if it was an affair, though, is it? Neither of us was seeing anyone else, we weren't married, so there really was no rhyme or reason behind any of it. It's just... well, you're right. We both know he wouldn't understand. It's just the way his mind works."

"Perhaps we should have gone to Wandsworth together... broken the news to him," she said.

"The opportunity never really arose though, did it?" he said. "The longer we left it the worse things got. If he found out now he would be apoplectic that we kept it from him for so long. I bet he thinks Max's dad just ran off, neglected his responsibilities and left his poor sister in the lurch."

"Probably, but that couldn't be further from the truth," she said. "You've given me everything I need: love, money... and him." She indicated to the door though Max had long gone.

"I can never see him mellowing, Anjie, not now," he said, switching the conversation back to Arnie. "I've heard through the grapevine that prison made him worse. What are you going to do, appeal to the good side of his nature? I'm afraid he buried that away a long time ago and even you would struggle to find it now, though you're closer to him than anyone."

"True. I can't help feeling, though, that he would rather his best friend was the father than some stranger." She was trying to convince herself but found it impossible to commit to the statement.

"I don't think it would work either way," said Gareth, who had always known he would need a clean break from the Boxer Boys if he was to succeed in his profession. It stood to reason he couldn't be seen harbouring close ties to gangsters. The real reason behind the move to Wales was that Arnie would be released some day and would be looking for his mate, expecting their friendship to take up where it had left off when he was locked away. As close as they had been, though, Gareth knew in his heart the relationship was destructive and to re-establish it would be to resurrect the past at the expense of the future. Changing the subject he said: "You've seen Mum, I hear."

"Yeah, she's fine. Questions, questions... you know what she's like. And she spoils him rotten whenever she sees him. I'm surprised, though, she's managed to keep the secret this long."

"My mum's good at keeping secrets – look how long she kept my dad's bloody womanising from everyone."

"I guess." Anjie patted him on the arm.

"The last time I spoke to her she was moaning on about Reg," he continued. "She told me that they'd split up and accused him of running off with her Status Quo tickets."

"Hey, that reminds me," said Anjie. "I saw him last night... Reg. He looked in a bad way like, I don't know, someone had given him a battering."

"She can be pretty tasty when her hackles are up!" said Gareth with a grin.

"Your mum didn't do it, silly! I don't know who did, but he was a sorry sight. I was going to ask if he was all right but when he saw me he crossed the street as if he was trying to avoid me."

"Embarrassed probably," said Gareth. "I expect he upset someone by beating them at pool down The Hope." Though he was trying to play the incident down, Anjie's revelation was making him feel uneasy.

Fortunately, she changed the subject. "What do you have planned for us then?"

"Well tomorrow I'll show you a bit of the real Wales. We'll go out to the valleys in the morning and have some brekky at the rugby club…"

"Rugby? You drag me all the way down here just for a sport you don't even like?"

Gareth looked hurt. "Well, it's growing on me to be honest and, anyway, all my friends will be there."

Her face cracked into a grin. "Had you there! It will be fun, I'm sure. Max will enjoy it, too, he's fascinated by all this fancy dress."

"Well, they're putting on a pre-game breakfast… full fry up, the works. It's very much a family affair. You'll be able to meet the Shakespeares."

"They're the people you lodge with?"

"That's right. They're fantastic. They've been really good to me. I never really liked the Welsh…"

"Don't I just know it! You grumbled all the way down for the interview and all the way back."

"Yeah, but these guys are different. I'm sure you'll like them, and I know they'll like you."

"And after the breakfast party?"

"I thought we could take Max for a bit of sightseeing, maybe down to Cardiff Bay for a boat ride or something… then perhaps you can meet up with Janie for the afternoon and I'll head off to the match."

"Sounds great."

"There's also somewhere I want to take you tomorrow night, but it's going to be a bit late for Max."

"Don't worry about that, it's why I bought Janie along. She'll be fine with it, particularly now she is in on the secret. I think she's thrilled, really. She was worried I'd copped off with some rugby hunk for God's sake. So, where are we going? Is it a surprise? A nice romantic meal or…"

"Actually, it's a night out at the wrestling," he confided, a grin creeping across his face.

46

"ABOUT BLOODY TIME, darlin', where are you?"

Jane Vickers felt a shiver pass the length of her body. He was being overly familiar, as if it was the most natural thing in the world for her to be talking to the man who had raped her and was threatening to wreck her marriage. She wondered whether she should lie, but knew he would find out the truth soon enough and punish her for her deception. She brushed a stray hair behind her ear and looked over at Max, who was perched on the edge of the budget hotel's bed, engrossed in cartoons on the TV. She felt an utter cow for betraying her closest friend, but what alternative did she have? She knew Arnie was not a man to renege on a promise and would follow through with the threats he had made if she didn't do as he commanded. Where would that leave her? A family ripped apart, a fallen woman dumped, her children turning against her once they recognised the depths of her betrayal.

She flopped onto the bed, phone to her ear, and fiddled with her troublesome designer shoe. It made her think of Pete. She already felt a traitor of the worst kind, a complete whore, for what she had done to him. She could tell herself it was rape, sure, but had she really put up a strong enough fight? A part of her felt she had brought it on herself, not being fully dressed when he awoke that morning, sending out an invitation. If it came to the crunch, who would Pete believe? He knew that in her younger days she'd had a thing for Arnie, and the bastard could be pretty persuasive at times. Her husband thought the sun shone out of his arse and, besides, she felt he wasn't strong enough to fight his corner against such a powerful personality.

"Are you there Janie, my little nymph? You going to tell old Arnie where you two have flitted off to? Good hen night? Have you seen the sights of Manchester or are you soaking up the summer rays?" In the silence that followed she could hear his breath, almost smell the scent of cigars on it which in turn brought a mental flashback to the scene in her kitchen where that same breath had been hot on her neck, loud in her ear as he thrust, the pain coming back sharply as she relived the whole disgusting scene in her head. What a bastard you are for doing that to me, she thought.

She didn't say what she was thinking though, just responded to his prompts with three words: "We're in Cardiff."

"Fuck off, really?" he said. "Little old Wales eh? Well, well! Laszlo doesn't sound a very Welsh name though, does it, babe? More your Eastern Europe type I'd have thought. What is he a Polish porter at some cheap hotel? An Estonian waiter? Strange. I blame the EU personally. Still, could be a Taff I suppose though if that was the case I'd expect him to be called something like Iestyn or Iolo or…"

"Gareth."

"Yeah, or Gareth."

"No. It's Gareth."

"Oh right, so she… wait. I don't get it. Is that supposed to ring a bell?"

"I'm telling you that Max's father is called Gareth… You know him better as Gazza, though."

Silence again. This time it wasn't for effect. She knew she had sucked the oxygen from his lungs, and for a moment it pleased her. It had been said deliberately in a way that would cause him maximum hurt, and it brought an abrupt halt to the easy-going patter, vacuuming his mind of scattergun nonsense. After what seemed like minutes but was barely a handful of seconds, he spoke again, the four words shouted so loudly she feared they would shatter her eardrums.

"The fucking traitorous cunt!"

47

MAX STARED in awe. His eyes weren't focused on the big screen, which was currently replaying great sporting moments of the past, but admiring the sight of a Welsh rugby crowd in all its glory. There were characters everywhere he looked. One person had painted his entire body green and dressed in rags like the Incredible Hulk while another group were pretending to be tribal warriors, paying tribute to the fact that Wales were up against South Africa in their first game of the World Cup. Chests bare and faces painted, they wore little more than loincloths. More Red Indian than African warrior, thought Gareth.

Others were resplendent in British Army battle dress from the turn of the 20th century, white helmets with red jackets and gold buttons. Their inspiration was Zulu, the cult film starring Stanley Baker and a young Michael Caine which immortalised the battle of Rorke's Drift where a handful of soldiers – many of them Welsh – kept hordes of savages at bay. Gareth guessed those soldiers must have possessed similar resolve to the under-fire bar staff in Pontyprenis Rugby Club, who were performing a sterling job keeping the howling mob at arms' length. Hell, he thought, this lot will be comatosed by the time the game starts at 2pm.

He described the mob as howling, but in all fairness they were pretty tuneful, belting out renditions of "Hymns and Arias", "Sospan Fach" and the old Tom Jones favourite "Delilah". The room swayed and heaved like a stormy Atlantic Ocean, sweeping everyone along with it. In the midst of the sea of bodies Gareth saw Jason and Will, arm in arm, using each other as human life preservers. Genuinely happy to be in one another's company they also looked delighted to be surrounded by their fellow villagers.

Sitting next to him was the Pontyprenis vicar, a genial fellow in his 60s called Gwynfor who had been more than happy to lend a bed to a troubled ex-rugby player. "You lot manage to generate a fantastic atmosphere, Gwyn," said the reporter. "Tell me... what would it be like if your boys reached the final?" He noticed traces of his newly acquired Welsh accent breaking through.

"Well, boy," said Gwyn, sipping an orange juice, "they would have to order a hell of a lot more beer." The two men laughed, easy in each other's company.

"Talking of beer, where is he?" asked Gareth, nervously scanning the crowd. "He's not going to make a 'special appearance', is he?"

"Oh no, he's given me his word," replied the churchman. "He's promised to stay in the back room behind a locked door with a TV, a phone and that notebook of his. They're going to interview him on the radio later – the BBC made a special request, so he's getting his ideas together before they call."

"Great," said Gareth, realising it would be good publicity for the paper to have their star columnist getting wider exposure. "Listen, do me a favour and keep an eye on Max for a bit. I want Anjie to meet The Legend... after all, she deserves to see the person who has been taking up all of my time lately."

"No trouble, boy, he will be fine with me." He ruffled Max's hair. "Isn't that right?" The boy nodded gratefully. He had been spoilt rotten that morning, having his own special viewing of Will's massive collection of model race cars.

Gareth whispered something to Anjie and she nodded, getting to her feet and grasping his hand. Gwynfor and Max watched them get swallowed up by the crowd.

GARETH UNLOCKED A wooden door at the side of the main hall. Careful first to check no one was watching, he slipped inside and pulled Anjie after him. "Hey!" she said, "What's all the secrecy. You're not thinking..."

"Umm, no, sorry," he said, his face colouring. "Not that. There's someone I want you to meet. He's a bit special, to be honest, he's kind of become my project."

Her eyes flicked around the room until they fell on a figure sitting at a chair sipping an orange juice and frantically scribbling notes, a telephone at his side. He had salt and pepper shoulder-length hair, white specks of dandruff decorating the collar of a stained blue jacket that had seen better days. He was wearing formal black trousers, as if en route to a dinner engagement, and he was so wrapped up in his work it was only when they were yards from him that he registered their presence. A red, slightly overweight face looked up and creased into a beaming smile. "So," said The Legend. "You have been hiding something from me or, rather, someone."

He rose from his chair, despite Anjie's protests, and delicately lifted her hand to his lips. "Delighted to meet you, my lovely," he said. "If you're a close friend of Geraint's here, then you are a close friend of mine." Anjie looked quizzically at Gareth and he briefly shook his head as if to say: "Yes, I know. He gets my name wrong all the time. It doesn't matter."

The Legend then pulled another chair from beneath the table. "Come on my lovely, take a seat. I've got a bit to do. I'm on the radio in a minute, then we can have a proper chat. Excuse me if I'm a bit excited, it's the curse of being Welsh on the day of a big rugby game."

"SO WHAT DOES the JW stand for?" asked Anjie. They had sneaked back to the Vicarage through a side door and were cosily ensconced in the front room with cups of tea and biscuits. Gwynfor had become quite attached to Max and had taken him out to see some of the animals in the nearby fields.

"It's John Wayne, after his father's favourite actor," explained Gareth.

"Oh I see," she said, taking a bite of her biscuit. "Get off your horse..."

"...And drink your milk!" JW and Anjie fell about laughing, The Legend's frivolity developing into a coughing fit. She walked over and rubbed his back.

"You should get that seen to," she said, waiting for him to bring it under control.

"Most kind dear," he said finally. "I can see you're an excellent nurse. Lovely bedside manner about you."

"Ahh, thanks."

Gareth had always suspected Anjie would get on well with the oddball Welshman should their paths cross. It was something which had attracted him to her in the first place. She was a kind, considerate person by nature who made it her life's project to defend and protect the underdog. Her job as a nurse indicated that plainly enough, but in other circumstances this need to repair damaged goods was all too evident. As an example he only had to consider his own experience, the care she'd shown him after the incident. She'd also stuck by her brother during his years behind bars and done the odd favour for Gareth's mother when she wasn't in the best of health.

The Legend, of course, would never countenance the idea he was damaged goods. Admittedly, the last few days had put his life into sharp focus, but he was still reluctant to face up to the whole truth. His father had bought him up to behave "like a man", to bury his feelings as deep as the coal mines that cut into the surrounding hills. This attitude had manifested itself over a lifetime and was not easy to change. There was his public to consider, too, even though he valued their view of him far more highly than they deserved. Gareth had come to realise that many rugby fans throughout Wales still admired JW Owens for what he did decades ago, but couldn't care less about his present state. They had moved on to newer, shinier heroes – ones that could realise their current goals and, frankly, had yet to become an embarrassment. If truth were told The Legend was a myth to them, as alive and human as those mugs, paintings and strange statues known as Grogs which had been crafted in his honour.

If JW was keeping up an image it was for himself... no one else. His daughter would want to see the person she knew as dad. If she wished to meet a Welsh entertainer she could go to the Sydney Opera House the next time Max Boyce was in town. JW's true friends like Will and, yes, Gareth, just wanted to see him living life in the moment. People at the paper, like Jacko and Lana, who wanted to milk his expertise while reimbursing him a pittance. Those boys he met at the pub? They could take a long walk off a short pier. They were users not mates, the damn lot of them. Real mates would never have let him get into this condition.

Gareth's thoughts were interrupted as Max ran into the room, a worn-out Gwynfor trailing in his wake. He did a quick lap of the furniture then disappeared out of another door at the far end of the room.

"He's a lovely kid," said JW. "Reminds me of my boy."

"You have a son?" she asked.

Gareth thought he had better jump in. "I don't think..."

"It's all right," said the old man. "I'm among friends. Gwynfor's been trying to get me in the confessional ever since I got here." He chuckled. "Maybe it's about time."

"I get a lot of people in the hospital offloading their troubles to me," said Anjie. "It always seems to make them feel better."

"My boy died," said JW bluntly, breathing a sigh of relief once the words were out. "A long time ago now. It was unfortunate, one of those million-to-one chances. Whenever I think about it I keep coming back to the fact he should never have been there in the first place." His mind drifted as he gazed out of the window. "Lovely boy, my Martin. A lot of people said he took after me. He wasn't bad at rugby either, but to be honest his real talent was comedy." He chuckled as if remembering a joke.

"He sounds easy going, like you I guess," said Anjie, gently coaxing the story from him.

"Oh no, love. He was much funnier than me. At the time I lost him he was coming up to 30 and making a name for himself doing stand-up shows, mostly around the rugby clubs in the area. He had just been invited onto one of those TV programmes that showcase young talent and a few agents were knocking on the door. His big break was long overdue."

"He stayed with you when your wife left?" asked Gareth.

"Yeah. He was a loyal boy. He had to put up with a lot, the bailiffs knocking the door, me having to move us at a moment's notice to various dodgy flats – the only places I could afford that would have me – but he took it all in good humour, said he couldn't move away from Wales, that he would be homesick, miss his friends. His mum didn't like it, of course, didn't think I could look after him. She was right, wasn't she?"

Anjie noticed the old rugby star's eyes watering, the tears starting to form. "It sounds like there was nothing you could have done, though," she said.

"I could have stopped him going," said The Legend.

"Going where?"

JW considered the question. "He usually played rugby on a Saturday, see, for one of the Cardiff village teams. At the last moment, though, he changed his plans. The game was cancelled: the opponents couldn't raise a side. Then he got a call from one of his old school mates, told him they were off on a trip and it would be a good laugh. What I think they really meant was it would be a good laugh if he tagged along because he could provide the entertainment on the journey..." He smiled briefly then his voice caught. "I never saw him again."

Anjie draped her arm around his bulky shoulders and gave them a squeeze. "Look," he said, "I can't do this now. It's always like this, I struggle to find the words. The story's all here, though." He put his hand inside his trademark blazer and pulled out a scratched leather wallet that had seen better days. Opening it, he dipped his hand inside and pulled out a well-worn scrap of paper. Carefully unfolding it, he looked at it briefly then handed it over to Anjie. As he sat back in his chair, The Legend's hand went to his temple as if shielding his eyes from the glare of the sun. Gareth knew, though, he was once again engulfed in grief.

Looking back at Anjie, Gareth saw that her mouth was hanging open and her eyes were wide in shock. Before he could ask her what was wrong, she beckoned him over and handed him the paper. It was a press cutting, from a local South Wales evening paper.

Out of a faded, yellowing page of newsprint stared the menacing mugshot of a face he hadn't seen for years. The headline that ran alongside it announced: *"Thug jailed after rugby star's son killed in football brawl"*.

The photograph was that of his best friend Arnold Dolan.

48

"LOOK AT AT these mugs." Arnie surveyed the battle zone which was the Cardiff Central railway station concourse. The sheer volume of semi-clad and drunken men and women amid the overall carnage astounded him, the aftermath of an international rugby match in the Welsh capital. "What have they got to celebrate, anyway? Have they won the FA Cup or something?"

"It's the rugby, Doles," pointed out Pete Vickers. "They played their first game in the World Cup today against South Africa, that's why we couldn't get train tickets until this late in the day."

"Rugby? That's a toffs game, ain't it?"

"National sport of Wales, apparently," said Fancy Man. "Don't ask me. I can't understand it, myself."

"Nah, right."

Two drunken men stumbled past them, arm in arm, knocking against Arnie as they did so. He gave one of them a sly dig in the ribs but his victim was too anaesthetised from the afternoon's alcohol intake to notice. "Stupid fuckers," sneered Arnie. "So I guess they won, right?"

"Not quite," said Tigger.

"You mean, they're all happy as Larry, celebrating and stuff, and they lost? Man, what kind of mixed up fuckin' country is this?"

They all nodded in agreement but no one uttered another word as they scanned the panorama laid out in front of them. A slightly slurred rendition of Hymns and Arias came from the direction of the bus terminals where hordes of locals ebbed and flowed like a red tide. "Anyway, we've got a schedule to keep," said Arnie, grabbing hold of an overweight girl who was hobbling past on one foot, a shoe missing from the other. "Oi, where's this Millennium Stadium?" he asked.

She adjusted the cleavage she was proudly displaying to the world from beneath what appeared to be a red basque. "You serious?" she asked, chewing her gum with manic enthusiasm. "Bleedin' Nora, you must be from another planet." He tightened his grip and pulled her closer.

"Oi! You're hurting me," she protested.

"Now if I knew where the bloody place was I wouldn't be asking you, would I?" he said through gritted teeth. "Now, pretty please. We are here for the wrestling and need to get to the Millennium Stadium."

She shook him off and gave him a confused look. "Wrestling?" she shrugged her shoulders. "OK... OK. Well, you just go straight on, through the terminal, across the main road and you can't miss it. Great big thing it is. Home of the mighty Welsh rugby team. Not wrestling, rugby. Now fuck off and let me celebrate with my pals." She hobbled away.

"Charming lot, ain't they?" Arnie said, turning to his entourage. He received grunts and nods in acknowledgement.

"You going to tell us what we're doing here, Doles?" asked Tigger.

Arnie swung his arm out and caught the drug dealer in a headlock. "Well, my old son, it's like this. I reckon we've found my rat thanks to that useful tip of yours and now we are here to trap him, you know. Then the plan is to establish his guilt, like in one of those TV courtroom dramas."

"The Cri... I mean Gary. It's him?"

"Yeah, well that's what we're here to find out."

"What you going to do if it's him, Doles? I mean, you don't want to end up inside again, do you?"

Arnie gave him a withering look. "Hopefully it won't come to that. I need to see what he says, but if it is him, I can't let anyone get away with something like that."

He put his hand to his chest, feeling the comfort of hard steel beneath the material before leading the way to the stadium, Tigger and the other Boxer Boys falling in behind.

IN A CROWDED function room in the bowels of the Millennium Stadium Gareth and Anjie stood at the bar. They were talking with a strangely dressed man who could easily have been mistaken for a Shakespearean actor. "I love your uniform," said Anjie, raising her glass of red wine in a mock toast.

"Thanks very much," said Will Shakespeare. "We're called the Bard Guys, see, and it all goes with the name."

"Well, I think it's terrific and I can't wait to watch you in action," she said. "I think it's great what you're doing: You being father and son. How old is Jason?"

"He's a mere pup – 16 at the last count."

"Well, he's certainly a big boy for his age, and a real tribute to you Will... and, by the way, I have to tell you: I love your accent!"

"Talking of accents..." a voice behind her made Anjie flinch. She span on her heels to see Jason standing there, dressed in similar costume. "Oh, er, sorry about that, didn't mean to make you jump," he said. "It's just I saw a gang of lads at the door talking very much like you two, what d'you call yourselves? Cockerneys?"

Gareth felt a wave of unease sweeping through his body. "Really?"

"Yeah," said Jase. "They were pretty insistent they got in, like. It's meant to be a ticket-only affair but I saw one of the bouncers pocket a wad of cash and wave them through. Think one of them mentioned boxing... probably got the wrong flippin' event. Strange names they had, too. One of them called another one whasisname, ah, Tigger, like out of Winnie The Pooh. Anyway, I thought I'd better tell you ... hey, where's he going?"

Gareth was walking off in the direction of the entrance, his head flicking one way then the other, scanning the crowd. "What's up with your bloke?" asked Will.

"I'm not sure," said Anjie, her eyes betraying her.

Will's interrogation was interrupted abruptly by a bell ringing in the distance. "Shit!" he said, "that'll be us, then. I hope you enjoy the show, lovely. It's been great to meet you. I'm sure there's something better you could be doing with your Sunday night than watching two fully grown men romp around in tights, but we're honoured you're here. I hope you'll find it entertaining."

Will indicated with his thumb and headed for the dressing rooms, his son following close behind. As she watched them go, she felt a vibration in the front pocket of her black trousers. Reaching in, she withdrew her phone and studied it. There was a new text message. It was from Janie and said simply: "Sorry Anj. They r on way & after Gaz."

It took a moment to sink in then the truth hit Anjelica Dolan like a sledgehammer. She wheeled around in panic, searching the crowd for Gareth. Taking the same route he had followed, she frantically bobbed up and down, peering over the sea of heads. She couldn't find him but what she did see sent a chill sweeping through her body. Two faces she knew well were scanning the crowd in the same way that she was, two faces that were completely out of place in this environment. One was her eldest brother Chuck, the other the bloke they called Fancy Man. She quickened her pace and seeing Gareth 50 yards ahead of her, broke into a run, pushing past the people queuing at one of the bars.

"Watch it lady!" an angry voice protested.

"Hey, there's a queue," said another.

"Gareth! Hey!" she shouted, closing the gap until she could reach forward and touch his shoulder. He wheeled around, fists raised.

"Oh, Anj, it's you. Sorry..." he said.

"You know, don't you?" she said. "You know they're here. I didn't tell them, honestly, and I'm pretty sure I wasn't followed. I've just seen Chuck and..."

"Janie," he said, resignedly.

"Yeah, looks like it. Sorry." She shrugged her shoulders.

Suddenly from their left came a familiar voice, cutting like a scalpel through the background hubbub of excited Welsh voices. "Well, fuck me old boots!" spat Arnie Dolan. "Look who we have here? It's my lovely sister and, well, I'm not sure, he looks a bit different, smartly dressed with darker hair and a bit chubbier, but it seems it might be my best fucking mate Gary Marshall. What's more, if I'm not mistaken they're sharing a cosy moment together. How bleedin' sweet."

Anjie stepped forward, putting her body between Arnie and Gareth. "Hi, babes, what a surprise! What on earth are you…?"

"Out of the way, Anj," he said, roughly shoving her aside. "You wouldn't keep your big bro from his best buddy now, would you? Gazza? It is you, isn't it? I didn't recognise you with that extra bulk and those luscious black locks. You in disguise? Come to think of it, I think I even heard my little sis call you Gareth. Strange. Hiding from anyone in particular?" Leaving no room for answers to his scattergun questions, Arnie moved forward as if to hug the reporter, then pulled back at the last moment, blowing air kisses like a celebrity chat show host.

"Hello Arnie," answered Gareth warily.

"Jeez, it's been a long time," said Arnie. "Buy us a pint would you? Lager, if you don't mind spending some of that hard earned dosh of yours – I haven't been out and about to earn any I'm afraid. It's a long story, but then again I bet you got tales to tell. We should sit down and do a swap. I'll tell you about my eight-year fight to stay alive in a prison where someone was always trying to shiv you in the back and you can tell me how you've ended up here, no doubt on a nice little earner – oh, and how you knocked up my little sis, too."

"Don't, Arnie…"

"Don't what?" said Arnie, his face hardening. "Don't feel a teensy bit miffed I've been shunted aside by the two people I care about the most? Don't feel slightly niggled I've been made to look a fuckin' mug because everyone knows something I don't? I'll tell you exactly what I can and cannot do. We'll have that catch up we should have had long ago, if only you would have had the decency to visit me in Wandsworth. Hell, I was used to people trying to knife me in the back there. I didn't expect it from my mates and family on the outside."

"I was gonna visit, Arnie…"

"Course you were, soldier, course you were. Let's sit here and you can trot out your lame excuses and lies. Vickers?" His friend appeared at his shoulder without giving Gareth a glance. "Entertain my little sis, would you? She loves a glass of red. Me and 'Gareth' need a private natter."

Anjie considered protesting but knew the situation was hopeless. Vickers, along with Fancy, Tigger and Chuck, blocked her path to Arnie and her boyfriend. She feared it wouldn't end well. There was a time, before the incident, when Gareth might have held his own. Now his movement was hampered and even if he got the better of Arnie, he was vastly outnumbered. A word from their esteemed leader and the other Boxer boys would steam in, too wary of what the consequences might be if they were to stand aside and let the situation unfurl. Her heart pounding, she looked around for allies. Too late, the lights were going down and the MC was announcing the main event.

"Ladies and gentlemen, I am delighted to present, for your entertainment, coming to the big city from the valleys, the poet laureates of the grapple game, the playful playwrights. Coming out of the red corner tonight, please give a big Cardiff welcome to… the Bard Guys!"

The cheers were deafening as Jason and Will Shakespeare leapt the ropes in unison then bounced around the canvas. Anjie wanted to grab their attention but realised she would be just one of hundreds of people throwing their arms in the air. Looking back over her shoulder, she realised Arnie and Gareth had been swallowed up by the crowd.

49

ARNIE TOOK A swig of lager and wiped his mouth. The two men were sitting as far from the wrestling ring as was possible. The gang leader didn't want any distractions. He leaned close, his eyes fixed on Gareth's. "So tell me... you and my sister. How did that come about?"

Gareth took a drink too. His knee was throbbing again and he needed to dull the sensation. "We fell in love, mate. Pure and simple."

"And when did this momentous event occur? I don't remember getting no wedding invite, or video of the christening. Oh hang on, you're not married and you're living hundreds of miles apart. Weird love affair if you ask me. I should expect betrayal from you, though. It's in the genes, ain't it? What with your old man knocking up anyone who took his fancy."

Gareth's face hardened. "Don't even think about comparing me to my dad! This is exactly why we didn't tell you. We thought you would act like this... that you wouldn't understand."

Arnie leaned forward in his chair. "Well, I can't lie, it hurts me. Even more so when I have to find out like this. Christ! All my life I been fed stories that ain't true, just to keep me sweet. Surely you knew I was always going to find out... you know I'm a persistent bastard when I want to get to the bottom of something. Still, enough of that. Tell me about the other betrayal... the one where you coughed your guts up to the Old Bill."

"What?" Gareth's disbelief sounded genuine.

"Ahhh, didn't think I'd find out about that either, did you? Well, your stepdad, good old Reg, spilt the beans. Can't trust parents can you, eh? First your old man does a runner with some old tart then good old 'uncle' Reg gives away your precious secrets. He told me you were pulled in by the Old Bill just after that bit of trouble we had at football. I wondered why you didn't make it to The Hope that night. Apparently you were released without charge. Then, lo and behold, the next day the police come and knock down my door! Coincidence? I don't do coincidences. I don't need no psychic to work out the two things are related."

Gareth took another sip of his drink. He realised how guilty he looked to Arnie, and wondered how he might change his friend's perception. "It's true," he said. "I did get picked up by the law, but I swear to you, Doles… your name didn't even come up. So, whatever happened, it wasn't down to me. Do you think I'd do that to you after what you did for me?"

"Honestly? I don't know, Gar, would you?" said Arnie. "There was a time when I knew exactly how your mind worked, but since Brighton I've been unable to figure you out. Maybe you did something to your bonce cos you fucking changed. Or perhaps you blamed me for busting your leg and wanted to get even. That would explain the Anjie thing, too. You wanna rub my nose in it, get back at me by putting my sis in the club. With me out of the way it gave you a clear run. The funny thing is none of it would have happened if I hadn't come to your rescue. Again! I pulled that big fucker off you and maybe saved your life. Strange, eh?" He looked around. "Here we are talking about this in Cardiff when it was these fuckin' Taffs that started the whole thing off."

His words triggered something in Gareth. "Look, there's something you need to know."

"Really? Bit late for confessions. I already know…"

"No you don't. Not this. Remember the bloke that died?"

"Some Cardiff mug? Not really. It was mayhem."

"I know, but do you remember the name – from the court case?"

"I'm hardly going to forget, am I? Owen it was."

"Owens."

"Well, if you know why you asking me?"

"Because what you probably don't realise is he was the son of Wales' biggest rugby celebrity who is somewhere in this building as we speak. Our papers didn't make much of the story, just an everyday football incident, but down here it was headline news. I ought to warn you that this bloke, JW Owens, carries the story of your court case in his wallet... together with a picture of you."

"Warn me? Warn me?" Arnie raised his voice. "You ain't in any position to warn anyone Gary fucking Marshall."

Gareth looked around, aware their raised voices had attracted an audience. Big mistake. Arnie took advantage of the distraction to launch himself across the table, grabbing the reporter by the tie and pulling it tight. Gareth started choking. "I don't want to do this... you know I don't," said Arnie. "But I got a whole team watching me, waiting to seize on any little weakness. I'm like the captain, like Kevin Nolan at the Hammers, leading by example. If I let you off, what are those boys gonna think? Arnie's gone soft? They'll all try it on... I've seen it happen in prison when the big daddy lets his guard down. You've made treachery fashionable, Gar – the next time one of them's in trouble what's to stop them stitching me up for it, eh? 'It worked for the Crip', they'll say. Lord, I just wish you'd have come in with me when you had the chance. I would have got you the best lawyer, it could have been sorted in no time."

His finger shot out, jabbing Gareth in the eye and temporarily blinding him. Removing a knife from his pocket he rammed the point ferociously into Gareth's hand, pinning him to the table. Pain came in waves and when the scream escaped it took seconds for him to register that it was from his own voice. Around them, people moved back hurriedly, frightened of being sucked into the fray.

"See? You see? You hurt me and I can hurt you!" said Arnie, whispering words through clenched teeth. "Look, blood brothers." He pulled out the knife and smeared the blade across his cheek, leaving a trail of red war paint down his face. Wide eyed, Gareth nursed his hand as he watched his own blood soak into the table top and realised how demented his friend had become. Arnie had always possessed an aggressive streak but there had been a semblance of underlying humanity if you looked closely enough. It seemed the real Arnie had been eroded during his time inside those prison walls.

Arnie pushed the point of the knife close to Gareth's eye and was about to strike again when a shriek came from behind them. A flailing, out-of-control figure jumped on the gangster from behind, punching him in the side of the head. Whirling, the gang leader stared in disbelief as an ageing cowboy fell from his back. Jabbing his knife in the air to keep the loony at bay, Arnie watched the cowboy regain his feet and back off, breathing heavily. "Run!" the cowboy shouted to Gareth, who was sprawled across the table.

"John Wayne?" the reporter was unable to believe his eyes.

"What the fuck is this?" said Arnie, aghast. "It's a bloody freak show. John Wayne? You're having a laugh... and there I was thinking it was Clint bloody Eastwood."

"Name's Owens," said The Legend, hands on his knees. "You should know it well. It was the name of the person you killed... my boy. I recognised you as soon as I set eyes on you. I've carried your picture around in my wallet for years. Manslaughter? You got off lightly. You're a bloody murderer."

"Christ," exclaimed Arnie, not looking quite so self-assured as the crowd's tension seeped through to him. "You couldn't make this shit up. I don't know what you're talking about, but I reckon you live in some kind of fantasy land. I wouldn't be shocked if the lone fuckin' Ranger and Tonto rode to the fucking rescue soon."

"Funny guy," said The Legend. "Well, my lad was funny, too. They said he was the life and soul. His mates took him to his first away football game ever just to liven up the journey. He never came back, though. Apparently they got themselves into trouble and, like a good mate, he tried to help them out. Trouble was, he ran into you."

"Jeez, you know nothing," said Arnie. "You weren't even there. Still, come on then, you want to do this now? Give it your best shot."

As The Legend straightened up, Gareth realised he had to take advantage of the confusion. He rolled from the table, biting back the agony as his bad leg made contact with the ground. Removing his tie and wrapping it around his injured hand, he hobbled his way through the crowd. The pain was excruciating, but he knew delay would lead to worse punishment. Looking over his shoulder, he saw Arnie's head jerking from side to side, trying to work out which battle to fight first.

"Vickers! Fancy! Chuck! Fuckin' stop him!" he shouted. "I've got some bloody cowboy nutcase to deal with here." The three men looked around, confused to see their leader in a face-off with a crazy old man in a stetson. They looked in the direction Arnie was pointing and saw The Crip hobbling towards them. Preparing to intercept him, none of them realised that Anjelica had slipped away to ringside.

Will Shakespeare had hold of the leg of an opponent in a Spiderman mask when he heard her shout. Seeing Anjie's anguished face below him, he twisted the limb viciously, not realising the pressure he was exerting. There was a crack and Spiderman banged the canvas. "For fuck's sake, Will, we're only supposed to be playing at this shit," muttered the injured wrestler effeminately. "I think you've busted my leg, bach!"

Will wasn't listening, though. He leapt from his kneeling position, jumped the top rope and shouted for his son to follow. The crowd turned to watch the Shakespearean tag team transferring the action from the ring to the auditorium, thinking it all part of the act. Assessing the situation, Will jumped onto Fancy Man's back, grabbed his head and thrust it forward just as Chuck turned to see what was going on. The crack was audible as their two skulls collided and they fell to the floor. The audience were hysterical, cheering and applauding.

"Fuck!" said Vickers, turning away from the advancing Gareth. At that precise moment Jason launched into a flying kick which connected with the Boxer Boy's throat. Vickers crumpled to his knees gasping for air. Both Shakespeares were on their feet now and Will started exchanging punches with Sly. Jason, meanwhile, turned his attention to drug dealer Tigger, who took one look and fled through the crowd. His getaway was halted, though, as a giant rugby-playing Welshman with a head the size and shape of a cinderblock stuck out an arm. Tigger's feet flew from under him. Landing in a dazed heap on the floor, he found the vice captain of Pontyprenis rugby team staring down at him. "Bloody English, coming over here causing trouble," he said.

Clapping and chanting filled the room. "Bard Guys, Bard Guys", the crowd repeated, thrilled at the value for money they were getting. Their attention switched to Arnie, who was circling a man dressed as a cowboy, jabbing at him with a six-inch blade. There was a murmur of disappointment as the older Shakespeare grabbed the cowboy from behind and pulled him away from the confrontation. Arnie swivelled, searching out his No. 1 target.

He caught sight of Gareth pushing his way through double doors to emerge on the main concourse inside the stadium. Hobbling forward the reporter searched anxiously for the best escape route as the shouts and cheers faded into the background. Not for long, though. Suddenly the door behind him burst open and Arnie Dolan emerged, knife in hand and blazing fury in his eyes.

50

GARETH CHANCED ON the nearest door to his left and pushed hard, emerging inside the main bowl of the stadium. He was in a hospitality box, looking out on the vast expanse of green where the Welsh rugby team had earlier performed in front of a packed crowd. He knew he had to put space between himself and Arnie and hope for the best. He was playing for time.

Using his good leg as a springboard he vaulted a barrier and landed in the main stand. Shuffling wildly between the seats, he reached a wider concourse leading upwards and began tackling the steep steps, wounded hand gripping his injured knee and leaving dark blood stains to congeal there. A voice behind him interrupted his stuttering progress. "You can't run forever, you fuckin' rat!" sneered Arnie, leaping the barrier from the hospitality box and joining him in the stand.

Looking down, Gareth realised how steep the steps were and how high above the pitch he was. It made him feel nauseous. He was struck by vertigo, a dizzy sensation that came on every time he found himself in an elevated position. He'd suffered from it ever since that balcony plunge, but knew he had to climb as far as he could go, the distance between him and his pursuer shortening with every painful stride.

Reaching the top of one flight of steps, he heard Arnie's heavy panting behind him and accepted the chase was over. Thoughts of escape perished, with no one on hand to rescue him. It was the old scenario, fight or flight, and he had done enough fleeing to last a lifetime. His chances on one leg against a knife-wielding maniac were so minimal even the most optimistic of betting syndicates would have closed the book on him, but he had no alternative.

He ripped off his black evening jacket and wrapped it around his arm as a flimsy customised shield. Looking up, he saw his childhood friend 15 feet away. "OK, Arnie, is this it... is this what you want?" Gareth shouted. "You won't listen to reason or believe my version of events, so let's have it. Come on!"

He braced himself against a seat in the back of the stand and waited for the inevitable attack. He was thankful for small mercies that Anjie wouldn't be there to see it. Arnie's dexterity with a knife was legendary.

"What the hell do you think you're doing, getting old Taffies to fight your battles?" retorted Arnie, slowly closing the gap. "Still, that cowboy bloke didn't give me too much trouble – it's just you and me now. For Anjie and Max's sake, I'll make it quick. They don't realise what a cheating, lying fucker you are."

Stoked up on adrenaline, Gareth felt a familiar sensation, anger rising within him. "You can accuse me of many things, but the truth is I owe you nothing," he spat. "Fuck all. If anything, you owe me!"

Arnie stared intently at him. "How the fuck do you work that out? I've always been good to you... more than necessary, some would say."

"Yeah?" spat Gareth. "Tell me this then. Why when I look back at my life are all the bad things that have happened connected with you? Before we met I was a pretty happy kid. After that it all turned to shit."

"You've lost too much blood, mate... your head's gone."

"No. It's clear as a bell," said Gareth. "Who cajoled me to take that pill, eh? The one that wrecked my football career? Oh yeah, good old Arnie Dolan. Who was always trying to persuade me to give up football and share in a lifetime of criminality? You've guessed it: Arnold fucking Dolan. Who's fault is it I have to live hundreds of miles from my girlfriend and child? Yeah, I think you get the picture.

The way you dominate people, run their lives… it ruins them, Arnie. To be honest, I can't work it out. Why me? It's as if you chose me as your best friend, that I had no say in it, as if it was your single-handed mission to destroy my life."

"Oh don't bloody flatter yourself," said Arnie, breaking into a run and slashing wildly with the knife. Gareth fended him off with the jacket and, like an angry bull being teased by a matador, the gangster overbalanced and landed on his haunches higher up the stand. Gareth readjusted, wincing as his knee reminded him of the strain he was putting it through. Arnie stood their panting, his hands on his knees.

"You want answers?" he said. "How about this? Maybe you've forgotten but you were about to get fucking lynched by a gang when I came to your rescue. I saved your bike and possibly your good looks. You seem to have a selective memory when you say everything I did was bad for you."

Gareth nodded. "I wondered about that," he said. "I mean, why bother? It was easier to walk away than take on some lunatic with a knife."

"Must be my good nature." Arnie raised himself upright and thrust the knife out in front of him. Gareth backed away but felt the back of his knees bump up against a plastic seat. Looking down he could see people gathering on the pitch, staring in their direction. The spectators looked like toy action figures at this distance.

"That's too easy an answer, Doles," he said.

The gang leader sneered. "Well, perhaps I just wanted to get next to the Special One." He jabbed with the knife again and Gareth parried with his coat, feeling the point rip through the material.

"What?"

"Work it out, you're the intelligent one, the bloke who has made something of his life. When you were growing up you had everything. New bike, constant attention, someone to encourage you in your football and your schoolwork. What did I have? A 'sham' of a father in prison and a mum too busy with all the other bloody sprogs to give a toss."

"And that's it… pure jealousy?"

"Sure, it played a part. I wanted to know why one son was so much more spoilt than another."

"You're just talking in riddles," said Gareth. "I can't be held responsible for your father's actions."

"Nor I yours, but can't you see? We were both victims." Seeing the baffled look on Gareth's face, Arnie raged on. "Hell, I thought you were cleverer than this. Some reporter you must be if you can't see the facts in front of your bloody face. I guess I'm going to have to spell it out. Let's start by talking about lovely Stan Marshall. Stan the man."

"Don't…" Gareth warned.

"Sorry, we have to, philandering arsehole that he was, because it didn't all start with that bird from Bolton did it? Nooo, it started long before."

Gareth felt his fists tightening. He had tried to expunge all thoughts of his father's cheating from his mind. "I don't know. I guess…"

"Take my word for it, he was one for the ladies even before you were born… for example, when your mum was six months pregnant he was playing away from home. Wife had a bun in the oven so he looked elsewhere. And don't look so surprised – in your heart of hearts you've always known what he was like."

"You're saying this just to hurt me," muttered Gareth through clenched teeth. "You know it's a sensitive subject."

"Hey, I'm trying to answer your question," said Arnie. "Simple as. You asked me about my fascination with you, well this is it… the full monty. Remember my old man chasing yours all over the Boxers that time? I saw it and I know you did. Know why?"

"Because he was a raving psycho?"

"Oh, that would be nice and simple wouldn't it? Just put it down to the fact that Mo Dolan's a nutter. Sorry to disappoint. No, the reason he was chasing your dad was because he had found out Stan the Man had been fucking his wife… my mum… for 14 fuckin' years!

While the cat's away, I guess they say… and our 'cat' was always away, locked up somewhere or other. He still found out though. I heard him and mum talking, just before he went and did that Post Office job which landed him 20 years. They were rowing about the time she had spent down the market, at the stall where they sold the cheap trainers, then he produced something from his pocket, a note she had written to Stan. He showed it to her and then started shouting and smacking her about, shouting: "That boy will never be a son of mine". Later, I retrieved it from the bin. In it she revealed she had given birth to Stan's son and how they would have to guard the secret or Mo would go mental."

Realisation dawned for Gareth in a bright glare as someone turned the stadium floodlights on. "No…"

His mind flashed back to all those years ago in Arnie's house. The bruises on his friend's body, the mother recounting her regular visits to Stan Marshall's stall at the market to buy trainers for her kids. His mum's animosity towards Arnie and the fact the two women refused to acknowledge each other's existence.

"Oh yeah," said Arnie, rubbing home his advantage. "I wasn't keeping an eye on you because I was entranced by your sparkling personality. I felt I had to intervene on the day that gang attacked because it's the sort of thing one brother does for another. I thought if I helped you then your dad… my real dad… would look at me in a better light. Maybe even acknowledge me. After all, the bloke I called Dad wanted nothing more to do with me, other than as a punchbag. A part of me said, 'get close to the golden boy and maybe some of the magic dust would rub off on me'. But all Stan did was warn you off seeing me. He probably made it out it was better for you when really it was better for him because it meant his secret was safe."

Gareth didn't know what to say. He just stared, a million more questions stuck in his throat. Arnie ploughed on. "When 'super Stan' did the dirty on you, though, showing his true colours I already knew what that was like, the rejection, so felt sorry for you, wanted to help you get over it… hence the Brighton trip. I figured the pill might just act like, you know, the one that bloke takes in that film The Matrix, which changes his life, brings him into reality and helps him escape the past. It just backfired, is all."

Imparting the tale had made Arnie Dolan look different somehow, a broken man, the spark having fled his eyes. "Why didn't you tell me?" said Gareth. He slowly advanced, his eyes pleading with the boy he now knew to be his brother, almost a twin considering the few months between them.

"What was the point," said Arnie. "You'd been hurt enough."

Arnie's head came up and Gareth stared into a shell, the soul long departed. He moved towards his friend, not frightened any more, his arms reaching out to embrace the brother he didn't know he had. Too late, he realised his mistake. If there had been a glimmer of despair in Arnie's eyes, it was a trick of the light. The gangster was like a faulty firework, his touchpaper still smouldering. He sprang to his feet and slashed a couple of times with the knife, connecting with Gareth's unprotected arm and forcing him back across the seats as the jolt of pain charged through his body. "You're just as bad as him, that fuckin' bastard of a dad we share," he protested. "Lying, stitching me up to the police, making my sister pregnant. I hate you!"

Arnie was above him, raising the bloody knife in preparation for the final plunge. Gareth closed his eyes.

"Aaaaaaaaaaaaaaaaaaaargh!" The noise split the chill night air, loud and guttural and from the heart. Gareth jumped reflexively, opened one eye and looked around. There was no Arnie, just a knife lying on the floor beneath one of the seats. What on earth?

Suddenly hands were lifting him, muscular arms cushioning his injured limb as he rose slowly into the crisp night air. Will Shakespeare's face looked down with concern. "You'll be all right now, son, we'll protect you. My Jase always told you we would, didn't he?"

Gareth nodded. "Yeah, but what..?"

"The Legend, mate. I've never seen such bravery, well not since the day he took down that rampaging Aussie back row forward on the Lions tour when he alone stood between defeat and victory. JW came out of an entrance above you and sneaked down while you were talking. When he saw that bloke was about to stab you, he threw himself down. They both tumbled down there." He pointed at the steep incline of steps. "Last thing I saw The Legend got to his feet and lifted him like a dumbbell, throwing him down one of those exit tunnels. Fuck knows if they're all right. We'd better find out."

Jason and Anjie appeared behind them as Will strode down the aisle, carrying Gareth as a soldier might transport an injured comrade. Reaching a stadium exit, they saw a prone body at the foot of a steep flight of steps. Will and Jason continued down towards the rugby pitch in search of The Legend as Anjie ran down to attend to her brother. He was barely conscious. "Sis?" he whispered, staring up at her. "I'm sorry. I had to… Eight years in hell and your bloke was the one who put me there."

"No, he wasn't," said Anjie, cradling his head.

"Oh come on! Should have known you… would… take… his side."

"No," she said. "You don't understand. It's more complicated than that, love. I know for a fact Gareth didn't turn you in because I did. It was me who told the Old Bill."

51

ANJELICA DOLAN and Janie Sullivan were wearing their best Saturday night clubbing clothes as they pushed through the doors of The Hope. Anjie's little black dress was low-cut and fell to just above the knee while Janie, forever the exhibitionist, wore a red micro-skirt above sparkling silver tights and high-heels. Her short lacy white top ended a good inch above her pierced belly button and her blonde hair fell in ringlets around her heavily made-up face. Her hands were covered in rings and a rosebud tattoo was visible on her shoulder. In contrast Anjie shunned jewellery, wearing just the bracelet her mother had given her on her 18th birthday.

At first the girls thought they had gatecrashed a male-only party. I'm Forever Blowing Bubbles was ebbing and flowing around the east London boozer, the boys swaying in time as they belted out the traditional West Ham United supporters' song with gusto. A familiar figure stood on a table at the centre of the group, leading the chorus. Anjie's brother Arnold looked manic, fuelled by too many pints and the rare feat of Hammers reaching the fifth round of the FA Cup. If it was a party, though, he certainly wasn't dressed in his best party gear. His retro West Ham shirt, the one with the number 10 on the back, was ripped at the collar and he had what appeared to be blood smeared across his knuckles. The girls pushed their way through to the bar.

"What are you having Janie?" asked Anjie, trying to attract the attention of the extravagantly overweight Irish landlady, who had to cope with a packed boozer with only a couple of bar staff to help. Janie requested a vodka and orange.

"Hey girls... looking good!" The two of them turned to see Pete Vickers approach. "Shit, Pete, more than can be said for you," exclaimed Janie, "what on earth happened?"

"Oh," he said, putting on a brave face and touching at an eye that was a mishmash of blacks and purples, as if a make-up artist had gone berserk on him for a Hallowe'en parade. His stonewashed jacket was badly torn and there was blood all over his denims. He smiled and Janie gasped when she saw one of his front teeth had been sheared off. "Bit of trouble with some Taffy bastards down the Boleyn today. No sweat, we sorted them good 'n' proper. You should have seen your Arnie, Anj. Tore into them, beat the living shit out of a couple of 'em. Don't think they'll come here with such a swagger next time."

Anjie tutted. "You boys and your little wars," she said. "What the hell's the point?"

"Oh, you know," said Pete. "Something to do on a Saturday afternoon, ain't it? We've got to protect our turf."

"It's not war, though, is it? I really don't see the point in all this fighting – all over football. My God, there are lads your age fighting real battles in Afghanistan." She took the drinks from Irish Mary and handed one to Janie.

"I don't know," said her friend, stroking Pete on the shoulder. "Kind of makes them more attractive when they're a bit naughty."

Pete beamed, but Anjie tossed her black hair back in disgust. "If you like that sort of thing; I'm more interested in a bit of intelligence and sophistication."

"Oh yeah," said Janie, "We know exactly which 'sophisticated' bloke you're talking about."

Anjie hit her friend playfully on the shoulder. "Don't!" she warned. Pete was baffled. The girls seemed to be speaking in some sort of code.

Sniggering, Janie asked him: "So where's Gazza tonight then, Pete? I can't see him anywhere."

"Nah. We lost him outside the ground," said Pete. "Think he got a bit of a shoe-in. Luckily Doles was there to rescue him. I was otherwise occupied."

"Yeah, getting your teeth rearranged," said Anjie. "Ah well, shall we get some seats?" Janie nodded, kissed Pete on the cheek and followed her friend to a section of the pub as far from the pool table as possible. They had just taken their seats when Arnie came across. "Right sis?" he asked, bending to kiss Anjie on the cheek.

"Sure am," she said, "And you look like the cock of the walk. What's been happening? Anything to tell me?"

"Not really, babes. Hammers won."

"And what's that you got tied around your wrist? Doesn't look like a Hammers scarf to me and it's got... Jeez Arnie, is that blood? Gross."

"Oh," he said, as if he had forgotten it was there. "Oh, that's just a little gift one of our Welsh friends gave me. Nice little silk scarf don't you think? Sadly the colours run... not like the claret and blue." He turned to Fancy Man, and they both laughed at the private joke.

"Mum will kill you if you've been in trouble again," said Anjie. "And Dad won't be happy either."

"Fuck 'em!" said Arnie aggressively. "What's the old man going to do? Slap me on the wrists? Tell me not to be a bad boy? He's a fine example, ain't he? He's banged up and we're supposed to act all goodie two shoes. He don't give a fuck about me, Anj."

"Oh there's no talking to you tonight, is there? Where are you off now?"

"Dunno. Thought we might hit the West End."

"Gary not with you?"

"Nah. Shit knows what happened to him. I called his house earlier and no one's seen him. He's a strange bugger at times. Disappears for days on end and then I catch up with him again. It's been that way ever since the incident."

"I suppose."

"Fancy taking us with you?" said Janie, her eyes sparkling as they always did when they landed on Arnie.

"Nah, you're all right girls," he replied, turning again to Fancy Man. "We don't want anyone cramping our style do we?"

For all Arnie Dolan's fighting prowess the thump on the arm from his sister caught him completely off guard. It would leave a nice bruise, to add to all the others.

"Come on then, guys, let's go!" he said, jumping from his chair. "See you later, sis." The gang pushed against the crowd and formed a column to the door, the sound of Bubbles rising to the ceiling again.

Anjie was at the bar a little while later when she bumped into Reg, the man who was dating Gary's mum. "Hey Reg, what's the hurry?" she said as he necked a glass of whisky and grabbed his coat.

"Oh hi, love," he said, "Bit of drama at home is all. Sheila just rang. The boy's got himself in bother. He's at the cop shop. She couldn't tell me what had happened over the phone other than we need a good lawyer. He was in a bit of a panic when he called, apparently."

Anjelica interrupted Janie's conversation with Pete Vickers, who had decided against following Arnie and the gang into the West End. Pete claimed he had money issues, but Anjie had a sneaking suspicion he had a thing for Janie. "Hey, something's cropped up at home," she said. "I've got to go. Sorry and all that, but some of the other girls are over there and I'm sure, umm, Pete will keep you company."

"Oh Jeez Anj! I was really looking forward to a night out with my best mate. Is it really that important?"

"Life or death," said Anjie, "you know me. I would never leave you in the lurch."

"ON MY LIFE, what am I gonna do?" Sheila Marshall pulled Anjie into an embrace. "He said it might be murder... apparently some kid died! My boy couldn't murder anyone, you know that, and, anyway, you should have heard the state he was in. By all intents, it sounds like he was the one who came off worst."

"Hey calm down, we'll sort it... what exactly did he say?"

"Come in off the doorstep and let's have a cup of tea. Reg? Put the kettle on. I need a chat with young Anjie."

They went into the front room and Sheila appeared to stop and mutter a prayer to a small statue of Jesus on the mantelpiece. She straightened a picture of the Queen and looked at the massive poster on the facing wall. "Oh Rick! What would you do?" she asked.

"I'm sorry Sheila but I doubt Status Quo can help," said Anjie. For the moment she felt uneasy as Sheila stared at her, but then the older woman burst out laughing. "You're right, love," she said. "I am silly! Look, this is the situation as I know it."

Sheila told Anjelica the whole story, how Gary had been chased and punched to the floor and how his walking stick had been taken and used to beat a Cardiff fan around the head. "Gary saw the boy lying on the floor covered in blood. Apparently he died in hospital and the police are saying it's manslaughter or, worse, murder. They've got DNA evidence off the stick and claim CCTV images show a guy wearing the claret and blue battering this poor boy senseless. God, I can't imagine how his mother must feel. Why do they do these things?"

"Male bravado," said Anjie.

"I know it's not my Gary, even though he was wearing his Hammers shirt," continued Sheila. "My worry is he has some work experience with the local radio station coming up in a couple of days. If they hear about this that's his career over before it's started. How much bad luck can a lad have? His injured leg means his hopes of becoming a footballer are wrecked, and now this. Mind you, if he did it I'll never forgive him."

Anjie was quiet for a moment, calmly patting the older woman's hand. Thoughts were tumbling around her head, visions of Gareth in a cell, then the fresh memory of Arnold standing on a table, leading the chorus of Bubbles, waving a blood-soaked silk scarf around his head. There was the assertion by Pete, too. *"You should have seen the way he tore into them, beat the living shit out of 'em."*

Anjie considered confronting Arnie, getting him to give himself up to the police, but knew he would never do anything like that willingly. He was leader of the pack, the head Boxer Boy, and would be afraid of his empire crumbling.

She thought about that empire. Would it really be a bad thing if the whole criminal enterprise collapsed? In the long run it might help Arnie grow up. In contrast, another blow for Gary in his seriously weakened mental state might be the final straw. He felt he could trust no one, but Anjie wanted to show him that wasn't the case. She had to make the ultimate sacrifice for the good of them both.

"Can you excuse me a minute, Sheil," she said. "I've got to make a call."

IN HIS CELL, Gary Marshall mulled over his situation. He was in deep water and didn't have a clue how to get out of it. If he told them what he had seen Arnie would be in trouble, but if his best mate hadn't intervened it might be him on the slab. After a wait of another hour the cell door opened. Expecting the worst, Gary was shocked by the policeman's words.

"You're free to go. There's a bloke out here, name of Reg… says he's your next of kin. You're lucky, mate. Must have a guardian angel. There was talk of charging you with affray at the very least, but the evidence suggests you were a victim… anyway, on your bike before we change our minds. We're keeping your walking stick, by the way… it's evidence. You'll have to get another."

Gary felt relief flood through him as he limped into the cold night air with Reg at his side. The older man hadn't commented, just collected his possessions and guided him to the car. When they got back to the Boxers it was gone 11 and Gary felt his eyes well up with tears as he saw his mother waiting on the doorstep. "Don't cry son," she said. "It won't look good in front of your visitor."

As his mother stepped aside, Anjelica came into view. Before he knew what was happening she rushed at him, wrapping him in a breath-stealing embrace. He thought she'd been crying, too. "Bloody hell, Gary Marshall, you're such a silly sod," she said.

52

Present Day:

"I JUST TOLD them the truth, Arnie, that's all, love. I found a phone box and made an anonymous call. I gather it was pretty easy for the police to work it all out from there. They spotted your Geoff Hurst top on the CCTV then when they raided the house the next day they found that stupid souvenir, that bit of silk scarf, by the side of your bed. It was pretty easy to match the blood to the victim and that did for you."

Arnie could find no words, his face a mixture of bewilderment and pain. Every time he opened his mouth, it shut shortly afterwards, no sound escaping. He was devastated, she could tell, and though she realised that nothing she said could ease his suffering or earn his forgiveness, she carried on talking just the same. "I love him, you see, Arnie? Always have done. Gary's my world now. Ever since you brought him around our house for tea in the old days I knew we had something. We were on the same wavelength, liked the same books and stuff, and when he asked me along to watch him play football I couldn't refuse. When the accident happened I felt I had to look after him. He was fragile, his dad having left and his career gone up in smoke... it was those visits to hospital that persuaded me I wanted to be a nurse."

Finally he managed to squeeze out a few grunts and she could only recognise the last word "... brother".

"Yes, you'll always be my favourite brother. I love you deeply, but in a different way. You're stronger than him, always have been. You can look after yourself and carry the burdens of others, too. I wasn't worried about you, Arnie, you always bounced back. I'm sorry, though, more sorry now than before, because I can see what jail has done to you. Horrible. What I would really like is the old Arnie back, not this new, callous version. I don't suppose..."

"You don't understand, he's... aaaargh!"

"Hell, what's wrong?" cried Anjie, turning to the bystanders looking down on the scene. "Has anyone called an ambulance? Are they coming? What..?"

Will Shakespeare put his arm on her shoulder. "There's one on the way lovey," he said. "We had to dial 999 anyway. The Legend hasn't regained consciousness."

"Really? What's wrong with him?" she asked. "You should have said something – I'm a nurse! Look after him, would you?"

Anjie mounted the steps and rushed down to pitchside, where she found the other victim. She listened to his chest then took his pulse. "Shit! Shit! It's very faint," she said. "He's in a bad way. Critical. If we don't get him to hospital soon..."

She was interrupted by the arrival of paramedics with two stretchers who pushed people out of the way before splitting up and moving in opposite directions to attend the victims.

GARETH PICKED AT the bandage on his arm as he wrestled with his thoughts. The knowledge he had gleaned in the past few hours had answered some questions but posed a lot more.

"Penny for them?" said Anjie, handing him a Styrofoam cup containing something murky, hot and brown.

"Oh, nothing and everything," he said. "Basically, I'm just worried about what's happening with him." He indicated towards the door. Somewhere behind it there was an operating theatre where The Legend had been wheeled after doctors had made their initial diagnosis of his condition.

"You said he's pretty tough," she pointed out.

"I know, but all that hard living is bound to take its toll. Sometimes I wonder if he's just looking for an excuse to give up."

"Hey, you've been there, haven't you? Remember, he's made a lifetime of fighting for survival. I'm sure he isn't going to throw in the towel at the first sign of trouble."

"First sign? Babe, this is the last rites."

"Yeah, but when you told me about him you said it yourself, 'however often he gets knocked down he bounces back the next day'. Hell, the first time you saw him you thought he was dead!"

Gareth chuckled at the memory. "I know, silly bugger," he said, the words catching in his throat. "How's Arnie?"

"He's got a problem with his spine," Anjie replied. "Doctors think he's going to spend the rest of his life in a wheelchair. I got a short, sharp text from Janie earlier, saying: 'It's all kicked off. We're heading home'."

"What about Max?"

"She's taking him with her." Gareth raised his eyebrows. "He'll be fine. She'll look after him until I get back. He loves it at her house anyway, practically lives there. He really looks up to her boy Simon, enjoys playing with all his toys."

"Shame I couldn't see him before he went."

"I know, but there will be other opportunities. Anyway, I don't particularly want him to see his old man all cut up like this." She pointed to his hand and arm, both wrapped in blood-soaked bandages, his tattered jacket hanging loosely from his shoulders.

Taking a sip of the coffee he looked back along the corridor. "Uh oh, here comes trouble."

She followed the direction of his gaze to see two figures approaching. A woman dressed for business in a black pleated jacket and skirt was striding out ahead, her 6 inch heels click-clacking on the tiled floor. She was being trailed by a man with wild-looking grey hair sprouting from the side of his head. He was dressed in what her mother used to call a pair of slacks which were partially covered by a black jumper that was far too long.

"Who's that?" asked Anjie.

"It's my boss, the sports editor Jacko... and the big boss is with him."

"What, that woman?"

"Oh yeah, she's a tough old piece of work. Her name's Lana Desmund. Half Scottish, half Spanish and all tyrant. My editor. I'm in big trouble."

As he whispered to her, Lana's eyes locked on him. "Ahhh!" she said in mock surprise, her exclamation far louder than necessary. "Here he is, Jacko. Our Mr Fix it – how are you, Mr Prince? And who is this?"

"A friend from London: My girlfriend. Anjelica, this is my editor Lana."

The Tribune Despatch editor gave Anjie a perfunctory handshake. "How cosy for you all. Now, do you mind telling me what's going on here? One minute I am discussing with Jacko how we might be able to take advantage of The Legend's insight and the next thing I learn from my TV is that he's in hospital after some dramatic incident in the Millennium Stadium. Care to enlighten me, Mr Prince?"

The look she now gave him could freeze lava. In the background, Jacko did his famous owl impression, turning his head to the side to indicate the situation had nothing to do with him. "You know about this Jacko?" Lana prodded.

Shocked out of his feigned indifference, he wasn't sure how to reply. He didn't want the editor to think he had no idea what was happening in his own department. "Um... ah..."

"Oh, never mind!" she said, losing patience. "Another rather alarming thing has come to my attention. Do you recognise this, Mr Prince?" She held out a small, black device. His Dictaphone. "There's an ugly rumour doing the rounds that you are getting that 16-year-old work experienced boy to do your work, dictating match reports into this. I've had a listen and it's certainly not your voice on here. Have you conned me? To think I had you down as some kind of journalistic genius for your work with The Legend."

As Gareth scrambled for an answer, an Asian man in a white coat pushed his way through the double doors and approached them. "Are you relatives of Mr JW Owens?" he asked.

Before anyone could speak, Gareth said: "Yeah, um, yes... I'm his nephew."

Lana gave him another scowl, but he ignored it and kept a straight face.

"And who can I ask are these people?"

"This is my wife," he indicated to Anjie, "... and these people are from the newspaper where JW Owens works. We're all keen to know what's going on."

"OK then," said the doctor. "Well, I'm pleased to say the tumour is definitely operable." He looked around the blank faces and realised he had said something to stun them. "You didn't know?"

"Um... no," said Gareth.

"Well, the truth of the matter is that your uncle has had a tumour lying dormant in his brain for, oooh, I would say around 30 years," explained the doctor. "It's absolutely astonishing that it hasn't been detected before, or that it didn't kill him. One in a million chance I would think. Anyway, I reckon it must have developed during his rugby days and it is only now, with all the state-of-the-art scanners and everything available, that we've been able to detect it. Fortunate he took that tumble really. Like I say, though, we think it is operable and have put him into a medically induced coma to relieve pressure on the brain. We have to let the swelling go down from his recent tumble before we do anything."

"Excuse me," said Gareth, "but would this tumour cause erratic behaviour?"

"Oh undoubtedly," replied the doctor, "and, from what I can gather, he's quite partial to alcohol, so I'm sure that wouldn't have helped. On occasion he probably felt paranoid, frightened, lost... he may even have had blackouts, forgotten people's names, that kind of thing. It's all quite common in brain abnormalities like this."

Gareth nodded. Missing pieces of the jigsaw were falling into place.

"Anyway, I must get on," said the Doctor. "Nice to meet you. I think it's going to be a while before we know anything more definite."

As the doctor departed, Gareth noticed Lana and Jacko wandering off into a corner to share a frank exchange of views. There were exaggerated arm movements on both sides before the editor clomped off into the distance.

"She isn't happy, mun," Jacko explained on his return. "She's considering a charge of gross misconduct resulting in instant dismissal. I've tried to argue but we'll have to let her sleep on it. She seems to have convinced herself that rather than a high flyer from London you're nothing more than one of those dodgy market traders we hear about up that way. Someone has convinced her you didn't write the Argentina report yourself... that it was all down to Jason. Can't see it myself... he's as thick as mince. Spends so long plugged into those headphones listening to his thumping music, I doubt his brain has got room for anything else. I don't know where she gets these ideas from but I warn you, Gareth, when she sniffs blood she goes in for the kill."

"Is there any good news?"

"Well, at this moment you're still in a job. She can't really prove anything though CCTV at the stadium suggests you were involved in this punch up and judging by the look of you it's going to be a tough case to argue otherwise. You can take a few days off to get yourself, um, straightened out, but be warned there could be some sort of disciplinary hearing."

When Jacko had gone, Anjie touched Gareth on the shoulder. "Are you still in a job?"

"It appears so... for the moment," he said, a puzzled expression on his face. "Do you know, I think he actually fought my corner there."

He sat back down and picked up the Styrofoam cup, sipping at the tepid liquid before screwing up his face and throwing it into the nearest bin.

"Listen," said Anjie. "I've been thinking. You obviously aren't suited to looking after yourself. If you are kept on, how about Max and I come down here and keep an eye on you for a while, nurse your wounds."

It took seconds for the thoughts to whirl around his head and click into place. "You mean it?" he said, wide-eyed. "What about your job?"

"I reckon I could get a transfer through the NHS, it shouldn't be too difficult." She looked around. "This seems a nice hospital, I just might make some inquiries before we leave."

Grabbing her in a bear hug he gave her a kiss which lasted so long that when they parted they realised they had attracted an audience.

53

ARNIE WAS DOZING when his right-hand man Pete Vickers pushed through the doors of his private hospital room, the eldest Dolan brother Chuck following close behind. Pete looked strained, as if he, too, had been the victim of trauma. His eyes scanned the various monitors and drips feeding into Arnie's body.

"What do the doctors say?" he asked.

Arnie seemed to be fighting an internal conflict. Eventually he managed to prize his eyes open and peer out. His face was a mess, bruised and bloody and through the swelling his visitors looked fuzzy and distant. "Ah, Vickers old mate," he said, trying to inject some lightness into the situation. "You always were the loyal one... forget the fucking rest. They tell me I've got some sort of back injury, son, something to do with the spine. I might struggle to walk again, apparently. Another crip, eh? Kind of ironic. Still, what do these doctors know?" He smiled.

"That's bad luck," said Pete Vickers. "Probably means you won't be able to fuck my wife again."

For once, Arnie was lost for words. He tried to push himself to a sitting position, using all the strength he could muster as beads of sweat formed on his brow. "What?"

"You heard. I said it means you won't be able to rape Janie again. You've no shame, have you, no idea what's right or wrong? You just take what you want to take..."

"Look," said Arnie, wrestling to get to grips with the situation. "It wasn't like that, Pete. She was begging for it. She's always..."

"Shut up! You were only kids back then when you did it the first time – and she reckons you forced yourself on her then, too. I know exactly what's gone on here and I trust my wife. God, she had gone a long way towards forgetting you and we were settling down to a proper family life together, just as she wanted. Then you come along and ruin everything... like you do with everyone: Gazza, Tigger, Anjie. We had a good heart-to-heart last night and Janie told me all about your little episode in the kitchen, how you forced yourself on her and wouldn't take no for an answer. You used a knife, for fuck's sake. I should kill you for that alone. Then, of course, there were the threats you made to get her to do your bidding. Well, you're on your own now. The lads were happy before you came out of nick, making a decent wedge, running the show. Fancy Man and Chuck built up a bit of muscle while you were inside – a pretty tasty crew – and Tigger hates your guts for the way you bully him. It hasn't been hard for me to persuade them it can be business as usual without you..."

Arnie's face changed, his bewilderment swapped for pure and undiluted contempt. "You won't last a fucking second!" he shouted. "You and that bunch of wasters. Where's the brains eh? What happened to loyalty? At least I got the power of family behind me, ain't that right Chuck? Go on, teach him a lesson here and now!"

He saw his older brother form fists and move forward. For half a moment he thought Chuck was going to do his bidding. Then he diverted his attention from Vickers and leaned over the bed.

"You think we're going to get you out of this one, bastard?" said Chuck. "You ask for loyalty, then go behind Pete's back and rape his fuckin' wife? That ain't the Dolan way, mate, but perhaps that's because you ain't a Dolan..."

"Oh come on Chuck you thick..."

"Bloody hell, you've always thought yourself better than us, ain't you? Taking charge of us, bossing me and Sly around even though we were older than you. I let you get away with it because you had a head for business and could talk people into things, just like that fucking market trader who fathered you. I only found out the true story when

Dad came out on licence. He hated you, you know? The fact that you made him look a right weak mug in front of his crew. Every time he looked at you he saw that fucker Stan Marshall looking back. He couldn't do nothing while you were home because mum was always keeping an eye out for you, but he still regrets that he didn't finish you off in prison when he had the chance."

Arnie was perplexed. "Oh yeah, that's right," continued Chuck. "You still haven't figured it out, have you? You thought it was to do with that Ilford mob, those black boys. Dad's mate Cozza did a pretty good job sowing that seed."

The words brought a vivid flashback. From the depths of Arnie's memory he conjured up the sight of his cell mate walking out, claiming he was going to learn about the bounty on Arnie's head. It was now clear who was the real rat – he'd set up Arnie for the attack, an attack arranged by the man he knew as big Mo Dolan, the man he had called Dad from the moment he'd been able to talk. He felt a prickling around his eyes.

"Stevo?"

"He hated that dog," said Chuck. "Stevo never bit anyone. Dad was seething, though. Having failed to get you in prison, he saw another way to hurt you. There's different ways to skin a cat, they say, or should that be different ways to kill a dog. Poor Stevo. I always thought he was a vicious little brute but in this case he was an innocent victim."

"Noooooo!" Arnie screamed, his eyes blurrily focused on two of his closest confidantes. He couldn't believe what he was hearing. All his life he had been guarding against an enemy easily identified by the colour of their skin, when his real detractors were much closer to home.

"Look at you," said Chuck. "You're washed up. Just an empty shell. There's nothing to you. You can't physically intimidate people and you can't play mental games with them. Everyone's wise to you. Anyway, we've no time for small talk now. I've got a train to catch and Pete has to get back to the wife and kids." With that he turned and headed for the door, Pete Vickers following.

"Vickers!   Vickers!" Arnie shouted, trying to get out of bed. "Come back you bastard. Vickers!"

Pete Vickers watched a stream of nurses rushing in the opposite direction, towards the ward, responding to a patient in distress. As he turned the corner he smiled. For the first time since childhood he felt free.

EPILOGUE

"FANTASTIC TO MEET you," said Gareth, taking hold of two heavy bags and dumping them onto one of the airport trolleys. He put his hand out to shake but she pulled him into a warm embrace.

"At last... Mr Prince," said the attractive, older blonde woman with the slightly Antipodean accent. "I can't tell you how much I owe you for looking after Dad the way you have. What's the latest?" Releasing him, Ellie Clifton stood back, a serious look on her face.

"It's great news, actually," Gareth told her. "While you were in the air they brought him out of his coma and the last thing I heard he was sitting up in bed chatting up nurses. They still have to do the main part of the operation and there's no telling how that will go but at least he's up and about and not looking any the worse for wear after his adventures."

She nodded. "I do feel guilty, you know, not coming over before. It always seems to be something like this that brings a family together. The good thing is I'm going to see him before... well, you know, worst case scenario, but I can tell him how much I miss him and love him."

"I know he feels the same about you," said Gareth. "Hell, John Wayne is always..."

"What?" Ellie Clifton wore a puzzled expression.

"John Wayne," Gareth repeated a bit louder. "That's what the JW stands for isn't it?"

She burst out laughing, a full belly laugh not unlike her father's. It attracted strange looks from those around them at the baggage carousel. When she bought herself under control she said: "He told you that?"

"He said he was named after his dad's favourite actor."

"He's a real joker my old man, isn't he?" she said. "Always pulling people's legs."

"You mean..?"

"Sorry, Gareth, but he's been taking you for a ride. He's not called John Wayne at all. His first name is John, yes, but his second is Wallace. John Wallace Owens. Still, I bet he had some fun with that."

Gareth could see the funny side, too. "Mostly at my expense. Damn."

Just then his phone rang, the Bubbles ringtone blaring out. He mimed that he had to take the call in private.

"Don't worry, I'll wait here for my husband and little John," she said.

Walking over to the corner of the room, he pressed the button and put the mobile to his ear. "You've got a guardian angel watching over you boy," said Jacko. Yes, thought Gareth, her name is Anjie.

"Oh?"

"Yeah… it seems Lana went in to see The Legend today. He was in great spirits and had a good chat with her. He offered her an exclusive. How he fought the bloke who killed his son at the Millennium Stadium, lived with a brain tumour for 30 years, and was reunited with his daughter… it's a real heart-tugger and he says he'll give us the whole kit and caboodle. We can turn it into a series. Of course, she snapped his hand off, but asked what it was going to cost."

"And..?"

"He said the only thing he wanted was his normal fee and for you to be the bloke who writes it. He told her he could go to the nationals but wanted to stick with the paper he knows and trusts and the reporter he gets on with the most. His exact words were, 'Gareth Prince understands me, I want him to write it'."

"Are you sure? He normally doesn't even remember my first name. Ah, hang on – did you put him up to this? He wouldn't have even known about my precarious position – he's been out of it for days."

"As if I… maybe the surgery sorted him out, mun," said Jacko. "Anyway see you in the office bright and early tomorrow…"

Perplexed, Gareth rang off and was surprised when he looked up to find Ellie standing there, a sandy haired, bronzed man alongside her pushing a little dark haired boy in a pushchair. He looked like his grandfather.

"As we're talking about names and you've just been discussing a similar thing on the phone, sorry, I couldn't help overhearing… I spoke to Dad briefly just before we arranged to come out to see him," she said. "He told me that if I was ever to speak to a bloke called Gareth I was to address him as Geraint. It was a joke he'd been carrying on for some time. He said it really got up the bloke's nose. I guess… it's you, isn't it?"

Gareth nodded and turned to push the trolley out to the van where Will Shakespeare, his new best friend, was waiting to drive them to South Wales. As he did so he let his mind slip back to his first meeting with The Legend. "Geraint," he muttered under his breath. "Bloody Geraint."

Then a smile creased his face, his head fell back and he roared with laughter.

THE END

About the Author

Nick Rippington is one of the silent victims of the News of the World phone hacking scandal, having been made redundant from his position as Welsh Sports Editor at the paper when it closed down with only two days notice.

In a previous life he was an Executive Editor at Media Wales - the organisation that produces the Western Mail, South Wales Echo and Wales on Sunday in Cardiff – and in his spare time has written several popular blogs - Frankie Prince's Bovver Boots is a weekly look at the misfortunes of his favourite football club Bristol Rovers, which goes out each week on the Bristol Post website, Imgoingtopublish.wordpress.com is a blog following his novel writing adventures.

He also wrote a tongue-in-cheek blog called whaticookedlastnight.blogspot.co.uk which recorded the day-to-day antics of staff on the Welsh Sunday newspaper. A father of two, he lives with his wife in London.

For more information on Nick go to www.theripperfile.com and for free offers and advanced warning of future work join his mailing list on the website

Printed in Great
Britain
by Amazon

32067990R00206